AGENT.

THE TIR-NA SAGA

MOTHER.

BOOK ONE

OTHER.

invoke
CREATIONS

SHARN LEE

First published by Invoke Creations, Canberra.
Agent. Mother. Other. Book 1 of the Tir-na Series.
Copyright © 2023 by Sharn Lee
First edition.
ISBN: 978-0-6456585-2-1

Requests to publish work from this book should be sent to:
info@invokecreations.com

Visit the author's website at www.invokecreations.com

Cover art by Nikki Jane Design.
Edited by Teaspoon Consulting.
Typeset using Atticus.

*To my younger self who once dreamed of
writing a book.*

Prologue

MOTHER

187 AC (After Colonisation)

M Y HANDS STRANGLED THE cold steel railing as I surrendered my body to another surge of crippling pain. The constant prickling of shower water hitting my skin numbed my senses. But not enough. I knew it was supposed to hurt, but I wasn't ready for the unrelenting intensity of the task. As a painful wave subsided, my head flopped on my arms, and every muscle cried out in exhaustion.

My mind slipped down a negative spiral of thoughts. *How much longer will this take? I can't do this. I want it to end!* Just as I felt my flimsy control slipping, there he was beside me, wiping my brow with a wet washcloth and rubbing my back.

'You can do this, Rach. You're doing so well. You've got this.' It was exactly what I needed to hear, and he was right. Every female in my family before me had birthed successfully, and I wouldn't let them down. I could do it. After a deep breath, I focused my way through another powerful surge.

My labour had gone for nine hours at that point, but from my perspective, it could have been three hours, or three days. Time had evaporated for me. It became a non-entity, a nebulous concept that had no meaning. All that existed was me, my mind and the rolling waves of contractions and releases. My midwife Anna pottered around, coming over now and then to poke and prod, giving a token comment of encouragement in passing. But the constant presence of Miles was my rock.

In that moment, I both loved him and hated him with all my heart. He was the reason I was in this situation. If we had been more careful, my body wouldn't

1

be trying to rip itself open so a baby could escape from inside me. But I knew that if he left my side, everything would fall apart. His warm and steady presence made me feel safe and free to give myself over to this incredible and challenging experience.

As my world settled once more between surges, I looked out the bathroom window and noticed Marher, the larger of Tir-na's two moons, tinted by orange and gold streaks of light that coloured the sky over the sprawling, plant-covered city of Crayn. It was beautiful, but the sight of the setting sun made me internally groan. It meant I had been in labour all day.

The doorbell of our apartment rang, snapping me out of my internal world. *Who the hell would visit at a time like this?* I thought. The muffled voice of Anna echoed down the hallway as she answered the door, and after a few indecipherable exchanges, her tone of voice became louder and more animated.

'What's happening?' I asked through gritted teeth as another contraction wracked my body.

'I'm not sure,' said Miles. He stayed by my side throughout the contraction, holding my hand and rubbing my back. Once the worst had passed and I slipped down from the peak of pain, he loosened his grip. He ushered me out of my safe place in the shower and kissed my forehead. 'I better go check things are okay.'

As the contraction subsided further and my senses returned, I realised I could hear Anna shouting at the unknown visitor.

'I'll see what's happening,' said Miles, as he wrapped a large towel around me.

'Just hurry back.' My words came out in an exhausted, nervous breath.

A loud crack echoed from the hallway, followed by the hollow thud of a body falling.

'Hide, Rach!' Miles ran out of the bathroom and down the hallway towards the front door.

Naked and wet, I tied the towel around me and shuffled to the bathroom door to follow, but found myself frozen to the spot as another contraction surged through my body. I gripped onto the doorframe to weather the storm and watched Miles turn into the smaller hallway leading to the front door. A heartbeat later, I heard a loud crack. Miles fell backwards and crumpled to the floor as a red liquid splattered across the white walls. I couldn't understand what I was seeing, but then blood started flowing from beneath him and I had a horrible realisation. Miles was dead.

My nails dug into the doorframe as I breathed through the peak of the contraction. The pain slipped away again, and I used it as a chance to figure out what to do. If my training was ever going to serve me, it needed to be now.

Clumping boots sounded from the hallway, moving closer. A black-gloved arm reached towards Miles with a handgun and loosed another round into his head. An insurance kill shot. The figure then started rummaging through Miles's clothes, as though looking for something. I bottled up the torrent of feelings coursing through me and grabbed my wrist-comm as I crept back towards the bathroom window. Just as I laid a hand on the window to prise it open, another contraction overtook me. I clamped down on my vocal cord and breathed as quietly as possible. Surging waves crippled my body, but my brain knew I didn't have time to deal with the contraction. I needed to get out. Through the fog of pain, I forced my shaky limbs to react to my command and opened the window.

The cold air hit me in the face, and I sucked it in, trying to take as much energy from it as I could. Through pure willpower, I lifted my pregnant body onto the windowsill and heaved myself out. My legs shook as I landed on the grass below and I was so grateful we lived on the ground floor of the apartment block.

Naked, wet and in the middle of a contraction, I couldn't have been a more vulnerable target, so I needed to move. As the contraction eased, I sucked in a breath and demanded my body obey me. I needed to get somewhere to have this baby. I pushed myself forwards and hurried towards the storage area access door at the rear of the apartment building. The door opened with a shove, and I quickly closed it behind me. There were storage containers for each apartment underground, and I hoped they would provide enough protection to get me through.

Gripping the handrail, I manoeuvred myself down the darkened stairs, terrified to pause even for a moment. My foot slipped on the edge of a step as my abdomen started twinging. Pain and fear flooded my system as I caught the handrail and righted myself. I couldn't stop. My legs threatened to buckle out from under me when I reached the bottom, but I pushed forward.

As the contraction subsided, I staggered through the darkened hallway as I typed an emergency code into my wrist-comm. The numbers of different apartments stamped on the storage containers flashed past me until I finally reached ours. I looked at it for a moment, then took a sharp left and beelined to my neighbour's container.

I rushed in and closed the door quietly behind me. Another contraction folded my body in half, causing me to collapse to the floor. This one differed from the others. There was a sudden pressure that needed to escape, and I instinctively knew I needed to push. My body seemed to know what it was doing, so I gave myself over to it, and on all fours, on the cold cement ground in the dark, I started pushing.

I don't know how long I was there, but the pain was nothing compared to the moments of silence after the contractions, as that's when I remembered what happened. Miles should have been there with me, but he was dead. He had been my entire world, but he was just gone. Back-wrenching sobs overcame me, but each time I was about to give myself to the darkness, another contraction would start and force me to focus. An involuntary scream left me and blue sparks filled my vision as the baby crowned, ripping open my body. The contraction halted, leaving me shaking like an injured animal in the dark. I was close, and I wanted this baby out. Another contraction rose within me, and I screamed in my mind, *GET OUT!* With all my strength, I pushed. I gave that push every droplet of my energy and felt a rushing of something sliding out of me, followed by pure relief.

I turned and frantically searched for the baby until my hand touched something warm, slimy and unmoving. My heart spluttered as I grabbed the baby and shoved it on my chest, wrapping the two of us in the towel. The silence of that moment still haunts me. There should have been the sound of a baby crying, but all I could hear was my breath in the dark. As I started rubbing the baby's back, panic and dread clawed at my heart. I couldn't handle losing the baby and Miles on the same day. In that moment, I was on the edge of a cliff, and if I fell over the edge and into the bottomless dark, there would be no way back.

A cough sounded from the small bundle in my arms as it wriggled. I let out a huge breath I didn't even realise I was holding. The baby was alive. I was alive. But Miles was dead. I held the baby tighter to my body and, to my relief, it suckled all on its own in the dark. My tears flowed harder in that moment as waves of emotions wracked over me.

'It's okay. Mumma's here,' I whispered through trembling lips. 'I'm going to love you enough for both of us.' My fingers started tracing the delicate outline of the tiny face and the tufts of stringy sparse hair plastered on its head. 'We even already have names picked out for you. Sam for a boy and Skye for a girl. When we get out of here and get some light, I'll let you know which one it is.' I pulled the large towel around us a little tighter, then closed my eyes and gave myself to the building, horrendous sadness inside me. Tears erupted from me as a burst dam, leaving everything destroyed in its wake.

I sat there for an indefinite time, crying myself dry, until I felt like a hollow husk. An echoing thud rang out through the concrete cavern, ripping me back to my senses. Footsteps were moving through the storage area. They paused close to where I was and ripped open what I guessed was our apartment's container. The footsteps shuffled around for a while in there, then moved back into the hall and paused. I held my breath. The sound of another container being flung open broke the silence and sent a shock of adrenaline through me. They were searching the containers. I stood up and grabbed the nearest thing I could find in the dark to use as a weapon. From my reckoning, I had grabbed a table lamp from the way its weight fell to one end. Curling the now towel-cocooned baby into the crook of one arm, I scooted behind the door and held myself ready to strike. It wasn't just my life I was now fighting for. This baby was the last part of Miles I still had, and no one would take that from me.

With a sudden crack, the door swung open. A dark figure stepped into the room, shining a torch light through the space. I took this distracted moment to strike. The blow sent the figure staggering into the centre of the dark space, then their weight shifted as they fell forward and smashed their head into a set of drawers at the back of the container, causing their neck to crack unnaturally sideways. It was confusing; I hadn't hit them hard, but then I remembered the placenta was still on the ground where they had stepped. I gripped the table lamp tighter and prepared to attack again, but they didn't move.

Peeking around the corner of the container's door, I saw there wasn't anyone else in the immediate surroundings, so I ran. Naked and with just a towel around my baby, I hustled around the corner, trying to ignore the tearing pain between my legs that made me run with an awkward, wide-legged gallop. I headed back towards the exit, but then noticed lights flickering across the stairs. I pivoted and ran back. At the end of the storage containers, I hurried around the corner and took a moment to gather my breath and thoughts.

'Rachel?' said an all-too-familiar, sickly-sweet voice from the bottom of the stairs.

'Vivian?' I sighed in relief. My emergency code had worked. Even though Vivian wasn't my favourite person, she was better than whoever was trying to kill me, and seeing her meant backup was here.

'It's just us. You can come out.'

My brain whirled. Was I safe? I couldn't believe that whoever attacked would just disappear. And why were they after Miles? Usually, these types of people were after me. Nothing made sense, but I knew I needed to get out, get my baby dry and warm, and get the tearing between my legs, which seared every time I moved, stitched up. But most of all, I needed to confirm if I had just dreamed Miles was dead. It couldn't possibly be true. Could it?

Taking a deep breath, I stepped around the corner. The first thing I saw was Vivian standing at the bottom of the stairs as her calculating eyes widened at the sight of me. I didn't care that I was completely naked and covered in bloody goo. At that point, I would have walked down the main street of the city and not cared. All I could think about was getting my baby safely out of there and checking on Miles. Nothing else mattered.

As I moved towards the stairs, a single figure came forward. They wrapped me in an oversized coat and ushered me past Vivian's judgemental gaze and out of the stairwell.

'Shit, Rach, you look worse than that time in Aeir.' It was Peter. My work partner-in-crime. We'd been through a lot, and I knew he always had my back.

I gave a slight nod in response, then fixed my eyes on the stairs as we walked out. I was aware of other people there, but truthfully, it was all a blur, except for the dust. The dust in the stairwell glittered in the artificial lights the group had brought with them. It seemed to dance in the air, weighed down by nothing as it swirled in hypnotic patterns. That image of the dancing dust has stayed with me forever.

The next few hours disappeared. I remember being looked over by a medical team and awkwardly stitched up, then the same team checking over my baby—that caused an anxious twist in my stomach until they confirmed he was a healthy boy and returned him to me. I remember insisting on seeing Miles, which part of me regrets to this day. But mostly, I remember sitting in the back of an e-vehic feeding my healthy baby while my head lolled against the cool glass. There was only Marher in the sky that night, and the surrounding trees cast long sorrowful shadows across the ground. They taunted me. Beckoning me to join them in their dark, depressing depths. It would be so easy to give in to the heavy grief that racked my body. But instead of succumbing, I killed off the part of me that wanted to wallow in the sadness. I had bigger responsibilities now. It was just the two of us, and I would make sure that was enough. I was a mother, and my son needed me.

1

Birthday

M IRRORS. DO THEY GIVE you an actual reflection of what you look like? Or do they just reflect your own perception? I certainly hoped it was the latter as I stood gazing at the ever-deepening smile and worry lines framing my face. I was proud of the wrinkles, though, as each one meant I had lived. The smile lines showed I had enjoyed my life, and the worry lines showed I had a twenty-year-old son. The teenage years hadn't been too stressful, especially compared to the experience of other parents I knew, but the inherent mother worry had done nothing for the elasticity of my skin.

With a sigh, I turned away from the mirror and headed down the stairs of our modest dome house and started making my favourite breakfast, eggy toast. Bio-eggs were a true treat, so they always helped start a special day the right way, and if you can't indulge on your forty-ninth birthday, then when could you?

I smiled as I heard Sam's rushing footsteps charge down the stairs. Late again. As always. I closed my eyes and inhaled the intoxicating cooked egg and toast smell. My mouth watered with anticipation. Popping our meals onto plates, I turned to welcome Sam with a beaming smile.

'Hi Mum. Bye Mum,' he said as he rushed past the kitchen.

'But I—' The door slammed shut behind him as he rushed off to university.

I tried not to feel completely dejected as I put the plates on the kitchen bench and instead reached up into my carefully curated hodgepodge mug collection to retrieve my favourite grey mug—the one covered in an intricate white lace pattern that sat in my hands just right. I filled it with hot caffeinated goodness, then leaned back against the kitchen bench, the mug feeling warm and comforting in my hands.

'Ah, coffee. My delicious, reliable friend. You'll always be there for me,' I muttered to myself.

The front door flew open again, jolting me out of my pity party.

'Geesh Sam! I almost spilled my coffee everywhere. How many times have I warned you to be careful?'

'Sorry, Mum. I just wanted to run back to give you this.' Sam's wavy flop of auburn hair was sticking out in every direction, and his grey-brown eyes sparkled as he pulled me into a slightly awkward hug. 'Happy Birthday Mum. I'll see you tonight for dinner.'

'Okay. Same time as always. Don't be late or the food will get cold.'

'I won't. See you later.' He waved and ran out of the house. He never could keep himself running on time.

Feeling thankful that I was hungry, I sat down at the table, ready to devour both breakfasts. Today was going to be wonderful. I could feel it.

· · · · ● · ● · · ·

The table was set with our best dinnerware and decorated with flowers from the garden. Dinner was bubbling away, timed to perfection, so it would be hot and ready when Sam got home. I loved our birthday dinner ritual. Each year, the two of us would eat a meal consisting of new recipes we had never tried. It was a fun challenge. The person whose birthday it was picked out the recipes, and then we set about attempting to cook them. Or more accurately, I ended up attempting to cook them. Sam helped where he could, but after one particularly disastrous and hilarious dinner he cooked all on his own, we reverted to me taking the lead. Unfortunately, an afternoon technical coding lecture had held Sam up, so I spent a leisurely day preparing the meal on my own, while enjoying a novel day off from teaching my movement and meditation class.

Time ticked away, and the sun dipped behind the horizon, but still no sign of Sam. I moved the dinner into the cooker to keep it warm and sat down at the dining table to wait. The waiting was awful. Even though Sam was always late, he usually called to let me know, but I hadn't heard anything. Worry started twisting my stomach.

I got up and went into the living room and, without thinking, began rearranging the blanket draped over the back of the armchair. After folding it, I placed it back on the chair and stared at the front door, hoping it would suddenly open. But the door didn't change. I looked out the front window, hopeful of glimpsing Sam rushing up to the house from his e-vehic, but there was nothing. As I watched the street, something glimmered in the corner of my vision. An e-vehic was parked on the side of the road with a figure sitting in the driver's seat. They just sat there. Unmoving. Something about the stillness sent a shiver up my spine.

Our house was in Forest Glen, a small, heavily forested suburb on the edge of Crayn. The homes here were all a similar dome style, common throughout the region, with the design directing nightly dew or rainwater into underground collection tanks to be used by the household. These self-contained domestic water collection systems enabled more of the city's water supply to be directed to the plants and trees that wound their way through the city. Branches and vines seamlessly melded into building designs across Crayn, with the wonderful symbiotic relationship between plants and humans being the cornerstone of our civilisation. We provided the plants the water they needed to grow, and in return, they provided us with oxygen. Crayn had benefited from being the first ground city established on Tir-na back when terraforming first began. It meant the plants around Crayn had been thriving for over two centuries, resulting in the thick forest setting I loved to call home. Forest Glen was a great place to live, and I was thankful every day for the beautiful scenery and privacy it gave us. The neighbouring houses were quite a distance from each other with a lot of well-established forest in between. Usually I loved that, but today the thought sent a nervous tingle down my spine as I stared at the unmoving e-vehic. It wasn't a common sight to see one in the area just sitting in the street, and something itched at the back of my mind because of it.

The ceiling lights flickered, as they sometimes did in our house. With more strength than needed, I whipped the curtain closed, then noticed I had folded the blanket into a tight, tidy rectangle. I strategically messed it up, so it looked like I had carelessly thrown it into the perfect relaxed position, then walked back to the dining table to wait. Nerves were eating away at my stomach as various explanations of Sam's tardiness bounced around in my head. *I'm probably being ridiculous,* I thought to myself, *but Sam is very late. A quick call won't hurt.*

I hit the button on my wrist-comm to connect to Sam. A green circle spiralled round and round as the device reached out to Sam's, but the call never connected. It just timed out. I tried again, but the same thing happened. On instinct, I pivoted and hit the button to connect to Sam's girlfriend. This time, there was only one dial tone before she answered.

'Hi Rachel.'

'Hi Lilli. Just a quick question. Is Sam there with you?'

'No, he's not. He headed off a while ago. Said he needed to get going to make it home for your dinner. Isn't he there yet?'

'No, he's not. I'm probably just being silly and worrying for no reason. I'm sure he'll turn up soon.'

'Okay. Well, I'll let you know if I hear from him. Oh, and by the way, happy birthday!'

'Thanks, sweetie. Are we seeing you this weekend?'

'Yeah, I'm planning on coming over on Saturday around lunch time. So, I'll see you then.'

'Okay, that sounds great. Alright, I better get going before I accidentally let this food dry out. I'd never hear the end of it if Sam comes home to charcoal. See you on Saturday. Bye, sweetie.'

'Bye Rachel. Have a great night.'

I hung up the phone and went to check on the dinner.

Lilli was a sweet girl. She and Sam suited each other perfectly, and my favourite thing was how she helped Sam be happy just being himself. He had been more

11

confident in his own skin since meeting her, and I couldn't thank her enough for that.

I poured myself a glass of local wine I had bought especially for tonight. I swirled the deep colour around the glass and inhaled its delicious perfume, then took a sip of the silken liquid, letting the flavours slide over my tongue. It was delicious, but it did little to dissipate my worry.

Frustrated, I sat down to wait. And so, I sat, and sipped, and worried, and waited, then waited some more. But as a mother with an active imagination, there is only so much waiting and worrying I could stand before it was time to act. I needed to be moving and doing something, anything, that would release some of the pent-up stress. I pulled out my wrist-comm again and hovered my finger over a contact's details that I had hoped I would never need to use.

The front door tumbled open, and Sam part ran, part fell into the room.

'Sorry Mum! I wanted to get you flowers, but the flower shop was closed, so I went to the general shop, but they didn't have any either. Then I ended up on the other side of town at a random corner shop where I finally got some, but then got stuck in traffic coming home. My wrist-comm was pinging, but I couldn't answer because I was driving. I'm—'

I pulled him into a tight hug, cutting off his words, and just stayed there. My baby was home. He was safe. His tightly wound body slowly relaxed into the embrace as his anxiety left him on a calming breath. We pulled away from each other and stood quietly as I wondered when he had grown so tall.

'The flowers are beautiful, darling. Thank you,' I said and kissed him on the cheek. 'Come on. I can't keep this dinner warm any longer, and I refuse to let your tardiness turn my delicious creation into one of our worst dinners on record.'

'Worse than my attempt at cooking last year?'

'Well, maybe not as bad as that.'

'I can't believe you didn't let me try to redeem myself this year.'

'You had university, so you couldn't. Your birthday isn't too far off. You can cook then. But right now, let's feast.'

I led him into the dining room for my long-awaited birthday dinner. But first, I put a vase in the centre of the table and filled it with the strangest and ugliest collection of half-wilted flowers I had ever seen. I had never been so annoyed and relieved about a silly bunch of flowers.

············

'That was the best,' said Sam with a satisfied smile. 'You're definitely getting better at that whole wrapping the bio-meat and simmering it thing.'

'Ha! Thanks Sam,' I said.

'But there is something missing.'

'And what's that?'

'Your favourite dessert, of course! Come on. Get your coat. I'm taking you out.'

'Is Jasmine's even open this late?'

'Mum, there are people on this planet who don't go to bed at grandma o'clock. Of course it's open. Come on, let's go.'

In a happy flurry, I grabbed my favourite old coat, which I lovingly called Old Blue, and headed out to our e-vehic. I found myself swept up in Sam's enthusiasm and counted myself lucky to have a son as loving and fun as him. Other friends' kids didn't want to know them once they were adults. But not Sam. He existed just to bring joy to those in his life. He might have been shy with everyone else, but with those he loved, he was the heart of everything.

We jumped into our e-vehic and started heading to Jasmine's. As we drove along our street, I searched for the dark e-vehic from earlier, but it was nowhere to be seen. I pushed the worry from my mind and drove us along the weaving forest road. Sam put on his current favourite music, some sort of jolting but rhythmic thumping, and as its strange bass vibrated across my bones, we sped off to dessert.

Half-way along the restaurant strip in Crayn's business district sat Jasmine's Bakery, an indulgent dessert café that was truly a destination. The star-shaped flower motif carved into Jasmine's polished timber door shone in the twinkling street lights. We walked through and the friendly staff ushered us to a polished wooden table with small flowers carved into it, next to the sprawling tree in the middle of the light-filled bakery. The tree was truly a sight to behold. Covered in a vine dotted with tiny white star-shaped flowers, the tree dazzled as its gigantic form dominated the central section of the bakery. There were rumours the vine had grown from a cutting taken from Ancient Earth. Jasmine's had become a favourite of mine, not only for the beautiful flowers covering the tree and vines but also for its boutique pastries. Dessert was Jasmine's speciality, and it had gained them quite a reputation. It was common around this area to see people ducking out from work to grab a quick sweet treat to get them through the day. My favourite was a chocolate cream-filled pastry with some sort of oozy fruit jam swirled through it. It was sweet and sticky and amazing. I would have easily eaten five of them, but contented myself with two.

It was such a happy outing. Admittedly, I didn't go out very much after the sun went down, so I had forgotten the buzz of having other people around you at night. I forgot the simple pleasure of just being out, having dinner where other people served you food you didn't cook yourself. It had definitely been too long since I had enjoyed the nightlife.

With our stomachs happily bulging, we thanked the wonderful staff, dressed in white shirts that matched the crisp white flowers, and headed back to the car. Before getting in, I stopped and pulled Sam in for a hug.

'Thank you. That was lovely. A real treat.'

'I'm glad you liked it. Hope you've had a wonderful birthday.'

'I really have. Thanks, sweetie. Love you.'

'Love you too, Mum,' Sam said before pulling away and jumping into the e-vehic.

On a happy sigh, I slid into the e-vehic and started our trip home. Sam pumped his music once again, and I learnt it was called electro-step. Who knew that existed? And where did they come up with the genre names? I didn't mind the music, truthfully. It was quite fun, but it made me acutely aware of how old I was, which I didn't appreciate.

Driving along through the dense canopy-covered streets, I noticed other restaurants closing for the night. Time really had gotten away from us. I decided to take the shortcut that wove through the maze of vine-covered office buildings and forested public facilities in the business district. As I took the turn, I noticed headlights flicker in the rear vision camera. Another e-vehic was following us. As

I took the next corner, I monitored the following e-vehic out of curiosity, and watched it leisurely take the same turn. It still could have been a coincidence, so I turned once more. Again, it followed. A gnawing started tingling in my stomach. I was probably being silly, but something wasn't right.

Well then, I thought, *let's do a bit of an experiment.* At the next intersection, instead of turning to the right as I usually would, I turned left. You would only make that turn if you wanted to loop back to the restaurant sector, as there were no homes in the area, just silent, dark buildings. As I made the turn, I watched for the e-vehic while nerves prickled up and down my spine. A few moments later, it made the same turn. The music playing flickered between static and Sam's pounding beats, making me flinch. Fear ripped through my gut.

Shit. Okay then, I thought. *It's been a while, but I know what to do.*

As Sam nattered away, telling me something about the lead singer of some band who studied the same subject as him at university, I increased our speed. Not enough to notice, but enough to expand the gap with the other e-vehic. Except it didn't. I experimented again and sped up further, but it kept pace with us. I needed to make another turn, so I slowed down. This time the dark e-vehic didn't change its speed as we took the corner. They ended up right behind us. I looked in the rear camera and noted the figure driving. Something about it was familiar. It had the same silhouette as the person outside our house. My hands gripped the steering wheel tighter as a wave of adrenaline surged through me.

Sam was still nodding away to his music, none the wiser as to our stalker. I didn't want to worry him, but he was an adult and there was something I really needed to know.

'Sam, have you got your safety belt on?' I asked.

'Yeah. Why?'

'Because there's an e-vehic following us. Sweetie, I recognise it from this afternoon. I know you'll think I'm crazy, but I need you to trust me.'

'Wha—,' started Sam as I smashed my foot down on the accelerator. Our e-vehic rocketed down the street. I made some slight acceleration adjustments and slid our vehicle around another corner, then stamped the accelerator to the floor.

'Mum! What the hell?'

'It's alright honey. I've got this,' I said with more confidence than I felt. I had worked hard to forget the part of my life where this came naturally. But in that moment, everything I had once lived and breathed, all the skills I had wished to forget, came rushing back.

'Hold on!' I said, as we drifted around another corner. Then I started planning. If I used the tree-covered grid streets in the business district to lose them, we could cut through the industrial zone to the Outskirts Road. That road had multiple turn-offs that would help cover our tracks. Then, taking the third left, we could loop around the new housing development and sneak in the back entrance to Forest Glen and our house. I had my plan. Now I needed to make it work.

After the fifth corner in the business district, we sped under the auto-rail bridge and headed into the industrial zone. Metal angular buildings, softened by creeping vines and snaking trees, streaked past the windows. It was late and there was no one around, so I let our e-vehic see how fast it could go.

The rear camera showed the street behind us was clear, but I knew the worst thing you could do was relax too soon. So, with a keen focus, I continued our manic drive onwards. We skidded around a turn as I cut our lights and finally reached the open and quiet Outskirts Road.

'Mum. What's going on?'

'I don't know, but I think we're safe...for now.'

Rain started to fall as we cruised along the quiet back road, passing narrow driveways that lead to houses hidden in the densely forested outskirts. My eyes frantically scanned, trying to keep my precious boy safe. There was no one else on the road as we looped around the new housing development and headed for the back entrance road to Forest Glen. We weren't too far from home now. We just had to make it there.

Our e-vehic's wheels slipped on the wet road as we turned into the heavily canopied back road that would lead us home. Without thinking, I recovered control and continued speeding along. We were only a few minutes from home. We had almost made it.

'Mum, where the hell did you learn to drive like that?' asked Sam, breaking my focused attention.

'Hmm?'

'How do you know how to drive like that?'

'What? Are you saying you think I'm usually a terrible driver?'

'No, of course not.'

'Can't mums have skills?'

'Of course, it's jus—'

A loud, crumpling noise rang through my ears as an e-vehic smashed into my door, throwing us off the road. Our e-vehic hit the edge of a fallen tree and shot into the air, flipping at an angle that had our bodies straining against the safety belts. Blurred, incoherent images assaulted my eyes as we tumbled through the air. A smash reverberated through the e-vehic as it landed on its roof and bounced to a jarring halt.

I hung upside down, my arms dangling like half broken tree branches. On a sharp inhale, my brain refocused, and one thought screamed in my mind. *SAM!*

Nausea crept up my insides, but I clamped down the burning acid sliding up my throat and turned to Sam. He was hanging upside down, held in place by his safety belt, but there was no movement. Panic slapped me in the face and cleared my vision.

'Sam!'

There was no reply.

I reached down and relieved the tension on the buckle, then channelled all my strength to click my safety belt open. A sharp pain to rippled down my arm as I fell to the ground, landing on my shoulder.

Now more free to move, I reached out to Sam.

'Sam! Wake up.'

There was no response. My body shook with pain and fear. Sam had to be fine. He was my son and I would protect him till I died. He had to be okay.

Taking a breath, I reset my thoughts and checked for his breath. He was breathing. He was alive. I sighed, releasing an immense weight off my chest. Now to get us out of here.

Crunching footsteps stomped across the grass. My insides constricted with panic. If needed, I would fight. I didn't care what happened to me, as long as

Sam was okay. I reached under the driver's seat and tried to grab a small black bag stored there.

The passenger side door ripped open, and two figures reached in and began manhandling Sam.

'NO!' I screamed as they cut his safety belt and pulled his unconscious body from the e-vehic.

My hand found the bag. I ripped it down and pulled out a small handheld firearm.

Blood from a cut on my head dripped into my eyes, obscuring my vision. I aimed my shaking hand out the passenger door, but then lowered it. I couldn't risk hitting Sam and making a fatal and unforgivable mistake.

Sam's legs dragged behind him as they threw him into the e-vehic. I tried to open the driver's side door to go after them, but it was damaged in the crash and wouldn't budge. I screamed out in anguish and frustration. My son. They were taking him.

I twisted and dragged myself out the passenger door onto the wet grass as tears mixed with blood dripped down my face.

The headlights of the other e-vehic blinded me, making the heavy raindrops glitter like a mocking shower of golden birthday confetti. As its doors slammed shut, I limped towards them, raised my weapon, and fired. The windscreen glass shattered.

I kept firing even as the e-vehic revved its engine, swung around and streaked away down the road, disappearing into the dark.

My body shook, and I struggled to breathe under the crushing pain. I don't know when my weapon ran out of ammunition, but my trigger finger continued flexing and releasing empty shot after empty shot.

A single thought thundered through my mind, *My baby. They've taken my baby!*

A streetlight exploded above me in a shower of sparks as a raw scream ripped from my throat. Its force stole away my energy, leaving an empty husk in its place. I fell to the puddled ground, cowering over my knees, and sucked in the cold, wet air. It felt like frigid knives against my throat. My eyes fixated on the shrinking rear lights of the dark e-vehic, not wanting to let it from my sight. And as it turned the corner and disappeared into the night, so too did Sam.

2

Belly of the Beast

I T WAS A LONG walk home through the relentless storm and my aching limbs complained with each trudging step. I burst through the front door in a torrent of water and wind, then pivoted and with a pained grunt kicked the door closed, the force knocking two family photos off the wall. The frame of my favourite baby photo of Sam smashed on the floor. Another blow to my already broken heart.

The house was quiet compared to the storm outside, and I let the thick silence wash over me, pulling me down into its dark depths. I crumpled to the floor. The car crash had left me battered but not beaten. My body ached from the whiplash, my shoulder joint was sore, and the cut on my head stung, but I was okay. I reached out and pulled the baby picture from the broken frame. Sam's tiny chubby face with his one tooth smiled up at me. A pained cry caught in my throat as I let the trembling ache roil all over my body. Everything hurt, and I let the pain pull me downwards as I lay on the ground and curled in on myself. Then, I let my feelings take me. Despite the urgency, it was important to feel. That's what makes us human, after all. I'm not sure how long I lay there releasing my torn feelings while my body shook with grief, but once I had expelled the initial fear and terror, everything snapped into sharp focus. It was time to act.

Time was critical. They knew where we lived, so I needed to get moving and get out of there. I put the baby photo in the pocket of Old Blue and ran to the hallway cupboard and moved aside a box of exercise equipment stored within. It revealed a hidden panel that I pulled off. I grabbed my hidden go bag, a purple backpack covered in peaceful mantras and symbols of mindfulness that I got from a conference years ago. I pulled out a code card from one of the internal pockets and ran over to the kitchen bench to flip a hidden switch next to the stovetop. A whirring metallic noise sounded as part of the bench slid sideways, revealing a hidden holo-projector. I pushed the code card into a slot and the holo-projector flickered to life. An interactive hologram login screen floated in front of me and without missing a beat, I held up my hand for a palm scan, followed by a retinal scan and voice detector. The familiar home screen loaded, and after acknowledging the current threat pop ups, I twisted my hand through the hologram and pulled up the wrist-comm tracking application I had uploaded long ago. It flickered to life and asked for a tracking ID. I entered 5^M##001 and hit *Run*.

A picture of Sam flashed up on the screen along with the words **SEARCH INITIATED.** A large circle with a thin arrow began rotating round the picture of Sam, an innocuous image that seemed at odds with the invasive search occurring in the background. I held my breath while terrible nervous anticipation ate me alive. A loud *BEEP* sounded as the display showed the words **NO RESULTS FOUND–SUBJECT NOT LOCATED**. My stomach dropped. Sam's wrist-comm tracker had been deactivated.

I closed the holo-projector and reset the kitchen bench, snatching my code card back and shoving it in my pocket. But then, I just froze. The sound of the rain streaming down the outside the house into the reservoirs was deafening, but the voice in my head screaming, *What am I going to do?* was louder.

A terrible idea started taking root in the corner of my mind. What other choice did I have? I couldn't find Sam on my own, not quick enough to make sure he stayed safe. And I knew some people who could find him, and they owed me.

• • • • • • • • • •

Grass whipped at my ankles as it danced in the frenzied storm. Precinct parking had always been terrible. With the night shift in full swing at the perpetually awake precinct, I had to park Sam's e-vehicle and trek through the rain to reach the Agency's Glen. Heavy droplets drenched me down to my bra and my favourite coat streamed frigid water that pooled around my cuffs before trickling down my numb fingers. I looked up and finally there it was. The great phallic obelisk. I really hated that thing, but I always thought it was an accurate reflection of the men who roamed the halls of this precinct of contrived power. When it rained, the depressed monolithic buildings looked like they were crying, stuck in a thick forested prison, screaming out for someone to save them from their life in this cesspool. I jostled my purple backpack into a more comfortable position and continued my trudge through the precisely cut grass that was quickly turning to sludge.

Before I knew it, I was standing at the base of the soaring obelisk. Taking a deep breath, I pushed escaped strands from my soaked curly bun back from my face and knocked on the hidden metal door. My stomach twisted, causing bile to cover the back of my tongue in a sour tang. I knew no matter how much I fought it, the dark underbelly of this place was about to suck me back in, and I would succumb to its siren call.

The metal door wrenched open with a stale hiss, revealing the frame of a tall, broad-shouldered figure that filled the entire doorway. I knew that figure.

'Hi James, I need to see her.'

'Rachel,' the crewcut security guard nodded at me. 'Haven't seen you in a while.'

'Twenty years.'

'That long.'

'Last time I saw you was on that mission—'

'Out to the forest encampment. Now that brings back memories. Blew my knee out a few years back though, so no more fun outings like that for me, unfortunately. Had it replaced it with a pretty sweet mechanical one, but they assessed me as being invalid for field work. I got this gig instead of medical retirement though, and it suits me just fine. Fantastic out-of-hours rates,' he said with a conspiratorial smile.

An awkward silence hung in the air, broken only by the repetitive drumming of the rain. I had never been close to James, but I did remember he was one of those people who loved to share their life details without prompting. Seemed like he hadn't changed.

'Can I come in?' I asked.

'Sure.'

James moved his hulking figure to the side, allowing just enough room for me to squeeze through. The door slammed shut, reverberating off the concrete interior. I winced internally at the sound, but kept an external veneer of calm. I couldn't show weakness here. I was in the belly of the beast and once in, there were only two official ways out; you either got spat out or shat out. Personally, I preferred the more creative, unofficial third option. Find a weapon and hack your way out. I really hated the place.

'Here, wipe yourself off,' James said, passing me an old towel that looked like it had seen better days from behind his little desk.

I took the towel gratefully, and with nerves pumping, I started drying myself, taking a moment to hide a deep, calming breath while drying my face with the greasy, chemical-smelling towel. I instantly regretted that breath. *You need to do this, so just suck it up and act the part*, I thought before plastering on a neutral expression and getting down to business.

'She in James?'

'Yep.'

'In the same office the old Head was in?'

'Yep. I better escort you down, though.'

'What do you mean?'

'No ID pass,' he nodded at my chest. 'You need one of these.' James threw me a bright yellow visitor pass and matching lanyard. No chance of subtlety now, everyone would know instantly I didn't belong here.

'Fine,' I said and handed him back the now saturated towel. 'Lead the way.'

We wove through a maze of claustrophobic elevators and narrow grey hallways, passing nameless doors that hid all manner of secrets. It was late, but I could already hear the quick echoing steps of people rushing around, doing whatever it was they thought was so important and worth trading their lives for. I used to be just like them. This used to be my home, and I cringed inwardly at the memory of how much I used to love the ego rush of knowing I was part of something so elite and secretive.

We halted, and James pressed a small button on a bland black door.

'Yes,' a voice crackled from a hidden speaker.

'Rachel Tomsen here to see you, ma'am.'

There was a long pause before a click sounded and the door popped open.

'Off you go then, and good to see you again,' said James, ushering me through before closing the door behind me.

I entered a small, beige office with an even more beige looking woman typing away at a desk. Without looking or losing a beat, she flicked her finger commandingly towards a secondary door.

Steeling myself, I puffed out my chest and strode over to the door. Then, just like ripping off a band-aid, I opened the door, ready to get this necessary evil over and done with.

'Rachel Tomsen,' came a shrill and commanding voice. 'It's been years. Please, come sit down.'

Vivian Wyrmstead, one of the most powerful people on Tir-na who didn't exist. She was a short woman with painfully white-blonde, thin hair that was always combed into a perfect blunt crop without a strand out of place. Dressed in a tailored skirt suit, she gestured gracefully with her manicured hand at a standard-issue brown armchair. Following her lead, I manoeuvred to the chair and sat down, assuming the most non-threatening and respectful body posture I could manage, while purposefully ignoring the puddles of water dripping off my clothes. I must have looked like a mess. Unsurprisingly, Vivian remained standing, linking her fingers calmly in front of her, and looked at me as though she could see into my soul. She always had a way of completely unnerving you while looking serene; a veneer she had carefully crafted to hide the fact she was a cunning predator who relished toying with her victims before biting them. It's not that I hated her, it's just that I never trusted her. She never did anything without a selfish motivation. And so, I was wary of her, and she made me uncomfortable. I would have much preferred for each of us to go on living our happy lives as far away from each other as possible, so we didn't have to cross paths again.

'I must admit, you are the last person I ever expected to come crawling back through our tunnels. From what I recall, you didn't leave here on the best of terms. So, I admit, I'm intrigued. Only something terrible would drive you back here, and I can't wait to hear the story.'

'Nice to see you too, Vivian. I'll get straight to it, so we don't have to pretend with pleasantries. My son was taken and I need the Agency's help to get him back.'

'Ah Rachel. It's always straight to business with you. It's a refreshing change from the usual political dance I play with most people around here. But I can't help you with a personal matter. You know that.'

'Look. I didn't want to come here anymore than you want me here. I understood when I left it was forever, and I understand this is the type of request even I would have rejected when I was here. But this isn't just a personal issue. You know who the father of my son was. I won't insult your intelligence by pretending you don't.'

Vivian cocked her head and gave a sly, smiling nod that dripped with curious disdain.

'Good. That makes all this easier. I left the Agency to help protect it, and my son. Unfortunately for all of us, it seems you can never really escape your past. This place owes me, and I had a promise of help should I ever need it. Well, I'm calling in what I'm owed. Help me get my son back. Do this and you'll never have to see me again.'

'I already thought I would never see you again.'

I glared at her as hairline cracks splintered across my cool business facade. I needed her help, but I couldn't let her know how badly I needed it. The silence crashed around us, its waves slowly eroding our resolve. It was a battle of wills, but she underestimated how desperate I really was. I would do anything to get what I needed.

Vivian broke first.

'Fine,' she said. 'If it was solely my decision, I would have you thrown out. But as it is, the decision was made long ago, and I am bound to it. The Agency promised help if needed, in exchange for the agreement, and I am nothing if not loyal to the rule of the Agency. Know this though, the agreement never stated we needed to help you more than once. You ask for this favour, then afterwards all contacts between yourself and the Agency are null and void. You will no longer have the Agency's support. You will be no one to us. Do you understand?'

'I do.'

'Are you sure you want to ask for this favour then?'

'I am.'

'Alright. What do you need?'

'I need help to find my son and the people who have taken him. He was kidnapped at 2200. We were rammed off the road, then two figures then approached our crashed e-vehic and took Sam. I need to find out who the kidnappers are, and I need to get Sam back ASAP.'

'So, tracking, intel, then extraction?'

'Yes.'

'I can assign one agent to assist you. You're lucky. This one just happens to be between missions. What he'll think about it, though, I'll leave up to you to find out.' She paused and inhaled a resigned sigh. 'The Agency agrees to provide you informational, material, personnel and monetary support. But once this is done, you are dead to us, and I will never see you again. Report to Mission Hub, I'll have your agent meet you there. You are dismissed.'

· · · · · · · · · ·

A nameless house of a man in a crisp uniform led me through the bland, identical hallways that twisted deep underground. My nerves threatened to bubble over. I shoved my hands into my pockets to hide their trembling and started subtle box breathing while maintaining my face in a frozen mask. I was in. It was the last place I wanted to be, but they had what I needed and would help me. I took more comfort from that fact than was warranted. Truthfully, helping me was the least they could do. Every passing moment left Sam in harm's way, so I needed things to move faster, but frustratingly, I also needed to play their game. I followed the nameless uniformed man and let the rhythmic echo of our feet drown out my thoughts. The momentary stillness in my mind quickly filled with sense memories. I saw myself running through the hallways in training gear, heading into briefings, limping to the infirmary after a disaster of a mission, and sharing a joke with a friend as we headed through the blue doors of Mission Hub, the never-sleeping nexus of the Agency's universe where we received our task briefings.

I was jarred out of the past as Mr Uniform halted our march in front of those same blue doors. He swiped his ID pass and punched a complex sequence into a keypad. The doors swished open with a loud breeze, revealing a room that, in another life, I would have called home.

Huge holo-screens covered almost every wall, with perfect rows of smaller control holos lined up in front of them. Analysts madly swished their hands through the projected controls, pushing data through AI processing and correlation algorithms. If the Agency was one huge beast, then this was its brain, and its brain never shut off. It was where analysts prepared mission briefings, analysed threat landscapes and provided succinct presentations for agents before missions. As I looked around the room, I noticed how much the technology had advanced since my last visit. I couldn't even name most of the equipment they were using to process and compile their reports. In the centre of the room, though, was something that looked familiar, a large oval table with a holo-board embedded in its centre. There were two analysts at the large table, heads together, talking in hushed tones while rushing to pull together a briefing pack. Lazing in a chair next to the two analysts was a third figure dressed in a very well-known mission jumpsuit that identified them as an agent. The figure reclined in the chair with their crossed feet resting on the edge of the table. Their body language was completely at odds with that of the analysts. While the analysts appeared uptight, with an essence of cold, processing calculation, the agent appeared open and smugly relaxed. They were even stifling a yawn as I entered the room. The large doors swished closed, alerting everyone to my presence.

'Well, well. Rachel Tomsen. That's a face I never thought I'd see again.' The agent slipped their legs off the table, stood up and sauntered over to me. He stuck his hands in his pockets, and gave me a once-over, pausing on my face. 'You look like shit, Rach.'

'You're still here, Peter? Are things so bad at the Agency that they have to send old men out on missions these days?'

Peter Brand, the second-best agent in the Agency, or maybe the best after I left, and my old partner. He had a natural swagger and the most annoyingly perfect, naturally coiffed hair in existence, that had turned a dusty silver since I had last seen him.

He smirked at my flippant comment, then grabbed my hand for a rough shake and a one-armed shoulder hug and back pat. That ridiculous, classic sign of male affection, where they care enough to make contact, but not enough to enter the other's personal space.

'It's good to see you,' Peter said while half hugging, half patting my back. The act of it shocked me, as he had never been one for showing any affection. Maybe old age had changed him. It had been twenty years since I last saw him. He pulled away quickly and gestured for me to take a seat at the table next to the analysts.

My blood fizzed in my veins. I didn't have time for the song and dance routine that was about to unfold. Sam could already be dead, and they were about to waste more time extracting information. But I needed them to help me, so I played along. For ten years, I played my role in this decrepit cesspool, maintaining a perfectly crafted image that helped me sail under the radar of all the crazy politics in this place. I made sure I was never too confrontational, so I didn't show up the men and make them feel inadequate, but I also couldn't appear weak. On top of that, I needed to appear supportive of others, and individually effective enough that people spoke well of me, both of which boosted my reputation and provided more opportunities. It was a hard juggling game, but it had worked like a dream. So, I needed to play my part again, and like zipping up a well-worn mission jumpsuit, I slipped straight back into it.

I strode over to the indicated seat with my chin high and prepared myself for the oncoming analyst grilling. They were always hungry for information, and they often lacked the emotional intelligence to notice when a subject was spent. This was going to be painful. It was only conditioning that momentarily held off the keen analysts. They knew their position in the pecking order. They would respectfully but uncomfortably wait until Peter told them they could start before they began the information extraction.

Peter sat with a flourish of bravado. 'You're lucky Rach, I happen to be in between gigs so you've been assigned the best agent in the Agency.' He flicked me a playful smile edged with a hint of challenge, but I didn't have it in me to rise to it. When I was young, I happily bantered with him all day, but right then, precious minutes were ticking by. There was no time.

I attempted a half-smile, but something inside me had fractured. Something intrinsic. Sam held my heart, and he was in danger. My false bravado shattered. Tears welled in my eyes and streamed down my cheeks, leaving salty trails in their wake. I was crying in Mission Hub. An old part of myself shuddered at the thought of showing so much emotion, but that was the old me and I left her behind when I found a better way of life for me and my son. They could take their lack of empathy and shove it.

After wiping my face clean, I raised my eyes to see their horrified stares. 'I'm sorry Peter, I don't have it in me to spar right now. I just need your help. I know it's late and a bit of a shock, but I'm desperate and have nowhere else to go. The execs always promised me help should I need it. So here I am, asking for help and happy to do whatever needs to be done. Can we start the brief so we can get moving? Every moment we waste is another moment my son is in danger.'

Peter's face transformed before my eyes. One moment he was joking and cavalier, the next ashen and serious. 'Of course we can start. Analysts, what do you need?'

The analysts glanced at each other before the thin, weedy woman of the pair began speaking in an automatic tone.

'We haven't received any prior intel on this operation. The only details we have are the mission task request from the Agency Head, and a statement saying it's about a missing subject.'

'My son,' I clarified with a bit more force than necessary.

'Yes. Your son.' She paused as if uncomfortable that the subject was a real person and not just data. 'Can you tell us exactly what happened?'

What followed was a standard but unnerving back-and-forth question-and-answer session as I slowly told my story. The analysts peppered me with questions ranging from what Sam was wearing when I last saw him through to what holo communities he was part of. It was an exhausting process, but I knew it was necessary. The analysts entered the information as I gave it to them, and in real time, pulled all available and relevant records. They even pulled his University ID photo and used it as the image for the file, resulting in Sam's smiling face staring at me from the holo-projector in the centre of the table. The sight of him compounded my worry and I couldn't breathe.

'That's enough,' Peter said, the quiet authority in his voice halting the analysts in their tracks. 'That's enough. We can't sit here any longer. This mission is to be registered as time critical. So, in the essence of time, let the AI process everything we have so far and simulcast your analysis into the AI channel while it's running. If you come across anything to help identify Sam's location, or if there are any leads worth pursuing, hit me up on my wrist-comm.'

Peter stood and ushered me out of Mission Hub. The blue doors swished closed behind us and we turned to the left, heading deeper into the belly of the Agency until we reached Mission Prep.

Mission Prep was an equipment storage room where agents outfitted themselves for deploying on missions. It was laid out in a large rectangle with equipment lockers lining three of the walls. The equipment lockers contained everything an agent could need. There were replacement wrist-comms, jumpsuits, civilian clothing, boots, high heels (with hidden features), ration packs, optical-tool kits, EMP disks, incendiary stickers, DNS bugs, AI deployment keys and a huge range of firearms and daggers. All things that were easily concealed under clothing or in a bag. Quiet stealth was the ethos of agents rather than bluster and gusto, so the smaller the kit, the better. In the centre of the room were a few bench seats where agents could outfit themselves. I had never really been comfortable with the lack of privacy when I was an agent, but I had just got on with it. The Agency definitely wasn't a place for modest people.

Peter threw me a bag and then began methodically selecting various items from the equipment stores. I followed suit and found myself fascinated by the new tech on offer. Things had changed since I was last here. Agents these days had a massive advantage. What I wouldn't have given when I was young for some of that tech.

I followed Peter around the room and collected an excessive amount of equipment. It would have been silly to not take advantage of the shiny new things on offer. Once my bag was full, I turned to Peter and was met with a jumpsuit to the face.

'Hey!'

'You're drenched, Rach. Put that on until your clothes dry off. You've been shivering for the last hour.'

I hadn't even noticed. I looked down and saw my discoloured water-logged pants and felt my toes shrivelling in my socks. Seeing me in my underwear was nothing new for Peter after a decade working together on multiple missions, so I started changing into Agency clothing without a thought. Although I'm sure I looked a lot less saggy back then.

'I think we should go to your house first,' said Peter, as though I wasn't standing in front of him in just underwear. 'I'd like to get a feel for things there and maybe have a look at the tracking system you already tried. See if I can boost it with the Agency's AI.'

'Sure. Okay.' I zipped up the jumpsuit and sighed in thanks as the smooth and warm fabric cocooned me. Peter was looking at me with a strange expression on his face that I couldn't read. It wasn't a single emotion, but rather like he was on the edge of something. I wouldn't have noticed at all if it wasn't for my training. Micro-behavioural analysis was actually one of my strongest skills when I was an agent. The awkward moment lingered before his expression reverted to its natural state of over-confidence.

'How'd you get here, by the way?' Peter asked, halting any further thoughts on the matter.

'Used Sam's e-vehic. Had to park on the other side of the precinct and walk through the rain.'

'How about we travel in a bit more comfort and get ourselves an Agency e-vehic? Then I can drop you off at Sam's e-vehic and meet you at your house. I'd like to do a thorough once-over of the place. If that's alright?'

'Sounds good. Let's just get going,' I said as I put back on the yellow visitor pass and shoved the drenched Old Blue in my backpack. 'Lead the way, Peter.'

3

Betrayal

WE WALKED UP THE path to my domed house, which glistened in the pre-dawn light with droplets from the night's rain. I loved my little house. It was nothing fancy, but it was more than enough for the two of us, and it was all mine. That meant more than anything to me. I had fixed it up myself, which had been an enormous project but was completely worth it. It had also meant I could add in a few extra unconventional features thanks to a friend who had become disgruntled after working in the Agency's tech department. Was it illegal for her to install an Agency holo in my kitchen eighteen years ago and provide me with a ghost proxy account? Most definitely. Was I going to say no when she offered to put it in after everything that happened to Miles? Of course not. Did I hope it would help me find out who killed Miles? Yes, I did. Had it? No. Unfortunately, the tech also hadn't been updated for eighteen years to not set off any alerts or network alarms. The last I heard, my contact had moved to Aeir, so I was stuck with the outdated backdoor legacy system, but it still should have been enough to find Sam.

We reached the red front door and quickly headed inside. Several lights had been left on in my earlier hurry, and the broken picture frame was still on the floor next to a puddle of water that had soaked into the carpet. Peter paused in the hallway and looked at the smashed frame.

'That was me, so don't worry about it,' I said over my shoulder as I walked deeper into the house. Everything looked as it always had, but felt completely different. The house was silent. No echoing noises from Sam's holo-games, no ambient music from a physical meditation I had been working through, no bubbling kettle, no news speakers updating us on the state of Tir-na. Nothing. There was no life in this house anymore, just the wreckage of my once-perfect life.

Nerves trickled down my spine, and I found my hand unconsciously holding the folded baby photo I had put in the jumpsuit pocket. Coming back here was a tremendous risk. They knew where I lived and there was nothing to stop them from coming back.

'I want to get changed. Sam's bedroom is at the top of the stairs, the first door on the left. Feel free to look around. Hopefully, you find something I haven't noticed.' I strode up the stairs to my room as Peter peeled off into the living room to begin a systematic, analytical search throughout the house.

I reached my room and closed the door, then let myself lean against the solid wood as I closed my eyes and sucked in a shaky deep breath. My bedroom had that comforting and familiar smell to it. Exactly what I needed. I opened my eyes and saw my reflection staring back at me from the floor-length mirror I had attached to my wardrobe door. Standing in the mirror was the memory of a strong and determined young woman who believed she was the deliverer of justice, an angel of retribution. In a blink of an eye though she was gone, and instead a strange hybrid old woman stood against the door looking haggard and stressed. Her hair was frizzy, curling up at crazy angles, and her eyes were bloodshot and hung with dark circles. She wore a jumpsuit I had never wanted to see again. My hand grasped Sam's photo out of my pocket and placed it on the bed. I took faithful Old Blue out of the backpack and hung it up to dry, before removing the vile jumpsuit and stuffing it in the dirty clothes bin. I then made fast time putting on my most comfortable outfit and a pair of waterproof boots containing hidden arch support. They weren't the prettiest, but I loved them, and I thought it would be smart to prepare for anything.

I pulled my tangled greying hair up into a messy bun and spent some time towel-drying Old Blue. The cuffs and neck were still damp, and the fabric had developed a musty smell that rankled my nose, but I put it on anyway. The way it caressed my body was reassuring somehow. I put the precious baby photo of Sam in the pocket. Once dressed, I grabbed my backpack and headed to the hallway. I strode down the hallway and paused at Sam's bedroom door. Peter was in there sitting at Sam's holo-projector on the opposite side of the room. He was casually reviewing Sam's detailed browsing history and files. I had forgotten how useless encryption and standard security were against the capabilities of the Agency. Sporadic items from throughout Sam's room were laid out on the bed, including a pamphlet from a music performance, his portable gamer, the holo-pad he used for university, a picture of his girlfriend Lillian, and two hard-copy books called *The Permafrost Saga* and *Ancient Earth–A History of Humanity's Expanse to the Stars*. The precise alignment and categorisation of Sam's belongings was evidence of Peter's methodical analysis. I took a deep breath and crossed the threshold.

'Found anything?' I asked. Peter turned to face me, completely calm, as though he had known I was about to walk into Sam's room.

'He was into gaming, wasn't he?' It came across as more of a statement than an actual question.

'Yeah, he was.'

'You know if he ever had any run-ins with other holo-gamers?'

'Not that I know of, but it's not like he told me everything.'

'Was he part of a holo-horde?'

'Yeah, he was. I think there were about eight of them he would regularly play with.'

A look of curiosity darkened his eyes. 'Did he ever talk to you about the tournaments he was in?'

'He mentioned something about a competition he was playing in.'

'The kid was making some pretty substantial coin playing as a gladiator for the highest bidder.'

'He...what? I knew he made some money from it, but I always thought it was just some extra spending money. The way he discussed the competitions made me think he was hiding something, but I never imagined he was raking in cash from them.' I couldn't keep the surprise off my face. How had I missed that?

'Looks like he used some of it to pay for his university fees, and the rest went into savings, which is surprisingly responsible for a young kid.'

'He always told me he got a discount on his uni fees for paying upfront. Why didn't he tell me what he was doing? I know money's a bit tight for us, but I told him I would manage to pay—'

The click and thud of a door being opened echoed from downstairs. Peter and I looked at each other, then pulled out our weapons. It was too early in the morning for visitors. I crept to the window and scanned the outside surrounds. Nerves bubbled in my stomach. The window looked out on the backyard, but there was no one there. Peter waited until I gave him the all-clear before he moved to the top of the stairs, his weapon held at the ready.

Footsteps echoed from the downstairs hallway and Peter signalled for me to move into my bedroom doorway while he pulled back into the upstairs bathroom. The footsteps continued in a steady rhythm as they walked up the stairs. There was a slowness to the steps, almost a hesitation. My hands shook and my lungs ached as I desperately tried to silence my breath. I snuck a look at Peter from my hiding spot. He looked perfectly at ease, but the taut muscle at his neck betrayed his calm exterior.

The figure appeared at the top of the stairs and took two steps into the hallway when Peter launched himself and tactically swept the legs out from under them. The figure fell onto the solid floor as a high-pitched scream escaped their lips. Peter was on top of them in a heartbeat, grabbing their arms to immobilise them. I hesitated as the speed of Peter's movements startled me, but then moved forward and aimed my weapon to give Peter some cover.

The figure had long dark hair that looked midnight black in the dim hall lighting. They were slight of frame, wearing simple sneakers and a very familiar jacket with a large Crayn University logo on the back. The figure was shaking, visibly terrified, and everything about them looked familiar.

'Lilli?' I whispered.

'Rachel!' said the relieved, familiar voice of Lillian Zinke.

'You know her?' asked Peter.

'Yes, she's Sam's girlfriend. Let her up.' I reached down and helped her stand. 'Lilli, are you hurt?'

'No, I'm okay. Just a few bruises. I caught myself before my face smashed into the ground, so that's good.' She always rambled when she was nervous. Sam and Lilli had been dating for two years. They had met through a mutual love of holo-games at a game convention, so happened to be at the right place at the right time. She had become like a daughter to me during those years. An overwhelming maternal impulse washed over me, and I pulled her into a tight hug.

'Lilli. I must tell you something terrible.' Peter's hard eyes bored into me in warning, but I pressed on and ignored him. 'Sam's been taken. I don't know who took him or where he is, but we'll find him. This is my friend Peter. He's going to help us.'

Lilli's eyes flicked to Peter, quickly taking him in. She then stared at the floor, and for a while I wasn't sure if she was in shock or just hadn't understood. Suddenly, Lilli looked me in the eye and gripped my arms. Her fingers tightened as though she desperately needed to hold on to something to stop her world from spinning. Then she slumped to the ground and wept as her entire body shook from the raspy, hyperventilating heaves.

'No. No. It can't. They can't. He wasn't—' The words came out quivering, with the final one cut off by a shocking inhale of breath. Her body trembled, so I crouched down and pulled her into a tight embrace. She was crying uncontrollable tears and all I could do was hold on and gently stroke her hair to provide some comfort.

'I know. I know, sweetie.' I hadn't realised I was also crying until a tear dripped off my nose and landed on the back of Lilli's hair.

Movement to the right caught my eye, and I looked over to see Peter standing awkwardly at the side of the hall. He gave me a nod and gestured that he would head downstairs to look around. I nodded in reply and focused again on the distraught girl in my arms.

'Lilli. Sweetie. We'll find him. Don't worry. We'll find him,' I stated, with more confidence than I felt.

'It's my fault. It's all my fault.'

'Shhhh,' I whispered, while stroking her hair. 'Don't say that. Of course it's not your fault. You couldn't have stopped this.' My mind flashed back to the car spinning through the air before coming to a jolting holt, the sight of Sam's body being dragged from the car, and the hopeless feeling of kneeling in the rain, screaming at the e-vehic as it disappeared into the night. 'It's my fault. I should have stopped it. I could have stopped it, but I didn't.' The idea splintered me in two, as I hadn't said that thought out loud yet.

'You don't understand. It's all my fault. I love him. But what else could I do?' Something in her words didn't sit right.

'Lilli. What did you mean it's your fault?'

'I love Sam. You know that, don't you?' Her eyes locked onto mine once more. They were crazed. Manic in their intensity.

'I do, Lilli. I know you wouldn't do anything to hurt him.'

'But it is my fault.' She sat up and pulled herself into a ball, her knees tucked up tight under her chin. 'It really is Rachel. I'm not just saying that.' She wiped snot from her nose with the cuff of her jacket.

I pulled back from her and heard Peter walking back up the stairs. He silently indicated everything was fine and took a position against the wall at the top of the stairs where he could see both us and the downstairs hallway.

I looked at Lilli then. Really looked at her. There was something about her emotions that didn't just echo sadness. There was something else at play.

'How about we head downstairs? I'll make us some tea.' I stood up and helped Lilli stand. I tucked my arm around her waist and started ushering her down the stairs. Peter just stared at me. I could tell he had been giving me space to take the lead with this situation, so as we passed him, I gave him a look I had given him many times before. A subtle look, perfected over many operations together, that alerted the other to something without needing to say a thing. It only involved the minutest movement of the eyes, but its message was loud and clear. Something was wrong.

· · · · ● · ● · · · ·

The water in the kettle rumbled and bubbled. I took the boiled kettle and filled up three mugs to make tea. Lilli sat at the kitchen table and stared at a large old scratch in the timber with a near-crazed intensity. Peter sat opposite with his arms crossed over his chest. He remained silent and simply observed. His message to me was obvious. *This is your show, so off you go.*

I carried over the hot teas and put them in front of Peter and Lilli before retrieving my own and returning to the table. I sat in the seat closest to Lilli, on the other side of a corner. It gave me the best view of her face while talking to her, while also establishing the physical closeness I needed to emphasise our connection.

I blew on my tea and took a tentative sip. It was ridiculously hot, so I gently put it back on the table and cradled the mug with my hands. I noticed Lilli's hands move out from under the table and she also cradled her mug, which was a sign she was relaxing. Whereas Peter, I noticed, hadn't so much as looked at his drink. I took a breath and began.

'Lilli. You said this is your fault. Can you tell me what you mean?'

Her fingers began fidgeting with the handle of the mug. 'I...' She paused, her eyes flickering over the table as if searching for something. She inhaled a sharp breath before continuing. 'You're going to hate me.' She looked at me with fearful eyes. I remained neutral and continued.

'Lilli. Tell me what happened. If you know anything that can help save Sam, I need you to tell me.'

'I never meant for him to get hurt. They promised me he wouldn't.' She looked up at the healing cut on my forehead from the car crash, then quickly averted her eyes.

There was a long pause, but I knew sometimes you had to give someone the space to tell their own story. I sipped my tea and remained attentive. Lilli took a sip as well, then began her tale.

'As you know, I'm from the Grove and only moved here for university. I'm studying to be a doctor.' Her pride in this was clear as she looked over at Peter, but he remained silent and unmoving, so she looked away and continued. 'There's a program in the Grove that sends secondary school graduates to universities across Tir-na. The Master pays for the entire degree and covers all costs. My family is poor, so I wouldn't be here without it. Since I was little, I've dreamed of being a doctor. So, I studied hard and made sure I qualified for the program. When I arrived at Crayn, I attended classes, made friends and met Sam. On my way back to my accommodation one day, two men stopped me. They told me I was indebted to the Master, that I owed him everything and if I didn't repay him, my family would suffer. I didn't understand what they wanted, so I offered them money, not that I had much. They just laughed and told me to keep an ear out for things I thought were interesting and report back to them. It sounded like something I could easily do to keep my family safe.'

Lilli took a shaky breath and continued. 'I started meeting with one of them, the one with fancy blue hair, and I would tell him random things, like who was in my class, and who my teachers were. I remember the first time I mentioned Sam, the man seemed more interested than usual and started asking more specific questions, like who Sam was, where he was from and who his family were. It was fine at first, but then the questions started getting more intense and I pushed back. I didn't want to betray Sam like that, but when I tried to say no, the man just reminded me of my family.'

'What choice did I have?' Lilli's hands flew into the air as she became more animated and more defensive. 'I love Sam, and it broke my heart to betray him. But my family was in danger. *Are* in danger! I've been reporting things about Sam the entire time we've been together, and the man even started asking about you, Rachel. He's become more demanding and threatening lately. I was scared, so I told him everything he wanted to know. I couldn't stand the thought of my family being hurt, but I never imagined it would lead to this. I'm so, so sorry!'

Lilli began weeping into her mug of tea. It was like she had been a vehicle running at top speed, only for the battery to have finally run out, leaving her stranded and desolate. Completely empty.

Panic ripped through my body as thoughts flooded my brain. *She's a spy. A spy for the Master!* The room began spinning. I let go of my mug on the table and gripped the side of my chair. I couldn't think. I needed to know so much, but I didn't know where to start or what to ask. My mind was a buzzing mess, and anger squeezed at my chest.

Peter cleared his throat and leant forward in his chair. 'If you really love him Lilli, you need to help us. Where and when did you meet your contact?'

Lilli used her sleeve to wipe her snot and then spoke in jolting sobs. 'I...I would meet them ev—every second day, at sunset. In the alley behind the book depository in the industrial zone. I'm supposed to go there today.'

'Who did you meet Lilli?'

'It was always the same man. He never told me his name. But he had purple and blue eyes. I'd always heard of iris tattoos but had never seen one in real life until him.'

'Is there anything else you can tell us about your contact?'

'He's tall. Large build. Doesn't have big muscles, but not fat either. He's just...big. He has blue hair, wears black boots and rides a two-wheeler that he would park against the wall and lean against. I never stayed long, and he didn't talk much. I just report to him, and he sometimes asked questions.'

'Why did you break in this morning?' Her head twitched slightly at Peter's question. 'Why did you need to come here? You said you didn't think anything would happen. But somehow you knew something has happened.'

'I...' The question startled her. 'I didn't. Sam didn't answer his wrist-comm last night, and never went on his holo so I was worried something bad had happened. My contact had been very interested that it was your birthday today, Rachel, so I wanted to come and check things were okay, but when I opened the front door and saw the smashed picture frames, I knew something was definitely wrong. I know all of this is stupid. I'm stupid. I'm so sorry.'

I sat for a moment and let myself process everything before speaking again. 'You spied on us.' It came out as a statement, not a question. 'I welcomed you into my home and you became part of my family, but you betrayed us.' I could see Lilli physically recoil with each accusation. My words hit home, and they hit hard. 'Why did they take my son?'

'I don't know.'

'WHY LILLI?'

'I DON'T KNOW!' She slammed her hands down on the table. A silence pulled through the space as I stared Lilli down. She eventually broke her glare and took a moment before conceding. 'They never told me why they wanted to know certain things. All I know is that for the last few months, all they have asked about is you. What you do, where you go and if I had noticed anything odd? They've been asking about you.'

'Don't you dare try to blame this on me! You don't know anything.' My emotions were at a tipping point, so I stood up and began striding out of the room to give myself some space.

'How can I help?' Lilli pleaded. 'Please, I need to help!'

'Just...just go home Lilli. You've done enough.' I stormed out of the room, leaving Lilli crying behind me.

4

Trapped

I STORMED OUT THE back door in search of fresh morning air to calm my emotions, and found solace sitting on the back step, watching the surrounding trees dance gently on a breeze. Eventually Peter appeared and let me know he'd disabled Lilli's wrist-comm before joining me on the back steps. Lilli's regular meeting with the blue-haired contact was the first genuine lead we had, and it just happened to be scheduled for tonight. With the plan agreed, we sat for a while in a companionable silence, and I realised how tired I was. I needed to sleep.

The door opened and Lilli came outside. Her eyes were still red from crying.

'Rachel, I want to help find Sam.'

I took a deep breath and stood to face her. She was only a kid, and she needed to hear from someone that she wasn't alone in this, and that someone cared about her. 'I know you do Lilli, and I'm sorry I yelled before. But the truth is, I can't lose you too.' I pulled her into a hug and both our bodies let go of the tension we had both been holding. 'I need to know you are safe and far away from the people who did this. Is there somewhere you can go? Somewhere out of Crayn?'

There was pain and fight in her eyes, but I could also see that she understood what I needed from her, so she nodded. 'Yeah, I know somewhere I can go.'

'Good, get there as fast as you can, and stay away from anywhere you usually go. As I said, I need you safe.'

When Lilli was ready, we said our tearful goodbyes, and I watched her walk off towards what I hoped was a safe future.

My head was pounding from exhaustion by the time Lilli left, and since we had the time, Peter and I agreed to take a few hours' rest. As I neared my bedroom, a sudden urge pulled me instead to Sam's. I went in and curled up on his bed and had the most fretful sleep I had ever experienced. After waking, we made quick work of getting ready, then got into Peter's comfortable Agency-issued e-vehic, instead of Sam's second-hand one, and drove away.

The sun was almost at its zenith as we drove through Crayn's industrial zone. It was a strange place where brutal facades of factories and warehouses competed with wild climbing vines and spindly trees. We still had hours before Lilli's usual meeting time, and we drove in silence while my mind questioned everything. I still couldn't fathom that Lilli had betrayed us. And worst of all, it made me question if she had ever really loved Sam.

We found the book depository building and did laps of the neighbourhood to check out the situation. There was a loading area behind the book depository, where Lilli usually met her contact. We found a place nearby to park our e-vehic and settled in to wait.

Peter handed me a snack bar, and I gulped it down while Peter nibbled on his.

'Rach,' Peter said between bites. 'I don't know what the last twenty years have been like, but what I do know is that we're about to go into an unknown situation with an unknown hostile. Can you handle it?'

'Of course I can.'

'Can you really? No jokes or judgement, but your life seems very different from your old one. The Rach I knew could handle this in her sleep. Can you do that? I guess what I'm trying to say in a stupid roundabout way is, I need you to dig deep. I need you to bring back the golden girl. Cause that girl always had my back, and I know she's still there somewhere. You just need to find her again.'

'I might be old Peter, but I'm still me. Having a different life for the last twenty years doesn't make me soft.'

'Good. You better not be, and you better have the stomach to do what you need to. If we're going into this situation, I need to know you are going to be an asset and not a liability.'

'I've got it.'

'Do you?'

44

'I said I've got it! You don't get to judge me. I could whip your arse back then, and I'll whip your arse now. You know nothing about my life, so don't underestimate me. I'll do what I need to. Now shut up and eat your snack bar.'

'Yes ma'am,' Peter mumbled.

We spent the next few hours in the car, waiting for the scheduled rendezvous. I fell asleep for most of it and was jolted awake by Peter shaking me.

'Thirty minutes till sunset. Time to wake up, Sleeping Beauty.' Peter got out of the e-vehic and opened its storage trunk. I took a moment to get my bearings, then wiped the dried saliva from the side of my mouth as I got out and joined him. In the trunk were the two weapons and tech cache bags we filled up at Agency HQ.

'What do you reckon? Stunner followed by a herding sphere?' asked Peter.

'I was thinking of a silencer trap. Then once we're in there with him, we pull out the intel-wrench. Just like the old days. Unless there is better tech these days for that kind of thing?'

'Sometimes you just can't beat the classics. Should get us what we need. You want me to run point?'

'I told you, I've got it.' I grabbed a sleek little device that I assumed was an updated intel-wrench, and two guns that I holstered in a gear belt. There was a lot of equipment in the bags I didn't recognise, so rather than risk learning something new, I threw on a bandolier of EMP dots, just in case.

Loaded up, Peter and I exchanged a nod and then began weaving our way through the back alleys and up the vine-covered fire escape stairs that led to the roof of the book depository. The roof was covered in rain collectors and various plants. It also provided a perfect vantage point, with an unrestricted line of sight to the specified rendezvous point. Just as we settled into position, a screech of wheels echoed off the surrounding foliage and buildings.

This area of Crayn was dedicated to the reuse and repurposing of resources, as nothing on Tir-na was ever brand new, including books, which were created from old paper products processed and recycled at the book depository. Materials were constantly reworked into new things, and since repurposed goods were constantly required, this area was always thrumming with noise from the factories and processing facilities that worked around the clock. The mechanical sounds from the surrounding buildings were deafening, with the trees here doing little to absorb the noise. It was the perfect rendezvous point; shipments were only loaded in the morning, meaning no risk of being disturbed, and the constant factory noise provided the perfect cover for conversations. These people knew what they were doing.

The two-wheeler revved into the small back loading dock area and parked directly below us. The rider took off his helmet and swung his leg over the wheeler before assuming a relaxed position resting against his ride. From what I could tell, he was a lean but strong-looking young man with cropped, inky blue hair with a shaved intricate angular pattern wrapping around his head.

I looked at Peter, who was holding the silencer trap. It had always been my favourite piece of kit. Just two little innocuous spongy cubes that, when activated, became an extremely effective and quiet trap. I gave Peter a nod, and he dropped the cubes off the roof with a deft hand. They landed on the ground on either side of the target and exploded on impact with a bright blue warbling energy that raced both outwards and upwards until they fused together to encase the target in a perfect dome.

The blue-haired man's shock was palpable. His mouth moved, but we couldn't hear anything, and he reached out to touch the blue energy field. From experience, I knew it was hard beneath his hand. In frustration, he smashed his fists on the side of the dome, but nothing happened. He was trapped inside the energy field.

We moved to the fire escape stairs and headed down to meet our quarry. The man was staring at us as his mouth moved with exaggerated expressions. He didn't look happy. The constant whirring, high-pitched mechanical thuds from the surrounding buildings reverberated throughout the street, but the sphere and its contents remained silent, although very agitated.

'You got a stunner with you, Rach?' Peter asked as we approached the sphere.

'No, I didn't grab one.'

'Here.' Peter tossed me a small silver rod around the size of a finger that I caught in mid-air. 'We enter on my signal from opposite sides, dual stun him, magno-cuff him, then it's over to you. Got it?'

I nodded.

'You'll need this too.' Peter held out an Agency wrist-comm. 'Press the green button to enable dome transit.' Peter moved to the other side of the sphere. Our target inside paced back and forth like a trapped animal, smashing his hands against the dome's wall every so often in frustration, while his purple and blue tattooed irises warily flicked between us.

'Ready?' Peter asked.

'Yep.' My reply sounded a lot more certain than I felt, as my insides roiled. A clammy tingle crept its way up my neck and my breath quickened. I had buried this life and this part of myself the day I buried Miles. This world had led me to disaster once, but I couldn't deny there was still something exciting and satisfying about it. Like a dull, inaccessible itch on the bottom of my foot that was finally being scratched. The idea made me recoil, but I would do anything for Sam.

Peter held up his hand and thrust it downwards in a signal that meant it was go time. We moved into the dome and activated the stunners. The poor guy never had a chance. Trapped in the stunner's golden electric streams, he collapsed to the ground like a corpse, with only his eyes and mouth able to move, making it easy to trap his hands in the magno-cuffs.

'Who the fuck are you people?' he screamed. I ignored his question and kneeled in front of him. His eyes were wild as he flung profanity after profanity at me, but it was nothing I hadn't heard before. In fact, it didn't even rate in the top ten worst things I'd heard. He needed to get more creative.

I pulled out the intel-wrench and set to work. With the stunners doing their thing and the magno-cuffs holding his arms behind his back, I easily extracted a droplet of blood from his finger using the wrench's hidden syringe. It retracted back into the main body of the wrench, and I quickly tapped a few commands on the control screen to start its processing.

One of the most useful parts of an intel-wrench was its DNA processor, which had instant reach-back access to the Agency's vast databases that held details of almost every person on Tir-na. I really didn't want to know how they got all the information, and it was something that had always made me uncomfortable, but it had helped save lives so many times when I was an agent that I learnt not to question it. After so long out of the game, though, my reservations had returned, but I needed to get Sam back. The end justifies the means, right? I think that's how the Ancient Earth saying went.

The intel-wrench pinged when it found a match. I hit the holo-projector option, and the details shone in front of me.

Enric Vasteros.

24 years old.

No parents.

Raised in a kids' home. Ran away when he was 12.

Lived on the streets, then joined a street gang.

Arrested twice for assault and once for possession of Euphoria.

Served two years in the Kid Hold.

Now in the employ of the black-market Euphoria distribution company Pleasure

Tech. Owner is Raph Merton.

Location and front of the Pleasure Tech Den is Fuse Bar.

So much information from a single drop of blood. It was terrifying, but now I needed more details. I needed to know what he knew. I sent a copy of the info to Peter's wrist-comm and then hardened myself for what I knew had to come next. Intel extraction.

My hands were shaking, so I clenched them shut to hide it. A memory ripped through me. A memory of a different time, and a different person. There was a faceless man curled over on the ground. He looked at me with pleading eyes, screaming and begging for death instead of what I was doing to him. I was relieved at his response as he was exactly where I wanted him. 'You want me to stop?' I had asked. 'Then tell me what I need.' I had known exactly what to do, and with a few deft flourishes of the intel-wench, I made him scream.

I pulled myself out of the memory. Blood was pumping through my ears, drowning out the metallic hum of the silencer trap. Cold sweat shot across the back of my neck and I tasted the sour tinge of bile at the back of my throat. I couldn't do this. I didn't want to do this.

Peter stood staring at me, his face clear of any expression, but I knew that look. It was the same look assessors wore at the Agency when we went through assessment trials. Analytical, cold and expectant.

I closed my eyes, and instead of the past, I thought of Sam's future. I needed to do this to make it a reality. My hand drifted to the pocket of Old Blue that safely held my treasured baby photo. For Sam, I would do it. I inhaled a deep breath, held it for four seconds, then released through my mouth. When I opened my eyes again, I was focused. I was ready. This was for Sam.

'Get away, you bitch!' said Enric. He spat at me and thrashed on the ground. That was the encouragement I needed. I grabbed his leg and forced it straight, then quickly stuck the tip of the intel-wrench into the back of his knee. He screamed, but couldn't do anything to stop the pain. I pulled the wrench back, leaving Enric panting and shaking on the ground, and I saw a vision of Sam in Enric's situation. Maybe the same thing was happening to Sam right now. Enric was so young. Only four years older than Sam. What was I doing? My hands trembled, and I crumpled backwards and just sat there, shaking. What had I done? I had just tortured a boy. I had promised myself I would never be sucked into the Agency's world again, but it had been so easy to slip back into it. That thought terrified me more than anything. I tasted the tang of bile again, but this time it was richer and thicker. I turned and vomited over the ground.

Peter swooped in and grabbed the wrench from my hand, then stuck his face right in front of Enric.

'I need you to tell me some things, Enric. Can you do that for me?' Peter's voice was a tingling mix of enticement and threat. The sound of it made me shiver.

'Fuck off!' Enric spat. Peter stuck the intel-wrench directly over the top of Enric's jugular. The effect on him was immediate. His face exploded in strained lines as veins pulled taut throughout his body. My stomach rolled at the sight of it, but I didn't want to vomit again, so I clamped my mouth shut and inhaled deeply through my nose. Peter released the intel-wrench pressure and let Enric's body slump to the ground. His breath was ragged, coming in great heaves that stunk of strong spirits. The smell of it crinkled my nose and did nothing to ease my queasy stomach.

'I really hate swearing, Enric. Something you should try to remember. Now, first question, why do you care about Sam Tomsen?' asked Peter.

'I ain't tellin' you shit!'

'This really would all be a lot easier if you just cooperated.' Peter pressed the intel-wrench to the vein in his wrist. Enric jolted as electrical currents shot through his body. The wrench was such an innocuous device, but it certainly had a punch.

After a sequence of intel-wrench pressure applications across his body, Enric finally agreed to talk. He his eyes were glazed and the little finger on his right hand twitched. My brow was covered in cold sweat. I couldn't believe I was complicit in something like this again. But I needed Peter to do it, and he had Enric exactly where we needed him.

'Enric. Enric, look at me.' His eyes seemed to see through a fog of pain, but slowly Enric focused his eyes and met Peter's gaze. 'Why are you interested in Sam Tomsen? We know you asked Lilli about him.'

'The boss.' Enric closed his eyes and let his head drop back onto the ground. 'The boss wanted to know about him.'

'Why did your boss want to know about him?' Enric responded by shaking his head. Peter brought the intel-wrench up into Enric's line of sight. 'Tell me!' Enric flinched at the sight and sucked in a sob. He looked so torn and terrified as Peter kneeled over him. Then Peter pressed the wrench to Enric's temple. Enric's face momentarily froze in a quivering silent scream, his eyes straining from the painful electrical current. Peter relented but was instantly in Enric's face again.

'Who is your boss? Tell me now or the next one goes on your balls.' The menace in Peter's voice made me recoil, and it had the same effect on Enric.

'Boss is Raph Merton. He owns Pleasure Tech.' Every word sounded like it was being dragged through Enric's teeth.

'Good. Now, what the hell does he want with Sam Tomsen?' said Peter.

'I swear. I don't know. They don't tell me. I just report whatever that annoying Lilli says to me. Then they tell me what to tell her next time. I'm a nobody, man. I'm nobody.' Enric started crying. My heart dropped. He was just a boy doing what he was told so he could stay off the streets with a full belly and a place to sleep. I couldn't blame him.

Peter's face had contorted, as though seeing this boy cry was personally insulting. Peter never used to look at people like that. The Agency had obviously wrapped its tendrils tighter and pulled him deeper into its core. A terrible thought crossed my mind. That's what I would have been like if I'd never got out.

A metallic bouncing sounded behind me, followed by a faint beep. The blue dome of the silencer trap disappeared, and the magno-cuffs holding Enric's arms together fell away. Enric was free. He pushed himself up to look at us, then his head snapped backwards as scarlet patches started appearing on his shirt in a vertical line upwards from his naval to his neck. He fell backwards, lifeless, with a glazed, shocked look frozen on his face. His body was covered in a line of slim metal daggers. No human could shoot at that velocity and strike in such an arrangement. It was like nothing I had seen before.

'Bots!' Peter yelled. His tone was enough for me to understand the warning. I spun around and saw three spherical drones hovering above head height in a perfect triangular configuration. They were completely silent and frighteningly deadly.

Thin metal daggers shot out of all three drone bots at once in an arc towards Peter. He dived behind a large trash collector, the sharp projectiles smashing into the metal in front of him. My brain took a second to shift into a state of mind that disconnected consequences from actions. The exact state of mind that would keep me alive.

I rolled sideways as the closest bot turned towards me. I spotted Enric's two-wheeler and leapt towards it as the bot released a stream of daggers. A searing pain cut through my right thigh and shoulder. I rolled behind the two-wheeler as daggers started puncturing the entire vehicle. The noise was deafening, and the scratching metallic thuds echoed through my brain. I sucked in a trembling breath and waited for a dagger to hit closer to home. I saw Peter limping slightly behind the trash collector as a red stain spread across his lower back and left leg. His wounds reminded me of my own and I reached up and found a thin dagger lodged in the meat of my right shoulder. Another protruded from the back of my right thigh. Blood was creeping across my clothes. I had been stabbed before, but I didn't remember the searing pain that went with it. I had a split second to think. I could pull out the daggers and risk bleeding out, or leave them, but possibly last longer to get out of here. It wasn't really a choice, so I left them, and if my old training had taught me anything, it was suck up the pain and do whatever you needed to stay alive, even if it caused you agony.

My hand drifted away from the dagger and hit the edge of my bandolier. The EMP dots. I knew what I needed to do.

'Peter! Catch!' I yelled over the thunderous clangs of the endless barrage. I risked exposing my arm and threw an EMP dot to Peter. A searing blade sliced across the back of my forearm mid-throw, causing me to flinch and lose my aim. The dot landed about a leg length in front of Peter, directly in the line of fire. Not ideal, but I could work with it. I pressed a hand over the wound on my arm as another dagger shot through a gap in the wheels and nicked my left shin. It was time to move.

I reached up exposing my hand, praying the daggers hadn't destroyed the two-wheeler's battery, and pressed its start button. A spark of hope grew in my gut as the engine rumbled.

The bot spun its firing mechanism to reload. I took that moment to drop an EMP dot at my feet, jump on the two-wheeler and smash my fist down on the accelerator. My sliced muscles quivered and screamed in pain as the wheeler shot forwards.

Two EMP dots were in position. I just needed to drop one more. I swung the two-wheeler around behind the drones and noticed they followed my every move. Wherever I zigzagged the two-wheeler, a stream of daggers followed, bouncing and ricocheting off the road. One caught me across the cheek, the sting of it making my eyes water. I exhaled a thankful breath that it had only cut my face as blood started running down my cheek.

I grabbed another EMP dot from my bandolier, smashed it against my leg to activate, and dropped it.

Five.

A torrent of daggers flew around me as two of the three bots turned their attention to me.

Four.

Another dagger hit in the back of my hip as my muscles shook.

Three.

I spun the two-wheeler around, narrowly missing the wall, and headed towards the trash collector.

Two.

I sped along and ducked another volley of daggers as the bots followed me.

One.

Once close enough, I jumped off the wheeler. I smashed into the road as the wheeler crashed into the back wall of the book depository. The daggers embedded in my muscles tore out as I rolled uncontrollably into the side of the trash collector.

Zero.

All three EMP dots sprang to life. A warbling beam of golden light shot out of each one towards a central point, encasing the pursuing bots. Everything electrical trapped within the pyramid of light was destroyed. The three bots crashed to the ground, their internal systems completely fried. The bots were down. We were safe. *It worked*, I thought, as my head flopped to the ground and everything went black.

5

Safehouse

E VERYTHING HURT, BUT MY shoulder, hip and thigh seared with an exquis-
ite pain that drowned everything else out. My head was swimming, and my
breath came in short bursts. There was a rolling, rumbling sound and the seat I
was in jostled and rubbed against my shredded muscles. I prised my eyes open.
It was dark. Lights sporadically flashed past the e-vehic, blinding me in waves.
I attempted to adjust my position in the seat to make everything hurt less, but
that was a terrible mistake. Each movement sent horrid shooting pains rocketing
through me.

'You still with me?' asked Peter.

A high-pitched grunt in acknowledgment was all I could muster. I focused my
thoughts on my breathing and blocked out the trembling pain that threatened to
overwhelm me. I felt weak from the loss of blood. It didn't help to think of how
much I had already lost as you can only worry about what you can control, and
in that moment, the only thing I could control was my breathing. So, I slowed my
breath and focused on that.

'Stay awake Rach. It's not far. We'll be alright.' Peter's voice held an edge of
tension. Maybe old age was making him soft and causing him to worry.

The e-vehic took a tight turn and rumbled down an empty, overgrown, narrow
back alley. We painfully bumped over wild-looking plants and vines that spilled
across the street as they slowly consumed the surrounding buildings. We came
to a stop and before I knew it, Peter was out of the e-vehic and ripping open my
door. He started to lift me out, and I tried to wave him off, but the pain of lifting
my arm made me shut up. After all, the real sign of an adult was knowing when to

accept help. I always told Sam that, so I thought I should follow my own advice. Now was not the time for bravado.

Together, Peter and I lifted my body out of the car. He wrapped one arm around my waist, threw my arm up over his shoulder, and began an awkward shuffle towards a flat metal door. The world was spinning as I clenched my teeth against the agonising, jolting steps. A pressure was rising from my neck towards my temples and soft ringing tolled in my ears. My vision shrunk and the world slipped away until I was nothing but my consciousness. As I was about to give in to the quiet comfort of the darkness, a blue flash sparked across my vision, jolting me awake.

Peter pushed aside some vines and quickly typed a code into a hidden access pad. The buttons on it blurred together as I looked at it, appearing as nothing more than a dancing pattern. My world began to shrink again. I closed my eyes to the foggy pain and tried to focus on my breathing. If I kept breathing in and out, I was still alive. The flat metal door popped open with a hiss and Peter jerked me over the threshold, causing a shock of pain to rush through my body in a surging wave. The pain made my head spin, and I desperately tried not to vomit as we continued down a hallway and up a flight of stairs. Peter scanned his eyes with a hidden retinal scanner before dragging me through another door into a functional and sterile-looking house. I saw the dining table and Peter helped me hobble over to it. I pushed Old Blue off me and let it fall to the floor before flopping down across the table. The pain from the movement was overwhelming as I sucked in a sharp breath through my teeth. Luckily, it didn't last much longer. Peter pressed a cylinder against my neck and clicked a button that shot a sharp spike through my skin. A heavy warmth spread out from the puncture site on my neck. The wave of warmth rushed over my head, down my chest and speared outwards along my arms. In its wake, it left nothing but a warm, numb peace that instantly soothed the large wounds that laced my body. The wave spread further, and I let out a heavy sigh of relief as it flowed across my hips and torn legs. Its numbing effects were intoxicating, but there was also something unnerving about it. I knew my body was in terrible shape, but I couldn't feel it.

Peter was watching me intently, observing my muscles slowly relax as he got busy tying large pads against my open wounds, then without a word, he walked away. I turned my head to look for him and saw him coming back with an Agency field med kit in one hand, and a piece of ice in the other. That med kit sent a jolt of panic through me as it was filled with everything you needed to perform quick and dirty surgery. I was obviously in worse shape than I thought.

'Alright Rach. I need you to tell me if you feel anything. How's this?' Peter pressed the piece of ice against my foot. I couldn't feel anything. There was pressure, but it was more like I had rested my foot against a hard surface rather than ice on my skin. My mind whirled with the cognitive dissonance of it all. I knew it felt fine, but I also knew it wasn't.

Unnerved by my extended silence, Peter turned and looked at me. 'No, I can't feel it,' I murmured and rested my head back on the table. I felt like it would go better if I couldn't actually see anything, so I closed my eyes and waited for his next test.

'Can you feel this?' A pressure appeared on my wrist. The initial unexpected pressure made me jump, but once again there was nothing.

'Nothing.' It came out as a whisper. I was too tired for anything more. Peter moved away and returned with an oxy-mask. He positioned it so that it rested just under my nose, then he flicked the switch to start the flow. The hit of oxygen sparked my system, and the world refocused. The shaking that I hadn't realised wracked my body subsided.

'You're cut pretty bad, Rach. Looks like they avoided any arteries, which is good. It will take a while to patch you up.'

'What about you? Are you injured as well?' I couldn't help but wonder how long he could perform field surgery before he started succumbing to his own wounds.

'Nothing so bad that a quick binder won't hold. You can finish it off once I get you up and running again.' I looked directly at his eyes, trying to find his hidden truth in them. He looked exhausted. Not physically exhausted, but rather something more insidious. 'Let's get to it, shall we?'

'Sure.' I closed my eyes and attempted to let my trained mind fall into that quiet zone. That place where it was protected and warm, and nothing bad could hurt it. I felt the rhythmic tugging and prodding of the various surgical instruments, but I let it wash over me and become just part of what I was.

I was calm and relaxed, but Peter's gravelly voice woke me from my secret hidden safe place. 'Just like old times, eh? I don't think I could count the number of times we've patched each other up with a med kit.'

'Probably too many.' I knew what he was doing. It was best practice to talk to the patient to keep them conscious, but I really just wanted to sleep.

'That's the truth.' A silence dragged out, and he continued his constant tugging and prodding with instruments I didn't dare look at. He then stood and began carefully cutting away my torn shirt that was stuck to my skin with sticky, dried blood. 'I'll need you to roll onto your stomach if you can?'

I gingerly rolled over as Peter removed the last of my top, leaving me in my bra. There was a long pause. I could practically feel his mind churning, flickering with questions at the sight of my body. The years had made me forget how shocking the scars were. They were littered across my back. Sometimes they were in tight patterns, while others were long scars with no rhyme or reason to their snaking pattern.

Peter got back to work, continuing to stitch and then seal my wounds together with a smelting stick. I was quietly shocked they still used smelting sticks. It was a horrible process, and the resultant smell of cooked flesh turned my stomach. After another few minutes of silence, Peter decided what he wanted to say.

'We worked together for a long time, you and me. Then one day, with no warning, you were reassigned to some super-secret mission. Tippity top secret, you might say.' There was a smile in his voice, amused by his own turn of phrase. 'I don't know what you did during your last two years with us.' I froze, staying silent and letting him get out whatever it was he was trying to say. 'But there were rumours about experiments to make the perfect agent. Crazy thing was, you already *were* perfect. Top of your class, highest number of closed cases. So, I couldn't believe it when people said the experiments were to make you better.' He took a long breath. 'I don't know what happened, but I was there the day

Miles died, and I was there the day you left. I remember it so clearly. It was the biggest shake-up the Agency had ever seen. It was like a black storm cloud had been released, blowing through the whole place. You came in with a full guard around you that herded you into the Head's office, but then you just left. After walking out, nobody saw you again. You just left.'

His voice was heavy with sadness, and it made a strange coldness settle over my body.

'I'm sorry I never said goodbye to you.' I closed my eyes, hoping it would make the words easier. 'You deserved better than what you got. You always had my back.'

'I'm not worried about that. It's just that I wish you felt you could count on me. I won't lie. It hurts thinking you didn't trust me.'

'Of course I trusted you. There was just too much at stake. Too much going on. Just...too much.' Silence settled over us. I closed my eyes to the scraping, pulling and burning from the med kit equipment and instead let myself drift into reminiscence.

· · · • · • · • · · ·

It had been a long twenty-four hours, and all I craved was a long hot shower, but I had someone to see first. My heart beat faster as I approached the nondescript white front door, its blandness masking what lay within. I paused and took a deep, shaky breath. I had just gone up against a highly trained terrorist cell with no qualms, but knocking on that door made my heart tremble. I closed my eyes, swallowed my stupidity and knocked.

The door creaked open and there he was. Miles Shawbank. His laughing golden eyes had always made me smile. His dishevelled, burnt sunset-coloured hair spiked in every direction, and we just stood there smiling at each other for a moment.

My memory then twisted and turned, pulling me forwards in time to a different moment.

I stepped out onto the patio of Miles' small, Agency-issued apartment and saw a table dressed with a simple blue cloth. Mismatched plates and cutlery were laid out, and a candle stood pride of place glimmering in the light of Tir-na's moons Marher and Inyon, and next to it all stood Miles in a clean shirt with a warm grin on his face.

He reached his hand up to the back of his neck and rubbed his hair, looking down at his shoes. 'I...umm...' he attempted to speak. His voice was jittery and warm. 'I thought...'. He couldn't finish his sentence; his nerves were practically sparking off him. His awkwardness melted part of my heart and I moved towards him. I paused and stared into his eyes, halting his nervous movements.

'It looks lovely,' I said, as I took hold of his hands. His face changed in a wave of relief, and he ushered me to the seat.

The memory shifted again, racing forwards through that night to a moment that changed my life forever.

We sat together, gazing up at the majesty of the moons. Their shining light turning everything a bright, glittering silver. I had never been more comfortable, rested or at ease. I simply had never felt more like myself. My eyes wandered over to look at Miles. To really look at him. He had a smile of wonder on his face as he stared at the beautiful night sky. He was just so perfectly him. Scruffy hair, soft eyes and a heart filled with hope. My pulse quickened and small goose bumps prickled along my arms as I came to a terrifying realisation. I was completely in love with him.

· · · · · · · · ·

A jarring beep pulled me from my nostalgic escape, causing the memory of the first sparks of love to dissipate into the reality of the here and now. I didn't know how much time had passed since I had first closed my eyes, but the sun was up, and high, Peter had finished his patching. I twisted around to locate the source of the noise. Remarkably, the movement didn't send sparks of pain across my vision. Peter's efforts were already helping. He sat on a chair near the table with his shirt off. It looked like he had been sealing his own wounds with the field smelt stick. My throat constricted at the lingering roasted-flesh smell. A new Agency wrist-comm Peter was wearing emitted a rhythmic, piercing beep. He hit a few buttons and a small holo-screen projected upwards from the device.

'Welcome back to the land of the living, Rach. Also, I hope you don't mind, but we put a listener on your personal comms line.' Of course they had. Privacy wasn't really a concept the Agency understood or valued, not when there was a mission to achieve. 'Looks like you've got an unknown caller trying to get onto you.'

Peter hit another button and the holo-screen filled with a vidcon image. A single figure was sitting in a chair in the middle of a darkened room. Their face listed forwards as though someone had sucked the energy out of them, and a dark wet stain soiled their lap. They looked tired, hurt and scared, but it was their wavy mess of floppy auburn hair that made my heart panic. No one else had that mess of hair. I knew my son. It was Sam.

I lurched forwards to get a clear look. A cracked, deep voice sounded from the holo. 'Rachel Tomsen. It was you who had it all along. You have lied. You have betrayed. So you will pay. Bring it to us and you might see your boy again. Use those old skills of yours and hopefully you'll find us in time.'

A figure entered the screen wearing a dark, vile mask and flowing black clothes. They paused close to the camera and dragged out a large knife. My stomach twisted as my nerves burned with fear. The figure relished displaying the horrid sharp knife to the camera before turning and walking behind Sam. With no warning, they grabbed Sam's face and purposefully sliced down his cheek. Sam screamed in pain. When the figure removed the knife, there was a deep red line that dripped down the side of Sam's face. He was crying, and as his tears fell, they mixed with the blood, making it stream across his skin. The masked figure returned to the screen, their face front and centre. 'Hurry, Rachel. Your little boy is missing his mummy.' The screen cut to black and the transmission ended.

'No!' I yelled and grabbed at the holo-projection. My hands swiped through nothing and instead began shaking. 'Tell me you know where that vidcon came from.'

'The listener we planted should record all comm end points and transitional hops. We should know where they are.'

'Find him, Peter.'

He started tapping his fingers on his wrist-comm and raced off to a state-of-the-art wall tech-capsule. He hooked up his wrist-comm and started typing on the capsule's control panel. I saw the Agency's logo flash up and a cold, robotic voice sounded. 'Please centre your eyes on the scanner.' Peter moved his head back and forth, trying to find the correct position, before the capsule's in-built camera sounded. 'Thank you, Peter Brand. Your identity has been confirmed.' The screen then faded to the Agency's homepage and Peter began pulling up various programs on the screen.

I took the moment to lie down with my eyes closed so I could analyse my thoughts, but initially all I saw in my mind was the blood sliding down my baby's face and the terror in his eyes. My heart constricted. He had looked so terrified. I suffocated a cry of pain from the thought and forced myself to suck in a breath. Now I saw the chair. It was metal, with a curved design. Not something often seen in houses, so they were more likely in a factory or office. It was completely dark in the room, apart from a light shining straight at Sam from above the camera. No windows at all. An internal room somewhere. The walls and floor were dark colours and made of a smooth, solid surface. It wasn't shiny, so it couldn't have been metal, but it had a gleam to it which made me think it was cleaned regularly. Then I saw the knife. Large and terrifying, with one side sharp and smooth, and the other jagged and serrated. The handle was a smooth black and moulded to enable a perfect grasp. That was no cheap knife. It looked like a custom design. Whoever had Sam had money behind them. Next, I saw the face of the figure. The mask they wore was grotesque. It had all the normal features you would expect on a face, but reimagined into a terrifying and unnerving configuration. With all of it tinged a deathly violet hue. This was no cheap mask. It looked bespoke, and something like that could only derive from the depths of someone's insidious mind. Costly mask and knife. Solid, private, clean location. Efficient and planned abduction. Connecting strings pulled across my mind.

A repetitive low beep sounded from the holo-capsule. 'Shit!' Peter turned slowly to look at me. 'Whoever they are, they know what they're doing. They blocked the bloody tracker. I've never seen one fail before.' It would have taken a lot of money to develop something to beat an Agency tracker.

'We should follow the money.' I ignored Peter's quizzical look and focused on moving myself off the table. 'Not just anybody can block a tracker, and those bots that came after us looked like some serious kit. It all points to money, and right now we've got at least one lead pointing at someone we know has money. Raph Merton, the owner of Pleasure Tech, and we know where his den is. I think we should pay him a visit.'

I stood on wobbly feet and made my way over to the field med kit, then grabbed an adrenaline injection and pressed it into my stomach. The sharp needle punctured through my saggy, stretch-marked skin, but a moment later my vision cleared, and control of my limbs came back to me. I grabbed a patch kit and headed over to Peter.

'Alright,' I said, 'let's finish patching you up then get to work.'

6

The Den

W E SPENT THE REST of the day resting and preparing; Peter gave me a new wrist-comm to aid with our research, since mine had died in the EMP blast. Then, once all the stand-up citizens had long gone to bed, we headed to the industrial zone to find Fuse Bar. We parked a couple of blocks from Fuse, where the industrial zone morphed into the more manicured and purposefully cultivated Crayn business district. This area of the zone had more shop fronts than factories, but all of them were closed for the night. Our feet clacked against the road as we strode down the dark and deserted wild-forested streets, until we turned a corner and found ourselves confronted with a crowd heading for a squat, rectangular building. It was covered in a tangle of vines, with a blue neon sign sticking out from the foliage flashing the word *Fuse*. I had reluctantly left Old Blue at the safehouse and instead agreed to dress all in black, which blended easily into the crowd that was steadily streaming towards the bar. It was a motley crew, some in suits, some in dresses and some in latex-looking bodysuits. We let ourselves flow forwards with the crowd, happy to blend in as we approached the bright blue Fuse sign.

A herd of two-wheelers was parked out the front of the bar, and two hulking bald men in puffy black jackets leaned grumpily against each side of the overgrown entrance. Keeping a keen eye on their processes, we watched the guards give every patron a once-over before nodding for them to enter. I looked at the revellers heading into the bar and one thing stuck out on most of them: the tell-tale sign of ruby spotters.

'Safe to say this is the location of the Den,' I murmured to Peter. 'Check out their temples.'

Peter carefully scanned the scene before sighing. 'Ruby spots.' He shook his head. 'Ruby spots as far as the eye can see.'

We made our way to the door and slipped into our planned act as an older couple out for an exciting night out on the town. I slid my arm around Peter's waist to add to the facade and noticed he had some surprisingly solid muscles for an old guy. I guess the Agency had been working him hard. The guards gave us a careful once-over while I purposely looked all around with wide eyes and pulled myself closer to Peter. With an unnerving synchronised curt nod from the two guards, they ushered us into Fuse. Playing naïve but excited had always worked, and it didn't let me down tonight.

After stepping through a weapons scanner, we crossed the threshold from the rough and wild streets of the industrial zone and into a dark tunnel with pulsing lights along the edge of the floor. It felt like a starship landing strip guiding us to our destination. A deep thumping reverberated through the floor as we walked forwards. There were closed double doors at the end of the hallway where a sliver of constantly changing light shone through a gap between the two halves, hinting at what might lie beyond. With each step, the rhythmic vibrations shot up my body, making my heart pound in time to the music's heavy bass. We reached the end of the tunnel and pushed open the doors.

'Whoa,' escaped my lips as we were overwhelmed with music that pumped through every vein of the building. The smell of stale alcohol, cheap fried foods and sweat assaulted my nostrils. Conscious of the numerous swaying bodies littered throughout the space, who had eyes everywhere, I plastered an excited expression on my face and grabbed Peter's hand to head deeper into the dark. Colourful light patterns flashed organically across the space. Each time it passed over us, it would blind us momentarily, before once again leaving us in the dark. Eventually, we manoeuvred through the space and found a small table at the back. We slid into our seats and took in our surrounds.

'What can I get ya?' said a waitress, who appeared from nowhere. She had white zigzag streaks across inky, sharp cropped hair that seemed to pulse with different colourful hues as the dance floor strobes cycled through a kaleidoscope of colours.

'Ummm. Whatever you want, honey,' I said, looking at Peter.

'Two Starfires, please.'

'Nice choice. Won't be a sec,' said the waitress as she disappeared back into the sea of gyrating bodies on the dance floor. It was hypnotic watching the lively Craynians writhing around. Their limbs swaying in a never-ending rhythmic trance. They moved as though the sun had just broken through clouds after a dark storm, the joy and ecstasy of it evident on their faces. But that's what Pleasure Dots did.

Pleasure Dots were small disks that attached to your temple with a simple adhesive. It was the adhesive that left the ruby-coloured marks on people's skin. The disks themselves looked innocuous enough, but once stuck on, they activated a small chip that sent electrical waves into the brain, stimulating the release of dopamine and serotonin, while also making the receptors more sensitive. In effect, it was a high-strength happiness and pleasure hit with a half-life of four hours. It sounded great, but was extremely dangerous. There were no direct medical side-effects from using products like the ones produced by Pleasure Tech, but you risked a psychological addiction to the highs.

When the tech was first invented, there were masses of people in the streets, all riding high and loving life. It didn't seem all that bad until the deaths started. People were being hit by vehicles or accidentally walking off buildings in the midst of their euphoria. Some people started selling everything they had just to get another hit, with many ending up living on the streets. Some people even died of starvation—begging for money, only to spend it all on another hit instead of food. That was the power of its addiction. It was now illegal, for a reason. However, you still saw people around with the tell-tale ruby spot, evidence of their out-of-hours activities. It perplexed me how companies like Pleasure Tech continued to run when they so obviously were involved in illegal operations. I could only assume there were political machinations and agreements at play that I wasn't privy to, and somehow, that was enough to protect this place and its boss, Raph.

The dance floor suddenly parted as a girl with spikey blue hair moved into the open space and began a fluid twisting set of dance moves that defied the expectations of flexibility. The crowd reacted instantly with cheers and hoots of excitement. This was definitely a different pace to my usual nights out at my meditation group.

The waitress with white streaked hair popped out of the dark carrying a tray with two electric-coloured drinks in tall, curved glasses.

'Here ya go. Two Starfires,' she proclaimed with a smirk of pride. As she placed the drinks on the table, she also pulled two long sticks out of her pocket, popped them into the drinks, and retrieved a lighter. With a deft hand, she set the sticks on fire. Flaming sparks flew everywhere. Even the top of the drinks caught on fire. I leant back and sat there for a moment, stunned. I guess they were called Starfires for a reason. Peter quickly blew the drinks out, and I remembered to maintain the charade, giving an appropriate light-hearted giggle. Satisfied, the waitress smiled and disappeared again into the chaotic light storm.

'Could you pick a more conspicuous drink?'

'Look, we're a couple out for a rare fun night out, right? I'm sure nobody noticed.' At least he had the decency to look embarrassed by the whole thing. I just shook my head.

'Alright. We need to find the entrance to the Den. There must be a doorway to the back area somewhere.'

'Like that one?' Peter inclined his head across the dance floor. Just through the swarm of bodies, I spotted a dark doorway with a burly black-clad guard on each side. 'Why do you think I sat us here? Perfect view.'

I kicked myself for not having noticed earlier. 'Fair enough. How are we getting in?'

'I was wondering: how are those old acting skills of yours?'

·········

We wove through the pulsating dance floor, then emerged out of the crowd near the doorway. As we walked, I took a deep breath, and channelled a sense of urgency into my steps as I began my act.

'I need to see the manager! My boy is missing. He works here. He works for you lot and you let something happen to him.' I waggled my finger earnestly at both guards, quivering my lip and drawing tears to my eyes.

'Honey, it's not their fault.' Peter stepped in and patted my arm.

'Don't patronise me! I want my boy home and safe. Now let us see the manager.' I didn't need to fake my tears as I channelled all of my feelings for Sam into my words.

The guard on the right cleared his throat. 'Ma'am, I'm sorry but we can't just let anyone in. It's orders,' he said in a quiet, uncomfortable voice.

'Anyone! I'm not *anyone*.'

'Ma'am, calm down.'

'I won't calm down. Not until you take me to the manager, and I'm not talking about the manager of the bar,' I ended with a knowing glare.

The rising volume of my voice had started drawing the eyes of other customers, making the guards twitchy. 'Harri,' said the one on the left. 'Just take 'em through to the waiting room. We can sort it out from there.'

'But the boss said—'.

'I know what the boss said, but he'll be fuming if there's a fuss. Take em inside.'

'Fine. But you can wear the blame if there's trouble.' Harri begrudgingly left his comfortable position and turned to face us. 'Follow me then.' He placed his hand against a palm scanner and the dark door slid open, revealing a dimly lit hallway. Harri ushered us along the passage into a small room with a beautiful leather sitting chair, and a shabby two-seater couch. 'Wait here. I'll get the boss.'

'Thank you,' I said, dripping sincerity into my voice. 'I'm sorry for the trouble. I just want my boy back. It's been an awful day.' Harri began to leave. 'Sorry to ask,' I said, pausing his exit. 'But is there a toilet nearby I could quickly use?' Harri ground his teeth.

'Down that hall to the right. Go and come straight back.' He turned to leave again, but a thought got the better of him. 'And don't go anywhere else!' Satisfied with his instructions, Harri left, slamming the door shut, leaving us alone in the room. We were in.

I nodded at Peter, then left the room. The hallway was empty except for a red carpet that ran its length. There weren't even any noticeable security cameras, which was unusual, although that didn't rule out the risk of unseen cameras.

I walked down the hall until I came to an intersection with one path leading right and the other left. The toilets were to the right, but that's not what I needed, so instead I closed my eyes and let the surrounding sounds intensify until I could isolate and categorise every sound. The heavy bass of the thumping music still reverberated through the concrete walls, the hallway lights hummed and a single set of pacing footsteps echoed faintly from the direction of the small room. Peter must be worried. Stretching my hearing further, I eventually picked up a faint rumble, accompanied by a whirring and electrical buzz that undercut the other tones somewhere down the right hallway. It had to be the server room, and it was just what I was looking for.

I turned to the right and promptly found the symbol for 'toilet'. To keep up appearances for potential cameras, I pushed on the door and entered. My belly was quaking with adrenaline. I hadn't snuck around anywhere in a long time. Luckily the toilets were empty, so I waited an appropriate amount of time and then headed back out, and headed further down the passageway.

I slapped on a confused look and strived for a lost old woman's appearance, hoping it would play well for anyone watching. I focused my hearing again, and there it was. The buzzing, rumble and whirl of the server room. I reached the door and grasped the cold metal handle, expecting it to be locked, but it turned easily. The door opened, and I dashed inside, closing the door behind me.

The room was tiny, with barely enough room for one person. A huge rack took up most of the space, with boxes of varying sizes inside it. Blue, green, red and yellow lights flashed on the boxes to their own unheard rhythm. Cables snaked out of every box, coiling and twisting together before heading up and out of the room through a hole cut into the wall. It was those cables that connected this Den to all the information in the universe. In case there were cameras, I maintained my act as a confused and upset old woman who wasn't thinking straight. I slid a sleeper dot into the palm of my hand and examined the boxes. It wasn't long before I found what I was looking for. The central comms box. Some other processors slightly obscured it, but it was still accessible. I forced a stumble and threw out my hand to catch myself while clicking the sleeper dot into a small hole at the bottom of the comms box. That tiny dot would give us a free path through their layers of firewalls and a provide us a copy of their crypto key. It would let us get in and see everything.

The door burst open. I spun around and found a gun aimed at my chest. 'What are you doing in here?' challenged a slender man with severe acne scars across the side of his face. He looked like a boy to me and was too young to be handling a gun.

'I'm so sorry. I...I needed the bathroom, then I got lost on my way back.' My words spilled from my lips a little quicker than usual as I began to cry. 'I was trying to get to the little room near the nightclub door. The guard—Harri I believe—said I could go to the toilet and come straight back. I tried to come straight back, but I must have made a wrong turn. The doors could all really benefit from some signs. Can you help me get back? I'm supposed to be meeting the manager.'

'Ma'am.'

'My son's gone missing!'

'Ma'am.'

'He works here, you know. But he never came home yesterday. It's not like him. Where's the manager?'

'Ma'am! Get out now and get back to the other room.' The boy pointed towards the hallway with the end of his gun. 'Now, ma'am!'

'Alright, alright,' I said, stepping back into the hallway. 'You just make sure the manager sees me soon. Now...which way do I go?'

He pointed in the right direction and escorted me the whole way.

'Here it is.' He opened the door and pushed me over the threshold. 'Now get in and stay here! The manager will be in soon.' The door slammed shut, leaving me and a surprised Peter on our own again.

'I got a bit lost on the way back from the toilet,' I said with a pointed look, 'but no harm done. I did what needed doing.'

Relief washed over Peter. 'Now we just need to see this manager.'

As if on cue, the door swung open, and another black-clad armed guard entered the room, followed by a small pig-nosed man with glasses that were too big for his face. The man sat in the pristine leather armchair and stared at the worn couch positioned opposite him. The armed guard pointed us towards the couch with his gun.

Once we were seated, the pig-nosed man pushed his glasses up with his middle finger, then folded his hands in his lap, letting a heavy pause settle over us. I resisted the urge to squirm in the awkward silence.

The man then coughed slightly and began. 'I am the manager, Raph Merton. I'm told you need to see me about your son. Who is your son and why would I be able to help?' His voice was pointed and nasally, and wasn't at all what I expected for the head of a drug den. Peter and I exchanged a glance before I began my rambling act again.

'It's about our son, Enric Vasteros. He's only twenty-four. But he works for you and we haven't seen him since yesterday morning. I'm worried. It's not like him not to call me. I was hoping you can at least tell me if he's, okay?'

Raph was perfectly still as he let another silence settle. The armed guard slid over to the manager and bent down to whisper in his ear. Raph's face was completely unreadable and remained that way even after the guard had finished and walked back to his post.

Raph sucked in a sharp breath through his nose. 'I didn't know he had parents. He has always led me to believe he was an orphan. Grew up in a kid's house, he said.'

'And you bought that?' I dropped my face into my hands and let tears gather in my eyes. 'I blame myself.' I sobbed and wrung my hands in my lap. 'I pushed him too hard. His entire life. Maybe I had too high expectations of him. I just wanted the best for him, you know? Wanted to see him be successful, and happy in himself. But he pushed me away. Started rebelling. I only wanted to get closer to him, but I ended up so much further away. I just I want to know he's okay? You don't need to tell me where he is. I know that could be...sensitive in this work. But just a word to let me know he's okay would be more than enough.'

'Ma'am. I'm sorry, but I'm not sure where Enric is right now.' My body slumped with disappointment. 'But,' he continued, 'I'm sure he will turn up. We're all family here, after all. You will just need some patience. I'm sorry I can't be more help, but I'm sure he will contact you when he appears. In the meantime, you must wait. I must leave now but you should go and have a drink on the house.' He rose from the chair and clicked his fingers. A second guard opened the door from the outside. 'The guards will show you to a table in the club. Sorry to not be of more service. It was nice to meet you.' With that awkward dismissal, the manager left the room, leaving us to be escorted back into the bar by one of the armed guards.

We followed the guard back out through the door guarded by Harri and his friend, then on through the throng of writhing bodies on the dance floor. The guard showed us to a booth near the bar and handed two small silver disks to us. 'Use these to get yourselves a drink,' said the guard before turning and disappearing back into the crowd. We spotted him again for a moment when he spoke briefly to Harri and the other guard, before heading back into the hidden world of the Den. I didn't know how deep those passages went, and I was almost certain I never wanted to find out.

'Alright,' I whispered to Peter, 'that part is done. Now, how do we get out of here? The manager seemed a calculating sort of man, and I don't believe he would let us out of his sights that easily. Especially once he hears I was in the server room.'

'Just wait and watch for now,' said Peter. I turned my head to see what he was looking at. From here we could see the entrance to the bar, and the entrance to the Den. 'Give it a bit of time. Then, if our charade worked, we could just head to the entrance and walk out. The blueprints I looked at before we came showed the only other exit points as a fire exit behind the bar, and windows in the bathrooms.' Peter left me at the table for a moment, handing over our silver disks at the bar.

Our two free drinks arrived at the table. I had no idea what they were, but they smelled strong. We sat for a while, trying not to arouse suspicion, watching as the heavy blaring music faded for a moment and transitioned to a dance song even I knew. It was the Tir-na Slide, and it had a dance to go with it that everyone learnt at school, although the version playing was a tricked-up dance club version rather than the one from my school days. The ruby spotters swarmed to the dance floor. That was the power of the Tir-na Slide. When you heard its nostalgic beat, it was hard to resist.

'Now,' Peter said and grabbed my hand, pulling me up. As we stood, we noticed two black-clad men run from the front entrance to the door of the labyrinth. They spoke momentarily before Harri opened the door and ushered them inside.

'I don't like that,' murmured Peter.

'Could they have found Enric's body already?'

'Probably. Not like we did a thorough job of hiding him while you were bleeding all over the place. We need to go now.' We wound our way towards the entrance, avoiding the flailing arms of the crowd's synchronised dance moves.

We were almost at the entrance when Peter paused. I smashed into the back of him, as the wayward arm of a dancing reveller whacked into my back. I poked my head over Peter's shoulder to see what was happening. There was a guard at the entrance, and he was staring straight at us. With his eyes locked on us, the guard reached up to his ear and began talking.

'Not this way,' Peter yelled over the music while turning and dragging me back into the crowd. 'Try for the fire exit.'

I nodded, and we ducked and weaved through the constantly moving limbs until we poked our heads out of the dancers near to the bar. I looked at the entrance to the Den. There were now four guards, and one of them pointed straight at us. Two of them raised guns and started shooting. The effect was immediate.

Loud cracks from the guns undercut the bass of the dance music. A glass on the bar near us smashed, and a hitched scream leapt out of the mouth of a young female on my left before she collapsed to the ground. Her friend stood in shock, their gaze fixed on the lifeless figure sprawled on the ground. A sinister pool emanated from the girl's chest, drenching her yellow shirt in an inky hue that shifted between shades of blue and purple under the ever-changing lights of the bar. I saw the girl gurgle a bloodied cough, then her eyes stopped seeing, and she lay still, surrounded by still-dancing revellers. Her friend started screaming. The writhing bodies on the dance floor slowed as another two loud cracks sounded. People looked around, dazed and scared.

Two more dancers screamed and fell. I grabbed Peter's hand and shouted at him over the chaotic noise, 'They're shooting everyone!'

'Come on! Get behind the bar.'

Peter crouched low and tugged on my hand, forcing me to follow him as he looped around behind the far side of the bar.

A body lay on the ground, blood streaming from a wound to a face framed with short spikey white hair. She was a waitress and couldn't have been older than Sam. The poor girl now stared at the back of the bar with unseeing eyes. We hurried past and reached the fire exit. Peter pushed on the door with all his might, but it didn't budge. I spotted a small hand-scanner pad and drew Peter's attention to it.

He let out an audible sigh. 'Well, I'm sure that's not aligned with the fire code.'

'Do you have a hacker on you?'

He reached into his pocket and tossed a small rectangular strip to me. I ripped off a piece of plastic to expose the adhesive on one side and slapped it on top of the scanner. Red lights began flashing on the rectangle. It would do its job and unlock it for us, but how long it took depended on the complexity of the embedded code.

Peter grabbed my hand and ripped me away from the door, pushing me down behind the bar as more bullets hit the wall. Peter looked at the hacker still doing its job and swore.

'Rach, I hope you've still got some fight in you. Two guards. Ten o'clock and closing.' Peter pointed at the hacker. 'If that thing hasn't finished in the next ten seconds, we're going to have to fight. I didn't bring guns cause of the weapon scanners, so all we have are these.' He held up his fists. I nodded in response; the simple action sent a stiff pain through my neck, which wasn't a good sign.

My heart pounded, and my fingers trembled. I hadn't fought anyone in twenty years, and now I was both older, and out of practice. I was screwed.

A guard lurched out of the darkness towards us. Peter hurled a bottle at them and used the guard's moment of surprise to disarm him. Now there was one less gun shooting at us, but Peter was stuck fighting the guard.

Something yanked the back of my shirt collar and flung me across the bar. I smashed into the glass storage shelf and fell on top of the dead waitress. The gunshot wound to her head was still oozing, with grey matter and blood covering the surrounding floor. I tried to twist myself to get to my feet, but my hands slipped on the waitress's internal fluids. It gave my attacker the opening they needed. A large palm grabbed the back of my shirt again and lifted me off the ground. I saw the world twirl around me as I was thrown against the side of the bar. The impact pulled at my recently sealed wounds.

'Who are you?' the guard roared. His breath stunk like a horrid blend of acid and mould. My eyes watered from the smell. I reached my hands behind me and found the edge of something upright and smooth. Something that fit perfectly in my hand. I gripped the object tightly and hiked my knee up between his legs. The guard curled forwards and slackened his grip. I smashed the object into the guard's face as hard as I could, the movement tearing at my shoulder's newly sealed skin. Glass shattered across his face, cutting his eye, as flowers and a yellow liquid sprayed across the area. A strong sour smell suddenly burned my nostrils. The flower vase I grabbed was filled with Stop-Grow, a potent liquid that preserved flowers perfectly, but stunk like a failed chemical experiment.

The guard screamed as the chemicals burned the lacerations crisscrossing his face. I twisted out of his reach and tried to run, but he swung out an arm and pulled me back towards him. My cheek bone cracked as the guard's fist stuck directly under my eye. The force knocked me across the bar and small black dots scattered across my vision. Everything was blurry, so I sensed rather than saw the next strike coming and ducked a moment before it connected. I struck out with a forceful kick aimed through the guard's shin bone just above the ankle and heard a horrid crack. The guard stumbled as a scream gurgled from his lips. I punched this throat, cutting off the sound. Looking around, I spotted a glass jar filled with Pleasure Dots behind the bar. Perfect. Holding it by two hands, I smashed it across his head, shattering glass and scattering Pleasure Dots everywhere. The guard fell to the ground, not unconscious, but looking rough, with Pleasure Dots scattered all around him. That's when a couple of enterprising ruby spotters noticed the scene and rushed over, frantically snatching up dots. I stood on wobbly feet as more ruby spotters rushed and clawed to get behind the bar. The draw of free dots outweighed any fear of the lethal fight. The guard's body quickly disappeared under the frenzied ruby spotters. I slid over the bar to the dance floor and noticed word was spreading about the free dots. Swarms of crazed ruby spotters were converging on the bar, trampling the bodies of the dead dancers in the wake of their hysteria.

The hacker finally flashed green as I weathered the flood of spotters flowing past me. I wove through the revellers and emerged to see Peter land a solid elbow to his attacker's throat. I remembered that move from my recruit training; it was a move that momentarily closed off the oesophagus. The guard wouldn't have a good time for the next few minutes, but would be fine tomorrow. Peter pushed the gasping man to the ground and headed to the exit.

More gunshots rang out, and another couple of ruby spotters fell to the ground. I crouched and ran towards the fire exit, but tripped on the dead waitress's foot. My ankle bent in a painful direction, but I heaved myself up and hobbled towards the exit. I slammed into the door, not wanting to slow my momentum. It swung open easily, and I had to catch myself before face-planting into the street. Peter ripped the hacker off the scanner pad and ran through, pushing the door closed behind him.

We were in a well-lit back alley that provided Raph and his security cameras a clear view of any loiterers around the Den. We slipped down a narrow access passage of a nearby building as two guards burst through the fire exit. Metallic thwacks echoed along the passageway as bullets smashed into the walls. We popped out the other end and, after taking another back alley, found our e-vehic. Peter rounded to the driver's seat as I threw myself in and slammed the door shut. I reached over and hit the start button to help get things going.

I looked back at the passage and saw figures coming our way. One lifted his gun and aimed directly at me. My breath hitched. The engine roared as Peter sped us away as a stream of bullets smashed through the back window and sailed over my ducked head. We turned a corner, and the pursuers were gone. My face and ankle throbbed, but we had done it. We were still alive, and I was one step closer to Sam. A relieved smile crawled over my lips as I sunk back into the chair and Peter drove us back to safety.

7

Encryption

P ETER SCANNED HIS RETINAS, and the safehouse clicked open. We hobbled over the threshold and slammed the door closed behind us.

'You start monitoring the Den's comms. I'll get the med kit,' I said. My ankle was stiff as I hobbled through the safehouse and I couldn't help but notice the 'functional' furniture choices made by someone for the safehouse. The Agency definitely wasn't a fan of creature comforts. Apart from our dining table-come-makeshift surgery table, the only other thing in the room was an ugly couch that looked like it was manufactured in bulk and sold off to large organisations at heavily discounted prices.

I grabbed the med kit out of a lower cupboard in the kitchenette and hopped over to the table, where I gingerly sat down and inspected my injuries. My ankle was strained, but nothing was broken. I drifted my fingers over my face. The left side where I copped a fist was inflamed and swollen. Even a feather-light touch made me wince. I tried to trace my eye socket, but instead found nothing but an enlarged mountain of puffy and painful flesh. I retrieved a small mirror out of the med kit and saw one bloodshot eye staring back at me, squinting through a narrowing slit as the eyelid swelled. The impact had connected with my cheek bone. Fear spiked through my blood. I had seen broken cheeks on others before and all of them had ended up needing surgery to prevent their face structure from collapsing. I carefully examined my cheek bone with my one good eye and traced the top edge of the bone with my finger. The good news was it hadn't sunken. It wasn't a full break that would have made my face collapse in on itself, but I was pretty sure it was fractured.

Resigned to my fate, I peeled off my blouse, leaving me in my under singlet, and sat down to inspect my previous wounds. Using the small mirror, I saw that the seared skin of my previous shoulder wound had held up to the fight. No blood was visible, but the skin had been pulled tight and thrummed with waves of painful inflammation. My hip and thigh were the same, and I thanked the stars Peter's surgery skills were up to scratch.

I placed insta-ice strips over my ankle and cheek, wincing at the initial contact that felt like a kiss from the icy expanse of space. I reached internally for my well-known breathing practices to help accept and adjust to the initial pain. It was something I had taught groups of people for over seventeen years every week at my job as a meditation coach. Shifting perspectives and controlling the breath went a long way to help get you through a lot of shitty circumstances. I knew from experience. But breathing only got you so far. I popped a couple of pain blockers in my mouth and forced them down. Things were now well beyond breathing.

I sunk into the chair and closed my eyes, hoping the pain relief would come quickly. 'How's the monitoring going?'

'Pulling the access feeds up now. I've set it to alert us to anything of interest. It'll look through all their records, finances and comms, and ping us on our wrist-comms if there's something we should look at. It will take a while to scour the system, so in the meantime,' Peter groaned, straining his body around in his chair at the tech-capsule, 'I'm going to make use of that med kit you have there.'

Bruises and swelling had started to bloom over his face. 'You've definitely looked better.' Peter ignored me and hobbled over.

'Have you looked in the mirror?' We both released a tired laugh that left us both exhausted.

'We're too old for this. I should be at home, with my son, sleeping comfortably in my bed. Not nursing my broken body back to health.'

'Speak for yourself. I'm still in the prime of my life.'

I gave Peter a judging look, but being too tired, I let the obvious banter fall into nothing. 'Do you need any help to patch yourself up? Cause if not, I'm going to have an ice bath.'

'Nah, I'm good. Just a few bruises and sore ribs this time,' said Peter. I nodded and pushed myself up to hobble my sad, broken, old body off to the bathroom.

Our wrist-comms pinged at the same time. Peter swivelled around and started pulling up various screens on the holo-screen. 'Looks like it found an encrypted communication.'

'That's not unusual though, is it?'

'Not really, but our system has pinged it because it is using one of the most sophisticated encryption methods around. Well above what I would expect from the Pleasure Tech Den.'

'What do you mean?'

'It says this type of encryption uses an advanced AI processor to shift encryption keys every nanosecond. You need a quantum partner key to decrypt it. Unfortunately, it's nearly impossible to grab the partner key cause as soon as you look for it, it changes this side of things. We could run it through the Agency's decryption AI, though. See if it can crack it. It should have a good shot. Vivian likes to prance around lecturing everyone about how advanced our systems are. Might as well put them to the test.'

'Can you do all that from here?'

'Yeah. Just got to open the AI connection. I'm not sure how long it will all take.'

'Maybe I will go have that bath then. Let me know if you get anything.'

'You'll get a ping if it works.'

I left Peter to hook up the connection to the Agency's AI. Soon, the complex living AI algorithm created in the belly of the Agency would be let loose, and commence a fierce invisible battle with the encryption's AI that would rage in the unseen void of data.

I locked the bathroom door and caught a look at myself in the mirror. An old woman stared back at me with a face smeared in bruises and a swollen, bloodshot eye. Her wiry curled hair sprung out at all angles, the grey colour in it creating a fuzzy halo. Who was that person staring back at me? It was the same face I had woken up to only yesterday morning, but so much had changed in such a short time. Curious, I touched my wrist-comm to see the time. It was only four hours till sunrise. Had it really only been forty-eight hours since Sam was taken? No wonder I felt like shit. I'd kept myself strong and lithe over the years with running, weight training and teaching movement and meditation, but I hadn't been pushed like this since my Agency days. Every muscle screamed and the patches of recently seared-shut skin were painful and red. I knew what I was about to do would be uncomfortable, but it will be worse if I didn't do it.

I started filling the bath with cold water, hitting the button to drop ice into the water at intervals, then switched off the bath and removed the rest of my clothes. With my clothes dumped in the corner, I took a moment and just stood, looking at myself in the mirror. My body was littered with marks from the past. Old scars, stretch marks, wrinkles, all of it combining to make a tapestry of my life. And of course, there were the recent injuries. All of them would fade in time, slipping to just a memory of a time, an event or a hardship I survived. That's if I lived through all this. I looked at my stretch marks, and my wrinkles, especially my smile lines. All of them were because of the crazy, wonderful ride of being Sam's mum. My chest felt hollow. The fear and dread at the thought of losing him started suffocating me. My breath was shaky, but I forced away any debilitating thoughts, and instead turned slowly to look at my back. Scarred lines and circles covered my entire spine in an intricate pattern. It was all that was left of Miles's experiments.

Maybe I had been a fool for volunteering for it, and I could still recall the pain that radiated through my core after every session. But I was a different person then. A person too motivated by not letting people down and always being the best. So, when the opportunity to increase my skills came up, I jumped at it. I couldn't really fault my old self. She had been an idiot, easily persuaded and completely misguided about what truly mattered, but all of her actions had led me to the most important thing that ever happened to me, meeting Miles. The scars on my back were my lasting connection to him. My proof he had existed, that I had once loved, and that he would always be with me. The scars proclaimed the turning point of my life, and in some awful way, I loved them for it.

My lungs deflated on a breath I didn't realise I was holding as I turned away from my reflection and the painful echoes of my past. Instead, I faced my next challenge, getting into the freezing bath. I sat on the bath's rim, my feet hovering over the top of the water, where clumps of ice silently drifted. I sucked in three deep breaths and slipped my body down into the bath's biting embrace. Air rushed from my lungs, leaving me gasping. I forced my shoulders under the water and stayed there. The rhythmic pattern of the forced labouring inhale and exhale of my lungs slowly numbed my brain to the burning tingle assaulting my skin. I closed my eyes and gave myself over to the numbness. I slipped into a trancelike state, the physical and mental exhaustion of the last day finally seeking its dues. An onslaught of memories began flashing before me. A timid hand reaching over to rest next to mine, the little finger brushing the smallest edge of my skin sending sparks up my arm, then looking up into Miles's smiling eyes that melted with relief when I reached my hand over and entwined our fingers. Laughing till my stomach ached while curled in bed together, talking till the sun rose. Miles holding my hands and looking me in the eye, telling me with wholehearted certainty that I would get through labour, that I could birth our child. Miles's unblinking eyes staring at nothing while blood dripped from the gunshot wound in his forehead. Trying to both give life to my son, while also keeping him alive in a dark, cold and empty storage room. My heart pounded in my chest, the pain of the memories gnawing at my nerves. I sucked in a breath through clenched teeth, and forced myself to go deeper within myself, to halt the flood of painful memories, and instead just let myself sink into nothingness.

Somewhere inside I found a peace, a quiet, and I embraced it with all of my being. I gave myself over to the nothing and slipped further and further until there was just darkness. I barely existed in this place, but I felt safe and free. Free from the pain of my past and the stress of my present. I couldn't even contemplate a future, because without Sam there was nothing left for me.

A voice whispered through the void, drawing my attention from my slippery dark slide into nothingness. *Rachel.* The familiar voice that was lost to me so long ago, Miles' voice, consumed the space. *Rachel, relax. Let yourself go deeper. Trust me, my love. Drift deeper within you. It has always been in you. You were always meant to be the one. You just need to know it in your own heart.*

I gave myself over to the void. I fell backwards without really falling. My essence drifting down like I had no weight. Down and down, my arms dragging behind me like a comet's tail during its constant fall through the universe. Then there was nothing. I was standing again, or was I laying? Directions meant nothing. I stood in the quiet, embracing the feeling of being wrapped in nothingness.

A soft blue light pulsed close to me. Its light brightened with each pulse, growing brighter and brighter until it was too painful to look at. I shielded my eyes as the unbearable brightness collapsed in on itself. When I risked a look, there was a floating blue orb, sizzling with light. As I watched, an inviting shimmer crossed its surface and gently pulsed. Fear had spiked through my limbs, making it hard to move. What was this thing buried deep inside me?

An awful answer rushed through my mind. I knew what it was. I think I'd always known it was here. I just didn't want to see it. *It's alright Rachel.* Miles's comforting voice sounded again. *It was always meant to be part of you. Embrace it and save our son.* I steadied myself and really looked at the orb. My heart was pounding as I watched it. With each throb of my heart, the orb pulsed. It was echoing my heartbeat. I reached out with a hesitant finger and took a shaky step forward. As I put my foot down, the void collapsed around me. Then the ground gave way, and I plummeted.

I smashed upwards through the surface of the ice bath, dragging in a huge breath. Panic passed over me as I realised I had slipped under the water's surface. A high-pitched beeping from my wrist-comm pierced the air. I pulled myself up and out of the bath. My entire body shook, and not just from the cold.

'Rach,' Peter's voice crackled over the comm, 'the ruddy AI did it! It cracked it! They must have some big-brained coder hidden away somewhere at the Agency. Come look.'

I wrapped myself in towels and turned on the gentle dryer. My brain was roaring and churning like it was set to hyper-drive. What was that? It must have been a dream. A case of delirium brought on by exhaustion and stress. Surely?

I left my clothes in a heap and instead padded in bare feet to the bedroom to hunt for more. There were three bedrooms in the safehouse. The first room was crammed full with a bunk bed and single bed, the second was a simple room with a double bed squished into the corner, and the third room was obviously the main bedroom. I pushed open the door and saw a sparse room with nothing in it but a chest of drawers and an enormous bed. I walked into the space and discovered another door. Opening it found a small room with a shower, basin and toilet. I knew which room I would claim for the night. I really needed to sleep. The bed was in front of me, taunting with its plush pillows and warm blankets. I would have given anything to just crawl under the covers and let myself drift into dreams, and I would hopefully realise that this is the dream when I wake up in my house, with Sam asleep in his room. It was a lovely hope.

I found a stash of clothes in the chest of drawers. I had to admit, they thought of everything at the Agency. There were clothes for almost any occasion, all ready to wear. I kept hunting and found what I needed, a simple but warm tracksuit and clean underwear. I got dressed and pulled on some thick socks to warm my feet. My body had stopped shaking from the bath, but I still had a chill prickling across my skin. I grabbed a large jumper and pulled it over my tracksuit top, just for good measure, then once wrapped up nice and warm, I head off to find Peter and the annoying pinging.

Peter was sitting at the capsule. My foot caught a creaking board that announced my arrival. Peter waved me over. 'Come check this out. The ruddy Agency AI did it. Looks like it's a one-off hack, though. The encryption key would have already changed at least a bazillion times by now. If we find something else that needs this type of decrypt, the AIs will have to battle it out again.'

I stood behind Peter to look at the screen. 'What did it find? Hope it was worth it.'

'You ever heard of La Panta?'

'The disgustingly rich company that seems to own everything? Yeah, I've head of them.'

La Panta was a vast conglomerate that owned companies in every industry but seemed to do nothing itself. Their whole business was based on buying and selling other people's businesses. There were rumours of La Panta strong-arming and threating brutality to other businesses during the company's early days, which probably contributed to their meteoric rise to power. It was a disgusting model, but admittedly, it worked; they were the wealthiest and most influential company on Tir-na.

'There's a message here sent from our buddy Raph to a Serena at La Panta. Looks like he didn't like us much.' The screen displayed a small white box with newly decrypted text that read:

Handler found dead. Two people sniffing around.

It barely said anything. Only two small sentences. But it was the lead we needed.

'Do you know much about the workings of La Panta and its executive? Any dodgy dealings in the past? Anything that would explain a direct connection between the black-market Pleasure Tech Den and a powerful conglomerate?'

Peter leaned back in his chair, thinking. 'Nothing off the top of my head, but you know me, memory like a black hole.'

I had heard some random phrases from Peter in the past. Throwing out an intriguing morsel of a statement hoping you'll bite and ask for more information was something he loved to do. Of course, it was all a ploy, so he could show off his wit. In the old days, I took pleasure restraining myself from ever asking for an elaboration, and instead watched him struggle to contain his pent-up excitement as it slowly fizzled and internally snuffed out. We knew each other too well and used to have so much fun playing off each other's quirks. It had been so long since I'd heard one of his silly metaphors, and I appreciated his efforts to make things like the old days, so this time I couldn't keep my mouth shut. I had to ask. 'Black hole?'

'Info is sucked in, never to be seen again,' Peter laughed.

'Hmmm,' was the only response I gave him.

'I've always relied too heavily on the tech in that department; it'll hold more info than my brain ever will. I like to think of my grey matter more like a library index. All I need to remember is where to go to find the info.'

I nodded then tried to drag the conversation back onto topic, 'So, La Panta...how do we find out who this Serena is and why they are interested in Lilli's handler? Raph is a big hitter with lots of lackeys, but that isn't a message to a minion and I can't imagine a giant corp like La Panta being happy in the passenger seat. To me, it reads like he's reporting up the chain. Giving a heads up to cover more tracks. And the brevity of it. No one talks like that. But short, sharp messages draw little attention zooming across the info-scape. He's probably been instructed when and how to get in contact.'

'Yeah, I agree. Well, lucky for us, we picked up this message. I've run a search for Serena, and guess what?'

'She doesn't exist? It's actually a fake identity?'

'Nope, quite the opposite. Serena Fabrica is the head of Client Management at La Panta. She even features all over their info pages. And she happens to be hosting a business afternoon tea for potential clients tomorrow.' Peter paused and looked at the clock. 'Actually today,' he corrected, surprised at how quickly the time had slipped away. 'Should we go to the afternoon tea? Sniff around?'

I stifled a yawn that swept over me from the mere mention of the late hour. 'Yeah, it's probably a good idea. It's also the only new lead we've got. Would be good to know more about what we're getting ourselves into though.'

'I'll get the analysts at the office to put together a briefing pack.'

'Make sure it has building info as well. I hate going somewhere I don't know.'

'Yeah, I remember. It'll take a while to get everything together. Go get some sleep. It's been a hell of a day, and you look like shit.' Peter twisted his head to the side, causing loud cracks to pop out of his neck. 'I'll hit up HQ and then head to bed myself.'

I found Old Blue where I had left it on the living room couch and dragged my tired arse back to the big bedroom, where the plush pillows and enticing blankets were waiting for me. With the door locked, I placed Old Blue on the bed, then stripped down to my singlet and underwear and snuggled under the blankets. The room was uncomfortably quiet. I reached over and pulled the photo of baby Sam out of the inside pocket of Old Blue. His chubby cheeks and huge smile broke my heart. I touched the picture, trying to imagine drifting my hand over his soft hair, something I hadn't been able to do with ease since he had grown taller than me. I held the picture close to my heart as a heavy sob bubbled out of my chest, releasing a cascade of tears that soaked the pillow. My other hand reached out and gripped onto the sleeve of Old Blue. It had been a gift from Miles, and I held it tight, trying to pull its memories back into existence. This was all I had left of my family, and that thought shattered my soul. I rolled over onto my side and, gripping my only physical connections to my family, sobbed myself into a deep, exhausted sleep.

Networking

To finish off my corporate costume of a basic pant suit, I tied my unruly hair back in a tolerable bun and set about applying makeup. I usually didn't wear makeup, but after a quick search through my wrist-comm for popular makeup trends, I was able to paint myself to look like a modern and serious business executive. The resources available to the Agency never ceased to shock me. Just in terms of makeup, there was every product you could think of in a case under the sink in my ensuite. All of them were new and from expensive brands, including a top-of-the-line makeup tech by Shimmer Skin Cosmetics that instantly covered all blemishes and ensured smooth, clear skin. Turned out it was also perfect for covering black eyes. After using the insta-ice strips to reduce the swelling, and the shimmer skin to cover the bruises, my face looked perfectly clear of injuries. I was impressed. Curious, I used my wrist-comm to look up the brand. A stifled laugh escaped my throat when the results flashed up on the holo display.

Shimmer Skin Cosmetics are a subsidiary of the La Panta Corp, based in Crayn City.

Of course. Almost everything was, it seemed.

I had never thought about the abundance of stuff readily available to the Agency. I never had a reason to when I worked for them. It was just part of the job. Whatever you needed, whenever you needed it, would easily appear at hand. But now, I couldn't help but wonder who looked after the safehouse when it wasn't in use. Who bought these supplies? Some of the makeup products had only come out last month. How big an unseen army did the Agency have at its disposal, sprawled across Tir-na? A prickle tingled across the back of my neck, but I shook it off and got back to the task at hand.

I grabbed a black, structured bag to go with my outfit, along with the business cards some analyst at HQ had created for us. Today we would be Tessa Pips and Darian Rockhurst, co-founders of new tech company Secfund, specialising in the production of secure protection code for implanted credit chips. 'We ensure you swipe with a smile every time,' I practised with a fake enthusiastic smile. Apparently, it was our fake company's catch phrase. I didn't know who had come up with it, but I had to admit, it was a believable cover, and exactly the type of small business La Panta would hungrily want to consume.

I threw on Old Blue and tenderly put Sam's baby photo back in the inside pocket, then headed out into the living room. Peter stood there waiting for me, fidgeting with his shirt collar. He was dressed in a similar sharp cut suit, but his hair looked much nicer than mine. His perfect coif seemed to have increased its buoyancy somehow, looking both fuller and higher. If I didn't know him, I would have thought he'd been styling it for hours. But I did know him, and irritatingly it was just the way it looked after being washed.

We eyeballed each other, appraising our costumes. Peter, I knew, had a much harsher and critical eye, so I was prepared for what was coming. 'You'll pass, I guess. But what's with the flat shoes?' He pointed at the comfortable black boots I had on under my suit pants. 'It's more traditional for women to wear high-heeled shoes to these things, isn't it? Makes you look more professional?'

'I would think that if it's the height of my shoes that determines whether someone takes me seriously or not, then I'm obviously not very good at my job.'

'Fair enough. But you kind of come across as one of those older women who've given up.'

'Excuse me?'

'You know the look. Flat shoes, dress like a man, with an easy-to-care-for haircut. You know, frumpsters?'

'Frumpsters?' I repeated.

'Yeah.'

I swallowed a list of profanities that rushed into my head and instead shook my head and walked over to the table to start compiling everything we needed for the day. 'Peter. I realised a long time ago how detrimental it is spending your life worrying about what other people think of you,' I said, while sorting papers. 'Worrying about what others think of the way you act, the colour of your hair, what you wear, it's all wasted energy. The people who care about that sort of stuff are not worth caring about. You might see what you call a "frumpster", but I see someone who has accepted who they are and refuses to let anyone make them feel bad about it. They do what they want to be happy and comfortable, and that's all that matters. They have their priorities in life straight. It's nothing to be sneered at. We should applaud them. We could all learn a lot from women like that and should be aiming to be like them.'

Peter looked at me with earnest eyes. 'You know I'm only joking, Rach. I didn't mean anything by it.'

'Yeah, but you kind of did. You're obviously spending too much time with women half your age instead of realising we're old Peter. We might not feel it, but to younger people, we're old. And I'm okay with that. It means I've lived, and that's everything.' I paused to reset, then clicked myself back into focused action mode and assessed the paperwork compiled on the desk. 'Do you have the tickets? Looks like we've got all the details here from HQ apart from that.'

Peter looked at me like he was trying to interpret an artwork, but then thought better of something. 'They just sent them through.' Peter walked back over to the tech-capsule and picked up a separate folder of papers. 'They sent through some other things, too. Looks like they got into the La Panta personnel files. Guess whose HR record we have a copy of?'

'Please let it be the only one we actually need.'

'A Miss Serena Fabrica. Looks like she's been there for a while. Joined the company as an apprentice, then had a meteoric rise to power. She's now thirty-seven years old and heads up Corporate Operations and Client Management, whatever that means.'

'Hmmmm. I wonder if that means she has oversight of corporate e-vehics?'

'What do you mean?'

'I was thinking about the e-vehic that ran me off the road and took Sam. They weren't your average shitty e-vehics. They were well looked after, and kind of reminded me of Agency ones. Any chance we could look into the records at La Panta to see if any made a significant trip a couple of nights ago?'

'I'll get HQ onto it.' Peter activated his wrist-comm and relayed the request directly to the analysts. A thin and reedy sounding woman's voice crackled over the connection and confirmed they would look into it and send a report as soon as possible. Analysts loved reports. I never would have made it as an analyst, as I didn't have the patience to write as many documents as they did. I'd rather be out and about than stuck behind a desk.

'It's a bit of a drive, isn't it?' I asked, already knowing exactly how long it would take us. 'We'd better get going.'

· · · ● ● ● ● ● · · ·

Peter had acquired us a new Agency e-vehic that didn't have a smashed rear window. The new one was shiny and complemented our appearance as burgeoning business executives perfectly. We used the drive to practise our cover stories and go over exactly what we were trying to find once at La Panta HQ. We knew Serena was connected to the Den, and they had monitored Sam via Lilli. But why would La Panta or Serena care about Sam? We needed more proof of any La Panta connections, and to find out exactly who La Panta was and why they were involved. Once again, we needed more information. More clues to follow. I internally groaned as I realised I would have to pull out my ignorant old woman routine again.

We pulled up our e-vehic a block away from La Panta HQ and stepped out onto the path. The plants here in the heart of Crayn's business district were artfully sculpted and carefully tended to, with the trees forming a perfect uniform canopy over the streets that protected Crayn's business elite from the dry season's harsh heat and the wet season's drenching rains. I cast my eye around and saw the normal bustle of bodies between the buildings, all hustling along with their heads down. All of them rushing to meet some unspoken deadline that most likely didn't matter in the scheme of things.

'Rach,' said Peter, hopping out of the car. 'You might need to leave the coat.'

'What?'

'Your coat. I don't want to be rude, but it looks like you got it from a second-hand clothes shop managed by a blind person. Probably not the type of thing Tessa Pips would wear, I imagine.'

I looked down at Old Blue. My well-worn, comfortable, reliable coat. My last tangible connection to Miles. I loved it, but Peter had a point. It didn't give off much of a business boss vibe. I sighed, conceding to Peter's point, and pulled off Old Blue, placing it carefully on the front passenger seat, making sure not to crumple the picture of Sam.

'Better?' I asked, showing my streamlined black and white outfit.

'Much. Shall we, Tessa?'

'After you, Darian.'

Equipped with minimal tech and one concealed weapon each, we made our way down the street and turned the corner to face La Panta HQ. The building soared sideways in each direction, before gracefully curving towards the sky in the shape of a huge egg. Rather than being solid, it was constructed of huge, vining tendrils, each containing multiple floors and office spaces, that twisted and wove together, forming a thatched nest effect. It was an architectural wonder begging belief. A large entrance faced the street with a white carpet spilling out onto the pathway like a lolling tongue. A stream of e-vehics pulled up next to the carpet, with La Panta employees eagerly opening the doors to greet the guests and usher them inside. Attendees wearing expensive business finery meandered up the carpet, nodding to each other and engaging in the type of light-hearted conversations only the wealthy could afford to have.

Peter's wrist-comm pinged, alerting him to an incoming call. He touched my arm to pause for a moment and lead me off the path, playing the role of businesspeople needing to take an extremely important call.

He put in an earpiece, then pressed a button on his comm and turned his attention to whatever message he was receiving. I stood nearby and absentmindedly scrolled through news articles on my wrist-comm. I couldn't hear the other part of Peter's conversation, so all I could do was wait. One news article caught my eye, though. It detailed the La Panta business afternoon gala we were about to attend and there, smiling in the promo photo, was none other than Serena Fabrica. Looked like our target would definitely be here.

'Copy that,' said Peter. He pocketed his wrist-comm earpiece then came close enough so we could talk without being overheard.

'That was HQ. They tried looking into La Panta corporate e-vehics. It took them a while to get into the system, but they did it. Looks like there were two e-vehics that made more significant trips than usual two nights ago. One of them was even sent off for repairs yesterday.'

My conviction galvanised. We were on the right track. 'Let's go then.' I turned on the spot and strode off towards the entrance. La Panta was involved. They had taken Sam, and I was going to find him.

• • • • • • • • • •

Afternoon tea was served in an opulent garden, cocooned in the centre of the intricate tangled building. Trees soared above us, some covered in soft flowers that draped like waterfalls, others curiously straight and so streamlined you struggled to believe it was natural and not man-made. There were swift-footed wait staff moving amongst the crowd, passing around exotic sparkling drinks imported from across Tir-na, along with small colourful delicacies tailored to please all palates. Music from an elegant band drifted through the space, softened by the luscious dense foliage surrounding us. It was beautiful, and the rich and powerful people networking around us were completely at ease here.

We each took a glass of the offered sparkling drink and set about fitting in. I had never seen anything like it. Life as a single mum with a minimum wage job didn't allow for many luxuries. I lifted the glass to my lips and sipped. The taste was like tinkling sunshine. It was delicious, and it made me hate this place even more.

On arrival, we had been issued a small earpiece that would scan the other attendees and automatically tell us who everyone was and what their company

92

did. It made it easier for attendees to avoid wasted conversations with people not worth their time. Luckily for us, the Agency had peppered our covers with interesting details that made us an intriguing investment or buyout opportunity for most of the attendees, provided the price was right.

We were approached by an endless throng of suit-clad old men, all eager to hear all about Secfund's offerings and the effectiveness of our secure protection code. My cheeks slowly ached from smiling and I hated the number of times I had to repeat 'We ensure you swipe with a smile every time'. We played our parts, both of us ensuring we came across as people with a great idea, but very little actual business acumen. It made us the perfect buyout opportunity and accordingly we had no lack of attention, which hopefully would get us to our actual goal.

We had been at it for almost an hour. Peter was busy talking to another grey man about the potential for expanding our portfolio when I noticed a beautifully suited and sleek young man walking over to us. As he approached, I noticed small lines around his eyes that hinted he was older than he seemed.

'Ms Pips?' The man's face stretched into an iridescent smile, the absolute image of charm and grace. He gave a curt nod in greeting, as seemed to be the way with these rich and powerful people.

'Yes,' I smiled back, giving a nod in response.

'My name is Garran Vertus. I hear you and your partner here have a very interesting company.'

'Oh really? You've already heard about us? That's awfully kind of you to say. We've just been so struck by the attention we've had from all these wonderful people. It's so lovely to be here.'

'I represent La Panta, Ms Pips.'

'Please, call me Tessa.' I tried to look slightly flirty, but I didn't think I could pull it off as well as I used to.

'Thank you. As I was saying, I represent La Panta and I must say we're keen to hear more about Secfund and your potential offerings.'

'Oh really! Darian!' I said, turning to Peter with a huge enthusiastic smile plastered on my face, and interrupting his conversation with an older man who, according to my earpiece, was Hedric Milman, the CEO of the Heatwave cooking tech company. 'Mr Vertus here is interested in talking to us. He's from La Panta.'

Peter made a polite excuse to Mr Milman and turned to join our conversation. 'Mr Vertus, was it?' asked Peter, nodding his head in greeting.

'Yes, that's right. Ms Pips, Mr Rockhurst, I'll be frank with you. La Panta is very interested in making an offer for your business. Whether it will be a full buyout, or if we just purchase a portion of the business, can be negotiated.'

The Agency had done a wonderful job creating a perfectly pitched cover company for us that was instantly enticing for investors. Knowing their methods, they would have backstopped the cover with multiple historical records to reassure potential investors that we were legitimate and perfect for the taking.

'Mr Vertus. I'll be honest,' I said, channelling my best business voice. 'We don't really know enough about La Panta to commit to anything. Secfund is our baby.' I turned and look at Peter, who nodded in agreement. 'We can't just give it up to anyone, especially when we don't know them.'

'Perfectly fair. What would you like to know?'

'I guess Mr Vertus, we would first want to know about the owners of La Panta, the type of businesses you have, and how large La Panta's footprint is,' said Peter. 'So, then we can understand how our little Secfund would fit into it all.'

'Of course. As you probably know, La Panta is one of the top five companies on Tir-na. We have connections into almost every industry, and it's all headed up and run by the Closman family and has been for five generations. The Closmans were part of the initial colonisation of Tir-na and were fundamental in the foundation of Crayn. Since those days, the Closmans have remained an essential element of Crayn, with strong functional relationships with sister cities and outposts like Uishka, Aeir and the Grove. La Panta's businesses help provide jobs for citizens and make products to improve our lives. I, for one, am very proud to be a part of it.'

'That's very impressive,' I said, earnestly.

'The current head of the family is Maxim Closman. He has been in the role for sixty-five years.'

'Wow! That's a surprisingly long time,' said Peter.

'Yes, Mr Rockhurst. It is. It's rumoured his oldest son, Felax, will take over soon. But it's just a rumour, and that rumour has been around for the past ten years. You can be assured, though, that the Closman family are smart, strong and would be fierce protectors and champions of your company, should you decide La Panta is the right custodian for Secfund.'

'That's great to hear!' I affirmed. 'That reminds me. I remember an article once popping up in a business feed I follow that I wanted to ask about it as I think the author works here. It was a very interesting article. I think the name might have been Serinia Farica. Yes, I think that was right.'

'Do you mean Serena Fabrica?' offered Mr Vertus.

'Yes! That's it. She wrote about modern people management and business strategies. It had some fascinating ideas, so I wanted to ask if she really does work here?' I had spent the morning studying Serena, including reading the article, which really did have some very interesting ideas on management.

'Yes indeed. Ms Fabrica is the head of Corporate Operations and Client Management.'

'Well, she sounded impressive. It sounds like you certainly have some great leadership here.'

'Indeed, Ms Pips. It is through the strength of our leadership that we succeed where many other companies have failed.'

'Can I ask a silly question? I can't help it, just ask Darian here. I tend to get a bit excited about little things. But were those company e-vehics I saw out the front? I can only imagine what it's like working somewhere like this every day. Does everyone get one?'

Mr Vertus laughed, 'If only, Ms Pips. La Panta has a lot of resources, but not enough to provide every employee a company e-vehic. No, they are only used for business-related events.'

A high-pitched ping sounded from Peter's wrist-comm. 'Excuse me for a moment. I need to take this,' he said, looking down at the alert before peeling off to the side to look at the communication. Mr Vertus nodded in acknowledgement and the two of us continued.

'Must be a lot of paperwork to manage all those e-vehics,' I said.

'No, not particularly. We pride ourselves at La Panta on streamlining processes as much as possible. The e-vehics are organised through Serena Fabrica's office, with all the management handled by her. We even have our own e-vehic maintenance crew who keep everything in perfect condition.'

I nodded in appreciation. 'That's smart.'

Peter headed over to us again, catching my eye in the process. 'I'm sorry, Mr Vertus, but I must ask to steal Tessa here away for a moment,' Peter smiled. 'There is some business we need to attend to momentarily. I hope you understand.'

'But of course. Let me give you my card so you can contact me directly. My details are on the back.' Mr Vertus held out a smooth, super-black card, the type of black that absorbs all light, with a stylised image on the front that echoed the tangled tentacles of the La Panta HQ building. 'As I said, La Panta is very interested in hearing more about your offerings, so please reach out to organise a time for us to meet and discuss what can be arranged.'

'Thank you, Mr Vertus.' I nodded.

'Not at all. It was a pleasure, Ms Pips.' He nodded and then turned promptly to begin moving through the throng of people to find his next potential target.

Peter gripped my elbow and directed me to an alcove off the main function area. I managed to keep my curiosity at bay until we were away from prying ears. 'What is it?'

Peter's face dropped, becoming deadly serious. 'You just got another video message. Came in three minutes ago.'

Fear turned my stomach into a frozen, knotted ball. 'Show me.'

'I'll send it straight to your comm, but put your earpiece in first so we won't be overheard.'

I nodded, put in my wrist-comm earpiece and prepared myself. A green alert button popped up on my wrist-comm. With shaking fingers, I hit it and turned myself to the wall to block the image from any passers-by.

The video started. Centre of screen was a small defenceless figure restrained on the same chair as before, only they looked like they had been put through hell. It was Sam. There wasn't fear in the lines of his muscles anymore, but rather an exhausted, resigned depression. His head hung low and there were bloodstains from his cheek that had dripped onto his shirt and large, dark urine stains stretched across his pants.

The same dark clad masked figure moved into the screen and spoke. 'Tick tock, Rachel. Time's running out. We thought you were better than this. I know your boy was hoping you were.' The figure moved behind Sam and wrenched his face upwards towards the camera. Sam's eyes were glazed, and thick blood had clotted along the rough cut that stretched from the top of his temple to his jaw. 'He's just dying to see his mummy again.' The screen cut to black, and the communication ended.

'They're taunting me. They say I have something that they want but won't say what it is. Why do they just want to hurt me?' I said to Peter through clenched teeth. 'Who the hell is doing this?'

'There are probably lots of potential answers to that question, but that doesn't really matter right now. We focus on getting your boy, then we figure out the why.'

'Fine,' I conceded, glaring at Peter. 'But we go in now. I want to see Serena.' I spat out her name as the taste of it became bitter on my tongue.

'Whatever you want to do. I'm with you.' Peter nodded at me, before adding quietly, 'it's the least I can do.'

I ignored his last comment and headed deeper into the alcove, where there was a side door that led to an emergency staircase. We prepped our concealed weapons and pushed open the door. It opened easily. We crossed over the threshold and began our trek deeper into the tentacles.

9

Client Management

O
UR TREK THROUGH THE building went smoother than hoped. Only a couple of staff stopped and asked us what we were doing, but we talked our way around them easily by confessing to be 'lost' and sincerely requiring their help to find Ms Fabrica's office as Mr Vertus had sent us to talk to her. I pulled out Mr Vertus's card, providing the extra legitimacy we needed. I had to admit, all the La Panta staff we encountered were extremely helpful and promptly directed us to the fourth floor, with one of them even insisting on leading us there.

We reached the fourth floor and found the Corporate Operations and Client Management section. The area had a hyped-up buzz of energy, as fashionably dressed staff with perfectly sculpted hair worked away at their crammed desks, their hands flying as they interacted with their holo-screens. For a moment, the sight of all these beautiful busy people made me wish I had worn the heels, but it was a fleeting thought. We wandered past the workers and stopped at a beautifully carved office door. The carvings showed a twisting maze of tentacles that reached upwards, as though desperately trying to grasp something, and there, in the centre of the door embossed in gold and caressed by tentacles, shone the name we sought, Serena Fabrica.

'Here it is. Ms Fabrica should be in there and will help you,' said our too-eager guide. She was a young woman who had been an intern for the past five months and had apparently been starved of anyone to talk to, as she ended up telling us her entire life story while we walked through the hallways. 'Do you need anything else before I head back to my desk?' she asked.

'No, that's it,' said Peter. 'And thanks, Carri. We appreciate your help. I hope your grandmother's knee surgery goes well.' We both gave her a warm smile of thanks.

'Not a problem at all, and thank you.' She smiled and waved before heading back the way we had come. Once her back was turned, I shook my head slightly. She was really too trusting and had told us way too much information, but she had got us where we needed to go, leaving us in front of the looming door.

I took a deep breath and knocked.

'Come in,' a crisp voice answered from within. We looked at each other, then pushed open the door, readying ourselves for whatever we encountered.

'Ms Fabrica?' Peter said tentatively. 'We're sorry to interrupt, but a Mr Vertus sent us up here. We are guests from the party. The owners of Secfund.'

'Oh, of course, please come in.' A tall, thin woman with wild auburn hair restrained in a messy bun sat at a delicately carved wooden desk. She gestured for us to enter and sit in the chairs opposite her desk. 'Garran did highlight you as a potential client of interest. I hope the hounds downstairs haven't given you too much grief.'

I entered first, with Peter holding the door open for me, and then stood there, reciprocating Serena's charming smile and acknowledging her attempt at being funny. Peter ensured the door was closed behind us, then after hearing the click of the door lock, we pulled our weapons.

'Alright Serena,' said Peter. 'We've got some questions for you. And if you don't mind, we'd appreciate you cooperating and telling the truth.'

Serena stayed sitting in her chair, her body not even flinching at the sight of the drawn weapons. 'I'm impressed. They must be some pretty high-tech guns to get past our scanners.' She leaned forward slightly and clasped her hands together just below her chin, elbows resting on the arms of her chair. 'Makes me wonder who the two of you really are.'

'We'll be asking the questions, if you don't mind.' Peter smiled at her, enjoying the high-stakes banter and the tension flooding the room. Meanwhile, my insides were quivering, but I focused all of my strength into my arm and core muscles to keep my gun steady to not betray my nerves.

'What's your connection to Pleasure Tech?' Peter asked.

'I don't know what you're talking about,' Serena lowered her hands behind the desk and leant back in her chair.

'Hands up, sweetheart,' Peter instructed while gesturing with his gun. 'Now, come on, we both know that's a lie. Why don't you try again? What's your connection to Pleasure Tech?'

There was a moment of silence as Serena crossed her arms and sat there critically, eyeing Peter. The uncomfortable moment stretched on until she loudly released a breath through her teeth and leaned forward, having made some internal decision. 'Alright then. I sometimes reach out to Pleasure Tech to acquire their product for some of our more influential corporate partners and VIP associates. Some of them enjoy mixing business with pleasure. And who am I to stop them?'

'Isn't it risky for a company like this to have dealings with the black market?'

'Let's just say it helps to have powerful connections who are happy to ignore matters that don't involve them.' Serena bared her teeth in a terrifying smile. Her eyes were cold and focused.

'Do you ever personally contact Pleasure Tech?'

'Of course not. I have people to do these things for me.'

'So, you've never had comms with Raph Merton?'

'Of course not.'

'That's interesting, 'cause we know that's not true. In fact, you were contacted by him only yesterday.'

Her eyes narrowed at the unspoken implication Peter had just laid out. La Panta's sophisticated AI had been hacked. I didn't want this conversation to get bogged down in those details. We needed to get moving. We needed to find out if Sam was here.

'The company cars,' I said, interrupting and taking the conversation in a new direction. 'Do you control the use of them?'

Serena turned her steely eyes towards me. It felt like a frigid breeze creeping over my skin. 'Ms Pips is it?' I didn't respond. 'You're not looking very good. You might want to sit down.'

Frustration bubbled within me as a cold sweat formed on the back of my neck. 'Just answer the question.'

'I do control company car use, but I don't police it. Staff only need to log into a system and book the cars. It's not a hard process. By the way, I really do think you should both sit down. You're not looking the best.'

My head was throbbing, making it hard to see straight. Risking a glance at Peter, I saw his skin had started to turn slightly grey, and there was a sheen of sweat across his top lip.

'Who took out the cars two nights ago?' I said, with frustration dripping off every word. The gun I held grew heavier, and the floor swayed.

'I'll need to look it up. It might take a while. Please, have a seat in the meantime.' She gestured to the chairs on the other side of her desk. Her hand looked strange and moved like it was being pulled through tree sap at a crawling pace, as though time had slowed down. The edges of my vision started creeping inwards, and my internal voice become my only reality as everything went black.

· · · • • • • • • · · ·

My eyes opened to a grey, clinical-looking room. The light above us was too bright and painful, forcing me to squint. Completely disorientated, and with my head pounding, I began twitching small, isolated muscles to test my situation. I couldn't move my hands or feet. My brain suddenly clicked back into working order, and I realised I was restrained on a chair, its hard surface pressing into my thighs and back. I heard a sharp intake of breath. Turning my neck painfully, I saw Peter restrained on a chair next to me. His breath was steadily speeding up as his body came back to consciousness.

The light was still too bright, so I couldn't see anything but the floor. Bland and grey. Smooth. Polished. I didn't know where we were or what had happened. The last I remembered we were in Serena's office. Then the world spun out from under me, and everything went black. How long had I been out? The thought of Sam stuck with his captors for a further unknown amount of time filled me with terror.

I pushed through the pain of the bright light and forced my eyes to open so I could absorb every detail of the room. The ability to recognise the stories told by the smallest of objects had always been one of my strongest abilities as an agent. However, that was a lifetime ago, and prior to seeing the video of Sam and the masked figure, I hadn't used my mind in such a way for a long time, apart from using it to check if Sam had made any effort to clean up his room. I needed those skills now, though, and I hoped they would be enough.

I drew in a breath and let every detail flood my senses. The room was constructed of solid floors and walls, all grey and oddly smooth. Two simple bar lights were attached to the roof. They weren't anything fancy, but they weren't the cheap versions. There were no windows, but there was a door looming in front of us. It was metal, solid and expensive-looking, with a simple push-down handle. This wasn't a room used for keeping people for long periods of time, as the door had an exposed locking device that could be easily bypassed. Next to the door was a tech-capsule built into the wall and a small metal table. In the corners of the room were cameras, and I found it interesting they hadn't chosen unseen cameras. The chair I was strapped to spoke volumes. It was made of a simple wood but was solid in its construction. It wasn't the type of wood easily sourced from the standard tree plantations. This was a specialised composite wood that harnessed the strengths of multiple tree species. The joints were smooth and of bespoke construction. My throat wasn't screaming out in thirst so we couldn't have been there for long, and when I sniffed, the air was filled with a gentle, hygienic, but clean, floral smell. It was the smell of a premium sanitiser. All this information whirled through my head. Various options and stories playing out in a heartbeat. Until a solidified picture clicked into my mind. We were most likely still in La Panta HQ, and I had seen this room before.

The door handle clicked, and the large metal door swung open. Serena Fabrica strode into the room like she was walking into a business meeting, carrying a metal case in one hand. Her pointed shoes clicked on the solid floor and behind her drifted in a figure clad head to toe in black with a hood shadowing their face.

'You're finally awake.' Serena moved to the small table and opened the metal case with her back towards us. 'I forget how long it takes for the gas to wear off.

Don't worry if you feel queasy or lightheaded for a while. It's a perfectly normal side effect that will dissipate in its own time. Or so I'm told.' I looked at Peter. His eyes were glazed with his head leaning to one side. They had gassed us. How had we not pre-empted such a possibility? The Agency was supposed to know everything.

'Luckily,' Serena continued, 'it's not something any of us who work here need to worry about. One little injection and you're immune for life. Quite a clever security protocol, really. I'm actually surprised neither of you noticed me activating it.'

We were idiots. I had been trained to leave emotions out of every job so they didn't cloud your judgement and put you at risk, but I had spent the last twenty years trying not to live like that. The life I had built for myself was rich and full, and I cherished my emotions and felt them every day, just like Miles had taught me. But look where that had gotten me. I didn't know what had distracted Peter, but I had charged in with no real thought except that I needed to get Sam, and now we were trapped. I had failed. The person I had become since leaving the Agency had failed.

Serena pulled out two long, thin silver cylinder and turned towards us. The sight of them shocked me. Intel-wrenches. She shouldn't have them. They were Agency equipment and weren't on the open market. There was no way the Agency would want to lose a tech advantage like that. So how did Serena have them?

'Now,' said Serena, approaching us with the grace of a relaxed predator, 'hold still for a second and we can find out who you both really are. Not owners of a new tech firm, that's for sure.' She stalked behind the two of us and I felt a sharp puncture on the side of my neck. She was collecting my blood. Serena did the same to Peter with the other intel-wrench, then strode over to the table where she watched the wrenches begin whirring as they processed our blood, and started reaching out into the intangible data networks to find the information they sought. While Serena was busy, I took a moment to look at the black unmoving figure that had taken up vigil in the room's corner. The hood completely shadowed their face, and they just stood there. Unmoving. Analysing. I couldn't tell anything about the person underneath, but the robes looked familiar. Then it hit me. It was the prick from the videos, or at least someone wearing similar clothes. Sam must be here. The thought lifted my heart. We might be close to him. We just needed to get out. My fingers examined my wrist binds, desperately trying to reveal a weakness that would set me free.

The intel-wrenches pinged, alerting Serena that they had finished processing, and I hoped the Agency analyst who doctored my records all those years ago had done a good enough job.

'Rachel Tomsen,' Serena announced. 'Forty-nine years old. Lives in Forest Glen on the edge of Crayn City. An office clerk for ten years, before becoming a movement and meditation teacher,' Serena's voice inflected upwards at this information, as though it was the most surprising thing she could have read. 'I must admit, I didn't pick that,' she said. 'One son. Sam Tomsen, who is—oh wait, that means you're the mother! Ha! How wonderful.' I jostled against my binds. The sound of Sam's name and Serena's condescending tone while she laughed ground my nerves. My facial muscles twitched as I tried to maintain a cold, unmoving expression. 'He's studying electro-engineering and robotics at Crayn University. You must be so proud.'

'Where is he?' I ground out between my teeth.

'Oh, he's long gone. You won't be seeing him.' The words stabbed through me. 'Now for you.' Serena turned to Peter. 'Peter Brand. 54. Lives in the South Quarter of Crayn City. Works as a security consultant. Well, that's handy,' Serena mocked, taking a moment to look at Peter. His eyes were still glazed, but his face was a mask. A slightly smug and amused mask with his mouth pulled to the side in a cocky smirk. It was his well-used veneer that he used on almost every occasion. Serena continued, 'No spouse. No kids. Sounds lonely.' She raised an eyebrow at Peter and studied his face. I may have imagined it, but I thought I saw a slight twitch in the corner of his mouth before he pulled it back under control. It was so fast most people would have missed it. I had no idea what it meant, but whatever it was, I hoped Serena hadn't noticed it. 'Now that we all know each other, why don't you tell me what the two of you are doing here?' Silence followed. Neither of us would disclose anything to this woman. Realising we wouldn't talk, Serena clasped her hands in front of her and began stalking around us, her heels clicking on the hard floor. 'Why don't you tell me what you were hoping to get from me, then? I'm just one woman, after all. How could I possibly have helped you?' Serena stopped in front of me and grabbed my face and came in close to stare into my eyes. She was trying to maintain a cool facade, but her eyes burned with excitement. She was enjoying herself. I remained silent.

'Fine,' Serena said, releasing my face with a forceful push. 'If you don't want to talk to me, maybe you'll be happier talking to him.' She inclined her head towards the hooded figure. At the suggestion of his involvement, the figure's entire body puffed up, and the fingers on his right hand twitched. Serena turned towards the figure. 'Alright. It's your turn. Just don't make things too messy.'

Serena sat at the table near the tech-capsule, while the figure who had come alive at her command started prowling towards us. They moved past me and stopped in front of Peter. The figure leaned forward and began examining every wrinkle and pore on Peter's face. Once satisfied, they then moved on to me.

I took a deep breath, but before I could do anything with it, the figure was there, and the light finally lit up their shadowed face. The same grotesque mask I had seen on the videos stared back at me. Up close, it was even more terrifying and reeked of putrefied flesh. This wasn't a fake. The mask was a patchwork of different pieces of skin stitched together. A wilted and stretched nose bobbed above the right eye, a skewed mouth that was sewn shut with a rough black cord wobbled back and forth with each inhale of breath, an ear flapped off the bottom of the right jaw, and two shiny dark eyes stared at me through holes hacked through the rotting skin.

The smell burned my nose and throat. My stomach clenched in response, but I kept my eyes locked on the figure and forced my face to show no response. The mask twitched from side to side as they examined me.

'Tell me, Peter,' the figure drawled as they suddenly moved back to Peter. 'What are you doing here?' Their voice was husky but in a rich, melodic way, which was both pleasant and unnerving.

'Sitting on a chair,' Peter offered with flippant charm. 'Can't you see through that ridiculous mask? Maybe you should ask for your money back, or was it a homemade job?'

The figure moved with unnatural speed and pulled out the jagged edged knife we'd seen in the video. They hovered, nudging the tip of the blade against the flesh of Peter's lower lip. 'Careful Peter,' said the figure. 'I need a new mouth for my mask. This one's getting old and floppy.' The figure reached up and carefully, lovingly, drifted a gloved finger over the sewn mouth. 'Your skin looks strong and nimble. It would make the perfect new addition to my creation.'

Peter froze. His face was still a solid mask of bravado, but I had known him too long. The pulse of his throat, and the strain in his muscles, gave him away. He was nervous, but didn't want to show it.

'Peter. Rachel,' the figure rasped. 'Let's try this again. What are you doing here?'

'We just really wanted to see you,' shrugged Peter. 'We'd heard about this curious figure who lurked the halls of La Panta. They say he eats the souls of anyone who refuses to let La Panta buy them out. It's really a great story, and I wanted to see if the legend was true. So, I grabbed Rachel here, and we came on an excursion. So far, you don't disappoint.'

The figure's hands moved faster than my eyes could track. They grabbed Peter's hair with one hand and ripped his head to the side, pinning it still. With the other hand, he slowly, tenderly, dragged the sharp knife blade across Peter's lower lip. The touch of the honed steel released a torrent of blood. Peter groaned. Finished, the figure stood to examine their work. The gratuitous mask slid around with every move. The figure reached out a gloved finger and touched the fresh cut.

'Thank you, Serena,' the figure said, turning towards her. 'This will be a lot of fun. Alright Peter. Let's continue, unless, of course, Rachel has anything to add.' The figure said it without even looking at me. His eyes were locked on Peter, who was sucking in controlled breaths. An internal war raged within me. My training taught me to never say anything, but I didn't want my friend to hurt.

'Don't worry Rach. I've got this,' Peter said with a fake smile in his voice.

'Do you, now?' taunted the figure. 'Well, this will be fun then.'

I didn't see the figure's next move. Instead, I closed my eyes and stared at the darkness behind my own eyelids while forcing my breath to slow. Peter's screams filled the room as I let myself fall into the deep inky nothingness, leaving everything behind. The room, the screams, all of it gone. I was nothing but a consciousness and I drifted down. Deeper and deeper where there was no stress or worries. There was only drifting downwards into the unending void. *Rachel.* It was Miles's voice again. It was always Miles's voice I heard when I meditated. *Go deeper. You have the strength and the power. Accept it. Use it. Embrace what has been there all along. It is your power. Only you can unlock it. Be who you are and save our son.*

My drifting downward halted with a jolt. The darkness spun all around me and I tried to orient myself. I stood for a moment, letting the inky dark wash over me, but then, in the distance, a speck of light flickered into existence. I hesitated for a moment, then put one foot in front of the other and moved towards the light. My steps made no noise in this space of nothing, and as I approached, the light grew larger and larger.

When I was close enough to reach out and touch it, I stopped. Up close, I could see the warbling ball of light was actually hundreds of sparking blue tendrils that snaked their way around each other. It hovered in front of me, bobbing gently to an unheard rhythm. As I stared at it, a torrent of painful emotions filled me. The pain was multifaceted and unrelenting. I was surrounded by the pain of pretending my previous life had never happened, the pain of losing my chance to have a happy life with Miles, the pain of having to hide my skills and abilities for so long, the pain of losing my son, the one true thing in my life. He was the one thing that gave all the lies meaning, and the reason I was happy to accept my lot and press on for as long as I had.

The rush of feelings and thoughts left me breathless as their depth and poignancy shocked me. I hadn't realised how much I had bottled up these feelings. It was completely at odds with the lessons I taught every week in my classes, and I couldn't be afraid of it anymore. I couldn't ignore who I had been or who I was now. On instinct, I reached out and thrusted my hand into the centre of the ball. A sharp pain seared through my skin as I watched the light contract, then snap into place in my palm. Tendrils of the blue light flexed outwards before twisting their way around my hand. The individual strands joined and created a glove of searing light that burned. It was painful, but not as painful as the emotions flooding through me, so I let it have me. The sparking blue light began creeping up my arms and seared along the scar lines across my back. The crackling light stretched around my body, forming a second skin that engulfed every inch of me up to my neck. I accepted the blinding pain and let the light rise past my neck. Moving higher, the light filled my ears and throat, drowning me. My entire body burned. Just when the pain became unbearable, I closed my eyes. The pain exploded out from me and then disappeared, leaving me in darkness. I opened my eyes and found myself illuminated by a gentle blue light. A light that radiated from the electric flames glowing in my eyes.

10

The Trip

I RETURNED TO MY senses with a jolt. Peter was screaming as the masked figure hovered over him, his body blocking my view of what he was doing to elicit such a response. I had only heard Peter scream once before, and that was a long time ago during a mission that went horribly wrong. Peter had been close to death, but I had got there in time. Now we were both stuck. What good was an old woman who couldn't even keep her son safe? I didn't want to be useless, and I couldn't stand being thought of as weak or incapable. I had loved my previous life, but I had to be strong and throw it all away to protect my family. I needed to be strong again, but this time, instead of hiding myself, I needed to bring everything I was to the surface. I needed to be me.

A drop of tingling energy blossomed in the palm of my hand, echoing my burning anger. I focused my mind and let the feeling burn into my body while everything else slipped away into nothing. A thin tingling spark rose from my core and speared out through my limbs. The pulsing light was everywhere inside me. But then it extended beyond me, and I could feel everything. The speeding data behind the tech-capsule, the electrical connections holding the door closed, the sleeping energy of the cameras, and the buzz of our hand-restraints. I even sensed Peter's earpiece. I looked at him and saw a ghostly blue sparking light around the earpiece lodged in his ear. Scanning the room, I saw Serena's wrist-comm, surrounded by the same pulsing blue light, along with everything else I had sensed.

I focused on my hand-restraints and felt a tenuous pulse keeping them in place. On an instinct I reached for that pulse and pulled, directing the energy to open the locking mechanism. They clicked open, and I grabbed them before they fell to the floor, while making sure the rest of my body stayed perfectly still. Questions rushed through my mind. Had I really just done that? *How* had I done that? I quietened the rising fear and instead sought the faint pulse of Peter's hand-restraints. Their electrical pulse buzzed quietly. I tried the same thing as before and reached out with my new sense. Peter's hand-restraints fell to the floor.

Serena's body jolted upright at the unexpected sound. I launched myself at the masked figure and tackled him to the ground. We fell in a heap of twisted hood and cloak, and the impact sent flares of pain through my joints. I rolled out of reach of the figure and pushed up into a crouch. Out of the corner of my eye, I saw Serena lift her wrist-comm to her mouth. The strange sparking energy already filled me, so I threw it towards her wrist-comm. The surge overwhelmed her device in a burst of crackling electrical streams. Serena screamed at the arching sparks as she desperately tried to rip the wrist-comm off. It eventually fell to the ground, but a lingering burn line circled her wrist.

Peter launched himself behind the masked figure and wrapped his arm across their throat in a rear naked choke, a classic move that was embedded in the muscle memory of every agent from years of drills. The figure flailed and scratched at Peter's face as they tried to escape, but Peter held them in place. Serena stood staring at the blackening electrical burn that engulfed her wrist, her hands shaking as she watched Peter choke out the masked figure. But then her eyes cleared with a terrifying focus. She spun on her heels and ran for the door. Without thinking, I grabbed my hand-restraints and sprinted over to Serena. I pulled her backwards, delaying her escape, and used my body weight to push her to the ground. She fought the best she could, but she wasn't trained. With an ease that surprised even myself, I manoeuvred her onto her stomach, ripping her hands behind her. I slapped the hand-restraints around her wrist and, without thinking, sent out another surge of energy that clicked the restraints shut. Serena screamed as the hard metal dug into the burns on her wrist.

Peter was on the ground, still holding the masked figure in a choke hold. Their desperate flailing was quickly subsiding into half-hearted slaps, and it wasn't long until their entire body went limp. They were out cold. Peter pushed them off him and stood up. Our eyes locked in an unspoken conversation as each assessed the condition of other and what we'd done. Peter was breathing in heaving, shaky blasts. He had always been the fittest man at the Agency. He barely used to break a sweat during our daily long-distance treadmill runs. Of course, we were both twenty years younger back then. The current intensity of his breathing wasn't like him, though, and it worried me. I took a moment and really looked at him. His skin was taut and pale and blood still trickled down his chin from his sliced lip. Then I saw what that figure had done to him. A precise rectangle of skin had been removed from his forehead. Blood dripped out of it and white tinged muscle glistened from the open wound. It looked like the skin had been cut and then peeled off. Nausea roiled in my stomach, but, with a synchronised nod to each other, we began moving again.

Serena was on the ground, yelling at us. 'You bitch! Let me go! You'll never get out of here without me! You have no idea what you're doing—' Her words were cut short as Peter grabbed her in a choke hold. Desperate to get free and unable to use her arms, her high heels thrashed at the ground. I stood there listening as her thrashing slowly settled, until finally stopping completely as her body went limp from the lack of oxygen, rendering her unconscious.

With shaking limbs, Peter stood and walked over to the masked figure. He bent down and pulled off the putrid flesh mask, revealing a skinny man with a nose too small and pointed for his face. His skin was slick with a shiny, acidic-smelling sweat. The hair was tousled, but carefully cut, and the top of an expensive shirt collar poked out from beneath their black robes. Something about the sweep of his high cheekbones and the thick-set eyebrows reminded me of someone. Someone I had seen recently, possibly in a photograph. Peter stared at the figure in silence. After a strained pause, he spat on the figure before shuffling off to look for a med kit.

I stared at the figure. Peter shouldn't have spat on him. He was better than that, but I also couldn't muster up any sympathy for the sycophantic vile creature laying before me. I watched Peter's saliva drip off the tip of the figure's nose. A thought suddenly twigged and started gnawing at me.

'He looks familiar somehow,' I murmured. I walked over to the unconscious Serena and riffled through her pockets until I found what I was after. Moving back to the now un-masked figure, I found an exposed point on his neck and pressed in the intel-wrench to extract a blood sample. Sucking the blood back into itself, the intel-wrench started automatically whirring and processing his DNA sequence. After a few moments, the device pinged, and I pushed the results up onto its holo-projector to read them out.

'His name is Velor Closman. His father is Maxim Closman, CEO of La Panta Corporation.'

'Shit.'

'Yep. That's why he's familiar. We saw him in that Closman family photo the analysts sent us. He's twenty-seven years old and the youngest of five sons. Works in Client Management. And that's all it says. The rest is redacted.'

'Stupid, spoilt, messed-up rich kid.' Peter wiped away the blood dripping down his forehead. 'How long do you reckon daddy's been covering up for this piece of shit?'

I didn't bother answering as my brain flooded with thoughts and the tips of my fingers tingled with an electrical buzz. A memory suddenly burst into my mind.

Miles stood in front of me. I sat in the corner of a large laboratory, leaning forward on a hard chair, engrossed by what Miles was saying. We hadn't started any procedures yet. It was just an information session. A holo-screen with a presentation on it was behind him as he excitedly described his proposed process to change me. To give me an edge no one else could have. I was excited. The promise of power and his enthusiasm were intoxicating.

I looked at my hands, remembering that initial information session all those years ago that had promised so much. I had never seen those promises come to fruition. But maybe something had changed. I could feel a hum throughout my body. Mile's dream might finally be reality. My hands shook as these thoughts rocked me to my core, but I needed to keep moving and keep taking the next step. Sam needed me.

I strode over to the holo-kit and, on reflex, reached a shaking hand out towards it and closed my eyes. A pent-up torrent of energy burst out of me and into the capsule, forging a seamless connection that pulled me into the tech-capsule's system, and further out into the connected world of data.

I could see it all. Every connection, every file. An endless stream of data that pulsed through the closed La Panta network. The data circulated the planet, reaching into every La Panta node across every city on Tir-na, and it pulled me along with it at frightening speed. As I sped through the network, I saw tiny data leaks dripping through weak security walls. My heart pounded, and I was overwhelmed by the volume of information. I could feel myself disappearing into the electromagnetic connections. With a huge amount of willpower I stopped, took a deep calming breath and pulled myself back. There I found my peace, and I found myself again, or at least the construct I believed was me. I opened my eyes and, with a sharp focus, sifted through the data deluge and found the security video footage I was after. I pulled it up on the tech-capsule's holo-projector so Peter could see it.

'Here. Look at this. They took Sam through the loading docks and loaded him into an e-vehic. The ID is 3679FD4. The company tracking system shows it is currently travelling full speed on the Connector, heading towards the Grove. They're approximately two hours ahead of us. There is also a comm that was sent to an end point in the Grove. It just says *Package is being shipped. ETA eleven hours.*' I paused, blinking as my focus softened, and turned to Peter, who was now standing next to me. 'Did you get the vehicle ID number?' I asked him.

'Rach...what just happened?' Peter's voice was both concerned and hesitant.

'What do you mean?'

'Your eyes. They...they were blue, and...shiny.'

'What are you talking about? We need to move,' I said, giving Peter no chance to think about things too deeply. 'We need to get to our e-vehic and get after them. Follow me and we'll get there safely. I know the way.'

With a pull on the electrical energy, I unlocked the door, and we tentatively peered into the corridor. It was silent. We moved out into the corridor and started snaking our way through the corridors along the path I knew we needed to follow. We paused at every corner to ensure we didn't run into anyone until we found a sign that pointed to the loading dock. The door to the loading dock was a dull grey sliding door that I opened with a small electrical pull on its locking mechanism before scurrying inside. It was quiet in the dock, apart from two guards who sat near the e-vehic entry point chatting amongst themselves. Shiny company e-vehics sat parked around the room. I closed my eyes and felt for the communications console near the guard's station. Finding its waiting energy, I pulled and sounded the comms alert. One guard walked over to the console and we used the moment of distraction to duck behind the parked e-vehics. The large roller door began rising with a groan and a pair of e-vehic headlights flooded the dock. In a panic, we ducked back behind the nearest parked vehicle. The e-vehic swooped past our hiding place without seeing us. Noticing a singular opportunity while both guards were distracted, I pulled on Peter's arm and stealthily ran to the closing roller door. We ducked under the lowering door and ran out into the fresh air. I did a quick mental calibration of our location, then led us on the most direct path to our e-vehic, cutting across automated traffic and groups of business workers scheming in the street. We spotted our vehicle and sprinted towards it, throwing ourselves through the doors that had opened on a command from Peter's wrist-comm. Without a glance behind us, we powered up and sped away through the canopied streets of the business district. We drove past the sprawling gardens that littered the community hub, through another residential zone where multiple domed dwellings raced past us, until finally reaching the Connector, which led straight out of town. And straight after Sam.

· · • •· • • • ·

The trip along the Connector felt long and endless. Dense thick trees in straight rows, surrounded by springy shrubs, spiky grasses and colourful fungi, flashed past as the AI that controlled all e-vehics on the Connector rushed us along at frightening speed. The trip to the Grove would take us eleven hours, including periodic stops, so we could relieve ourselves. So, with our e-vehic in the AI's capable hands, I activated recline mode, rearranging the vehicle's seats into beds and repositioning them around the outside of the cabin. Then, I set about patching up Peter. His condition had started deteriorating as soon as his natural adrenaline wore off, which was when he had gone silent and still. He stared at the window, unspeaking and blank-faced as blood trickled down his forehead from the perfect rectangular wound where a strip of his skin had been pulled away. My stomach churned at the sight, but, determined to help, I plastered a neutral expression on my face and got to work. I grabbed a pain blocker and injected it into Peter's leg, the sharp point puncturing through his pants and skin to release a soothing cocktail of drugs that would block the pain and relax his muscles. He flinched on impact, but as the medication began doing its job, his tension dropped away. I wrapped Peter in a blanket and encouraged him to lie down on the reclined seat at the front of the e-vehic. Peter's distant eyes slowly closed as I disinfected his wound and applied a healing strip. By the time I had finished, Peter was solidly asleep, so I left him to rest and laid down on the opposite seat.

I watched trees surrounded by tangled beds of ferns and spindly plants flash by. Random plants that I assumed some scientist once decided were optimal for producing oxygen and supporting tree growth. Without them, life here wouldn't even be possible. Everything I have, and everything I have lost, would never have been possible. I couldn't help but wonder if everything in my life had been worth it. I could see every decision I had ever made falling out behind me, with it all forging an inevitable path that led me to this situation. It was my fault Sam was gone. It was my fault Miles was killed. I had tried to turn my back on it all and run, but things have a way of circling around on you. I had already tasted the bitterness of something you love turning foul in your mouth. Something you idolised and adored suddenly appearing before you, covered in filth and exposed as the hideous monstrosity it truly is. I had loved my life working at the Agency. Once, it had been my one and only dream. But it had betrayed me. At the precise moment when I felt I had more than I had ever hoped for, it was all ripped away. That experience had taught me never to trust again. Never to believe things could remain as good as they were. Sam had been my saviour throughout it all. My one beacon of light and love. He forced me to disregard my own circumstances and focus instead on making sure he was okay. But I even failed at that task. Saving Sam on my own was beyond my abilities. So, I needed Peter, but trusting him and everything he stood for didn't sit well with me.

I looked over at Peter sleeping peacefully. With the mixture of medications pumping through his system, he would be out for hours. I pushed away my thoughts of who I had been and who I was now and instead began searching for that strange blue flicker. The flicker Miles had painstakingly worked to create, foster and inflame. I had smothered it after he had died, as it was too painful to think about it without him. But now, as I closed my eyes, there it was. It was small, but it shimmered brightly, like an ember waiting to be fuelled. I had agreed to this. I had wanted this. But what had I really done all those years ago? I reached for the spark roiling in my core. It came easily to me, and I let myself dive into it. The world suddenly expanded beyond my comprehension. Reverberations were everywhere, and I could feel the engines speeding us along, controlled by the precise Connector AI. I reached into that controlling connection and found the electromagnetic wave that handled the data flow to adjust our speed. I urged it to let us move faster, encouraging the code to change a few numbers. The e-vehic lurched forwards in response, picking up speed and beginning to gain ground on the other e-vehics on the Connector. The AI was still carefully guiding us safely down the road, but it now let us travel faster than the standard enforced speed. I opened my eyes, releasing my connection to the data. Our e-vehic continued at its increased speed. Sweat beads dripped from my temples, creeping down the nape of my neck. Had I really done that? A tingle fizzed up and down my limbs. I felt heavy and jittery, and my mind was like mush. Exhaustion washed over me as I blinked my eyes closed and happily let them stay shut as I was pulled into a heavy sleep.

· · · · • · • • · ·

My eyes sprang open. Trees were still speeding past the e-vehic, but they had changed. They no longer looked like the large, gnarled and greying trees we passed near Crayn. These trees were paler and thinner, owing to their younger age. Their branches were straighter and reached upwards instead of twisting outwards like the Crayn trees, that had to compete each other for sunlight. Thin grass covered the ground, with small wiry ferns popping out randomly. It took my brain a while to remember where we were and what we were doing. It flooded back in a shuddering wave that threatened to consume and drown my core. Tears welled. I sucked in a sharp breath and sat up to shake off the wave of feelings, rubbing my face to soothe my emotions.

'You alright?' said Peter, breaking the constant hum of the e-vehic's engine.

I took a moment to orient myself. I didn't know what to say. What was the right answer to that? Sure, I was alive, but was I actually okay? Definitely not. I chose to just ignore his question.

'How's your head?' I asked.

'Sore. The healing strip helps. Thanks for that.'

Silence fell over us like a wet blanket. Heavy and uncomfortable.

'You hungry?' Peter asked.

'Yes, actually.'

'Great, 'cause we have the choice of reconstituted bio-meat, or reconstituted veg-mix.' Peter held out two silver squishy packs and shook them in a mock attempt to make them look enticing.

'Veg-mix. Always the veg-mix for me. Who knows what scraps of bio-meat they put in those packs, and I'd rather stomach a veggie cocktail than—'

'Miscellaneous artificial meat?' Peter offered. 'Yeah, I remember.' We smiled. The familiarity and brief reminiscing was comforting. 'How many times do you think we've shared food packs like these?'

'More than I can remember,' I replied. 'You really should opt for the veg-mix sometimes.'

'And you should try the bio-meat mix. You really do get used to it.'

We ate in silence, sucking in as many nutrients and energy as we could, while ignoring the terrible flavour.

'Imagine how many of these we would have shared if you hadn't left,' said Peter, shattering the comfortable quiet that had fallen between us.

'I imagine you've had a lot, having never left.'

'You know, the Agency has changed a lot since you left. A lot less...what did you use to call them? Oh yeah, back-slapping dickwads.'

'Well, that's good to hear. You managing to stay there the entire time makes more sense.'

'You mean I'm not a dickwad, so staying was easier without them around? Or you think I am a dickwad, and I'm just a relic that slipped through the cracks but enjoyed being the only dickwad around?'

I smirked at the potential trap of a question. 'I guess you'll never really know.'

'I'm going to take the first option. Better for my ego,' said Peter with an air of fake self-importance that made me laugh. We settled into silence again that started out comfortable, but as the seconds ticked away became stretched and unnerving.

'Hey Rach,' said Peter, breaking the silence. 'What is it these people are after? They mentioned you already have something they want. Is it something you don't want to tell me about, like some sort of cool object you've had hidden away all this time?' I raised an eyebrow at his last remark. 'What? I don't know. You left in such a rush and simply disappeared, so my mind couldn't help but wander and come up with theories. You were the subject of some hot gossip at the Agency for ages after you left.'

'Really? What were some of the best theories?'

'One was that you stole a priceless object that you were supposed to retrieve on a mission. One was that you were in an awkward love triangle with the high-ups, and you were made to leave when it got too messy.'

I couldn't keep the shock off my face at the last one. 'They were all a million years old! I do have standards.'

'Don't blame me. I'm just telling you what other people were saying.'

I took a shaky deep breath and felt fear bristle inside me. It had been a long time since I had spoken honestly about my past, and it scared me. 'You already know the crux of what happened, Peter. You were there. I remember you gave me your coat when I walked up those stairs. After all of it, I realised I had to prioritise raising my child, and I couldn't do that and work at the Agency. So, I left. I also didn't feel safe there anymore, not after what happened to Miles. The Agency had promised to protect him, and they failed. I knew I would be better off keeping myself and my son safe on my own, in a new life. And that's what I did.'

Peter nodded, looking like the memories of that night were playing through his mind. 'You just left, though,' he said in a quiet voice. 'After I visited you in the med-ward, you just disappeared.'

'I'm sorry I didn't say goodbye. I needed to leave quickly and quietly. The Head knew the Agency had fucked up that day. Miles was a valuable asset, so there should have been a protection detail already with us, but there had been no one there. I could have died that day. I have never felt so scared and so vulnerable in my life, and there was no one to help me. I couldn't trust the Agency anymore, so I needed to get out, and the Head offered me a onetime deal to help me do it. He helped set up a new life for me as compensation for everything, provided I never talked about what happened to Miles. He acted like his generous offer could somehow fix it, but I couldn't say no. So, I left for my new life, and tried to never look back.'

Peter stared at me with a neutral expression, his elbows resting on his knees. He leaned forward and rubbed his hands through his hair before leaning back and looking out the window. I could see him thinking, like he was trying to decipher what to say. I left him to his thoughts and turned to look out my own window. The spindly ash and green trees continued to whip by as we overtook other e-vehics at our increased speed, and I noticed the trees getting younger as we raced towards the Grove. It was like a trip through time, racing forwards towards today.

Peter cleared his throat, cutting through my thoughts. He was still staring out the window. 'How did the handcuffs unlock back there? What actually happened? There's something you're not telling me.' He looked at me now like his eyes were trying to see into my mind. 'I saw Serena's wrist-comm blow, and I can't shake this feeling that you did it somehow. I just don't know how.'

'Truthfully, I don't know either.'

'Is whatever caused it related to what happened back then? To when Miles was killed?'

'I don't know.' I didn't want to talk about it anymore, so turned my body away from him and looked out the window. Peter stared at me for a moment as he internally wrestled with whether to push me further or let it go.

He moved suddenly and laid down in his chair. 'How much further to the Grove? The trees and vegetation are starting to look pretty fresh, so can't be long now.'

'Another one or two hours, I think.' I actually knew precisely. It was another hour and twenty-seven minutes. The AI was streaming all of that information straight into the e-vehic and I could feel and understand it all.

'We should rest up while we can. We'll take the turnoff on the left, five clicks out from the Grove and walk in. Agency personnel aren't supposed to go through the front door without prior approval, which, of course, we never have. The forward operating base and safehouse were compromised on a recent mission and haven't been reestablished, so we won't have access to supplies or support once we go in. We'll be on our own. Until then, I'm going to sleep and let this healing strip do its thing. You've got the con.' He rolled over in his reclined seat and turned his back to me.

I leaned forward and manually programmed the e-vehic to alert us when we were twenty clicks out from the Grove. With nothing else to do, I laid down and let myself sleep, a wave of exhaustion once again pulling me under.

11

The Grove

WE PARKED THE E-VEHIC behind a rocky outcrop to obscure it from view and changed out of our business attire into more comfortable, utilitarian clothing. Peter put on his faithful tool belt, inconspicuous and ready. After adding a couple of weapons to my ensemble from the Agency cache in our e-vehic, I put on an oxy-mask and paused for a moment to appreciate the strange sight of the expanse of immature trees planted in perfectly straight lines that sliced across the landscape. Terraforming was a slow and painstaking process. One day, these trees would produce enough oxygen that oxy-masks wouldn't be needed here, but for now, their job was to keep growing. Their small and weak stature brought tentative hope to my heart, as it meant we were near the edge of the Tir-na forest, which meant we were close to the Grove.

With barely a word between us, we grabbed our pre-packed bags filled with basic supplies and double-checked the flows from the small oxy-canisters we wore in holsters under our coats. As you got closer to the edge of the Wastes, the air grew thinner and there wasn't enough oxygen to breathe without an oxy-mask and a sufficient supply of oxy-cannisters. Even in the new arbour region surrounded by juvenile trees, there wasn't enough oxygen to move around without a mask. For those living in the Grove, the small tubing that wrapped from the canister up behind the ears and under the nose was just a normal part of their everyday wear.

I threw on Old Blue, then with a nod we began our hike towards the ever evolving and eclectic movable city of the Grove. My hand gently touched Sam's picture, still safely tucked inside the pocket of my coat. We were coming.

Row upon row of trees passed us by as we walked through the arbour, being careful not to damage any irrigation systems or the trees themselves. Each one was crucial for ensuring the longevity of our society, as humans on Tir-na couldn't survive without them. We crested a small hill and saw a unique vista spread out before us. The trees grew smaller as they stretched their way to the edge of the Wastes, and there, cutting a jagged silhouette against the sky, stood the Grove. Individual parts of it were slowly moving even as we gazed upon it, as it crept its way forward, claiming more of the desert to turn into forest. We continued down the hill, taking the most direct path rather than the winding one that had been cut through the plantation for workers, and only stopped twice to drink water and check our oxy-mask supplies. We had a lot of ground to cover and needed to keep moving.

After a couple of hours walking, the Grove loomed before us, and we could hear sounds carried on the breeze of machines whirling and voices shouting or laughing. My ears pricked up at an unexpected and much closer sound. Footsteps to our left on the other side of a small embankment, crunching loudly on the soil enhancer that was spread all over this region to help the trees grow. I reached forward and grabbed Peter's shoulder, motioning for him to veer off towards the embankment as the tiny trees that surrounded us provided little cover. We crouched down and prepared to duck, weave and run as required to escape from whoever was approaching, but the footsteps stopped. Instead, we heard a tapping followed by a rhythmic hollow ringing. My mind raced at the possibilities of what the person was doing until I realised they were working on the condensation irrigation pipes. We stayed still as statues until the work had been completed and their footsteps retreated away from us again. My body relaxed as the sounds of the worker dissipated. Then the tapping sounded out again, somewhere further off to our left.

'Oi! Come give us a hand, will ya? This one's got a nasty case of the rusts,' the worker called out to someone. 'Bring a spare pipe with ya, too.'

'Yeah, alright,' came a voice from somewhere further off. We heard rummaging around in a vehicle and then plodding footsteps crunching across the soil.

I risked a look over the edge of the embankment and saw two workers about a hundred metres away from us, completely distracted by whatever they were working on in the ground. To our right, only fifty metres away from us, was their large utility e-vehic. I gave it a once-over and something caught my eye. Two worker coats were hanging on the e-vehic's equipment tray. The temperatures were often more volatile and unpredictable near the Wastes because of the competing ecosystems, so you often found people in the Grove carried multiple clothing options. An idea popped into my head at the sight of the coats. Looking back at the engrossed workers, I picked my moment and tiptoed around the rocky outcrop towards their vehicle. Peter tried to grab me, but I waved him off and gave him a direct and pointed look. Keeping my eyes on the workers, I hurried across the ground, jumping between the soft ground coverings around the base of the trees that insulated my footsteps better than the rockier soil. After several deft manoeuvres, some of which were only possible because of my years of movement teaching, I reached the e-vehic. I snuck around the back to shield myself from view, then reached over the rim and grabbed the two coats. After checking on the progress of the workers, I retraced my steps and was back with Peter before I knew it, with our newly acquired loot in tow. Peter looked at me with a judging glare that I knew meant 'what the hell was that'. He was too scared to make any noise in case the workers heard, but conveyed a lot with his scowl. I gave him a dismissive eyebrow raise and settled in to wait for the workers to finish.

We finally heard the two workers' footsteps as they made their way back to the e-vehic. My heart leapt as their doors slammed shut and the engine hummed. Only once their vehicle had sped off into the distance along the established plantation work roads did we finally stand up and stretch our aching limbs. Older bodies definitely don't enjoy being stuck in awkward positions for long.

'What the hell, Rach!' Peter finally snapped, unleashing the pent-up thought that had been hidden beneath his scowl.

'Now we can just walk right in,' I said, shoving Old Blue into my pack and then shimmying myself into the worker coat. With the coat on, I looked no different from any other worker in the field. 'You can thank me later.'

'Smart,' Peter reluctantly admitted in a mumble. 'Wish I'd thought of it.' He reached out and took the coat I offered him, throwing it on over his clothes with more dramatic flair than necessary. 'Alright, let's get moving. I reckon it's only about an hour's walk.' I nodded in agreement and we started moving.

As we walked, I watched the natural comings and goings of traffic in and out of the Grove's wall. I spotted a side entrance that all worker e-vehics gravitated towards, so I lead Peter that way. As we got closer to the Grove, we were forced to walk near the worker roads. We kept our head down and did our best to blend in as just two workers heading back in after a day in the fields.

A humming e-vehic engine rumbled along the road behind us. I pulled my worker coat around me tighter and continued trudging forwards with my head down. The e-vehic pulled up alongside side us as a voice called out.

'Hey!' It was the same workers that we had seen in the field. My blood prickled beneath my skin as my hand drifted to the concealed gun holstered beneath my worker coat. 'You guys need a ride back in? We've got plenty of room.' Peter was the first to respond, as my brain took a moment longer to process that it wasn't a threatening situation.

'Sure,' Peter replied in an extremely happy tone. 'Appreciate it. My feet could use a break, if ya know what I mean?'

'We definitely do,' said the older greying worker who drove the e-vehic. His whitewashed hair coiled into strands that wrapped around each other in an intricate pattern. It was mesmerising to look at. 'We've all done our time walking the arbour before getting the privilege to use this beauty,' he said, gesturing to their e-vehic.

'I can only dream,' said Peter as we hopped up into the back seat.

'Not long now and we'll be home,' the driver said, revving the e-vehic along the road again. The passenger was a younger, shy man whose only interaction with us was to throw a few furtive glances our way from the safety of his seat.

I settled in and let my head rest against the glass window as I watched row after row of young saplings rush by. Those trees would never know the pressure on them to protect the future of life on this planet.

The utility e-vehic continued bumping along the road. I could see the Grove's entrance, where the Connector finally reached its destination. It was heavily crowded and busy, with Grovian guards positioned everywhere. We were headed for the quieter and more run-down worker entrance.

We made our way to the gate, then pulled up at the threshold. There were only two guards positioned at the entrance and from their relaxed postures, they didn't seem to pay much attention to the comings and goings of the workers. Our driver lowered his window and called out to the closest guard. 'Hey mate, we right to go through?'

The guard was a scruffy-looking man with a uniform covered in dirt. He had about three days' regrowth sprouting on his face, and overly judging eyes surround by deep, weathered creases. The guard cast his eyes over both the e-vehic and us before answering.

'Yeah, you're right,' he said with a dismissive nod of his head towards the Grove entrance. 'Get on your way.'

'Will do,' said our driver. The utility e-vehic started up again and continued rumbling through the entrance. We drove past numerous storage and staging areas for the relentless tree planting undertaken by the people of the Grove. Movable demountables used for administration activities and large storage sheds lined each side of the road. Our e-vehic kicked up dirt as we drove along. Unlike the softened and rich soil enhancer we had been walking and driving along around the sapling plantings, the ground here was a compacted bed of sterile soil, the same soil that stretched across the Wastes.

We pulled into a parking warehouse and jumped out.

'Thanks for the ride, guys. Really appreciate it,' said Peter, giving the e-vehic a friendly pat.

'Well now, you just make sure you give a hand to any worker who could use help in the future, and we'll call it even,' smiled the older worker. The younger passenger continued to just stare at us.

'Done. Thanks again,' said Peter.

I waved briefly, and then we turned and walked out of the parking area, and into the crazy sprawling streets of the Grove.

Dirt roads stretched out in all directions, branching off into the distance before disappearing behind towering, rusted buildings on giant wheel treads. Stacked along the edge of the roads were grey dirty containers that held supplies for the city, and between them rushed people in various worker uniforms.

'Any thoughts on where to go?' Peter asked.

I didn't know, but my instincts told me I knew a way to find out. 'Let's find somewhere quiet and I'll see if I can figure it out.' Peter looked at me with a quizzical look, but followed as I walked down a road to the right. Not far along, we found an angular alcove that blocked us from people's view.

'Give me a minute. Can you keep watch?' I asked.

'Sure. You going to tell me what we're doing?'

'Just keep watch.'

I leant against the rusting wall at the back of the alcove and closed my eyes to release my awareness into the air. Thousands of signals pushed and prodded against my mind. There were so many waves in the air. People were using wrist-comms and tech-capsules everywhere, for every type of activity imaginable, and all that data swirled around without getting tangled in an improvised, frantic dance. The waves whipped around in a dizzying whirl. I couldn't feel anything but the waves, not even the ground beneath my feet. My head was faint as the tangible world slipped away and my knees buckled.

Firm hands violently shook my shoulders and wrenched me back to my senses. 'Rach!' came a loud male voice. I stared at the face for a moment, letting my brain catch up. It was Peter. A rush of thoughts I already knew, but had somehow forgotten, clicked into place. I'm Rachel. We're in the Grove. I have to find Sam.

'I'm fine,' I stammered. 'Sorry. I'm fine.'

'You don't look fine,' said Peter, steadying my weight with his hands. 'What the hell are you doing?'

'Just trust me. I'm going to try again.'

'Is that such a good idea?'

'I just wasn't prepared. Get back over there and keep a lookout.'

Peter begrudgingly walked back to his post. I inhaled a deep breath and drifted into my central core, before taking a moment to centre my thoughts on what I needed to find in amongst the chaotic data spinning through the air. Rather than opening my powers, I let go of the strong connection to my core, and instead speared it outwards to search for the tracker on the La Panta e-vehic that took Sam. My senses flew through the air, ignoring anything large, and instead focused on the tiny. There, on the edge of my consciousness was a faint rhythmic pulse. A ping that sounded out into the ether, calling back to its home in Crayn. I locked onto it and zoomed forwards. I could feel it. It was stationary. The e-vehic's engine was quiet and cold. I expanded my attention and searched around for identifying marks and found nearby security cameras. Jumping into their data stream, I felt it fall into a picture in my mind. I saw a grand courtyard. Multiple guards walked around wearing finely adorned uniforms. I reached for another camera and I saw mosaic stairs leading up to shimmering coloured glass doors that threw rainbows across the ground. The entrance to a building I had seen many times in info-sheets during my time at the Agency. The Master's Palace. A ramshackle collection of building materials and architectures smashed together into a gaudy, opulent palace. I had what I needed.

I let go of the data and floated back into myself. 'The e-vehic he was in went to the Central Grand Plaza. He's been taken to the Master's Palace.'

'How can you possibly know that?' said Peter. He was suspicious, and rightly so. I just didn't know what to say to him, how to explain something I didn't even grasp myself.

'Just trust me.'

Peter let out a frustrated exhale. 'Fine. But you need to give me something soon, Rach. You need to explain...something...anything...'

I just nodded in agreement. What else could I do? I owed him a lot, but I also owed him nothing.

'I was here not too long ago,' he continued, 'so I know the way through the new street configuration. We should dump these though,' he said, pointing at the worker jackets. 'People don't really wear them around.' We shrugged out of our jackets and left them in the corner of the small alcove, away from the passing glances of Grovians. 'You'll actually blend in fine with that old thing,' he said, indicating Old Blue. 'Whereas, for me...' he said, looking around to appraise what was around us, 'this will have to do.' He reached down, grabbed a handful of dirt and rubbed it into the fibres of his thick grey coat. Satisfied with his work, we set off through the warren of buildings, where citizens of the famous movable city lived and breathed with the aid of oxy-masks.

12

Vantage Point

BUILDINGS OF VARIOUS AGES were layered upon each other, squished together in a jumbled mess with narrow, winding dirt streets between them. The buildings were rough and rusted, but the most striking thing was how every single one of them was on wheels. Each building had large supporting beams stretching up their sides with bulbous welding scars caused by the Grovians needing to expand the supports each time they slapped another layer on top of the old ones. It was an amazing thing to behold. I could only imagine the spectacle when every building in the city activated their wheel structures and moved forward on their terraforming journey across the Wastes.

We pushed onwards along a narrow twisting path until reaching the edge of a large open space. The Central Plaza. It was surprisingly empty of people, with only a handful of Grovians wandering across the expanse. Usually public spaces were filled with life and movement, but not here. No one wanted to loiter in the strangely quiet space. The randomly parked buildings surrounding it created a strange organic shape, with something about the way the buildings were angled, drawing your eye to the far end of the plaza where unfurling majestically with its hodgepodge beauty was the Master's Palace. Designed to be moved and rebuilt over and over again, the Palace rose like a monolith, twisting and bending in on itself as it snaked towards the sparkling sky. A rainbow cacophony of colours shimmered across its surface, making it appear as though the building was alive. It stood like an exotic predator asserting its dominance over the town, and guarding the beast was a full unit of guards carrying auto-hit guns. I rummaged through my pack and pulled out a sight-enhancer. On closer inspection, I saw the guns looked remarkably similar to those used by the Agency. These weapons enabled the user to lock onto a target and tag them so that every shot was a guaranteed hit. They were a top-of-the-line model, and I was surprised to see them in the Grove.

'We'll never see anything good from down here,' said Peter as he looked around the plaza and surrounding buildings. We had popped out of a strange slit of an opening between two towers on wheels that soared upward on either side of us. 'The angle from these will be too tight. If we want a better vantage point, we need to get closer. The top of one of those should do.' He pointed at a discoloured metal building on the other side of the plaza. 'If we backtrack a bit, we should be able to loop around the outer-rim and keep out of sight.'

'Agreed.' I let Peter take the lead and followed him back through the labyrinth of narrow dirt passageways. As we walked, I caught glimpses of the plaza through the forest of sprawling buildings, which helped me track our progress. We cut a sharp left and popped into a laneway, and at the end was the plaza again. The view was from the opposite side to where we began, and from my reckoning, we had to be close to the building. I turned and looked at Peter behind me, who was standing at the base of the building we were after. It had rusted sections that were bolstered by shields of welded metal above the giant wheel treads. A lot of work, it seemed, went into keeping this menagerie of buildings stable and functional. As long as the building was sound enough for us to spy from its roof, I didn't care if they had stuck it together with glue.

Peter assessed the building, then indicated that we should enter through the emergency exit door at the back side of the building, underneath one of its giant wheels. The wheel was remarkable, and I could only imagine it slowly being lowered when the time came to grind the entire building forward. The engineering feat of holding that much weight boggled my mind. We opened the door using an electro lock pick Peter pulled from his well-worn tool holster. The satisfying click of the door unlocking reverberated off the surrounding metallic surfaces. Peter pulled the door open cautiously before we both rushed inside. We entered onto a winding stairwell and looked up to see the central shaft stretching the entire height of the building. Peter had already begun racing upwards. With an exhausted sigh, I ran to join him. This was going to hurt.

Twelve storeys later, we emerged onto the roof. My muscles and joints ached from the monotonous and relentless plodding upwards, and my poor oxy-mask had to work overtime to keep up with my heaving breath. A choking thick film of saliva had formed across the top of my mouth making it hard to suck in a proper breath, and every time I swallowed it just added to the sludgy gunk. As soon as we were clear of the door, I swung my pack off my shoulder and found my water bottle. I swished my first sip of water around in my mouth and spat out the thick, grimy saliva. The next sip was magnificent, as the cool liquid flowed across my tongue and down my throat.

Peter had paused in the centre of the roof and began crouch walking over towards the edge. I followed suit and crouched down beside him once he had settled into a position. Sneaking a peek over the edge, I saw that from here we had a clear line of sight into the central courtyard of the Palace and the grand entrance stairway I had seen on the surveillance footage. Sam was close.

Peter sat with his back against the roof's edging and gulped down water. There were days long gone when the two of us would run up the same number of stairs as a warmup. Time does strange things to the body. I dug out the sight-enhancer and looked over the edge. We had a much clearer view of the guard unit and their equipment from this vantage point, and I had been right. Those guns were extremely advanced tech, the type of thing I wouldn't have expected out here. Maybe there were big perks for the Master in having the livelihood of Tir-na rest in your hands.

'What should we do?' I asked Peter. 'Scope out for a while to find a way in?'

'I don't know. Is that what you want? To go in all guns blazing and rip Sam out of there?'

'Part of me says yes, but the trained part of me says that would just get us killed.'

'Glad to hear you still remember some basic training.'

'I could try something again.'

'Are you going to go all weird on me again? Doing something and then knowing things but not telling me shit?'

'I can try.'

'What happened to you, Rach? How are you doing any of this?'

131

'I promise when we're not in the middle of this shit, I'll tell you what I know.'

Peter lent his head back against the wall in frustration. 'Fine. I'll keep a look out.'

I settled against the wall and directed my mind internally. My body was a mess. I was exhausted and hurting. But I pushed those thoughts and feelings away. All of it would pass, just like I would pass in time. All I had was right now, and right now I needed to be strong and hold on to myself. I anchored to my core, then released my awareness outwards, aiming it in the direction of what I thought was the Palace. An overwhelming volume of data instantly bombarded me. The air was thick with it, but using the link to my core, I shielded myself from the noise and speared towards my target. I reached back into the surveillance feeds and started sifting through what felt like an endless flood of video data. Sweat dripped down my brow as I anxiously searched for the one face I desperately wanted to see. Then finally, just as my body began to shake from exertion, I found something that made my heart stop. In an internal room of the Palace compound, I saw footage of Sam locked in a room. He looked tired, but alive.

My grip on the video feed data slipped away as my mind became cloudy from excitement and relief. Before I knew it, a random data stream smashed into me. Details of financial transactions showing regular payments between La Panta and the Master. A moment later they were gone and instead I was left with a regular beep being broadcast to network monitoring systems. I'd accidentally set off a data breach alarm. I felt rather than saw the entire Palace react to my intrusion. The network began rebooting with every password changed in the process. Diagnostics were running in overdrive, trying to isolate the intruding code. But it wasn't code, it was just me. I let my connection go and slammed back into my body. My consciousness was back where it should be, but my body was exhausted and slow to respond. I could barely open my eyes as I slunk backwards against the railing. The shock and the effort of reaching that far into the network had sucked all the energy out of me, leaving me drained and weak. It took a while for my brain to work again and remember what I'd seen.

'Peter,' I forced out with my jaw slack and hanging from exhaustion. He was already at my side, helping support my weakened body. 'Sam's okay. He's in the Palace.'

'That's good!'

'Yeah, but I also set off some sort of alarm. The Palace is going into lockdown.'

Peter looked over the edge of the roof with the sight-enhancer. 'You're right. Something's up. There are more guards marshalling in the courtyard. One of them has some sort of sensor. Most likely an elecrto-magnetic emitter sensor. Shit!' Peter said, shoving me sideways. 'They're pointing it this way.' He turned to look at me. 'What did you do, Rach? How can they be tracking us?' I waved him off, not having the energy to respond. Peter looked back at the courtyard. 'There's a guard unit leaving now and heading this way. We need to move. Now!'

'I don't think I can. I can barely open my eyes.' My body felt heavy and I couldn't imagine trying to stand, let alone run.

Peter reached for his tool belt and pulled out a familiar long silver cylinder. 'You'll thank me later.' He slammed the sharp end of the adrenaline pen into my leg. The powerful jolt to my body was instantaneous, as the world around me crystallised into sharp detail. Peter used the strap of my backpack to pull and guide me across the roof. My feet slipped, and I fell, smashing my hip and knees into the ground that shot a reverberating pain through my joints. Peter kept dragging me and before I knew it, we were flying through the stairwell door and charging downwards two steps at a time.

The door at the bottom of the building slammed open and footsteps thundered up the stairwell. Peter halted mid-stride, and I froze. He threw me something that looked like a circular bracelet with a looped tail hanging from a small storage cylinder. I caught it mid-air and looked at the words scrawled across the side of the device. It said *magno-hoist*. I watched as Peter opened the bracelet of his magno-hoist and wrapped it around the stairwell railing. He flicked a switch to activate the extremely powerful internal magnet and then placed his wrist through the loop. I quickly did the same as my brain caught up to his unspoken plan. Once we both had our hoists activated, we moved onto the outside of the stair handrail, with nine storeys of open air looming below us in the central shaft. The footsteps thundered louder as the guards approached.

'They're on the fourth floor, I reckon. Will be on the fifth by the time we get there. You ready?' Peter said, pulling out his gun with his free hand.

I followed suit and pulled out my gun from its holster. I didn't feel confident about this plan, or in my ability and strength to hold on for the entire trip to the bottom of the shaft. Nerves started eating away at my stomach as I worried this trip downwards might be my last. I took a breath and nodded that I was ready. Peter counted down from three. We hit a button on the wrist loop to let a thin metal rope uncoil from the magno-hoist's storage cylinder and began our fall through open air. We aimed our guns at opposite sides of the shaft and readied ourselves for the guards. Numbers painted on the floors streaked past us.

8

7

6

I could hear the guards running up the stairs. They had no idea we were coming to them. A large number *5* flashed in front of me and I saw three guards sprinting up the stairs. I began firing. The shots were deafening as they hit the metal stairwell. I don't know how many shots I fired, or even if any of them hit as our window of attack only lasted three seconds, and then we were past the guards and on our way to the ground. I heard moans echo from above and took it as a sign that at least one bullet hit its mark. Our controlled fall down the shaft left us as open targets from above, so I hoped more than one was down. If a guard looked over the handrails, we would be both exposed and easily trackable. Speed was our only hope, so we needed to move. I ignored the burning pain from my wrist and counted the floor numbers as they flashed past.

4

3

2

1

The hoist slowed us the last couple of metres until we gently reached the ground. We let go of our wrist loops and ran to the door just as someone started firing from above. At a full sprint, we smashed through the door and stumbled into the dirt alley. We looked to our right and, hovering ominously in the middle of the path, were two sleek, smooth and deadly drone bots. My still healing wounds from the last one we encountered ached at the sight of them. We turned on the spot and sprinted in the other direction.

13

Flight and Flame

THE MOTORS OF THE drones whirred as they chased us along the narrow, dirt-covered street. Without knowing the new city configuration, I could do nothing but follow Peter. We ducked our heads and ran around the first corner, taking a turn so sharp I slammed my shoulder into the edge of the building's huge wheel. Two metallic *thawacks* reverberated behind me. I glanced back to see two large, pointed shards embedded in the metal rim of the wheel. I sprinted on and tried to ignore the growing dread as the flying death machines pursued us.

We slipped down another alley and cut back across our path before taking another tight left turn. Peter was taking every corner he could as he led us deeper into the sprawling mess of the Grove. Buildings of all shapes and colours whizzed past as we ran, and each tight turn forced the drones to slow down, giving us a moment to gain some ground. Tall buildings with doors covered in bright filigree and rust-coasted buildings with flaking paint streamed past us in a blur of colour and texture. We passed a smattering of Grovians in the streets who wore either worker uniforms or patchwork outfits, as you did in the Grove. Those that saw us coming pulled themselves out of the way as we sprinted along. But those that saw the pursuing drones jumped for cover.

I zigzagged as I ran, trying to throw off the drone tracking systems and increase my chance of avoiding any fired shards. My muscles ached and just as my body started struggling, Peter pulled me into a hidden alcove to hide behind a large street bin. My breath was heaving, and the world swam in my vision.

'I know somewhere we can go. We just need to lose these things for long enough to get away,' said Peter, while using his sleeve to wipe sweat from his brow. 'Do you think you can make it?' I nodded weakly in response. Even though I felt slow and old, what other choice did I have but to make it?

A whirling sounded down the street and echoed in our little alcove. We hugged ourselves to the ground, making sure we concealed every body part from their scanners. As I lay in the dirt, I noticed my hands were shaking. The adrenaline shot warred with my exhaustion, and my body didn't like it. I knew then that we wouldn't survive this if I didn't try something. Maybe just something small. Something that would give us the precious time we needed to survive.

I closed my eyes, tethered myself, and reached out into both drones' central processors. I couldn't hold it for long, but I managed just long enough to alter one programming code. The effort of the change drained me instantly, and I lost my grip on the power, causing my head to slump to the ground as I shot back into myself.

Peter stared at me with scared and worried confusion in his eyes. A huge crash pulled his attention away, and we looked around the corner of the bin to see that one of the drones had crashed backwards into a wall and now lay in the dirt with its circuitry sparking. The second drone hovered nearby and turned towards us. We were outside its shooting range, but it had spotted us. For an awful moment, I just stared at the floating sphere, waiting for the inevitable end that would come as soon as it moved forward. The engine revved as the drone tried to rush forwards and attack, but instead it shot backwards at full speed and crashed into the edge of a building's huge wheel. Sparks and dust flew everywhere as it ricocheted onto the ground. I had changed their programming so that the command to move forward moved it backwards.

'We need to run,' I said. My voice was a gravelly murmur, and I felt the tendons in my hands twitching. I was close to collapsing, but knew I needed just one more big surge to get through this. Peter reached down, grabbed my forearm and, with a grunt of effort, heaved me off the ground. We left the alcove and ran down the street and around a corner, quickly removing ourselves from the scene of the crashed drones. As we ran, Peter placed a supportive hand on my back to help me whenever my balance wavered. My feet kicked up dirt in a brown cloud as I shuffled along. We continued onwards, taking too many turns for me to track. The streets rushed by in a flash of dulled, muted colours, and I felt the eyes of strangers tracking us as we sped past. I turned up the collar of Old Blue against the feeling of their eyes creeping across my skin. Suddenly, we popped out into another open expanse, similar to the Central Plaza. It was cradled by hodgepodge tall buildings, their huge wheels covered in dirt. However, the space was completely different. Where the plaza was quiet and empty, reserved for official gatherings only, this area was alive with colourful stalls and crowds. We had found the famous Grove Market.

Stalls around the edge of the market used the huge dirt-covered wheels on the surrounding buildings to form part of their stalls. Sellers called out to passers-by, advertising their heavily discounted prices. The air was thick with aromas of spiced stews and smoke from wood-fired grills, and I heard various vegetables sizzling on open flames. We ran into the space and instantly lost sight of the surrounding buildings. The stalls were tightly crammed together in what felt like a never-ending maze, with only narrow paths between them. We slowed our pace as we entered the market and slipped into the stream of bodies walking through the stalls. The first few rows sold hot food, and the smells made my tummy rumble, reminding me we hadn't eaten since leaving our e-vehic. As we continued deeper into markets, the stalls slowly shifted in their wares. The hot food made way for fresh produce like tubers and herbs. Then we reached the overheated bio-meat production stalls. The air was heavy with the metallic, acrid smell of artificial meat growing in portable grow-tanks. A cold sweat prickled on my neck from the intensity of the scent.

'You okay?' Genuine concern rang through Peter's voice. Obviously, I wasn't as good at hiding my internal feelings as I thought. I was scared to speak, in case something that wasn't sound came out of my mouth, so instead I just gave a small nod. 'Don't worry. I know someone here who can help us,' said Peter, 'and they don't live too far away.'

We continued through the markets and found ourselves in the dyers' section. It smelled even worse than the bio-meat section, but thankfully, it soon gave way to rows of stalls selling cloth, clothes and other accessories. Here Peter paused to purchase a couple of blue and green patchwork fabric wraps made of intricately embroidered smooth materials. The type of wrap that was common amongst Grovians. We didn't have time to barter, so Peter offered a price for the two long pieces of material that instantly brought a smile to the face of the young woman running the stall. The woman bowed her thanks over the top of the small baby she had strapped to her front with a beautiful, shimmering fabric. After covering ourselves with the wraps, we continued through the overcrowded market until popping out the other side. Then we re-entered the sprawling and twisting streets of the Grove.

Peter led me up the stairs to the second floor of a squat building covered in rusting joints. We paused in front of a solid metal door, with crimson paint flaking off its hinges that revealed a cold brushed surface beneath. Peter appeared frozen to the spot, and just stared at the black number twenty-two in the centre of the door. I looked around, hoping no one had noticed us. Peter took a deep breath and knocked on the door twice, then pulled himself back sharply and waited. From the tension around his shoulder, he appeared to be bracing himself for something. A clanking sounded from within, then the door opened to reveal the face of a woman with cropped, spiky black hair and a swoop of a fringe that waved across the outside corner of her left eye. She had piercing blue eyes that made your skin tingle with her gaze, and fine lines that crept across her skin. Her strong high cheek bones reminded me of a feline creature, and I watched as the muscles around her neck went taut at the sight of us. Actually, not us. They went taut at the sight of Peter. It was only a micro-movement, but it told me a wealth of information. This wasn't a random contact.

Her hands moved faster than I could register, and before I knew it, a gun was in the woman's hand and a loud crack hurt my ears. Peter screamed. The woman had shot him in the leg. I moved quickly, grabbing her wrist and smashing her arm into the doorframe to make her drop the gun. Then, I threw my entire weight into a tackle that sent both of us falling back into what I could only assume was her home. I had her off-guard, so I smashed an elbow into her nose, causing blood to splatter over the entrance carpet. She grabbed my hair and ripped my head backwards, my neck craning and muscles firing at the sudden awful angle. Then a fist cracked across my nose. It ripped the cartilage sideways and let loose a stream of warm blood that pulsed over my lips. With my depleted energy, I grabbed, poked and punched the best I could while taking my fair share of blows.

'Enough!' Peter yelled from the door. We both stopped mid-wrestle. Our eyes drifted to Peter, who stood clutching the gunshot wound on his thigh, dripping blood. 'Enough.' He gripped the door frame to steady himself. 'Rach, meet my ex-wife Megan.'

'I told you, Peter Brand. If I ever saw you again, I would shoot you,' Megan said, her melodic, raspy voice cutting through the tension.

'I know. I wouldn't have expected anything less. Now, do you mind if we come inside? I'm sure your neighbours don't need to see all this, and I'm bleeding all over your rug.'

'Fine. Get in here. You can clean up the blood later,' Megan snapped. Peter hobbled further into the house and closed the door while Megan and I untangled ourselves. Megan reached out a hand and helped me off the ground. 'Sorry about that. No hard feelings. I'm sure it was a bit of a shock.'

'Just a bit.'

'I'll get some ice for your nose.' Megan began turning towards a small kitchen area off the hallway, but then paused and faced Peter. 'You can sit over there,' she said, pointing at a chair in a small dining room. 'And try not to get blood everywhere.' She headed off to the kitchen and disappeared from our sight.

Blood dripped down my face and my nose stung with a sharp pain. I grabbed a wipe from the pocket of Old Blue underneath my elaborately embroidered wrap and held it to my nose to catch the blood, desperately trying not to drop any on the rug. Carrying wipes with me everywhere I went was an old hang-up from Sam's baby days when it felt like I was always wiping snot or food off his face. I gingerly touched my nose and realised it was dislocated. I took a deep breath, closed my eyes and let my mind wander into the dark, then I moved without specific conscious thought and cracked my nose back into place. The pain shot stars across my closed eyes, and a strange yelp left my lips. But soon the pain settled into a manageable, pulsing throb.

Peter hobbled over to a dining room and fell into a waiting chair with a grunt of pain. I wandered over and joined him.

'Your wife?' I questioned. During all the time I had known Peter, he had always been a bachelor, and seemed to like it that way. He was always off on multiple dates with ever-available companions waiting for him across the planet. I had never imagined him as the marrying type. More intriguing, who was this woman that had caused Peter to settle down? And what the hell had happened to make her shoot him?

Megan came back with a med kit, and a cloth she held to her bleeding nose. I had to admit; I was kind of proud I got in the hits I did. Megan easily looked years younger than me, and much stronger. Even in my exhausted state, it looked like some of my skills hadn't left me after all.

She dumped the kit on the ground next to Peter and set about working on his injury. She jabbed him with a pain-inhibitor before cleaning and patching up the wound. Peter's face was a strained grimace throughout, and he regularly ran his hands through his hair to distract himself from the pain. Watching Megan work, I noticed her muscles pulling under her skin. They constantly looked taut, like she was ready to sprint away at a moment's notice. Her bedside manner also left a lot to be desired as she roughly applied med strips to Peter's wound. She definitely wasn't being gentle. Her fringe swung back and forth as she worked, exposing the ghost of a faded ruby spot hidden beneath. The sight of it sent my mind whirling at the stories hidden behind this woman's rough demeanour.

'You must be in some real shit if you're willing to rock up on my door again,' Megan said as she slapped on the final bandage.

'I wouldn't have come if we weren't,' Peter replied. Megan stood up and went to a cabinet in the corner of the dining room, where she began clinking things around. She returned with two glasses of liquor in her hands. She took a seat at a table and pushed one of the glasses towards me, blatantly ignoring Peter.

'No hard feelings about the nose,' Megan said, raising her glass at me.

'Back at you.' I raised my own glass, and we both drank.

Megan sat back in her chair, leaning her head back to staunch the flow of blood from her nose. 'Was that you guys then with the bots?' Peter and I exchanged a look. How could she already know? 'The rumour mill works pretty fast here.

141

There is talk all over town of the bots being deployed and two figures running through the streets away from them.'

'Yeah, that was us,' Peter said. 'Nothing to worry about, though. Just some usual Agency stuff.'

'You shouldn't be bringing any of that Agency shit here. Only silent ops in the Grove. You know that. At least that was the case when I was still there. And you're a renown stickler for the rules Pete. So, what's really going on?' Peter and Megan just stared at each other. An entire exchange occurring in just a look.

'It's my fault,' I said, breaking the tense moment. My voice was high and nasally as I pinched my nose to clot the blood. 'Peter's helping me.'

'Well, now I'm intrigued. Peter isn't one to just walk around offering to help people. What's the deal?'

The look Megan gave me felt like it stripped the clothes from my body. I felt vulnerable and exposed, but there is only one thing to do when you feel that way. You lean into it and own the vulnerability, because then you control it. 'You just mentioned you were at the Agency?' I asked.

'Yeah,' replied Megan, a dubious hesitation in her eyes.

'Well, so was I. I used to work with Peter. We were actually partners. But that was all a long time ago.'

'Partners.' She looked at Peter. I could practically feel her mind recalling distant memories and snippets of information from the past. 'You're THE Rachel.'

'What do you mean *the* Rachel?' I asked, confused.

'You're a bit of a celebrity at the Agency. Well, more like a myth. Everyone's heard tales from your career. Although I'm pretty sure most of the stories were spread by this guy, since he appears in almost all of them,' she said, pointing at Peter. 'But the most exciting and enthralling story was about your departure. Present and pregnant one day, evaporated into thin air the next.' It was weird hearing someone fictionalise my life, making it sound dramatic and exciting, when the truth was just ordinary and painful. 'Peter loved boasting to everyone how you learnt everything you knew from him.'

'Did he now?' I said, cutting a critical side gaze at Peter. 'Bit of a bold claim, as that's definitely not how I remember our training going down when we were recruits together.'

'I used to ask him about you all the time. I desperately wanted to know more about the mysterious legend. But he never told me anything. Nothing of substance, anyway. Any stories he did tell were always filled with his own heroic exploits.'

'Everyone is the star of their own show,' said Peter.

Megan let out an irritated huff. 'You really haven't changed at all, have you? You always justify yourself and your selfish perspective.'

Peter sucked in air, ready to throw back as good as he was getting. I could tell this was an old sport of theirs. But just as he was about to speak, Megan lifted her hand in a halting movement. 'But I digress. I don't care as much about the past. Not right now, anyway. You need to tell me what the hell is going on right now, and why did you think rocking up on my doorstop was a good idea?'

I took a deep breath and told her everything I could. I told her how I left the Agency twenty years ago after giving birth to my son. Then about my wonderful low-key life, and how it shattered when Sam was taken and forced me to reach out to the Agency. A brief summary of everything else caught her up to us sitting wounded and exhausted in her small apartment.

Megan sat perfectly still through the story, while her cold blue eyes seemed to cut through and analyse every sentence. When I finished, she simply sat and stared at me, leaving a lingering and uncomfortable silence.

'Yeah, okay. But what else?' Megan said after the quiet tension had built for too long.

'What do you mean?' I asked.

'Well, sounds to me like there are a lot of people involved in this song and dance.' Megan leaned forward in her chair and spoke directly to me. 'Awful lot of powerful and rich people involved, if what you say is true. Now why would all those people give a shit about you and your son unless there is a lot of crap you're not telling me?'

I didn't know what to do. I felt like what I imagined a ship stuck on the event-horizon of a black hole felt like—under a huge amount of pressure and not knowing if you were going to escape or be sucked in. This was just like owning my feelings of vulnerability though, as I realised I needed to own my story. I needed to accept it and harness the power in it, so I veered into the hole.

'Are you really ex-Agency?' I asked.

'Bonafide class two field agent. Ran jobs with this guy here after you left,' she said, indicating Peter. 'I've got no love for that place, though. They abandoned me when I really needed them, so in turn I abandoned them right back.' I couldn't stop my eye twitch wider in surprise. No one left the Agency. Not easily anyway, as I knew too well. 'Your story put the idea in my head that it was possible to get out, so I did. Best decision of my life. But it cost me.'

I knew that was true. 'Can you help get us into the Palace?' I asked.

'I could. But why should I?'

We sat staring at each other, sizing up how much we could trust each other. There was something about her that resonated with me, so I sighed and began to tell them both my tale. The real tale.

'The last time I was at the Grove was probably about twenty-three years ago. I was on a routine mission to get some intel from a contact about the goings-on in the Grove. One of them told me about a man they thought the Agency might be interested in. They said he wasn't from around here and no one had managed to figure out where he was from, but there were rumours he was from Aeir. I did my due diligence and went to check it out. That's how I met Miles. He was a scientist, with an understanding of bio-tech the likes of which I had never seen. He was also tall, svelte, with uncontrollable red hair that kept flopping into his face, and the most striking golden eyes I had ever seen.'

I lost myself in my reminiscing. I could see his face so clearly. Peter cleared his throat, alerting me that I had paused for longer than intended. 'He told me he escaped from an organisation; one he wouldn't say the name of in fear of them finding him. All he would say was that they were dangerous. I always suspected it was one of the underground crime rings, but nothing ever confirmed my suspicions. Seeing a potential asset in him, I offered to bring him to the Agency, where we could provide protection. He wowed the seniors straight away with his theories and was offered permanent protection and lodgings at the Agency's base. In return, he agreed to continue his research and give the Agency all proprietary rights to his intellectual property. He signed on so quickly, he really just seemed happy to have escaped wherever he was. I was assigned as his handler, and later on volunteered as his test subject. He was working on an experimental program that implanted and synthesised what he called *electro-tech* into humans. Volunteering sounds so stupid when I think back on it, but I was a different person back then. I was at the top of my game, the best agent in the Agency, and I felt pressured to stay that way.'

'You never told me that.' Peter stared at me with sadness in his eyes.

'There are lots of things I never told you. I've had lots of time to contemplate my past shortcomings, so I'm not afraid to say I made some mistakes. I was strong-headed, too easily persuaded by flattery or encouragement, and I leant too far into the masculine culture. I should have tried to carve out my own unique place in the organisation, but instead I just conformed, and part of that involved trying to be the best. So, when I heard Miles talking about giving someone powers, I jumped at the opportunity. The idea of being the most powerful person on Tir-na was extremely tempting, and I didn't care what it risked. As I said, I didn't have my head on straight back then.'

'You were fine, Rach. You just weren't who you are now,' said Peter.

'Maybe. It's a nice thought.' I took a breath before continuing. 'Miles had warned me the entire process would be very hit and miss. He had only done a few preliminary trials before we picked him up. He said it would be a long and painful process, and my body would most likely reject the tech multiple times. He couldn't guarantee anything would work, but I didn't care. I was too blinded by the promise of being the best. So, we began. He wasn't lying about the pain, though. You would've seen the scars on my back when you patched me up,' I said, inclining my head at Peter. 'Because of the process, and how it was kept strictly need-to-know, Miles and I spent a lot of time together, and over time, he became more to me than just an asset. We used to talk about everything during the long sessions. It helped take my mind off the pain. The talking lead to a real friendship, and from that sprouted something so much more. He was quite simply the best man I had ever met. He wasn't full of bravado or ego. Instead, he was curious and wanted to help make the universe a better place.'

'That's how I remember him too, Rach,' offered Peter.

I nodded in appreciation of his confirmation and continued. 'Each painful session brought us closer, not just to the end goal of my body accepting the tech, but also to each other. I don't know when it happened, but suddenly I found myself in love with him. I even moved into his residence with him. He taught me so much and I think he saw something in me that I couldn't see myself. Then one day my body seemed to accept the electro-tech. We were so happy, and not long after I found out I was pregnant. Those months were the happiest of my life. Then it was all torn apart. Miles was killed. Armed people broke into our apartment, killed Miles and then came after me while I was in the middle of labour. I still don't know who they were working for. I managed to escape, and my son was born. The Agency had promised Miles protection, but somehow he ended up dead on their own premises. It was a massive cock-up. The Agency tried to cover up the whole thing. It would have caused irreparable damage if the Tir-na Collective had found out how much they'd failed. So, still being an Agency girl at heart, I became complicit in their cover-up. I signed a fake testimony saying Miles had died from an accident during one of his experiments. I hated myself for it. The next day I quit the Agency, but not before forcing an agreement on the old Agency Head to help create a new life for myself and my son, along with the promise of a favour whenever needed. After all, it was only my compliance that kept the Agency out of shit. So, then add on multiple years of being a single parent and that leads us to the here and now.' I finished my tale and looked up at Peter. 'I'm sorry I never told you about this.'

He just looked at me, his expression empty. 'Shit Rach. I'm sorry I didn't know, and that I didn't help more.'

'What about the experiments?' Megan leant forward as she lowered the bloody rag from her nose. 'You said they were successful, but I can't imagine the Agency just letting you go if they knew that.'

'Well, that's the thing. We never reported that the experiment worked. According to the official record, it was a failure. Miles said he didn't want to get anyone's hopes up, so we kept the truth hidden. I really didn't believe it had worked. The entire time I was pregnant, he kept getting me to try impossible things that never worked.'

'Is that what you've been doing?' asked Peter. 'All the weird stuff, like the knowing things you shouldn't know? Or our e-vehic making record time along the Connector?'

'I thought you hadn't noticed that one. But yeah. All of a sudden, reaching for those impossible things worked. I don't know what it all means and truthfully, I don't care. My only focus is figuring out how to get my son back.' The cold knife of panic scraped on the back of my throat, threatening to make my voice warble. 'I can't lose him. He's all I have.' Tears had been welling as my mind churned over the pains of the past, and now they tumbled out freely. My hands started shaking as I stood up and left the room, to calm myself.

I went into the kitchen Megan had disappeared into earlier and found her water source to splash my face. The water was cool and soothing as it calmed my nerves.

Footsteps padded towards me. 'Careful. We're on strict water rations out here,' said Megan. I promptly turned off the water and faced her.

'Sorry. I wasn't thinking,' I said. Megan wordlessly handed me a small clean rag to dry my face.

'Like I said, the Agency screwed me over too.' Her words piqued my curiosity, as I couldn't imagine anyone getting the upper hand over a woman like her. 'Just when I really needed them, I learnt the hard way that they didn't have my back. The Agency only looks after the Agency, not its agents. Seems like you really hit my weak spot with that story of yours.' She leant back against the metal kitchen bench and looked right at me, her eyes both tired and wary. 'What is it you guys actually want from me?'

'I don't know what Peter is thinking, but what I need is help to get into the Palace. Get in, get Sam and get out again.'

'Palace runs pretty tight security,' she said, deflating my misguided hopes of an easy mission, 'but I know some people who might help us. You happy working with that guy, though?' she said, indicating back to the room where Peter was.

'He's had his uses so far, and I need his access to the Agency's AI. Truthfully, we wouldn't have gotten this far without it.'

'You trust him?' Megan stood perfectly still and stared at me, trying to read any micro-expressions that escaped my control. Luckily, I had nothing to hide.

'I don't think I really trust anybody anymore.' The truth of what I said made my heart sad.

'Good, you shouldn't. Trusting people isn't a smart move in my experience. I'll help you, but first I need to know everything.' Megan stuck out her hand, and I readily grasped it, closing the unspoken deal. 'Alright,' said Megan, nodding at our show of solidarity. 'Let's get planning.'

14

The Palace

T HE BURNT-SKIN SMELL LINGERED in Megan's apartment. It was always a smell that was hard to shake and made you equal parts revolted and hungry. Once Peter was patched up, the three of us schemed and planned until night approached and I couldn't stave off exhaustion any longer. Peter had already fallen asleep on a lounge chair in the small lounge room, aided by the assortment of pain relievers circulating through his system. His wound had been cleaned, sealed and helped along with the application of a healing strip. Over the next few hours, the bio-tech in the healing strip would start binding his muscles back together. It was a remarkable but exhausting process, so it was no surprise he was dead to the world. My eyes were struggling to stay open, and I felt like I had been hit by an e-vehic. I fell into the bed in Megan's spare room and wrapped myself in its blankets. Every muscle in my body throbbed with pain, but I was happy because I would soon be making my way to Sam. Exhaustion then grabbed hold and pulled me into a deep, unmoving sleep.

The next morning, we set about our work. Megan left early to reach out to her network of contacts, while I set about gathering supplies and packing bags. The three of us reconvened at lunch and set about finalising our plan. After filling our bellies and packing our bags, Megan gave us Palace Food Supplier uniforms she had acquired through unknown means, and we began our slow journey back through the winding streets of the Grove towards the Palace. We moved silently through the dusty streets. I noticed Peter limp a couple of times, but it seemed the healing strips had done their work. There was also only a faint rectangular scar outline on his forehead, the only evidence left of our experience at La Panta. While

I was looking at Peter, a swish of green-coloured movement over his shoulder caught my attention, but then disappeared just as quickly. Something about it made the back of my neck tingle, but I just filed it away as a mental note and didn't interrupt our journey.

The sun was starting its descent towards the horizon and Inyon, the smaller of Tir-na's moons, was already winking at us in the sky. We arrived at the Palace perimeter and paused a couple of buildings back from the main plaza to wait for Megan's contact. Partially hidden beneath the stairs leading up into a red, rusted building on huge caterpillar treads, we had little to do but bide our time and check our weapons. Megan had a surprising number of concealed guns within her apartment.

Someone wearing the same green fabric I had seen earlier appeared momentarily on the other side of the street before whipping back behind the corner of the building. We were being followed. I indicated to the others to pull back against the building and ready their weapons while I checked out the situation. On other occasions, it might have been an overreaction, but I wanted to be as careful as possible, which meant eliminating any possible threats. With a small handgun at the ready, I darted over to the other side of the road and pulled tight against the wall, the corner still between myself and the figure I had seen. I crept along the wall, scraping away dirt and paint as my clothing brushed against it. Then I was there, at the corner. I looked at Megan and Peter. They indicated that they still couldn't see anyone, but I knew someone was there. I revved up my courage and, in a swift movement, spun around the corner and aimed my weapon at a green-covered figure crouching in the dirt.

'Stand up and show yourself,' I demanded, forcing some fake bravado into my voice. The figure stood and pulled the hood of their cloak back, causing a shock of long midnight black hair to cascade around their face.

'Lilli?' I said, lowering my gun. 'What the...?'

'I want to help, Rachel. Everything is my fault, and I want to help get Sam back. After you disabled my wrist-comm and left me, I didn't know where to go, so I came home to the Grove. I couldn't believe my luck when I saw you in the markets yesterday. So I followed you, and kept following you. I don't know what I can do, but I want to help. Just tell me what I can do.'

'Lilli…you can't help us. It's not safe. You can't—'

'Don't. Please don't, Rachel. I need to help. I can't live with what I did. Please give me the chance to fix this in whatever way I can.'

We stared at each other, and I didn't know what to do. Her eyes glistened with tears. I was torn. My head screamed that she was a liability, but my heart argued in her favour. I remembered the feeling of losing Miles and the lengths I would have gone to get him back. 'Fine. But you do exactly as I say, okay?'

'Of course! Thank you!' Lilli sprung over and wrapped her arms around me in a tight hug, her tears spilling onto the front of my uniform. I hugged her back and stroked her head until the tears subsided. Then, with a renewed determination, we walked back across the road together and joined Peter and Megan.

'Who the hell is this?' Megan asked with crisp judgement in her voice.

'Lilli. She's with me,' I said and left it at that. Peter and Megan looked at each other as an unspoken assessment pass between them. I ignored it and pulled Lilli further into the gap under the stairs.

'So, what's the plan?' Lilli asked once we were settled.

'All in good time,' Megan said. 'First, if you're really coming with us, you need to put on one of these.' Megan pulled an extra Palace Food Supplier uniform from her pack. Lilli looked at me for reassurance. I nodded, and she took the uniform and began donning the brown jacket and matching pants with long red stripes down the sides. The uniform was a sack on Lilli, and she stood there pulling at its sides. I walked over and placed my hands on her shoulders to stop her fidgeting, then helped roll up her cuffs and pants. I handed her a strip of fabric to tie her hair up in a bun. Food suppliers would never wear their hair long and risk contamination of their products. Successfully dressed, we huddled together and waited for the next part of the plan to appear.

'They should be here soon,' said Megan. As if they had heard her, around the corner of the building came a large e-vehic. It pulled up a few metres from us, and its door rolled open, revealing a man with slick black, hair dressed in the same uniform as us. He waved us towards him, and after a confirming nod from Megan, we ran and jumped into the van, the door slamming shut behind us. Then we were on the move again.

'Strict schedule,' said the man as though he was answering a question someone had asked. 'How's it Megan?' The man spoke with a heavy accent and a huge smile.

'I'm alright Alfoz, how're you?' answered Megan. They obviously had crossed each other's paths before.

'I'm alright. Usual. This, though, this ain't usual,' he said, indicating all of us. 'Tell me, what's this all for?'

Megan cracked a secretive smile at him. 'You know me Alfoz, I'm always up to mischief.'

'True that. As agreed, I'll take you to the supplier loading dock. What you get up to from there is on you. We got thirty minutes to unload, then we're gone.'

'Understood,' said Megan.

'We be approaching the entry checkpoint soon. They check cargo and staff. Put on these badges, then you can be real Alfoz's Fresh Food workers.' He handed out badges with his shop logo on them and we each pinned them to our jackets. 'Looks great,' he beamed at the sight of us. 'Okay, you lot keep quiet now. I'll be up front with our driver Savi.' Alfoz stood and climbed through a small gap in the cabin into the front seats.

'Alright you lot,' Megan said, looking at us. 'Time to look like happy, helpful workers. I'm looking at you Peter.'

'What? I'm happy.'

'Hmmm,' was Megan's only response.

The e-vehic slowed and came to a stop. Muffled voices spoke at the front of the e-vehic.

'Of course, go right ahead and check out my beautiful produce,' Alfoz's voice sounded loudly. The roller door ripped open and two Palace guards holding auto-weapons stood there staring at us. I smiled, stood up and made room for them to jump into the back of the e-vehic, positioning myself so they had free access to the food crates surrounding us, but also so I had a clear view of them. My fingers drifted unconsciously in the direction of my weapon, just in case. The guards opened the lid of a few crates and checked them from top to bottom. My pulse quickened under their gaze, the back of my neck tingling.

'All good. Get on your way,' yelled one of the guards, making me flinch. Then, just as quickly, they jumped out of the e-vehic, slammed the door shut behind them and thumped twice on the side of the vehicle to let the driver know he could continue.

We rumbled through the gates and towards the loading docks, as a temporary relief washed over me. It didn't last long; the gate was only our first hurdle. Alfoz's e-vehic reversed into the loading dock and once parked, we opened the roller door and got to work helping unload the crates. It was tiring work, and more than once I felt my joints ache and my muscles twinge in objection to the manual labour. After most of the crates had been loaded onto waiting transport trolleys, we then set about our real mission.

The loading dock was alive with movement and people. Multiple guards patrolled the area, keeping an eye on the comings and goings in the dock, while other Palace staff busily assessed the stock of multiple suppliers and directed people around. We blended in perfectly. Alfoz and Savi led the way as we pushed the loaded trolleys towards the kitchen supply depot. Turning a corner, Alfoz whispered to Megan, 'Guards have got no direct view of this hallway. Break off here and do what you've got to do. We leave in thirty minutes, and if you ain't here, we're leaving without you.'

With a nod from Megan, we left the trolleys to Alfoz and his driver and began dashing down the hallway. Soon, we found ourselves in a stairwell that led higher into the Palace.

'Where now?' asked Peter, as we paused at the bottom of the stairs.

'I'm not sure. I've never actually been in the Palace,' replied Megan. 'Rach, you got any idea where we need to go?'

I looked around, trying to search for anything that would help, and spotted an electrical switch box embedded in the wall of the stairwell behind us. 'Give me a moment. I have an idea that might help.' My stomach clenched with fear at the thought of what would happen if this didn't work, but I stretched my neck to each side and rolled my shoulders to calm my nerves, and then got on with it.

I reached out with my power and connected with the system. It pulled me into the highly connected power grid of the Palace. All I needed to find, though, were the Palace cameras and comms. As I had before, I searched for the security monitoring centre, racing through the currents and waves until finally finding what I needed. There was a wall up, though, blocking my entrance. Evidently, my earlier obtrusion had caused them to increase their security measures. I looked at the wall, then let myself take a moment to feel its construction, running my awareness over every facet until I saw it. Hidden in a small back pocket of code, I found a small weakness. With a flick of thought, I manipulated it to create a tiny tunnel. I slipped through the hole in the wall and found exactly what I needed. Every camera feed and microphone across the entire Palace was before me. I scanned them all, searching for Sam. I saw countless rooms and faces. Alfoz and Savi were talking in the kitchens. Guards still wandered around the loading docks inspecting delivery e-vehics. But then I found what I was after. There, on a floor above us somewhere, in a large circular white room, was Sam. I grabbed the location details of which camera was showing the feed and used the cameras in the surrounding hallways to check for guards and figure out how to get there. Then, with all the information I needed, I let the connection go and turned back to the group.

'He's on the third floor, in room 313 of the south wing,' I said. Lilli stared at me in confusion, while the others looked wary, but nodded.

We took off up the stairs. While running, I opened myself up to the hallway cameras I knew would be ahead. I projected outwards and looped their feeds to shield us from any observant eyes.

We reached the stairwell door to the third floor. Before going through, I reached out to a camera on the other side to check the hall was clear. A small droplet of sweat slid across my right temple from the exertion. The hallway was empty, so I gave the clear signal to Megan and Peter. The three of us pulled out our weapons, then Megan opened the door. We entered a hallway coloured like a kaleidoscope, with stained-glass windows down one side that glowed in the afternoon sun. The floor was covered in a rich green carpet with intricate golden loops woven through to emphasise its opulence.

We padded down the hallway as I continued to block our journey digitally from any unseen eyes. The sweat on my temples was beading faster now and made my hair stick to my face. As we moved along the hallway, I watched the door numbers slowly count down to what I needed.

Room 319.

Room 318.

Room 317.

We paused at a corner just past room 316. We were so close, but I could feel the camera feeds alerting me to slight movements. There were guards. Two of them. I gave a signal to Megan and Peter, letting them know what was ahead. Megan held up her gun and made a show of changing her weapon setting to stun. Peter and I followed suit. Lilli stood nervously, scratching her thumb on the cuff of her jacket.

Once prepped, Megan indicated she thought we should layer our attack, with me going low, Megan going high and Peter protecting us from behind. My heart was pounding as I crouched down in the corner and watched Megan count down from three on her fingers.

When she hit zero, the two of us slipped around the corner in perfect synchronisation, aimed and let loose a round each before the guards even noticed we were there. Both guards barely had time to flinch from the stun before they collapsed in a heap. Peter stood behind us ready to fire, but instead let out a small, surprised 'Huh' and lowered his weapon.

'Nice shot,' said Megan.

'You too,' I said.

We headed round the corner and there before us was room 313. My heart was racing. After what felt like an eternity, we finally reached Sam's location. Without hesitation, I strode up to the lock pad beside the door and let my power spread into it. With a simple exertion of will, the door unlocked and vanished into the wall. I felt like I had stopped breathing and my nerves were pulsing faster than the speed of light. There before me, in the corner of the room, huddled and alone, was Sam.

He sat with his forehead resting on his arms, propped up on his raised knees. His gaze lifted. 'Mum?' he hesitated. I ran across the room and threw myself onto him, holding tight to whatever fit in my arms.

My chest heaved as relieved sobs escaped in ragged breaths. 'Sam,' was all I could get out. I kissed the top of his wavy auburn hair, then trapped his face between my hands so I could really look at him. As my hand brushed against the crusted wound on his cheek, Sam winced in pain. Velor Closman hadn't even bothered applying a healing strip or anything after slicing my boy with his hideous knife. It was as though he wanted his mark to leave a permanent scar on Sam's face. My stomach tightened in anger. I looked into Sam's eyes. Dark circles surrounded them, and the usual sparking grey-brown colour had a tiredness and an age to them that wasn't there before. 'I found you,' I said, reassuring myself more than him.

'Sam!' Lilli exclaimed behind me and raced over to steal him away in a tight embrace. He turned and held tight to Lilli. I sat back and let the two kids reunite, secretly missing the days when my little boy would give me squishy cuddles.

Megan came up behind me. 'We need to move if we're going to get back to Alfoz in time,' said in a quiet voice. I nodded and set about getting the kids moving.

'Sam, sweetheart. Are you alright to move?'

'Yeah. Yeah, Mum. I can move,' he said in the same hopeful tenor as his father.

'That's great, 'cause we need to leave now.'

Sam nodded and stood up with the help of Lilli. With her on one side and myself on the other, we began heading towards the door. Peter stood just inside with his back turned from us, keeping an eye on the hallway. He looked over and nodded, indicating the hallway was clear. Peter waited for us at the doorway, prepped to take point, while Megan slipped behind to take the rear. As we crossed the room, I pulled my weapon out and felt its cold metal press against my hand while a steely resolve echoed through me. I had my son, and no one would take him from me again. Peter was about to step into the hallway when the door on the opposite side of the hallway swished open. Four guards dressed in clean white emerged and aimed weapons at us, follow by a shadowy, grey-hooded figure, and then none other than the Master himself.

No one knew what his real name was. From what I had heard, he just appeared one day as the appointed master of the Tir-na terraforming efforts, which is how he got the moniker the Master. I had seen pictures of him previously, but his appearance was more striking in person. He echoed the electric vibe of the city he ruled over perfectly. Just as the Grove was a strange hodgepodge city of dirt, grit and intricate colourful details, so was the Master. His clothes were extravagant and colourful. He wore a green, hooded cloak with golden embroidered patterns adorning the trim. His shirt was a deep purple that contrasted with his black tight pants and shining black knee-high boots. His hair was a long monochrome brown that hung in limp oily strands swept across his head. There was an unusually angular cut to his nose and jawline, which made his face look like it had once been stretched uncomfortably, with pinched, cracked lips that outlined his large, crooked teeth. He was a walking juxtaposition of colourful, grotesque beauty.

'Friends. Welcome,' said the Master with a subtle nod of his head. His voice had a strained, sharp tone that resonated at an octave higher than normal. It was odd, sounding both sharp and pointed, yet with a lilting and unsettled musical tone. 'We've been expecting you. Rachel, Peter, Megan, I'm so glad you were prompt and didn't keep us waiting. Sam here has been a wonderful guest.' He waved his hand towards Sam. 'And you must be Lilli, of course. Now, if you could please put your weapons down, it would be greatly appreciated. My guards are highly trained and effective, so I'd hate for anyone to get hurt.'

Megan had moved up beside me during his speech, and I saw her hand twitch on her gun. In response, the weapons of the four guards whirred in synchronisation as they armed and then aimed them straight at us. Our smaller hand weapons wouldn't stand a chance against their large auto-fires. I knew what those weapons were capable of and there was no way I wanted my son anywhere near their line of fire.

I slowly and purposefully held my weapon out in sight of the guards, making an effort to show I wasn't holding the trigger, then carefully bent to place it on the ground. Peter quickly followed suit. Megan, however, stood staring at the guards.

A wordless challenge radiated off her. She wasn't one who liked to lose a fight. I was about to pull Sam down to the ground to cover him from what would surely ensue, when Megan relented and reluctantly held out her weapon, and carefully lowered it to the ground.

'There now. Isn't that better? I'm sure we all feel safer now,' said the Master with a crooked smile on his face.

My eyes scanned the room, and I extended my power in search of an escape. As my senses focused, I felt the door and its control mechanism that I manipulated earlier, and realised I could close it with a mere push of my will. With this ability, I could block us off from the Master, his guards and his silent, hooded companion. I reached out to it, ready to pull on the waves to make it move.

'How rude of me! Rachel. I believe you know my companion here.' The Master held up his hand, presenting the hooded figure. The figure reached up and pulled back their hood. My body froze. My mind went blank, and my connection with the door control was completely forgotten. Nothing made sense. Breathing didn't even make sense. Because there before me stood Miles.

'You...you can't be here,' I gasped. My insides were constricting from the stress. Above me, the room lights began flickering as my powers flittered away from my control, swirling and stretching around me in sporadic pulses.

The Master smiled and looked up at the flickering lights. 'It's perfect.'

'Rachel,' said Miles, pulling my focus to him. 'You need to calm down.' His voice was the same as I had remembered. It sounded like warmth, laughter and home.

'But you died. I saw it.' My brain felt cracked in two. I couldn't rationalise what I knew to be true with what I saw before me.

'Mum, who is this?' said Sam, moving closer and holding my arm. He was exhausted, but he still had enough in him to put on a show of protecting his mum. I grabbed his hand and turned my eyes to his.

'Sam. This is your father.' I didn't know what else to say. We held each other's gaze as he searched for an understanding of what I had just said, but I'm sure all he found expressed in my eyes was bewilderment.

'I need to get you out of here, Sam. It's not safe anymore. You both need to come with me,' said Miles. I couldn't figure out what was happening. His voice was filled with genuine concern and love.

'What...what do you mean?' I stammered.

'You all need to come with me now. It's the only way to keep you safe. I've made a deal with the Master here to get all of you out. But we need to go. Now.'

I looked at Peter, trying to get a read of what he thought was happening. But he was just staring, blank-faced at Miles. I looked at Megan and tried to non-verbally ask her what she thought, what we should do. She just shrugged at me.

With no one to guide me, all I could do was go with my head. Unfortunately, my head wasn't working at full capacity. So, my heart was left to fill the void, and my heart was screaming with all its might to run to Miles. To hold on to him. To finally feel his embrace and kiss again what I had too often dreamed about and longed for.

'Okay,' I said and moved towards him. As I approached, my eyes found his, and I disappeared into them again, as I had in the past. The curiosity and wonder were still there, even though there were a few more wrinkles and grey hairs than the last time I had seen him. He reached out his hand, and I willingly grabbed it as he led me out of the room. I could do nothing but follow.

'Yes. Yes. All of you make haste,' The Master said with a stilted flourish of his hand. 'You have far to travel, so be on your way.' The Master ushered all of us out of the room.

Our small group of six headed down the hallway with two guards trailing behind us. Whether it was for our protection or as a threat, I wasn't sure. I looked back and saw the Master standing in the middle of the hallway, flanked by the remaining two guards. He was smiling at us and even gave a farewell wave, but the whole time his lips were moving. Whether he was talking to the guards or someone else, I had no idea. As quickly as the oddity of this hit me, we had already moved into another hallway and hurried along until reaching an elevator that took us to the ground level. The guards exited the elevator first and herded us in the opposite direction to the loading docks, leading us instead towards the side of the Palace compound closest to the brutal and sterile Wastes.

The guards opened a door and lead us into an e-vehic housing area. But these weren't just any e-vehics: these were all-terrain e-vehics, designed for traversing the ragged and desolate expanse of the Wastes. They were similar to the workers' utility e-vehics, but their wheels were bigger, their cabins elevated and reinforced, and they were equipped with enough oxy-canisters to supply an entire high-rise building in the Grove. These e-vehics were designed to survive whatever was thrown at them. The e-vehic housing was open to the air, and before us rolled out the endless dusty brown and red soil of the Wastes. It stretched out to the horizon, with nothing but a few rocks and cracks breaking up the rubble.

We were ushered through the parking area, winding through numerous hulking vehicles, until we reached one on the precipice of the Wastes. The guards directed us with their guns into the e-vehic. Miles hopped up into the driver's seat, followed by Lilli, Megan and Peter, who all moved hesitantly into the main cabin. It was only then I realised I was holding Sam's hand. I couldn't even remember grabbing onto him. It felt good to have him close to me, but my eyes were trained on Miles.

'Mum?' Sam asked, trying to pull my hand to get me into the e-vehic.

'Yes, of course.' Things were moving too fast and my brain wasn't keeping up. I took my pack off and climbed into the e-vehic like an automaton. My body moving without conscious thought. I sat in the front in the seat next to Miles, and Sam climbed into the main cabin and sat next to Lilli.

I looked at Miles. He was prepping the e-vehic, moving confidently and efficiently. I didn't even know he could drive. The whole time I had known him, we had been confined within the Agency compound and only left when I drove us into the centre of Crayn for brief outings.

'You ready?' he said, turning to me with his loving smile. His eyes sparkled, filled with life.

'I don't know.' My answer was drowned out though, as the engine screamed to life and the e-vehic's door whooshed shut and locked with a solid clunk.

'Let's get out of here,' said Miles as he pushed the accelerator and drove us into the Wastes.

15

Family Reunion

THE ALL-TERRAIN E-VEHIC SPED across the rocky terrain, shooting out a trail of dust in its wake. Glancing out the window, I caught sight of the dilapidated Grove wall. Towering three stories tall, the wall curved around the Grove, shielding its inhabitants from the harsh storms that lashed the Wastes. Though I couldn't see it all, I knew it formed a circle, the only gaps in the barrier being the Connector entrance and the workers' exit, where the workers left to undertake their endless task of planting and tending the forests. Patches of the wall that had recently undergone repairs glimmered with a silvery sheen in the light of the two moons, Inyon and the larger Marher, who had just crested the horizon on her nightly journey. The rest of the wall reflected a ruddy hue, showing the rust and corrosion from the relentless, battering winds of the Wastes. Thick red dust accumulated against the wall, forming small hills that were whipped up and over the top by strong winds that raced across the barren expanse. Each of those mounds had to be manually cleared before the rolling city could continue its journey across the continent. Life in the Grove was tough and strange, and I was grateful we were leaving it behind. I understood why Lilli had wanted to get out.

I turned and looked forwards, letting the Grove disappear behind us. Our e-vehic sped onwards, its huge flood lights illuminating our way as we rumbled over the broken and destitute ground. I couldn't see where we were going, so I had to trust Miles. It used to be such an easy thing to do. I looked at him then. He was completely focused on driving. Fixated on some unseen destination on the horizon. I couldn't help but notice wrinkles around his eyes that I had never seen before.

'What?' he asked with a smile when he noticed me watching. 'Why are you staring?'

'I just...' My hand began drifting upward to touch his face, but something held me back. A fear, a trepidation. It had been too long. 'I was looking at your wrinkles. At your grey hairs. You didn't have them the last time I saw you.'

'I imagine I look a bit different.' An awkward silence fell. I looked away from Miles and stared out into the darkness, watching boulders, rocks and crevices rush by.

A hand from behind me touched my arm, a gentle caress to get my attention. 'Mum, what's going on?' Sam whispered in my ear.

I put my hand on his as I turned towards him. He looked like he had aged so much over the past few days and exhaustion hung heavy around his eyes. But those eyes were wide awake, and he stared at Miles like he was a strange science experiment he half expected to explode at any moment.

'Sam, this is your father, Miles Shawbank.'

'But he's dead.'

'I thought he was.' I looked at Miles, waiting for an answer, willing him to give some sort of explanation. But he said nothing. 'But obviously not.' I turned back and looked out the window again as happy and painful memories swirled through my mind in equal weight. It was all so strange, and my head and heart were at war with each other.

'Do you remember when we first met Miles?' I said, looking back at him.

'Of course I do,' he said with a wistful acknowledgement.

'You looked so handsome in your suit. I think part of me fell in love with you straight away.'

'It was mutual, darling. Love at first sight.' He said it like it was a matter of fact.

'The stars shone so bright that night over the Gala in the Grove's Central Plaza. But then a gust of wind from the Wastes blew a torrent of dust over us. I got some in my eye, but you were there next to me, ready to help with a clean cloth from your pocket. There was dust everywhere, all over my beautiful red dress. I would have hated to ruin it. You really saved me that night.'

Miles smiled and nodded at the happy remembrance. 'You looked beautiful. I couldn't let anything spoil that.' He reached out and squeezed my hand before focusing on driving again. Silence fell. Sam's arm reached up and brushed my arm in support. I patted it again and tried to pull some courage from it.

'Where have you been? How are you here?' I asked with all the strength and conviction I could muster.

'All in good time,' Miles said. 'First, let's find somewhere to set up camp for the night. I think there are some cave structures up ahead on that hill.' Miles pointed through the darkness to our right, where the distant outline of a solid hill rose from the horizon.

I looked at everyone in the main cabin behind me. Megan and Peter sat at the back, leaning into their respective corners, letting their bodies rest while keeping a wary eye on the surrounds. Sam was laying with his head on Lilli's shoulder, her head resting on top of his. Their clasped hands rested between them with their fingers entwined like a knot. Exhaustion was evident on Sam's face, and his cheek wound was a fiery red. His tired eyes met mine, and I smiled at him. On impulse, I took off my seatbelt and climbed into the back cabin to sit next to him on the other side to Lilli. He sat up and then circled his arms around me in a hug. I held onto him like he was life itself. He was my life. We just sat there as tears streamed down my cheeks. I kissed the top of his head and pulled back, holding his face so I could really look at him. He would need support and it would take a while to come to terms with everything that had happened, but he was in one piece. He would be okay. First, though, I needed to clean his wound.

We continued our journey through the night. The dark shadowy outline of the hill grew larger and more solid as the enormous wheels of our all-terrain e-vehic churned up the desolate soil on our journey towards it. At some point after patching up Sam's cheek, I drifted off to sleep, the monotonous sound of the droning engine and exhaustion combining to pull me into unconsciousness. An unknown time later, a huge thwack and bump ripped me from my sleep. I desperately looked around, searching for any threat, but there was nothing outside. Just rocks and dirt rushing past in the light of the e-vehic's headlights. In the cabin, Sam and Lilli were both asleep next to me. I turned and looked at Megan and Peter. Both were keeping a watchful eye out their windows as Miles continued driving us deeper into the night. Peter noticed me and gave a brief nod of acknowledgement. I nodded back and turned my attention back to the front of the cabin. My neck was sore and stiff from leaning uncomfortably against the e-vehic's solid metal frame. I rubbed at it as I climbed back into the front passenger seat.

'It won't be too far now,' he said as I settled into the seat and strapped on the safety belt. 'We're just rounding the edge of the hill's base.'

I nodded and just let the journey unfurl, relieved to not be desperately rushing somewhere. I had so much to ask Miles. So much I needed to know in order to shake the gnawing in my stomach, but it could wait. I looked up at the night sky instead. Inyon was already dipping towards the horizon, while Marher still shone brightly overhead. Their thin, silvery light illuminated the world in a hazy glow. It was beautiful, in the way cold ice crystals are beautiful—they looked magical, but behind their beauty was an icy burn.

The e-vehic slowed and changed its course as it looped around the back of the hill and began heading upwards until I finally saw the caves. Three gaping dark holes that looked like maws stretched up the side of a cliff face that stretched across the back of the hill. Our e-vehic's headlights washed over them as we slowed to a stop. Two of the caves were only shallow shelters, whereas the middle one appeared to stretch deep into the hill. Perfect for providing not only protection from the elements but also from any searching eyes.

'How do you know they're safe?' I asked Miles. I hated not being able to see all the way into the middle cave. Anything could be lurking there.

'It's safe. Look for yourself.' Miles unhooked a comms pad and handed it to me. 'Standard issue for the all-terrain e-vehics. It's got a modified radar built in that shows your surroundings, no matter the conditions.' This was how he had been traversing through the Wastes with relative ease, he could see what was coming.

'Does it only show rocks?' I asked.

'No. Organic matter will also show up in yellow, and inorganic matter is outlined in red.' I nodded faintly. He knew so much about all of this tech and the Wastes. But how? I pushed the thought aside and started using the radar to scan the cave. Its small screen lit up with red outlines showing the surrounding rock formations. Looking at the central cave, I could see a clear path between some tight, dense stalagmites that led to a larger opening within. There were no other shapes in the cave. Only the rocks and the ground. It was safe.

Miles hopped out of the e-vehic and headed to the storage, where he started unloading various equipment. I climbed into the main cabin and gently shook Sam's shoulder to wake him. He twitched before turning his head with his eyes still closed and letting out an irritated groan.

'Sam. You need to wake up. We're setting up camp,' I said. He let out a large sigh and sat up, rubbing his eyes. His movement also woke Lilli, who sat yawning next to him.

'Where are we?' Lilli asked.

'At the caves Miles pointed out. Looks like we should be able to make camp safely in the middle one,' I said. Both Lilli and Sam made to get out of the e-vehic, but I stopped them. 'Make sure you have a secondary oxy-mask canister hooked up before you get out.' They both looked at me oddly. Oxy-canisters typically lasted three days. 'Just in case, and so you don't have to rush back to the e-vehic if something happens.'

Sam gave me an assessing look, then grabbed a canister from the supply dispenser under the seats and hooked it up to the refill holder on the back of his oxy-mask. Lilli followed suit, then opened the e-vehic door and jumped down onto the gritty sands of the Wastes, followed closely by Sam. I grabbed a handful of canisters while their backs were turned and shoved them into my pockets.

'I'm going to check the back of this thing for supplies, maybe even a weapon if I can find one,' said Megan.

'I'll help. I hate feeling so exposed with no protection,' said Peter as they both exited the all-terrain e-vehic and started searching the storage trunk.

Sam and Lilli were already heading towards the cave, so I grabbed my pack from the front passenger seat and climbed out of the e-vehic to catch up to them. My steps kicked up small clouds of dirt and I had the passing hope that the inside would give some protection from the unrelenting dust that seemed to be everywhere. A warm light from within the cave suddenly broke through the darkness with a hiss. It was the sound of a cracker-light. Miles was setting up camp. My eyes squinted from the glare and took a moment to adjust after being in the dark for so long. I moved to the front of our little pack and walked through the mouth of the cave, my shoes squeaking as they rubbed against the dirt. I looked up and noticed stalactites lining the ceiling. Their presence made me uneasy, as they seemed to hang precariously over us. With a watchful eye, I led us under their looming shadows and deeper into the cave. The further we ventured, the more the air became stagnant, cut off from the outside winds. Despite the stale atmosphere, we pressed on, following the faint glow of light, until the cave unexpectedly opened up into a vast internal cavern. The rough, jagged rock walls that framed the space were bathed in an orange glow emitted from the cracker-light. At the centre of the cave sat Miles, fussing with the construction of a campfire pit.

We walked over and I settled Sam and Lilli on one side of the campfire, then walked over towards Miles and placed my pack on the ground. I pulled out Old Blue and wrapped myself in its comforting rough fabric. It was a small comfort. Every joint in my body was aching, and the night wasn't over yet.

'Do you have any food supplies? I think we all need something,' I asked Miles as I walked towards the large bags he had hauled in from the e-vehic.

'Yeah. Once I get this lit, there are some food packs we can heat.' I nodded and started busying myself with getting the food organised. Miles flicked a switch on a lighter and the prefab logs he had piled on each other roared to life. 'These things should give us about eight hours of warmth. Enough to get us through the night.' Sam and Lilli shuffled closer to the fire. The wind that ripped across the Wastes at night was cold, and even inside the cave where we were protected from the brunt of it, icy tendrils still slipped in and nipped at exposed skin. I placed the food packs on the edge of the fire to warm, then passed out blankets before sitting in the large gap between Sam and Miles. Then, I pulled up my knees and made myself a blanket cocoon, both for warmth and to steady myself.

Footsteps crunched from the entry of the cave as Peter and Megan walked under the stalactites and into our camp. They walked confidently holding a large bag each, which made me wonder if they had found a weapons cache after all.

'Nothing moving out there. It's as quiet as space,' said Peter, walking over and taking up a spot by the fire opposite me. Megan followed suit. Although she appeared quieter than I had ever seen her, her sharp and focused gaze revealed that her mind was working in overdrive, processing every minute detail. She settled herself between Peter and Lilli, and I couldn't help but notice her hand resting just above the top of her boots, where I suspected a weapon was concealed.

An awkward silence fell. I had always hated silence, so I took a deep breath and let loose the questions I had held in since I saw Miles at the Palace.

'Miles.' His gaze swivelled from the fire to face me. 'Where have you been?'

'I guess I really owe you an explanation.' He looked down at his interlocked fingers where his thumbs twirled around each other nervously, then paused and looked up at Sam. 'The both of you.' I pulled the blanket around my shoulders a little tighter before he continued. 'I used to work for a group, an entity if you will, who were very interested in my work, as well as the work of the Agency. So, they sent me to the Grove to find an agent, and that's where I met you.' Miles looked at me before staring back at the fire. 'I didn't have plans to meet a particular agent. It just happened to be you. I convinced you I was a persecuted scientist, with valuable information, who wanted to help Crayn and the Tir-na Collective. Thankfully, you believed me and took me straight to the heart of the Agency. The plan was to find out as much as I could about the Agency while continuing my work. The one thing I didn't plan on was falling in love. When it was time for me to return to the Entity, I refused. I didn't want to leave you or our child. They threatened to kill you both if I didn't go with them. So, I agreed. We faked my death to tie up the loose ends, and I disappeared, and you both got to live happily.'

'But where have you been?' asked Sam, his voice containing an icy anger. 'You've missed my whole life. How could you just leave?'

'It was the only thing I could do to keep you safe,' said Miles.

'But it didn't, did it? Look what happened!'

'And that's why I'm here. I got you out. I got you both out of there.' Miles gave me a directed look. I didn't know what to think.

I tensed, my fingers digging into the scratchy blanket, then asked him again the question he hadn't answered. 'But where have you been?'

Miles picked up a stick and poked at the fire. 'I went back to the Entity.'

'Did you continue your work?' I asked.

'No. I let all that go.'

A whistle sounded, pulling my attention, as steam from the food packs poured out through small heating vents. I stood up and, using my blanket to protect my hands, moved them out of the heat to hand them out to the group. With hungry anticipation, I sat down again and pulled the top of my food pack. The smell of the gravy, with unidentifiable vegetables mixed through, made my mouth water. I slurped some of the brown-coloured stew, being careful not to burn my lips. It was bland but filling, and exactly what my body needed.

Everyone sat, quietly eating for some time.

'I'm going to keep watch outside,' said Megan, breaking the silence. She pushed up to her feet and pocketed her empty food bag in her pack. 'I don't like being holed up in here.'

'I'll come too. If that's alright?' Peter asked her. He genuinely seemed unsure of himself around her, which was amusing to watch.

'Yeah, sure. Two pairs of eyes are always better than one, I guess.' She said it with such flippancy that I needed to bite my cheek to stop from smiling. The two of them headed off back into the night, leaving just our family and Lilli.

I swirled the thick gravy around in my food pack and used the moment to contemplate my next questions. 'So,' I said, turning back to Miles, 'you left us and went back to the group you used to be with. You told me you hated them. Why the change of heart?' I asked with a pointed glare. 'And what's it got to do with everything now?'

'I wanted to come back to you sooner,' said Miles, 'but you were being monitored. Staying with the Entity was the only way I could find out about you. I couldn't get anywhere near you without people knowing until now. You might not realise, but you have both been monitored the whole time.'

'I know about that,' I said.

'I don't mean the Agency.'

'What?' His reply caught me off-guard and made my skin prickle.

'Let's just say my experiments caught the attention of other people and they have remained interested.'

'Interested enough to take Sam?'

'I'd say so. It's because of them I couldn't get back to you. Until now, that is.' A painful silence fell upon us. My thoughts raged at everything Miles had said and not said as I methodically chewed my warm meal.

A crack of rocks echoed up out of a tunnel near the back of the cavern. The sound bounced up out of the depths of the hill and froze us to the spot.

'What was that?' asked Lilli, voicing what all of us were thinking.

'Do you still have that radar, Rach?' asked Miles.

'Yeah, I do.' I pulled out the radar and hit the sweep button. The screen lit up with red glowing outlines of the surrounding rock formations. As I aimed it at the tunnel near the back of the cavern, something else showed up. Something lit up green from deep within the tunnel. Something large with four limbs was padding slowly towards us through the dark. 'There's something there. Something coming straight towards us.' I jumped into action. 'Lilli, Sam, get over there behind those rocks,' I commanded, pointing at a cragged stone that created a hidey-hole with the cave wall. 'Miles, please tell me you have some weapons in those bags you brought in.'

'Already on it,' said Miles as he pulled out two large, long weapons from a bag, each with an electrified poker on the back end. He threw one to me, and I caught it mid-air, then pulled it in close to my body, before anchoring it in the crook of my arm. It felt heavy and cold. Instinctively, I flicked the switch to prime it. It hummed with an unnerving purr, slowly building until it was ready to discharge.

Miles moved to the edge of the gap in the cave wall and peered into the darkness of the descending tunnel. A low, deep growl reverberated up towards us. I gripped my weapon a little tighter.

A flash of fur, teeth and claws leapt out of the gloom, along with a deafening roar that ripped through the enclosed space. The roar quickly turned into a squeal as Miles landed a blow mid-leap with the butt of his weapon. The weapon let out an electrifying jolt that shocked the beast. I raised my weapon, tracking the beast as it landed in the centre of the cave near the fire and turned, rearing its head and raising its hackles towards Miles, before letting out a low, vicious growl.

The huge animal was illuminated by the fiery glow of the flames. Its four limbs ended in clawed, padded feet, and its back legs curved, showing off sleek, powerful muscles. Its withers came up to my shoulders, and it was covered in wiry, dusty brown fur that intermingled with black stripes down to its long, black tail. And at the front, crowning this powerful beast, were two large ears that twitched at every sound, two keen black eyes and a powerful nose above a maw filled with teeth that looked perfect for ripping flesh.

The skin pulled back on its maw, exposing its teeth, as it let out a rumbling howl that echoed throughout the chamber. It leant back on its powerful legs and growled, looking ready to strike out at Miles. I felt the vibrating hum of my weapon as I took aim and fired a blast of burning electricity. The weapon's kick pounded into my shoulder, but the shot hit true. Yelping in pain, the beast turned its head to look at the smoking burnt crater on the side of its chest, charred skin fragments and sinew hanging from the wound. The smell of burnt hair and flesh started filling the chamber. I could see the beast's body shaking, then a deep guttural sound erupted from its throat as it pinned me with its eyes before charging. The subdued hum of my weapon recharging a blast vibrated against my fingers, but I knew it would take too long. I flipped the weapon around and flicked the taser switch. The beast launched itself at me. I rolled to the side, whipping the end of the taser and struck the beast in its neck as it landed where I had been only a heartbeat before. Its body shivered with the jolt of electricity, but still spun and turned back towards me. I crouched and readied myself to move. My knees ached from the crouching, yet I persisted, holding onto my weapon with a vice-like grip, as if it were a lifesaving space tether. With the main blast function still reloading, the weapon was practically just a stick with a slight shock effect, but it was all I had.

The beast sprang towards me. I tried to step out of the way but my left knee stuck momentarily, interrupting my momentum. It was the opening the beast needed. Its front paws crashed into my shoulders, knocking me to the dusty ground. Its sharp claws tore into my skin and I screamed from the pain. I held out my arms and shoved the butt of my weapon into its open mouth and pushed with all my strength to hold its jaw at bay. Its hot breath drenched my face, stinking of corroded carrion. Its nose dripped and hot snot smeared across my face. I clenched my teeth and pushed harder. 'Mum!' I heard Sam call out. I couldn't let him watch the beast kill me, but my strength wouldn't hold out much longer. Hot anger started building in my gut and I sensed the prickle of the electric spark from the taser. With a blast of fury and desperation, I released another blast of electricity from the taser down the throat of the beast. It yelped and leapt backwards, giving me an opening to roll away and get back to my feet. The beast was shaking its head, as if trying to throw something off itself, then a loud crack rung out followed by another howl from the beast. Miles had hit it with a blast shot. Its flank began oozing a dark liquid from the open wound, the edges smoking from the electrical burns.

Angry and in pain, the beast whirled and ran at him with a desperate, renewed strength. Miles watched it leap towards him and flipped out of the way at the last moment, causing the beast to career into the rocky cave wall. Miles landed gracefully, then swung out the butt of the weapon in a flying arc that smashed into the interlocking bones of the beast's left hind leg, causing it to stumble. The hit had been perfectly aimed at the weakest viable point on the hulking animal. Miles moved with a fluidity I had never seen before.

I heard a beep from my weapon. It had recharged. I lifted it up and just as the beast turned towards Miles, I let loose a shot straight into the side of its head. It screamed again with a strangled, crisp sound, and swayed, but didn't fall. The beast was seared, limping and oozing blood from multiple wounds, but it was still up. I flashed a quick look towards Sam and Lilli. Both of them were peeking over the boulder. There was pure fear in their eyes, and I knew I needed to end this. I reached out with my senses and felt the hum of both weapons. They were in the process of recharging, but I could feel the sharp electrical energy spikes stored in the taser ends.

The beast gnashed its teeth in anger, then turned and leapt towards me. I closed my eyes and reached out my hands towards the weapons. I pulled the electrical sparks away from the tasers and willed them to me, feeling their pulsing energy flow through me. Then, in a fit of rage that released all the stress from the last few days, I slammed the pulsing energy together in my hands and flung it straight at the beast's face. It hit straight into the beast's mouth and disappeared down its throat. The hit faltered the beast's momentum as it leapt at me. I dropped to the ground as it sailed over my head and crashed into the rocky wall behind me. The force of the impact created a resounding crack that reverberated throughout the cavern before the creature crumpled to the ground in a twisted heap. I pushed up to my feet and picked up my weapon again, ready to attack, but the beast didn't move. Its head lolled sideways at an untenable angle and its eyes, that once burned with a predator's hunger, stared at nothing.

My breath came in heaving gulps as my body shook from exertion. Slowly, I inched towards the animal. Once close enough, I kicked its leg with my foot. It didn't respond. Its lifeless form was gigantic up close, and it was unlike any animal I had ever seen. I had heard rumours of beasts prowling the Wastes, but I had never seen one myself.

'Is it dead?' I heard Sam ask.

'I think so,' I said as I looked at the beast's chest, searching for any twitch of life under its rough and matted fur, but there was nothing. 'It's not breathing.'

'So, we're safe then?' asked Lilli, her voice sounding like a hushed squeak. She was still terrified. My mind buzzed at her question. *Were* we safe?

'I don't know about that yet.' I took a deep inhale and drew up my grit, then backed away from the beast and walked over to Miles. He had barely even raised a sweat after all his acrobatics. I stared at him, then in a fluid motion I had perfected through years of practice, I punched Miles in the sternum.

16

A Decision

AFTER LANDING A SOLID punch to Miles's sternum, I took advantage of his shift in balance and knocked out the back of his knee with a sharp heel kick. He toppled backwards, but somehow spun himself to his right and landed on all fours. He flipped further sideways, rolling out of my range, and jumped onto his feet to face me.

I stood stunned. My Miles could barely walk upstairs without tripping over. It had been twenty years, but I couldn't put together what I was seeing now with what I remembered from the past.

'Mum! What the hell?' I heard Sam yell at me, but I couldn't pay attention to him because Miles was poised and ready to strike. This was all wrong.

I lunged toward Miles and began a physical and dangerous dance that I used to know so well. I faked a move to the left, breaking his stance, then followed up with two punches. The first cracked against his jaw, sending a shooting pain through my knuckles. The second smashed into his stomach, causing the air to escape his lungs. My moves were stilted, but luckily my body still remembered them. As I went in for a hard kick to his chest, he caught my foot just before impact and threw me off balance. I hit the ground hard, but kept rolling to make sure I was out of reach. I pushed up to my feet, my joints straining and grinding from the effort. Then I faced him again.

'What are you doing, Rachel?' Miles asked, holding a defensive stance. His voice was even but curious, and it had an unsettling effect. There were so many tiny differences to the Miles I knew.

'You're not Miles. Not the Miles I knew and loved.'

'Of course I am,' he said with a warm smile. 'It's me.' He stayed perfectly poised in his defensive stance the whole time, never breaking his body's preparedness to attack. That made up my mind.

I raced at him once again, grabbing a handful of dirt on my way and flung it at his face as I approached. He screamed and reflexively reached up to his eyes, but I was already on him. And then I released my pent-up anger. All the cumulated rage and hurt I had pushed deep down inside me was released in a torrent of blows. My fists and feet flew as they hit their mark again and again. Miles eventually manoeuvred away, then threw all his weight into a tackle that smashed us both into the ground. I felt the sting of his punches against my body as he sat on top of me. He grabbed hold of my hair and ripped it painfully sideways while smashing his other fist into my cheek. I screamed from the pain, but pulled my knee up between us and kicked him off as hard as I could. The force flipped him off me and he released my hair as he tumbled towards the boulders where Lilli and Sam looked on with pure horror on their faces. A strange metallic crack echoed in the cave as the back of Miles' neck smashed into the jagged side of a rock.

I landed on top of him and watched as his face flickered with static for a moment, then settled again as Miles. Shock and anger pulsed through me, but I pushed through it and grabbed his head with both hands. I smashed it with all my strength into the rock again. It let out a huge metallic crack, then static fizzed across his face before the visage of Miles completely disappeared. In his place was a tanned, dark-haired man with a hard-worn face, with an unforgettable viciousness in his eyes. I looked at his neck and saw a small black box on a thick collar. The box was split along the edge, revealing broken metallic wires beneath. It was some sort of high-tech holographic mask. I had heard rumours of such tech being developed, but never seen it myself, and the Agency never had tech like it when I was there. Relief washed over me that this wasn't my Miles, but I also felt a deep crack form in my already fractured heart. Only a few hours ago, hope had started to fill it, but all that was now gone. Just like my Miles.

The fake Miles let out a raging snarl and threw me off him. I rolled with the momentum but my hip caught on a rock, sending a piercing pain through my bone. I ignored it and found my feet again to stand and face the fake Miles.

The first thing I noticed were his eyes. They were like slits holding only darkness behind them. His dark hair was short and spiked, creating a pointy crown that sat on top of a stretched, oval face with features that pulled downwards. It was an unnerving configuration. Blood trickled out of his nose. He reached up and roughly wiped the blood with his sleeve before spitting a mix of saliva and blood at the ground between us. I ignored it and looked at him in the eyes. He snarled a smile in response.

'No more playing house I guess,' Fake Miles said with a voice that grated against my insides, making me shudder.

'Who the hell is that?' I heard Sam exclaim from where he and Lilli stood on the other side of the large boulder.

'I would like to know the same thing,' I said in a slow and forced even tone. 'Who are you? And how dare you pretend to be Miles.'

'I'm happy not to be. He was such a wimp. Hard to believe the two of you were ever really together. He was such a sack of nothing.' My upper lip twitched in rage. 'Great brain, don't get me wrong. Everyone is killing to get their hands on what he created. But he wasn't much of a man, was he? I would have thought you'd go for someone more masculine. Because, well, you know, you're Rachel.' He lifted his arm and gestured towards me. 'You're the infamous Agent R. There's never been anyone like you. You're a legend. I feel sorry for the poor agents having to run around in your shadow. You made it hard for any of them to measure up.'

'Shut up,' I said, the words squeezing out through my teeth.

'I was rather hoping you wouldn't find out about my little disguise. What gave me away?'

'I was wearing a blue dress the night I met Miles, not red.'

'I knew I'd forget something. Shame though, as I was hoping you might be up for a romantic reconnection with your long-dead lover. It would have been an experience to brag about to the lads. But I reckon I still can. I mean, you won't be around to say it never happened since I'm going to kill you. So, all the better for me.'

He whipped out a gun from a back pocket holster. Reflexively, I charged at him and knocked his aim to the side as he fired. The noise of the shot filled the rocky chamber, followed by a crack of rock as the projectile smashed into the ceiling. A flurry of fine dust and rock rained down on us, temporarily blinding me. I grappled with Fake Miles, yanking violently backwards on his gun hand. His wrist hit its stopping point, but then broke past it. Fake Miles howled and reached up and grabbed hold of my hair with his other hand. He ripped it forwards, causing a sharp pain to shoot across my scalp, as he used my body weight against me and threw me over his hip. I landed hard on my shoulder and only just managed to roll and avoid snapping my neck. But I had kept hold of the gun. Fake Miles loomed over me. A loud cracking suddenly reverberated all around us as small rocks fell from above us. I looked up and then threw myself sideways just as a huge stalactite cracked off and smashed into the ground where we had been standing. Fake Miles had also moved, using the distraction to his advantage to race towards Sam and Lilli. I stood up and raised the gun, ready to fire. Fake Miles grabbed Sam and pulled him in front to block my shot. Faster than I imagined possible, his good hand reached to his side and whipped a knife out of a concealed holster and placed the blade over Sam's throat.

'Make another move and your precious boy is gone,' spat Fake Miles. His frenzied eyes froze me to the spot. Their intense, frustrated anger triggered a warning in my brain, prompting me to take caution.

I hesitated for a moment. Fake Miles pressed the knife closer to Sam's throat. I saw Sam tremble as a thin drop of blood slipped out from under the knife and his eyes filled with terror.

I threw the gun aside and held up my hands. 'Please,' I begged, 'let him go.' Fake Miles just stood there watching me with his raging eyes. He didn't move a muscle. 'Please!' I begged. 'Please!'

Silence descended on the cave. He had the upper hand, and I couldn't think of a way out of this. Fake Miles's lip twitched upwards, curling its way into a sneer. He knew he'd won. My blood ran cold as I saw a decision flash across his face.

'Nah. Fuck the runt,' he said as his muscles twitched, preparing to slice my son's throat. A strange scream escaped my lips. There was nothing I could do. He was killing my son.

A huge rock appeared behind Fake Miles's head and crashed down with an almighty fury. Lilli had found part of the fallen stalactite and bashed it into his head as hard as she could. Her blow knocked him to the ground and Sam fell sideways, clutching his throat. I ran forward trying to get there to help eliminate the threat of Fake Miles, but as I ran, Lilli just kept smashing. The first two blows caught Fake Miles unawares, and by that stage, it was already too late. Lilli kept smashing and smashing. Blood sprayed her face, twisted with disgust and hatred. She kept smashing until Fake Miles finally stopped twitching, and instead lay silent and still.

I got to Sam and braced myself for the worst. Blood covered his neck, and I quickly checked him over before letting out a breath I didn't realise I'd been holding. He wasn't badly wounded. The blood was from a shallow scrape caused by the knife sliding off him and would heal easily with no issues. Something in me broke, and I grabbed hold of Sam and held him in a tight hug, filled with all my love and fears, all my pain and relief. A heavy clump in my chest broke apart, and before I knew it, a flood of tears poured out of me. I looked over at Lilli. She stood slightly shaking, staring at the body of Fake Miles, the rock still in her hand. I squeezed Sam tightly and gave him a kiss on his head, then stood and went to Lilli.

As I approached, I could see the body. Fake Miles's skull had caved in. There was so much blood along with bits of white bone, nerves and grey matter poking out amongst it all. I took a breath and pulled my attention away from the body. Nothing good would come from looking at that.

I put my hand on Lilli's shoulder. Her entire body was trembling. 'Lilli?' I said, purposefully using her name. 'Lilli, sweetie. Look at me.' She didn't move. I stepped further around so my face was in front of her eyeline and blocking the body. I cradled her blood-splattered face with my hands. 'Lilli. Look at me,' I commanded. Her eyes were glassy, but with time they broke from their glazed focus, quivered and slowly raised to meet mine.

'It's alright. Everything's okay.' I had seen this before in new Agency recruits who were taken out on their first real job. The first kill was always the hardest. It broke some, while others almost relished it. Both of those extremes were a worry, and anyone showing those tendencies were promptly let go. Sure, the Agency needed you to kill, but taking a life is no small task. To completely snuff out a lifetime of memories, of love, of heartache, of stories and dreams, is a serious thing, and always deserves reverence. I hated the Agency for what it did to people. Pulling them in and spitting them out again as tools for use by the faceless men and women pulling the power strings on Tir-na. People who were always above getting their own hands dirty. I pushed these pained memories and thoughts from my mind and focused on Lilli. She needed me now, and truthfully, I was relieved taking a life pushed her into the broken camp. It showed me she had a heart and that taking a person's life didn't leave her unaffected.

I brushed my hands down her arms and held onto her wrists with a strong but gentle grasp. 'Lilli,' I repeated. Her fingers twitched, and the bloodied rock she had used as a weapon fell from her hands onto the dusty floor. I just managed to get my toe out of the way so it didn't get smashed by the gore-covered stone.

With a gentle tug on her wrists, I led her across to the other side of the large boulder, blocking the gruesome sight of the body. Although Sam had turned pale at the sight of it, he followed us, clutching his bloodied neck the entire way. I guided Lilli's shaking frame into a seated position and helped her rest her weight against the boulder. She moved the whole time without a word and her eyes appeared to be fixed on something unseen. Sam sat down and shuffled in next to Lilli so their shoulders were touching. I left them sitting there in silence and started rummaging through the supply packs that were now strewn across the ground from the two fights. My body was aching as I bent over each bag, then I remembered; I shouldn't have been doing any of this alone. Where the hell were Peter and Megan? It took a while to search through the bags, but I finally found what I needed. I walked back to Lilli and Sam and kneeled down beside them. The cave was so quiet, but I let the silence sit. Instead, I tended to Sam's wound. It was shallow and relatively clean, which made it a quick patch-up job. Then, with care, I poured water onto some scraps of cloth torn from a packed blanket and used them to wipe the blood away from Lilli's hands and face. The sounds of my actions had become a welcome ambient distraction, and as I finished wiping the last of the blood away, Lilli's head drooped as she fell asleep. I guided her to the ground and placed a second blanket over her. Sam just watched Lilli's chest rise and fall as she slept, his face filled with both concern and fear.

'It's alright, honey,' I said, hoping to provide some reassurance. 'Shock often does this to people.' He looked up at me, then without a word laid down next to Lilli and pulled the blanket over himself as well.

With the two of them resting, I stood up to take stock of the fallout of what happened. The carcass of the beast sprawled across the cave flow in a crumpled, hulking, furry mound. The smashed hologram mask was in the dirt, near to us. And there, on the other side of the boulder, were the lifeless legs of Fake Miles. I only realised then that I didn't know his real name and I probably never would.

As I stood there, the quiet became overwhelming, and my mind became acutely aware of the throbbing pain pulsing through my body. It felt like I was being punched over and over again on my hip, shoulder and cheek. I looked down I saw that my hip was bleeding from when it caught on a rock. The scrape looked rough and dirty and needed to be cleaned. I reached up to my shoulder next, where the beast's claws had landed. I still had movement, but the entire area was tender to the touch. There would definitely be a bruise there tomorrow. My cheek, though, was a whole other level of pain. Through gritted teeth, I gently touched the bone and found it was fractured. I walked back over to the kids, grabbed the med kit and sat down next to them to patch myself up for the umpteenth time. I didn't know how much more of this I could take. Luckily for me, the med kit had everything I needed, including a body reset injection.

It came in a long, thick canister, with a serum inside that, when injected healed any damage your body sustained within the last 72-hours. However, to do that, it also knocked you out for six hours. I closed my eyes, assessed the state of my body, and wondered if I could delay taking it until Peter and Megan returned. The kids couldn't be left with no one looking after them, but I was on my last legs. The physical and emotional stress from the last few days had worn me down. Not to mention the heavy exhaustion that hung over me from the electrical power exertion during the fight with the beast. I didn't think I had the energy to protect the kids, even if I needed to.

A shuffling of footsteps echoed through the cave. My body tensed in response until a recognisable voice let out a soft, 'What the...?' Everything relaxed instantly, as the sound of that voice meant I could use the injection.

'Over here,' I called out. Peter appeared around the side of the boulder and stopped for a moment to figure out the situation.

'Are they...?' He pointed towards the kids.

'They just sleeping. I'm not sure if they're fine, though.' I pointed over at the rock Lilli had used on Fake Miles, still sitting on the ground covered in blood and brain matter. 'That was Lilli.' I didn't want to go into detail in case the kids were still awake and overheard, so instead, I gave Peter a knowing look. He thankfully seemed to get my meaning and nodded back. 'Where the hell have you two been? I really could have used your help. My body is not coping well with this.'

'We headed higher up the hill to get a better vantage point,' said Megan, 'but obviously that decision lost us the ability to hear what was happening inside the cave.' She sent a judging look in Peter's direction, then bent down in front of me. 'Are you alright?' she asked in a quieter voice.

'No, I'm not,' I said. 'I'm on my last legs and I think this is the only thing that will help.' I waved the body reset injection at her and she nodded in understanding.

'We'll keep watch over the kids and yourself,' reassured Megan. I hadn't known her for long, but I instinctively felt I could trust her. I also didn't have many options available to me, so I nodded. 'Before you nod off, can you tell me quickly what happened? And who that random guy is?'

I quietly told them everything, leaving out some of the finer and more gory details to not trigger the kids if they were awake. Then, with the story told, Megan and Peter on guard, and exhaustion gnawing at me, I went to Sam and woke him.

'Sam, sweetie,' I said, shaking him awake. He grumbled, but stirred and turned to face me. 'I'm going to sleep as well and probably won't wake up for a while, okay?'

'Okay', Sam nodded sleepily.

'Megan and Peter are here keeping watch, so if you need them, they're here.'

Sam gave a tiny nod in response, then laid down to sleep. I kissed his head and shuffled myself to a comfortable position not far from him. With everything set and taken care of, I took the cap off the end of the canister and pressed it against my arm. A sharp piercing sensation let me know it had worked as the world slipped away and I was pulled into darkness.

17

The Unknown

T HE SOUND OF SHUFFLING shoes and a murmuring voices pulled me back into consciousness. I heard Sam's voice, followed by Lilli's. Although I couldn't make out what they were saying, their calm tone surprised me, given what had happened. Megan's voice suddenly overpowered the kids' hushed whispers from somewhere closer to me.

'She's been out for a long time. Maybe we should wake her?' she said. There was a squeaking of a shoe as someone walked across the sandy dirt ground.

'Better not,' came Peter's voice. 'She's already had at least two adrenaline shots in the last couple of days. I think her body just needs to rest. Let's leave her for a bit and check back later.'

What Peter had said caused snippets of memories from the last few days to rush through my mind. It had been a shitty couple of days. My heart spluttered and went numb at the memory of losing Miles for a second time. Even though I had known it was too good to be true, a tiny flame of hope had briefly flickered inside me.

Life seems to have an annoying way of never leaving the past behind. Ripples radiating from your history might not surface for years, but they eventually catch up with you. As soon as you're lulled into a sense of safety, thinking you are free forever, that's when the ghosts from your long-forgotten days rear their ugly heads and pull you back into worlds you had hoped to leave behind.

I kept my eyes shut and did a full-body scan. The process of focusing solely on one part of my body at a time while calming my breath helped push all the troubling memories and worries out of my mind. Good old compartmentalising.

It wasn't the first time it had helped me. I started the scan at my feet and worked my way up. Almost every joint ached from exertion and stress, but that was it. The serum had done its job well. There was no pain left in my hip or shoulder, and the heavy weight of exhaustion was gone. Instead, I felt revitalised, so I couldn't begrudge the lingering aches and pains. They were a small price to pay for getting Sam back, and I would willingly do it all again. I looked deep within myself and checked to see if the spark I had only just found had been extinguished. But I needn't have worried: there it was, burning away in my core, ready to obey my command.

My body was ready to get up and carry on with whatever lay ahead, but I didn't want to open my eyes yet. The surrounding sounds had already brought the world into sharp focus, and I absentmindedly tracked them while imagining their associated images. It was a nice distraction, but then I heard Sam's hushed voice again. I needed to get up and see him. Both the kids needed me. I slowly opened my eyes and rolled cautiously onto my side. Every movement was painful, but I pushed through it. The hushed murmurings stopped suddenly and were replaced by quick movements through the dirt.

'Mum!' Sam rushed over to me. His eyes were haggard with dark circles of worry. 'Are you okay? You were out for a long time.'

'Yeah,' I choked out, my voice rough from not being used, 'I'm okay, sweetie.' He helped me into a proper sitting position, and Megan handed me a hydration pack.

'Sip on this,' Megan instructed, 'you need to keep hydrated.'

The next few moments passed in a blur. I slowly sipped the flavoured liquid from the pouch while looking around the cavern. The blood splatter and gory remains of Fake Miles were gone, and the beast's hulking body had been removed. Looked like Peter and Megan had been busy on the clean-up while keeping a careful watch over us. My muscles relaxed slightly at the thought, but then I spotted Lilli. She hovered behind the others, seeming unsure and skittish. Despite her restlessness, her eyes were hazy, like she was present but wasn't really seeing anything clearly. It was one thing to kill a person when you had trained for it, but it was a different thing entirely to have that situation and choice thrust on you without warning. Discovering you could cross a line you thought was impenetrable could do some severe damage to a person if not managed. I needed to look after her.

I put down the hydration pouch and stood. I could feel everyone's eyes on me as I made my way over to Lilli, hobbling slightly on my stilted legs. She looked at me, unsure of what was happening. I pulled her into a hug and held onto her. She hesitated at first, but as I continued to just hold her in silence, her muscles drooped and her back started to quake. I moved one of my hands up to stroke her head in a soothing motion, as I had with Sam when he was a small boy frightened by a bad dream. We stood there until Lilli had cried out the tension from her body and her eyes had run dry. I slowly pulled myself back, placed my hands on either side of her face, and locked eyes with her.

'Thank you, Lilli,' I said with all the power in my heart. 'Thank you for doing the hardest thing when it was most needed. I know it doesn't make it easier but, you saved us all, and I will forever be grateful.' I saw the meaning slowly filtering into her.

She nodded and whispered, 'Thank you.'

I turned from Lilli, leaving her in the care of Sam, and went to talk with Megan and Peter about the situation. They told me they had taken the bodies outside the cave and buried Fake Miles while we slept. Sam came over and interrupted us mid-way through Megan and Peter's report on how many food packs we still had.

'Mum,' he said, demanding my attention with a strange conviction I hadn't seen in him, 'you need to tell me what is going on. No more avoiding it. Tell me the truth about why all of this is happening. You're supposed to just be a meditation and movement coach, but apparently, you're not...And I saw what you did with those electric prodding things. What is going on?'

I looked at Peter. I wasn't even sure why. For reassurance? Permission? Maybe from an imagined feeling that I was back under the Agency's command structure?

'You need to tell him everything, Rach,' Peter said with an encouraging nod. I knew Peter was right. I had spent a large portion of my life trying to bury the past, to forget it ever happened, but that didn't matter now, because Sam deserved the truth. He was an adult now. I didn't need to protect him anymore. He could make up his own mind and forge his own future. But he did need my honesty and love.

I turned back to Sam. 'Let's sit down first, then I'll tell you everything.'

And I did. I told him everything. Every detail of my past that had led us to that cave. But most importantly, I told him about the powers I had recently discovered. I confessed that although I knew the experiments were aiming to spark these powers in me, the twenty-year delayed onset had taken me by surprise, and I was still figuring out what they really meant or what the consequences might be.

Sam sat silently as I spoke. I could see thoughts spinning through his mind, as though I had just pulled the rug out from under his relatively simple and normal life. He had no idea how hard I worked to give him that quiet life. How hard it had been to keep us off the radar and keep him protected from this world. But he was a man now, not my baby boy. He hadn't really been my baby for years. So, I needed to trust in him and hope I had done enough to give him the best chance. I realised that all a parent can do is teach your baby bird to fly so that one day they can soar. Nerves fired through my body in fear of his response. I had lied, and that was unforgivable. But I hoped he could see what I tried to do, and that maybe, just this one time, the means did justify the ends.

'Mum...' Sam said, looking me directly in the eye, 'I don't know what to say. I'm so sorry you had to carry all that on your own. You should have told me. I could have helped.' He stood up, moved over to sit in front of me, and grabbed me in a tight hug. I had been so scared of how he would react, and I definitely didn't expect this. But I should have known. He was so much like his father, after all. So much compassion and warmth. My hand drifted upwards and absentmindedly stroked his hair.

'I'm so sorry, Sam,' I whispered. Tears slid down my face and I held onto my son as though nothing else mattered in the world, because truthfully, nothing else did.

We pulled apart once my tears stopped spilling, and I used my sleeve to wipe my face. All of a sudden, I became acutely aware of the others watching us.

'Why is all this coming back now, though?' asked Megan. 'I mean, everything you have told us, the whole story, it all happened so long ago. So why is it being brought up again now? Who would even know about any of this and want to rake it all up? You don't go to the lengths these people have without a good reason.'

'Megan's right,' said Peter. 'Something sparked this off again, and from what we've seen, these people won't let up until they get what they're after.'

'That's just it,' said Megan. 'What are they after? What are they trying to get? They kidnapped your son and let you chase them across Tir-na. But to what end?'

'Maybe they want the two of you,' said Lilli. We all stopped and turned to face her.

'What do you mean?' I asked her.

'Well...from everything I've heard, the whole story revolves around you, Miles and Sam. The experiments, your relationship with Miles, Sam's birth, Miles's death, Sam being taken, your powers appearing. It all seems connected.'

'You're right,' said Sam. 'So, if we work it back to the start, then who knew about the experiments? If we figure that out, then maybe we'll know who is doing this?'

While the others were dissecting my past, a terrible realisation hit me about why this was all happening. 'Lilli's right, they want us,' I said.

'What?' asked Sam.

'They want us,' I repeated, looking straight at Sam. 'All knowledge of how I got these powers died with Miles. What if they're trying to get us so they can reverse engineer the powers?'

'Who would have known what happened to even think of this?' asked Megan. 'And why not just take you and Sam initially instead of only grabbing Sam?'

'I don't know.' I said in frustration. 'It just doesn't make sense.'

'You said your powers kicked off when we were being held by Creep Face,' said Peter. 'What if the high-stress situation sparked your powers to life? Could this whole thing be designed to do just that?'

'That feels like a leap. How would anyone even know that would work?' I asked, my mind racing with snippets of memories and information, trying to piece it all together.

'I don't know,' said Peter, 'but it could explain why they only grabbed Sam and sent you on this trek across the continent.'

'Again though, it comes back to who would do this?' said Megan.

'I don't know, but I want to find out,' I said. Details flew through my mind until one crystallised into place. 'The e-vehic,' I said.

'What?' asked Sam.

'The e-vehic. It might have a programmed destination in it. We could find out where Fake Miles was taking us, then if we follow it, maybe we can find out who's behind this.'

'You want to go after whoever it is?' asked Peter. 'Seems risky.'

'If I don't, I'm scared they'll never leave us alone. And I don't want that for either of us,' I said, looking at Sam. 'I've been avoiding this for far too long. I've kept you in the dark, and it's time for me to face the truth and make things right.'

'First step then,' said Megan. 'Let's go check the e-vehic.'

Our small party stood, clicked on new oxy-mask canisters, and headed out the cave entrance, back into the plains of the Wastes. My eyes squeezed shut as I adjusted to the outside light that was blinding after the dark internals of the cave. The sun hung in the afternoon sky, its light visibly dissipating with each passing minute as time rushed us towards nightfall once again. Its presence in the afternoon sky made me realise how long my body had been still while I was unconscious. No wonder my joints ached slightly, even though the rest of me felt remarkably better. I pushed the niggling pain from my mind and hoped moving again would work out the stiffness.

We crunched through the sandy dirt. Peter and Megan kept their weapons armed and pointed outwards, mirroring each other in a smooth, protective formation just in case another beast reared its head. We reached the e-vehic, and I opened the driver's side door. I jumped in and started trying to figure out how to access the e-vehic's central processor. Next to the driver's console was a small rectangular touch screen, but there were a couple of custom modifications that made me hesitate. I couldn't just sit there though with everyone watching me, so I decided to try activating the screen to pull up the details. A login screen sprung to life.

PLEASE CENTRE YOUR EYES IN THE SCANNER, came a clipped monotone voice from the screen.

'Well, that's unexpected,' I said. I'd never seen a central processor with an eye scanner before. Why would you modify the kit to make it hard to access in the field? There was a moment of pause before a sharp click.

SORRY. YOU ARE NOT IDENTIFIED. ALERTING CENTRAL SECURITY OF UNAUTHORISED ACCESS ATTEMPT.

My mind screamed in panic. I may have just blown the whole plan up in smoke.

'Shit! Mum! Stop it somehow,' yelled Sam.

'I don't know how!' I said, my mind whirring.

'Try a reboot or yank out the data cord!' said Sam. I grabbed the cord on the back of the unit and yanked, but it was locked in place. Shit.

'If that thing alerts security, then we should head back to the Grove now as fast as we can,' said Megan.

Not knowing what else to do, I took a breath and reached out to the electromagnetic streams. I could feel it all. The data moving in waves through the system and out into the air. I sifted through and found the stream containing the security alert. I focused and began changing the data, nudging it into a new shape. Into a report of a system malfunction so that any alert that had already been sent would be dismissed as an error. Once a few malfunction alerts had been sent, I cut off the communications. I then pivoted my attention and dived into the pre-programmed guidance system. That's where I found the details we needed. The location of something deep in the Wastes. A location Fake Miles was trying to take us to. I sucked in another breath and let go of the currents, pulling my awareness back into myself. Every step of what I had just done felt forced and laborious, but I realised it had all occurred in the space of a single breath. These powers were still a complete mystery to me, but luckily, my instinct seemed to be getting me through. For now, at least.

I turned to face the others. 'I mitigated the alert, and even better, I know where he was taking us.' The others just stared at me, their faces contorted with shock and wariness. 'What's wrong?'

'Mum, your eyes are glowing. Well…not glowing actually, but kind of like, sparking, but inside your eyes,' said Sam, his face crinkled in a look of uncertainty. 'It's fading now, though. Are you okay?'

'I'm fine. Peter, you've been with me when I've used my...whatever this thing is. Have you noticed me look like this before?'

'The blue sparks in the eyes are new,' said Peter.

'Well...that's something to think about later. Right now, we need to decide how all of you are getting back to the Grove while I go on. I can take some ration packs—'

'Mum, what are you talking about? We're all coming,' said Sam.

'No. You need to be safe,' I said with perhaps too much force.

'Mum. Stop it. This has to do with my past and future as much as it has with yours. I'm coming. I won't let you do any of this on your own,' said Sam.

'I'm coming too,' said Lilli. 'I want to make everything up to you still. So, I'm coming and I'll help however I can.' Sam pulled her close to him and kissed her hair. She blushed slightly at the overt sign of affection.

'I said I'd help you, Rach, and I'm a man of my word, so I'm in,' said Peter. I nodded at him, grateful for some additional adult supervision since both Sam and Lilli were so determined to come along.

'I only met you a day ago, so I'm not invested at all. I've got nothing to gain and probably a lot to lose if I come along,' stated Megan. 'But, as I told you, I got screwed over by shitty organisations who don't care about people, and obviously whoever is behind this is pretty shitty and can't be up to any good. So, I'm in too.'

I hadn't expected this type of response. I had spent most of my life bearing the brunt of responsibility by myself, so I hadn't realised I wasn't alone anymore. Maybe I hadn't been on my own for a while and I was just too stressed and worried to notice.

'Well, alright then,' I said, trying to keep the almost overwhelming emotions out of my voice, 'I guess we better get going.'

We gathered up everything from the caves and piled it into the e-vehic. On the way out, I paused for a moment at the small mound outside the cave where Megan and Peter had buried the body of Fake Miles. I knew it wasn't my Miles, but emotions and memories pulled me to stop and reflect briefly on the twisted feelings seeing his face again had caused. A chilled wind slapped sand and dirt against my cheek, causing me to pull the well-worn fabric of Old Blue a little tighter around me. Miles was gone. I had known it all along, but a tiny kernel of hope had been growing in my heart since I first saw Fake Miles. That small flicker of hope was now extinguished, and instead, I grasped onto my old feelings of pain and sadness, holding them tight. They hurt, but at least I knew they were real, and that made them endlessly precious to me.

I walked to the e-vehic and discovered Peter and Megan arguing over who should drive. I didn't have the energy to get involved in it, so I sat in the front passenger seat where I could help with the guidance or comms systems, and patiently waited them out. Finally, their tense exchange came to an end, with Megan proclaimed the driver and Peter riding up back. I turned and looked at Sam and Lilli sitting in the back row of seats. They both had a nervous energy about them, but I noticed they held hands with a strong and comforting resolve. There would be no convincing them to stay.

I turned back and looked out upon the bleak and desolate world before me. Jagged rocks emerged from the ground like knives and the constant wind whipped dark clouds of dirt and sand through the air. It was also ominously quiet, apart from the skittering sound of sand and the whistle of the wind. I hadn't spent any real time out here in the Wastes, and I wasn't sure what to expect when we headed deeper into this landscape.

I reached out to the e-vehic's comms pad and pulled up the programmed destination coordinates. A map with a dotted line marked over it flashed before changing to a visual of the land ahead of us with a green arrow superimposed over the image. The arrow showed the direction and timing of our turns. It pointed in a hooked direction, signalling for us to turn around near the massive, lifeless body of the beast, which Megan and Peter had dragged out of the cave and left outside in the elements so it could return to the Wastes.

The e-vehic roared to life, and as we turned near the dead beast, the arrow changed, leading us down the hill and out deeper into the Wastes. It was a slow journey, and I noticed that the environment began shifting. As we progressed, it became rockier, with bogs and stringy low-lying vegetation spread across the desolate landscape. A few small scurrying animals I had never seen before darted out of the way of our rumbling e-vehic. I had always thought the Wastes was completely devoid of life, but after the beast's attack and unveiling Fake Miles, it seemed to be the day for my perceptions being shattered. Thankfully, the e-vehic's scanner showed no signs of any major life forms out there.

'Did you guys know there is a children's rhyme from the Grove about this place?' said Lilli, breaking the quiet companionship that had fallen over us. 'I've never really thought about it too much until now.'

'How did it go?' I asked.

'Go on,' Sam gently encouraged. With everything of late, I had forgotten how shy and quiet Lilli usually was. She hesitated but took a breath and in a clear, sweet voice sang a song from her past.

'Where the dirt and mud get high,
And boulders reach to the sky,
Watch where the secrets lie,
For if you don't, you'll die.'

'Sounds ominous now that we're out here. There were stories, too, of creatures that lurked the Wastes that would eat anyone that entered their realm,' Lilli said. 'I guess they weren't actually stories after all.'

'Sounds about right,' said Megan. 'Wrapping scraps of truth in a children's song that is easy to remember and pass down to generations of kids is an age-old practice.'

We rumbled on further, and I watched as the outcrops of rocks morphed into huge columns that shot up on all sides of us. Our journey slowed as the giant rocks jutted together to form an impenetrable barricade. If it wasn't for the map leading us along a tight and narrow pathway through the base of the tall spikes, which quickly became solid cliff faces, we would have been lost in the rocky labyrinth.

'Map shows we're not too far from our destination. Only another two rock-mountain-spike-things over,' I said. 'Maybe we should find somewhere to leave the e-vehic and do the rest on foot?' I asked Megan.

'Yeah. I think that'd be best. Maybe it's just the rocks slowly closing in around us that's putting me on edge a bit, but I'm starting to get a bad feeling about this,' Megan said.

'Me too. I keep checking the scanner to make sure we're not about to be ambushed or anything, but it still shows no other signs of life.'

'How about that turn to the right up there and that little road?' Megan asked, pointing up ahead. 'Reckon that will get us somewhere with a bit of cover?'

I quickly pulled up the map and confirmed that it led to a small alcove area that theoretically should have enough room for us to park the e-vehic.

The 'road', if it could really be called that, narrowed significantly after we took the right turn. Cliffs shot up on either side of us, forging unscalable walls that reminded me of a waterfall, except brown and craggy instead of soft, bubbly blue. It was a tight fit, but the e-vehic made its way over the rocky surface until we popped out into the larger alcove. We swung around in a tight turn and Megan cut the engine. The silence of the place instantly became apparent. I opened the door and hopped out, each sound reverberating off the huge stone walls that soared towards the sky. But the sounds were contained and trapped, which hopefully worked to our advantage.

I didn't know what we were about to walk into, and that terrified me. In the past, all our missions were carefully planned, with backups and redundancies built into every step. We would spend hours analysing locations and targets, so we knew exactly what we were facing. Today, everything was an unknown.

I set about helping Peter unload the gear we would need and handing it out to everyone. The work was slow and mechanical, but it's what I needed to stem the worry building in my stomach. I pulled the weapons cache towards me and looked in. After hesitating for a moment, I reached in and pulled out two handguns for Sam and Lilli.

'I don't know what we're going to face, but I want you to be as prepared as you can be, so you need to learn how to use these,' I said, and handed them each a handgun. 'Megan, can you help Lilli?'

'On it,' Megan replied, jumping down from her perch on driver's seat where she had been curiously watching us. Megan began by talking Lilli through the mechanics of the gun. I turned and began the same with Sam.

It was a strange and unnerving experience, and part of me hated that I had to show my son how to use a gun, but I needed him as prepared and self-reliant as possible. I ran him through how to aim and fire, the main target points on an adversary, and most importantly, how to safely store and handle the gun so he didn't hurt himself. His hands shook slightly throughout it all, but his eyes were set and focused. We couldn't risk the sound of using bullets, so instead a rhythmic *click, click* echoed around us as we put the kids through dry drills. Once we were sure they knew the basics, we geared everyone up. Peter, Megan and I started strapping on everything we had. The e-vehic didn't have the spread of options Peter's Agency car did, but it had some of the same equipment. We busied ourselves with loading everything onto our person, then I turned to select Sam's equipment.

'Keep these with you, and always be ready,' I said to Sam as I handed him a taser, holster and rounds for his gun. He nodded, his floppy hair bouncing with the movement. For a moment I saw him as a three-year-old who was too scared to go down a slide without me, but then the flash of memory was gone and instead the grown man stood in front of me. I couldn't help myself and pulled him into a tight hug.

'I love you, Sam,' I whispered to him.

'I know Mum. Love you too,' he replied in a genuine, casual, slightly exasperated voice, like it was the most obvious thing in the world and he was sick of telling me. He would never know how much it meant, though.

'Alright then,' I said, turning to everyone. 'I don't know what we're going to find, so I don't want anyone taking unnecessary risks. We stay low and quiet. We're ghosts, and we want to keep it that way. Hopefully, we won't have any need for this stuff,' I said, pointing at my weapons pack, 'but in case we do, kids, follow our instructions and stay close. Megan, can you take point and lead the way with the map? Maybe change it over to the geo-scan as well, just in case the other map is hiding anything.'

'Can do,' said Megan before walking over and pulling the map out of the front of the e-vehic.

'And Peter, you know what to do.'

'Of course,' stated Peter, 'be useless if I didn't.'

'Alright then,' I nodded. 'Let's go see where that fake son of a bitch was taking us.'

18

Mud and Rock

W E WOUND OUR WAY through the maze of soaring stone walls and gritty mud. It was slow going, but we got into a rhythm that helped calm the nerves radiating off Sam and Lilli. Megan led the way as the comms pad map from the e-vehic quietly beeped, leading us deeper into this natural labyrinth. I looked up towards the top of the cliff faces but couldn't see anything, not even a plant dangling over the edge. It was barren here, and part of me couldn't shake the unsettling feeling that this whole place was an unescapable trap. I had to admit, though, there would never be much traffic here, so it was the perfect secret location.

We had been walking for an hour, having weaved our way back to the main path and then continuing along it before following the map down a smaller path to the left. The path started to blur into a never-ending mess of brown as it twisted and turned ever deeper. Suddenly, the song Lilli sang to us began looping in my mind.

Where the dirt and mud get high.

My boots squelched in the strange silty mud that sucked at my feet as I trudged forwards.

And boulders reach to the sky.

I looked up at the soaring rocky cliff faces that enclosed upon us, seemingly forcing us onwards to some unknown destination.

Watch where the secrets lie.
For if you don't, you'll die.

The words put me on edge. It was never a good idea to discount children's nursery rhymes too quickly, for as Megan had said, there was often an essential nugget of truth in them.

I kept a keen eye out for anything out of place in this organic landscape, anything like evidence of struggles, or signs of anything mechanical or crafted. There was something about the rock face's colours and textures that niggled at me. I moved closer and reached out to touch the rock. Some parts of it were strangely smooth, in vertical strips with long scratches scattered across the surface, as though something had shaved layers off the rock. I stepped back and looked at the wall, craning my neck until my oxy-mask tubes pulled tight from the strain. The entire surface was covered in the same markings. My mind raced back to analyse the landscape along the main path and where we had hidden the e-vehic. There were more jutting rocks, debris and spindly clawing plants along the cliff walls back there; a much more natural environment. My mind raced forwards, trying to pinpoint when the landscape had changed ever so slightly. Then it was there, clear in my mind. The fork off the main path where we turned down this smaller twisting path. At that junction there were still craggy rock faces shooting up to the sky on the main path, but the edge, where the smaller path broke away, looked like it had been hewn out of the rock face, and that crafted facade had stayed the same ever since. It was a subtle difference, done carefully to look natural, but the evidence was there. Someone had created this path.

'I think we should get off this track as soon as we can,' I said in a hushed voice, trying not to set off an echo in the chasm. 'If anyone comes along, we'll be caught completely in the open with nowhere to go.'

'Yeah, I don't like it. Sooner we're out of here the better,' said Peter, who was trailing at the rear of the group.

'The map shows a small crack in the wall or something just round the next bend to the right,' said Megan. 'Looks like it winds back in the same direction as this path, but probably has less chance of traffic.'

'Sounds good,' I said. 'Lead the way, Megan.'

Our group continued our quiet advance along the path until we turned the corner and saw the crack in the rock that led to the smaller path. It was a tiny narrow gap filled with a latticework of jutting rocks that would only allow one person to slide through at a time.

'It's not like this the whole way, is it?' I asked Megan, heading over to look at the map.

'Looks like it opens up once we get through this first part.' She pointed out the path on the comms pad geo-scan and she was right. If we could get in, we would be safe.

'I'll go first,' said Peter, taking off his pack and getting ready to slide through, 'then Sam and Lilli can follow.' The kids nodded, and we watched as Peter slowly manoeuvred through the narrow cliff opening. It was slow going, especially as he had to awkwardly alternate between dragging and lifting his pack through the gap. But once Peter was in and consistently moving forwards, the kids headed in after him and quickly caught up, their bodies still pliable and nimble with youth. In comparison, Peter looked like a rickety robot. His movements were stiff and stilted, while Sam and Lilli seemed to flow through the narrow spaces. It made me miss my old body, the one that moved like that without any creaks or pains. But there is no point in wishing for the past when you've still got the here and now to deal with, and if anything, I was proud of my older body. It showed I had survived.

I indicated that Megan should follow next, and with an agreeing nod, she slipped into the crack. Her movements were smooth and calculated. It was impressive to watch, and it made me wish I had known her when I was at the Agency. We might have been good friends, and goodness knows, I could have used more close friends back then.

Lilli's song popped into my head again. It made me nervous, so I tentatively reached out with my powers, just enough to feel for anything around us. Anything electrical, any signals, any electronic signatures, anything. The idea that I could operate as my own radar system was exciting and worrisome. What was I becoming? I pushed the worry away and instead let myself flow outwards, as gentle as a breeze. My power drifted in every direction until a strong ping pulled me further ahead along the path we had been travelling on. It took me awhile to interpret what I was sensing, but then I realised I had seen similar electronic signatures before. There was an e-vehic heading our way.

My muscles responded instantly, and I rushed into the crack to get off the path. It was incredibly tight, but even with a few joints and muscles protesting, my years working as a movement coach helped me wind through the space with relative ease.

'Move!' I commanded Megan. 'There's an e-vehic heading this way.'

The tight gap disappeared to the left only five metres ahead. Peter and the kids had already gone around the corner, but Megan and I were still moving through the narrow space that, although small and craggy, had a direct line of sight to the path. We rushed through the space. Megan reached the corner and disappeared around it. My senses pinged at the e-vehic as it rounded a corner and sped straight along the path towards us. I flung myself forwards, throwing my pack ahead of me through a small gap between a boulder and an overhanging jutting rock. I could feel the e-vehic's approach and leapt through the gap after my pack. My skin scraped across the rock's surface as I fell forward over the boulder and crashed on the other side. The sound from my landing echoed along the cliff face. I froze on the ground, not daring to make another sound. The engine of the e-vehic paused suddenly. Sam's face popped around the corner just ahead of me, but I waved him back and then kept perfectly still in the mud that covered me in a slimy caress. Footsteps echoed from the path where the e-vehic had stopped, as they started scanning our area with their radar. I reached out desperately and found the signal for the organic matter map overlay. With a few forced tweaks to the system, I made it display everything as inorganic, so everything looked the same as the mountainous rocks all around us. We stayed silent, not daring to move. Eventually, footsteps squelched their way back towards the e-vehic, then the engine sprang to life again and it sped off down the path.

I took a calming breath in, then rolled over and stood up.

'Mum! Are you okay?' Sam asked.

'Yep, I'm good.' My voice strained a little with the actual effort of standing and I could tell I was getting tired again. I brushed off my clothes, but really, I used the motion as an excuse to assess the damage from my rough landing and scraping across the rock face. My hand brushed against sticky, torn fabric on my stomach and thigh. When I looked at my hand, though, it was covered in mud instead of blood. I sighed with relief, but the skin under the mud was tender, meaning there were still wounds under the muck that would need to be cleaned to avoid mud infection. I hobbled around the corner, trying to move as smoothly as possible, but my body didn't want to cooperate.

'That was a sweet move, Rach. I especially liked the landing. It was like you haven't aged a day,' laughed Peter. I gave him a withering look, and Megan punched him in the arm.

'Says Mister "I can only move like an old rusty robot." Don't be a dick,' Megan jibed.

'That's fair. My joints are a lot less pliable than they used to be, unlike these two mountain goats who just bounded through without a care in the world. Ah, to be young again,' Peter said while handing me a field med kit.

I sank down against the side of the cliff and started tending to my dirt-covered scrapes while also enjoying the slightly embarrassed and proud expressions that swept over Sam and Lilli. They looked at each other smiling, and I knew that look. At least I remembered that look. I used to look at Miles that way once. It was a look filled with pure love and pride of the other person, and astonishment that out of everyone on the planet, they chose you. It's a wonderful look.

'I'm guessing you did your hoozy-whats wibbly-wobbly thing to know that e-vehic was coming?' said Megan. It was part statement, part question, but I enjoyed her twinkling fingers for the hoozy-whats part. I couldn't help but giggle.

'Yeah, I did. I'm getting better at being precise with it. It's also more instinctual now, so doesn't need much thought. Like it knows what I'm thinking, or at least what my intentions are, and then just does it. I know that's a terrible expla-nation, but that's what it feels like,' I said, rambling as I roughly wiped the dirt and mud from my wounds. Cleaning out small wounds always hurt more than expected, so I welcomed any distraction.

'So, you think you can keep doing that, then? It's pretty handy having our own early warning system,' said Megan. She smiled at me, her cool icy blue eyes crinkling at the sides, while a trickle of blood suddenly oozed its way across her brow from a scrape sustained from the rocky edges during our hastened dive through the gap. Peter noticed it too and was already there handing her a steri-wipe. They barely looked at each other, but moved instinctually, as if they knew each other's movements before they happened.

'I can certainly try, although every time I do it, I feel drained after. I'm okay at the moment as that wasn't too much, but anything more and I start to fatigue,' I said.

'You're probably just old and unfit,' laughed Peter.

'You'd know all about that, wouldn't you, Peter?' fired back Megan with a look that made Peter squirm. She began cleaning her own wound. I found the process mesmerising to watch as my thoughts started wandering. She was such a cool woman, but for the life of me, I couldn't figure out the dynamic between her and Peter. He looked at her now with a strange look that I hadn't seen before. Was it pained concern on his face? Hopeful sadness? Whatever it was, it was a strange mix I couldn't read, which was annoying, as I was usually great at reading people.

'You all right, Mum?' asked Sam, cutting through my thoughts.

'Yes, sweetie, I'm okay. Can you pass me a sealer-strip please?' I asked him. He already had one in his hand.

'Let me.' Sam started gently applying the strip. It was a weird experience. I had always been the one to heal his wounds and make him better. He moved with care and precision, his hands solid and soft at the same time. A wash of pride swept over me. Once finished, he helped me to my feet, and we all regathered our stuff, ready to continue the journey.

'This path get any bigger Megan? I'm not going to have to pull out any acrobatic ariel manoeuvres like Miss Gymnast here, am I?' Peter said, flashing me a cheeky smile.

'As I said, it opens up from here. No need for you to break a hip,' she said it all with such seriousness I almost missed the dig. This was probably the most I had seen them interact. 'Can you do your radar thing, Rach?'

'Not all the time, but I'll try every now and then,' I replied.

'That will do. Let's go,' Megan said, and started leading the way along the path. The kids took off after her, then I followed, with Peter at the rear again. I reached up and held onto the straps of my backpack as I walked. The weight of it brought me comfort somehow.

We trudged onwards, twisting and turning with the strange flow of the narrow path. This was definitely a naturally made gorge. No sentient being would decide to purposefully build something like this.

Every five minutes or so I would let off a gentle feeler ping. I detected nothing as we hiked onwards, but then, after forty minutes of trudging and pinging, I felt a faint buzz from something around the next corner.

'Stop!' I said. I focused my attention and reached out to determine what the buzz was and whether it was a threat. Two points emitted an electrical hum, one a camera, and the other a mechanism of some sort that I couldn't identify. I reached out and just like at the Palace, found the camera's electrical feed and put its data on loop, so it broadcast nothing but an empty path. With the camera taken care of, I turned my attention to the other mechanism but couldn't get a good read of it. We would need to investigate closer.

'Alright, we should be good to keep going. There is a camera ahead, but I've taken it out. There is something else up there as well, but I can't get a good read on it, so we need to be careful,' I said. Megan gave a thoughtful nod and continued along the path, the others following close behind, trying to avoid the grippy mud that sucked at their shoes.

As we rounded the corner, I sent out a ping to identify the exact location of the mechanism. 'Here,' I said, walking past Megan to the far cliff face. I lifted my hand and placed it on the wall. It was cold and rough to the touch, and a faint electrical hum tingled my skin. I let my hand drift over the surface towards the tug of electricity, following the pull of intensifying pulses. When my hand moved over a smooth part of the rock face, I felt what I can only describe as a screaming electrical buzz. When I moved my hand away, the hum faded, but returned as soon as I put my hand back. I carefully inspected the area until I found a latch hidden below a small rock protruding from the wall. I flicked the latch, and a small rectangle of the smooth rock surface popped open on a hinge. It was so well camouflaged that it had been impossible to discern it from the rest of the natural rock surface. The craftsmanship to accomplish such a thing was impressive. I pushed it open and revealed a red and a green button. When I turned back to the others to get their opinion on what to do, they were just staring at me, mesmerised.

'Told you your powers were handy. The original path on the map would have led us to the other side of these cliffs. So, maybe this is a back entrance to whatever this is? Or an escape route,' said Megan, looking at the map she carried.

'Well, I've got two buttons here. Red and green,' I said.

'Open and close?' asked Peter.

'That's my guess. I can't feel anything else beyond it, not even a sensor or camera. What do you reckon? Want me to hit the green?'

'Well, we're not going to achieve anything standing out here,' said Peter.

'Do it,' said Lilli with a certainty that surprised me. She had been so quiet that her input shocked me. 'Let's get this done.' Her drive to find a resolution to all this was palpable. I couldn't blame her either. In that moment, I would have given anything to be back in our normal lives where Sam was safe, rather than stomping around in the Wastes, but I couldn't deny I loved the excitement.

Megan gave an encouraging nod, and I hit the button. A rumble sounded from inside the wall, then a section on our right shifted and retracted sideways into the cliff face. It rolled along a small track embedded into the ground. Someone had gone to a lot of effort to make this place. I couldn't even fathom the resources needed to build it. The wall opened before us, revealing the start of a dark steel hallway hidden behind the rocky facade. I took a breath, then stepped across the threshold. Lights slowly turned on along the length of the hallway, illuminating a long tunnel with another doorway at the far end. I sent another sensing ping outwards and picked up a couple of cameras and an alarm in the hallway. I quickly manipulated the cameras and placed a small bit of code in the alarm that made it delete any trip alerts. My instinctive efforts even surprised me.

We began moving tentatively up the hallway. The loud of our echoing footsteps reverberating along the metal surface sent a nervous tingle down my spine. We pushed on and with nothing but hope and curiosity driving us forward; we entered the unknown base.

19

Base

THE METAL TUNNEL ENDED at a sealed door. The nullified camera was perched on the wall above the door, its power light blinking at us.

'You sure that thing isn't working?' asked Peter, following my gaze towards the camera.

'Yeah. I left it running so any diagnostics would see that it's functioning, but the input data is on loop. All they see is an empty hall. I'm not sure about this lock though,' I said, indicating a data scanner and keypad next to the sealed door in front of us.

'Can you do anything about it?' asked Megan.

'I can try,' I said. 'This is going to sound stupid, but do you think I can have a food pouch while trying? I'm starving.'

'Here Mum.' Sam passed me a small food pouch. I opened it and sucked in the slightly sweet, congealed liquid. Using my powers on and off throughout the day had sapped my energy. Apart from having a snack, I couldn't do anything about it, so with the pouch in my mouth, I set about trying to unlock the door.

I placed my hand next to the pad on the wall and let my senses open to it. I could feel the data paths running to the door's opening mechanism, as well as deeper into the building. With focus, I found a data path leading back to a server and blocked it. All I had to do was short the lock mechanism and it would open. Before I did that, though, I reached out to sense any cameras or alarms on the other side, but I felt nothing.

'Strange,' I said out loud.

'What's strange, Mum?'

'I can't sense anything past the door. There must be stuff in there, but I can't feel any of it.'

'Look at the wall and the door,' said Lilli.

'What?' I said, turning to her.

'Look what it's made of. The door and surrounding wall are a different metal to the rest of the tunnel,' she said. 'It's copper, which means—'

'It acts like an old school faraday cage!' Sam interrupted in an excited burst.

'Exactly!' said Lilli. 'You think your powers have something to do with electromagnetic waves and electricity, right? Well, this stuff won't let any of that through.' She was right. How had I missed the change in the metal along the hallway?

'I could follow the data cables of the camera on this side to figure out if there is one on the other side,' I said, 'but it might take time to work back through the internal system. If I don't manage it, I'll have to mitigate the cameras once the door is open, but I can't guarantee it will be fast enough to avoid someone spotting us.'

'We'll be fine,' said Peter. 'We don't have time to wait. It's risky loitering here, so what choice do we have?'

'Peter's right. We'll deal with whatever comes,' said Megan in a strong and comforting tone. She definitely had a way of making you feel like everything would work out because she had it all under control. 'Get your weapons ready, kids,' she said to Sam and Lilli.

'Done,' said Lilli, holding hers up and making a show of turning the safety off so it was ready for use. Sam wasn't as confident with the weapon, so just nodded and continued to point his weapon straight down by his side, his white-knuckled fist holding the grip tightly. He had kept it like that for most of our hike. I probably shouldn't have gone so hard on the gun safety lecture, as it seemed he had taken its seriousness a bit too much to heart. He looked so uncomfortable holding the gun.

'Alright then,' said Megan, 'do your thing, Rach.'

With the alert signal already blocked, I reached into the control pad and overrode the locking mechanism. The door unlocked in response, and with an acquiescent nod from everyone, I pulled the door open a crack with my gun at the ready, and peered in.

There was a camera opposite the door, so I quickly reached out and looped its data starting from before I opened the door. The hallway on the other side was silent, with brightly lit white passages leading off in three directions. The brightness hurt my eyes after being in the dim metal tunnel and I had to squint, but an idea popped into my mind.

I stuck my head back into the metal tunnel. 'Megan, pass me the comms pad for a sec. I have an idea that may or may not work.' She passed me the pad, and I got to work. Now that I could access the camera though the open door, I reached out to find its main data feed, and followed it back to where all the video feeds were stored. With a few tweaks, I directed a copy of all the data to our comm pad. The pad flashed and then showed numerous camera feeds we could cycle through. 'Live camera feeds straight to the pad. That should help us,' I said, handing it back to Megan.

'Brilliant,' said Megan. She began quickly cycling through every feed. 'There are guards around the place. I don't have a map of the layout, but we can slowly form one once we get in and start moving about.'

'Okay, great,' I said.

'We just want to know what's going on, don't we?' asked Lilli. 'So, maybe we could find the main server room and access their data. Find out what's going on and who is doing it, then get out?'

'Server room. Alright. I could find that. I like that plan,' I said. 'We get in, we get the information, then we get out. Then we'll have more time to figure out our next move once we have the information.'

'Can't argue with that,' said Peter.

'Alight then,' I said, pulling out my weapon. 'Stay close, stay quiet and, Megan, lead on.'

We carefully began our journey through the hallways. Megan used the live images on her comms pad to avoid cameras, which I appreciated as it meant I didn't need to expend any more energy messing with video feeds. When there was no other option, though, I would pause and loop the camera image of an empty hallway before we walked through the space.

As we moved, I let my power radiate out as a sensor again. Gently feeling through the cacophony of signals that traversed this place, I eventually locked onto the busiest and noisiest point, which had to be the server room. It was only a guess, of course, but it was all we had. I worked with Megan to lead us safely towards it. Luckily, the building seemed strangely quiet. The hallways were immaculately clean, with bright white walls and a glossy grey floor that reflected the bright glow of strip lighting stretching down its length. It took my eyes a while to adjust to the constant glare as we quickly slipped past various doors, labelled as storage cupboards and accommodation rooms.

I could feel the server room humming loudly not far off on our left somewhere. I relayed this to Megan, and we paused at the next junction. She cycled her pad to the video feed of the camera in the next hallway. When it flashed onto the screen, we saw two guards positioned outside a door, chatting with each other. We hadn't seen any other guards outside doors, so with the added security and the screaming electrical hum coming from its direction, all evidence told me it was the server room.

We backed ourselves away from the corner, a safe enough distance to make our plan of attack.

'Whatever we do, we need to be quiet,' I whispered. 'We're just here for information, remember? Maybe me and you, Megan, can get the jump on them somehow, then take them out.'

'I was thinking the same thing. But how do we get close enough to do that?'

'I could cut the lights? But then how do we see to get close enough?'

'Would these help?' asked Sam, opening the top of his bag and showing us inside. He had dark-vision goggles in there.

'Where did you get those?' I asked, reaching for the top one.

'There was a box under my chair in the e-vehic,' said Sam. 'I opened it up and found these, so I grabbed them. Thought they might come in handy.'

'Good job kid,' said Megan. 'Alright. So, you'll take out the lights, Rach?'

'Yep, then the two of us sneak down and take them out. Quietly.'

'Agreed,' said Megan.

'Why don't I get to sneak down and take them out?' asked Peter.

'I think we have this one sorted,' I stated. 'From what I remember, you were never the quietest during ops. It's not your fault, you're just not as lithe as others.'

'Ouch, Rach,' said Peter.

'Well, it's true, and we don't have the luxury of taking any chances.'

'What makes you think you're still up to it?' he said.

'Probably my twenty years as a movement and meditation coach.'

'Alright. Let's stop talking about this and just do it,' said Megan. 'Kids, you don't come down the hallway until we say it's clear. Peter, stay and keep them safe.'

We geared up with the goggles and crept back to the corner. I reached out and put the hallway's security camera on loop, then on Megan's signal I cut the lights. The hallway was instantly plummeted into darkness. I could hear the instant unease and urgent chatter of the guards. Not wasting any time, Megan and I peeled off to either side of the hallway and slid ourselves along the walls to our targets.

'Who's there?' yelled out one of the guards. 'Stop or we'll shoot.' I heard them ready their guns. When I looked, they were pointing their weapons straight at us. My heart skipped a beat and then it fell to my stomach as I noticed their faces. We hadn't counted on them having dark-vision goggles. We now had no other option than to attack. I swung my gun up and aimed at the guard closest to me. I let off a shot, then tumbled to the side. My acrobatics caused the guard's shot to miss, but my shot was accurate and hit the guard's hand that held the gun. They screamed in pain and dropped their weapon to the ground. The other guard let out a similar noise as a shot from Megan smashed into their lower left leg. Before the guard could process anything, though, Megan was up and charging at them, and I followed suit. I didn't want to hurt these guards, but I didn't want to risk the kids getting hurt. With a deft and practised twitch of my finger, I flicked my weapon to the stun setting and ran at the guard. Using my momentum, I dropped and slid feet first directly at the guard's legs. I crashed into their ankles, then quickly clasped my legs around their shins. I held tight and rolled sideways. The force pulled the guard off balance and they tumbled to the ground. I whipped my gun around towards them and let off two stun shots. As they fell to the ground, their body jerked uncontrollably, the sound of their gasps of pain filling the air before they lay completely still. I looked over and saw Megan tussling with the other guard. Without thinking, I aimed and let off another two stun shots. The angle was tight and there was a high chance I could have accidentally hit Megan, but the shots were true. The guard she was fighting began quaking before falling to the ground unconscious. Megan picked the gun out of the guard's hand as her breath came in fast, adrenaline-filled gasps.

'Thanks,' Megan said. I nodded, then jumped up and grabbed the other guard's gun. I took off the dark-vision goggles and indicated for Megan to do the same. Once they were off, I turned the lights back on. There were bright red splatter marks over the surrounding white walls, and blood continued to seep out of the guards' wrist wound. I didn't want them to bleed out or get an infection, so I rummaged in my pack, found my field med kit, and began applying a wound seal to the guard.

'What are you doing?' asked Megan.

'I don't want them to suffer. They're just guards. It's not their fault for any of this. Not ultimately anyway,' I said. Megan looked at me with a strange expression that I couldn't read. Possibly something between incoherence and awe. I ignored it and focused on patching up the guard.

Running footsteps sounded from the hallway ahead. I looked up towards the sound and didn't have any time to react as another guard popped around the corner into the hallway. My gun was in my holster and my hands were busy applying the wound seal. I was completely exposed. A crack sounded from the hallway behind us. A perfectly aimed stun dropped the guard like a puppet with its strings cut. I turned and looked behind me, and there was Lilli holding her gun just like we'd shown her. Peter was standing behind her. It looked like he had started reacting to the guard, but had only raised his weapon slightly in that time, unlike Lilli, who had acted immediately. Peter must be getting old.

With all three guards down, I waved the others to come down the hall. 'We need to get these guards out of sight,' I said.

'There's a storage cupboard here,' Megan said, opening a door behind her.

'Let's get them in there,' I said, grunting with effort as I started dragging the guard I had been patching up by their legs. They were heavy, and I wasn't making much progress, but then Sam appeared next to me and helped.

'Thanks Sam,' I said.

'You okay, Mum?' he asked. When I looked at him, his eyes were wider than normal, and stress poured off him.

'Yeah, I'm okay. Are you?' I asked.

'I'm fine. This guy is really heavy, though,' Sam said through a grunt of effort. Together, we slid the guard along the floor and hauled him into the storage cupboard. The two of us were puffing hard by the end. Somehow Megan moved a guard all on her own and did it with such ease that I started thinking I should learn more about how she keeps fit since my weekly sessions of weightlifting, running and stretching weren't giving me the same results. The stun used on the guards wouldn't last forever, but putting them in the cupboard would at least give us more time, so once Peter and Lilli had dragged the last one into the cupboard, we closed the door and sealed it, using my powers to fry the lock mechanism. Those poor guys would be in there for a while.

With that done, I went to check on Lilli. 'Are you okay?' I asked. 'That was an amazing shot. I couldn't have pulled that off my first time with a weapon in the field.'

'I managed to keep it on stun,' she said in a tone of panicked reassurance. 'I didn't spill any more blood.' She was shaking, so I pulled her in for a hug, then put my hands on her shoulders and looked directly at her.

'You were amazing. Who knows what could have happened to us if you didn't take that shot? That guard definitely didn't have their weapons on stun, so thank you,' I said. She nodded in response, then went back to Sam.

After cleaning up the scene of the encounter the best we could, apart from a few blood smears that were impossible to wipe away, I walked over to the server room door and reached through with my power to feel for security cameras on the other side. I looped the feeds of the cameras I found, then with my hand resting against the door, used my power to unlock it. There, behind the door, was the central information hub of the secret base.

The room was alive with racks filled with servers and closed metal boxes. Small green or yellow lights flashed to their own beat in the racks, lighting up the room in a strange pulsing glow. A quiet hum from data whirling through processors reverberated in the air, as a shiver ran down my spine from a blast of cooled air that stopped the servers from overheating. The sight of it all made a small ember of hope grow in my stomach. We would find answers here.

I walked over and sat at a tech-capsule nestled in the back corner. Staring at its blank screen, I felt a wave of hesitation wash over me. 'What should I look for?' I asked the others, as they crushed into the cramped space.

'Look for anything about us, I guess,' suggested Sam. 'We're here to find out why everything happened, aren't we? So, see if you can find any trail connected to us.'

'I don't think I know how to sort through data like that. I could maybe bypass the security features and any access restrictions, but in terms of searching for data, I have no idea where to even start,' I admitted.

'Let me do it, Mum,' said Sam. 'You do remember what I study at university, right? This is my thing,' he said in an upbeat, reassuring voice while ushering me out of the chair. 'You just take care of those security features you mentioned, then I've got the rest.' Sam tapped on the capsule's attached data entry pad. 'First hurdle, Mum, help me log in. Preferably with full admin access if possible, and without alerting anyone to the session. You'll need to block session logging, so no one knows we're here.'

'That's a lot, Sam,' I said as my thumb absentmindedly scratched at the fabric of Old Blue. 'I'll do my best.'

Without thinking, I started to sit down on the ground. 'Oh, sorry Mum!' exclaimed Sam as he jumped out of the seat and moved it against the wall on the side of the capsule. 'You should have this chair. I can just stand and use the tech-cap.' Part of me hated he was treating me like an old woman, but I was incredibly sore and tired, and it would be better than sitting on the floor. I swallowed my disdain at being treated as old and sat in the chair.

'Thanks Sam. Alright. Let's see what I can do.' I reached out with my electro-sense and could feel the flow of data and electricity around the room. It was everywhere. This room was alive with electrical currents and data paths. It was overwhelming and started to make my head ache. I closed my eyes and forced myself to stop and focus, then pulled my attention away from the room and instead homed in on the tech-capsule. I isolated the data path that validated login details and followed it. As I rushed along the path, I found an attached alert system designed to flag when someone was working at the tech-capsule and kick off a session log, just as Sam had predicted. I blocked the data to both functions and reconfigured the system into auto-deleting any alerts or logging details. Once I had stopped the alerts, I set about finding the operating functions and forced the tech-capsule to start up in administrator mode. I opened my eyes and released my connection to the strange world of electrical signals as I turned to Sam. 'That should've worked. Have at it,' I said.

Sam started tapping away on the data entry pad, but I was too tired to watch. Instead, I followed through with my original plan of resting. My head drooped back against the cold, smooth wall as I closed my eyes. I was exhausted.

The endless black was comforting, and I let it take me. In the darkness, small streams of golden light began floating past me. First, it would just flit by, but slowly the streams became stronger and longer. They converged and entwined until I saw things in the streams. The faint ghostly outline of a rectangle appeared and became stronger as the lights swirled together, forming the picture of a document. The image rushed towards my face, halting abruptly when the words were close enough to read. Scanning through the words, I saw it was an official contract, an agreement for the Master to provide La Panta with an advanced artificial intelligence system called OmniAI. I looked for a date and found the agreement was from four months ago and had been signed by Maxim Closman. As I watched, the date changed and showed a contract date from five years ago, then it changed again, and again, at a rapid rate. Dates and contracts between the Master and the La Panta family flashed before me, showing a decades-long history of working together. As I scanned through other related documents, I started to form a picture, one of a company that has been paying exorbitant amounts to the

Master in exchange for AI. The recently provided OmniAI appeared to be the most sophisticated and broad-reaching one yet. It was a system that enabled the company to collate and absorb information from everywhere, effectively enabling La Panta to monitor the transactions of everyone on Tir-na. It also provided access to every competitor's private information, with the AI promising to break through any security systems without a trace. This type of information would ensure La Panta trade dominance. It was industrial espionage on a grand scale. Unfortunately, I didn't find myself surprised by it. If anything, it helped explain how La Panta had stayed ahead of its competitors and grown so big. What did stand out was the way the Master signed all the contracts. He signed his name with extreme flourish, but next to his signature was a small circle with a line horizontally through it. I had seen something similar when looking at a focal measure through imagery goggles, but I couldn't figure out why a symbol like that would accompany the Master's signature.

The image of the documents suddenly changed and morphed into a written communication dated from last week. It was sent from the Master to Serena Fabrica, our old friend and head of Client Management at La Panta. Since we had to follow Sam to the Grove, it wasn't surprising the two of them were somehow linked, but I was intrigued by what they discussed.

My dearest Serena,

I hope this finds you well. I'm sure by now you are across our required commodity, but I wanted to confirm some logistics. Rooms are now ready at the Palace to house our guest before further transport to the site, but first, I need the commodity here. Be a darl and make sure my expected guest arrives promptly. I'm sure you understand the pressures I'm under, so the sooner our guest arrives, the better.

As mentioned, the method of collection is completely up to you. Maybe that man you baby-sit can be put to some use? I will leave it to your discretion. Just remember, we need the commodity relatively un-harmed, as this package is our ticket to the real prize. Of course, I will be reporting on all your wonderful work, and I'm sure our enduring partnership can continue to be one of cooperation and prosperity.

Make sure you visit again soon! Some of the dust storms are particu-larly lovely this time of year and I'd love to show you them next week. Also, tell your friend his space is finally complete and has really come up a treat. Not long now and he can come and play.

See you soon!
Master ☉

It was the evidence we needed. Although veiled in the Master's flowery lan-guage, it wasn't hard to interpret the 'commodity' as Sam, then myself as 'the real prize'. What did concern me was the mention of a space being ready for 'Serena's friend' to come and 'play'. Something about that made my skin crawl. And there was that symbol again next to the Master's name. Maybe he just liked it. He was a very flamboyant man, but I couldn't shake the feeling there was more to it. From what I knew, the Master was a very precise, put together man. Things with him always happened for a reason. The communication was dated from early last week, so Serena should be looking at 'dust storms' right now.

I opened my eyes, hoping I had just fallen asleep and been dreaming. But as I came back to my senses, I heard Sam speaking, reciting the same communication to everyone that I had read. I hadn't been dreaming. My powers were obviously changing, and it scared me.

Hunger gnawed at me, so I pulled out another snack ration from my pack and munched on it while everyone finished reading. The salty flavour of the snack helped soothe my insides as it slid down to my belly, its energy rejuvenating my muscles, and slowly bringing my mind back into focus.

'What's OmniAI?' I heard Lilli ask.

'It's a myth,' said Sam. 'Or at least I thought it was. I learnt about it at uni. OmniAI is a hypothetical AI system that computes and gathers information using swarm quantum computing. It uses any server, anywhere, for its processing power, and uses attack vectors to access and collect information from any source or target. It literally hijacks other servers to use for its own bidding. Once it reaches into a server, it drops a bit of code that gets the server to work for OmniAI. Effectively, it's like a virus, or a plague. It spreads and transforms everything it touches into its minion, but it does it with such stealth and ease that it is practically undetectable. The data it can collect, process and analyse is staggering. But it was always spoken of as a theoretical concept, one deemed too dangerous to create, as no one should have that much power. The lecturers literally used it as a hypothetical example of how programmers could go too far. The costs involved in setting it up and maintaining such a network would be staggering. No company could afford it.'

'Unless you are a huge conglomerate that owns everything, with apparent linkages to the only terraforming company on the planet.' The words slipped out in a harsher tone than I meant. I was tired, and the idea that there were companies playing some game for their own benefit that somehow involved capturing my son really pissed me off.

'So, what are we looking at here? The Master has been providing La Panta with advanced AI for decades, and it looks like it is about to be upgraded to this OmniAI?' stated Megan.

'That's what I think this shows,' said Sam.

'And then the communication has the Master asking La Panta to bring the commodity to him at the Palace,' continued Megan as she paced in the tiny room, lost in thought. 'Then they mention dust storms and play spaces.' She stopped and spun around to look at me. 'You followed La Panta to the Grove, didn't you, Rach?'

'Yeah,' I answered. 'We literally followed a La Panta transport that was carrying Sam from their HQ to the Grove.'

'Could the dust storms and the play space be referring to whatever this place is? Like where we are now?' asked Lilli. 'We are in the middle of the Wastes in some random building. Who knows what's in this place?'

'I think you're right Lilli,' I said. 'Those veiled references meant they were going to bring you here regardless, Sam, but there is still something that doesn't sit right. This is all looking a lot bigger and messier than I thought.' I stood up and looked at Sam. 'I think coming here might have been a huge mistake. We should leave.'

I exchanged a look with Megan. I could see the pieces trying to fit together in her mind as a furrow of concern slowly deepened across her brow. 'You're right. We should go,' said Megan. 'Come on, kids. Let's head back the way we came calmly and quietly. We should be fine if we just follow the same path back out again.' We all stood up, gathered our things and headed back out through the door, following Peter into the quiet hallway.

20

Confrontation

THE HALLWAY WAS STRANGELY silent, and the cold glow from the strip lights bounced off the sterile white walls and sent an uneasy shiver down my spine. I reached out with my powers and confirmed all the cameras along our path remained on loop. There were still no sounds from the guards enclosed in the storage cupboard, so at least we had some time until they drew attention to our location. Our group followed Peter up the hallway. His body looked tense as he held his gun at the ready and moved along the lifeless corridor. When we reached the end, he paused at the corner to check the way was clear, then with a nod of confirmation, led us down the next hallway. My nerves were tingling down my back. Something was wrong. I looked at Megan. Her hand was too tight around the grip of her weapon. Obviously, I wasn't the only one worried.

We continued along, following Peter back through the labyrinth of hallways. We passed a numbered doorway that set off an alarm in my mind. I didn't remember seeing that number before. I reached out with my power and sensed that the cameras in this section weren't ones I had already put on loop. We were going the wrong way.

'Peter!' I whispered. 'This isn't the right way. We need to go back.' Peter just kept moving, not having heard me, but Megan had heard. She pulled out the comms pad and found the map she had pieced together on the way in. A deep line of concern formed between her brows.

'Peter, stop!' she said while pulling up the live camera feeds. 'This isn't the right way.' Sam and Lilli jolted to a halt and turned to face us. 'The cameras ahead are live. We need to go back.'

We started turning to race back the way we came, but Peter kept going, encouraging us to follow. 'No, this is definitely the way. I remember,' he declared in a strained, overly confident tone.

'Peter! Get back here now!' Megan snapped, but he kept moving forwards. My nerves fired stronger than before. I moved to Sam and Lilli and started ushering them back the way we came. Peter just kept walking forward.

Multiple doors around us swished open, their collective sound like a beast sighing. Guards flooded the hallway, in front and behind us. I whipped out my weapon and pulled Sam and Lilli closer to me, manoeuvring so I was between them and the guards in front. I saw Megan spin around to cover Sam and Lilli from the rear and face the guards behind us. We were completely surrounded, with no obvious way to escape. Over the shoulders of the guards, I saw Peter stop moving and turn to look back at me. He stared at me, his face contorting with a look of pained shame. But he didn't move. He didn't even raise his weapon at the guards. My stomach dropped.

The door next to Peter opened and echoing footsteps spilled into the hallway. Every clack of a shoe against the harsh, pristine floor spiked nerves through my body. The Master and Serena Fabrica walked through the door. They ignored Peter and instead turned to look at the four of us. The Master's mouth twisted into a deep smile.

'Ah, my friends, you found your way here. Thank goodness! I was so worried about you. I'm assured you know my friend Serena,' The Master said gesturing to the weedy figure of Serena. Her hair was free of the tight bun, and instead she looked wild, reminding me of a crazed beast from the Wastes, and I noticed a burn line around her wrist poking out from the cuff of her tailored blouse.

I held my weapon taut and ready to fire. 'What is this?' I demanded, my gaze flicking from the Master to Peter, who was standing behind them, dedicatedly staring at the ground.

'My dear Rachel. You really are quite the hot property around town, aren't you?' said the Master. 'Oh, how cute! Look at that brow furrow. I think we've genuinely confused her. Isn't it adorable, Serena?'

'I thought you told me she was the best agent of her time,' sneered Serena. 'It's a bit of an indictment on the Agency, if it's true.'

'Now, now. No need to be rude. She's just a bit puzzled. Understandable when your trusted ally reveals their true self, and our tentacles finally wrap themselves around you in their entirety,' said the Master, his perfectly manicured hand curling in a flourish to emphasise the point. He cocked his head to the side, his eyes sliding over my skin as he examined me. 'You really didn't suspect a thing, did you?'

I kept my mouth shut in response. In truth, I was only half listening. My mind was too busy racing as I desperately tried to find a way to get Sam and Lilli out.

'How perfect!' continued the Master. 'I love a surprise, don't you? Peter really is a perfect and loyal agent, isn't he?' His unnerving words finally cut through and pulled my attention to him. 'He was so helpful in giving those powers of yours a kickstart. Stress was the easiest way to spark those bio-electromagnetic chips Miles put in you, and what better way than by taking your only son? Oh, and the few little drone bot attacks I threw in there to spice things up! I do love those little drones. You see, your dear Miles was a smart boy. Left a failsafe that wiped all his records if anything happened to him, so all that was left of his research were shattered data fragments of test dates, and even those took over ten years to piece together. Then we realised: instead of piecing his research back together, we needed to look at his test subject and reverse engineer what he did to you. That's where my dear friend came into it. Didn't you, Vivian?' said the Master, turning to the door he had walked through.

The squat figure of Vivian Wyrmstead entered the hallway. Her perfectly sculpted short hair complemented the crisp cut of her tailored suit and shined shoes, in an annoyingly clean and polished way. I felt the weight of the dirt and grime all over Old Blue at the sight of her crafted perfection. My heart sank. I didn't like Vivian, but I had hoped for better from her. The enormous implications of her being here spun out before me, and my mind churned with information and connections.

'Well, when you come to me with a simple request and an offer I couldn't refuse, I just couldn't say no. And I am forever grateful for your help, Grand Master. I wouldn't be where I am today without it,' Vivian said with a slight bow.

'You have been useful, Vivian, but you still have a way to go to gain admission. Keep providing us fun like we're having on this little adventure, and I'm sure we can progress your admittance.'

'Yes, Grand Master,' said Vivian, bowing her head in deference. Terrible strings started connecting in my mind between my past and all the players before me, with everything leading back to Miles.

I looked at Peter. He was my oldest and only real friend from my time at the Agency, but now he just stood there looking at me, the wrinkles of his face pulled taut. At least he had the guts to look at me now. I reflected on the last couple of days and realised he had been relatively quiet. Not as quick with a funny line or his jovial mocking. I should have noticed it. I'm sure I would have when I was younger. Maybe I had been too long out of this world to notice such minor details, but I should have remembered to always take note of the little things, because often they can mean everything. I pulled Sam closer to me in response to my thoughts.

The Master noticed where I was looking and turned to follow my gaze. 'Ah! Peter. I must say thank you again, as we couldn't have done this without you.'

'You're right Grand Master,' agreed Vivian. 'Peter is a loyal and dedicated agent, and it was only through his close knowledge of the subject and his extensive skills that we were able to bring you not one, but two subjects.' An audible hiss escaped Megan's lips, and I noticed her take a small step closer to the kids. 'One of which I am told is already reporting signs of powers being activated by the stress response.'

'Magnificent. Thank you, Peter. Your service won't be forgotten,' said the Master as he unconsciously wracked his fingers back through his oily, limp hair. I just stared at Peter. How could he betray me and put my own son at risk? Rage flooded my system, and I hoped he burned with the hatred in my glare. Peter visibly recoiled and directed his eyes back to the ground. His face twisted in a manner I had never seen before, but I didn't care what he felt. I hoped it was shame. He had led us straight to this, and I had followed like a stupid beast of burden. If he died right then, I wouldn't have cared.

'Yes, it was a wonderful plan, Vivian.' He looked at Vivian, who stood with a tight, proud smile on her face. 'I will ensure I report that you came up with it, except of course the part with Miles coming back. That was all me. I love a good bit of drama and I just couldn't resist throwing in a real curve ball to really kick that stress response into overdrive. A twist in the second act. Yes, that's the way it should be. Did you really think Miles had come back? You don't have to answer that. I saw your face at the Palace. It was magnificent!' The Master laughed with delight. 'You know, you only have yourself to blame. Miles was happy here working for us, until he decided to run off, leaving us quite upset. We brought him here to conduct his experiments, but then he betrayed us. Something about him not liking our method of acquiring test subjects. That's why, when we heard he was hiding away with the Agency, brazenly continuing his work without us, well, he just had to go. We had an agreement. It was our tech, our proprietary information, and he gave it away. That was against his contract. I admit, I might have been a bit overzealous and probably shouldn't have had him killed right away, but I was angry. Luckily, his experiments worked on you, and now we have our second chance. So, welcome, Rachel and Sam, to our humble base, of which you are both now honoured guests. I hope your stay here with us will be...enlightening.'

I was ablaze with anger. A shimmering spark tickled under my skin. I felt ready to explode. 'Now,' I whispered to Megan, then I ripped away the electrical connections from all the lighting in the hallway. I grabbed Sam and pulled us down, as Megan did the same to Lilli. I slid on my dark-vision goggles, readied my weapon and turned to face the sea of frenzied movement coming towards us.

'Run the first chance you get!' I told Sam, then launched myself at a guard who had put on dark-vision goggles and was aiming their weapon at us. I smashed into their arms, sending the shots wide, then pulled them down to the ground and released my anger in one unhinged punch. Their nose cracked from the impact and sprayed my face with a warm liquid. I rolled off and shot them without a thought.

The emergency base lighting suddenly kicked in, blinding me through the goggles. I pulled them off and found the hallway bathed in a sickly orange light. A wave of three guards rushed towards me, guns at the ready. I tumbled sideways and with a deep exhale of breath, shot each of them in the neck. It wasn't pretty, but it immobilised them instantly. They hit the ground, exposing two more guards behind them. They could have instantly shot me, but they didn't fire. I realised they needed me alive, but the others may not have that luxury.

There were sounds of fighting behind me. I turned and saw Megan locked in her own battle with a guard and Lilli right behind her, their backs exposed to the two guards racing towards me. 'Sam, go!' I yelled, then charged at the guards, letting out my fury in a scream that successfully drew their attention away from the others.

A huge weight suddenly tackled me from the side, smashing me painfully into the ground and sending my weapon skittering across the floor. I rolled out from under the hulking weight of the guard, then dived on top to pin him to the ground. With as much strength as I could muster, I smashed my fist into his face, then violently yanked back his wrist, holding his weapon. The uncomfortable pressure released his hand just enough for the weapon to fall to the ground. Then I unleashed my fury on him. I rained down punches. The guard managed to get a few retaliatory powerful hits on me, but his moves were scrappy, and I was more calculated with my attacks, keeping control of the fight.

I chanced a brief look at the others. Sam was in his own battle against a guard. His technique wasn't bad. Maybe some of those basic drills I taught him as a child had actually stuck. Another guard ran towards Sam. He was doing okay against one, but I wasn't sure he could hold off two.

A flash of movement from near Megan caught my attention, and a shot rang out. The guard running towards Sam tumbled to the ground. I looked over and saw Lilli standing there holding her gun and aiming just how I taught her. Then she fired again and took out the guard attacking Sam. She moved her aim once more, but this time pointed it straight at the Master. A crack rung out from the other end of the hallway and Lilli collapsed to the ground. I looked up the hallway and saw Vivian holding a weapon aimed at the fallen figure of Lilli. A pained wail escaped from Sam as another guard grabbed him from behind. Peter rushed past me and tackled Megan to the ground. He pinned her to the ground and pointed his gun at her head.

'STOP!' rang the Master's voice. I let my concentration slip for a moment and the guard I was wrestling with punched me in the side of the head, sending me careening off balance and tumbling to the ground. The guard picked up his gun and aimed it at me. My head was pounding, but I could see through the pain that I was outmanoeuvred, and Megan and Sam were captured. My rage flared. I couldn't see any way out of this. This stupid quest to chase the truth had doomed us all. I turned and looked at Lilli. Her eyes were fixed, and blood trickled out of the corner of her mouth. She was so young! I choked on a thick sob, then looked over at Sam. He was a mess. Frenzied tears fell from his face as he tried to fight and claw his way out of the guard's vice-like grip and towards her body. Sam landed a solid blow that knocked the guard backwards, leaving him free of the guard's grasp. He flung himself over to Lilli and desperately held onto her. The guard was quickly back on Sam and pulled him away from her body. Sam didn't fight it this time. All of his spark had left him when he had confirmed the horrible truth. Lilli was dead. I went numb with the realisation, and all the fight drained out of me.

'Take them to the lab,' commanded the Master, pointing at myself and Sam. My weight shifted suddenly as I was pulled to my feet and ushered down the hallway, my arms pinned behind me by the escorting guards. I looked for Sam and saw he was being dragged the same direction as me, but his body was limp, and his eyes stared at the unmoving body of Lilli.

'What about this one?' asked Peter, indicating Megan, who he still had pinned to the ground with a gun against her head.

'We have no need for her. Take her away and dispose of her,' said the Master. 'Just stop getting blood all over the place.'

Peter heaved Megan to her feet. He opened one of the hallway doors and dragged her inside with him. The door sharply closed, then there was a loud crack and the sound of something heavy crumpling to the ground. A sound unsettlingly like the hollow thump Lilli's body had made when she fell.

My heart shattered. The guards dragged me forwards, their hands pinching my skin roughly and the point of a weapon stabbing into my back. I tested their grasp by shifting my weight, but they held firm. I couldn't escape. All hope started slipping away, and instead I only felt darkness. When we got close to Vivian and the Master, that darkness rose inside me in a violent wave. I ripped myself free of the guards and launched myself at Vivian. I wanted to grab hold of her throat and squeeze the life out of her. Adrenaline and rage coursed through my body, and my internal spark flared in response. I could feel everything on her with an electrical component, and I willed them to release in hopes that her own devices would fry her. Vivian yelped, but then something heavy smashed into my head. I remember falling sideways, but nothing more.

21

Lab Rats

A LIGHT SHONE ACROSS my eyelids, turning my world from black nothingness to a strange brown and red glow. A throb sparked painfully through my head, and a faint rhythmic beep came from somewhere nearby. My skin was chilled, and it tingled as flicks of cool air swept across my exposed arms. I was wearing a hospital gown, and I vaguely wondered what had happened to Old Blue as I carefully opened my eyes to let in a sliver of light. There was a lamp positioned directly over me, and the brightness from the bulb stung my eyes, causing them to water. I blinked through the pain, hoping my pupils would adjust quickly. I turned my head away from the light, but the movement was restrained. A strap pressed down against my forehead, holding me in place. I tried moving the rest of my limbs, but they were tied down. My heart sank and a niggling panic bloomed in my stomach. I closed my eyes and took a moment to make sense of everything. Then it all came flooding back. The ambush, Peter doing nothing, Lilli's death, Megan being shot and Sam being taken away.

My eyes flew open. 'Sam!' my rough voice choked out. I frantically peered through the light, trying to make sense of the room around me, desperately searching for another figure in the dark. The rest of the room was saturated in darkness, like an impossibly inky veil had been draped over it. I reached within myself to that strange blue flickering spark inside, and gently sent it out in a wave all around me, hoping it would unveil what was hidden in the dark. All I could sense were battery-powered lights and some sort of medical monitoring machine, but nothing more. Not even anything outside of the room, as my senses seemed to stop at the walls. A tightness spread across my chest. There was something too structured about where my power stopped.

'Ah! Finally. You're awake,' said a familiar voice as the spindly figure of Serena stepped out of the shadows. 'You've been out for quite a while, and we need you awake so the good doctor here can get to work. I believe you remember Velor, don't you? Graduated medical school only last year. He's really very talented, but you could say his skills are...niche.'

Velor slowly stepped into the light, the same skin mask stretched across his face. There was a new patch on it though, a tightly stretched rectangle strip of skin that was the same colour as Peter's. The sight, mixed with the rotting flesh and formaldehyde stench, made my stomach churn. Stuck as I was, I didn't want to vomit on myself, so I swallowed down the burning bile that was threatening to escape my lips.

'Hello again,' his raspy deep voice uttered through the mouth slit of his stretched skin mask. 'I'm Doctor Closman, and together, we're going to figure out why you are the way you are.' He moved out of my line of vision, and I tried to turn my head to follow him, but my view was restricted by the strap across my forehead. Metal clanged and scraped together, setting my nerves on fire as my imagination started picturing horrid instruments of torture. He reappeared holding a large needle. 'Do you have any question before we begin?'

'Where the is my son, you piece of sh—' Velor roughly stretched a gag over my mouth, cutting off my words.

'No questions? Good, let us proceed. This will hurt a bit.' A sharp pain shot up my right arm from the crook of my elbow. I tried to look at what he was doing, but all I could see was the top of the syringe and my own blood filling the attached tube.

The needle slid back out of my arm with a sharp sting. 'All done,' Velor said, sounding happy with himself. 'I'm going to run a full blood screen with this, but I also want to conduct a few more tests to ensure we are thorough in our data collection. All of them, of course, will require more samples, and some will hurt. So, settle in, because this may take a while.'

I pulled against my restraints in vain, then reached out again with my power to latch onto something. But there was nothing. There was no hope. Velor appeared with a large nasal swab. 'Hold still,' he said. 'This will tickle.' My eyes watered as he inserted the swab deep into my nose cavity and spun it around. It felt like it was almost touching my brain. I stayed completely still, scared of what he would bump if I moved. 'This will provide me some cells to analyse and also test for traces of viruses or microbes that could be linked to this power of yours.' He pulled the swab out, scratching the full length of my nose, and placed it in a collection bag.

'Alright. Next up, skin sample. My favourite one,' he said with a chilling smile in his voice. 'Serena, scalpel please, if you will.'

Serena emerged from the darkness holding a small silver tray with various sharp tools and collection jars on it. She stood, holding it perfectly still as if it was a well-practised occurrence. Velor drifted his hand over the top of the tools on offer before choosing a small scalpel. He held it up and assessed its sharp lines.

'Thank you, Serena, this will do nicely,' he said, content with his choice. He stood back in front of me with the small scalpel in his hand, holding it gently with an almost loving caress. Without meaning to, I tensed and pulled against my restraints. 'Don't worry, I won't take anything off your pretty face like I did to Peter.' His hand stroked my cheek before drifting lower. His hand continued downward along my neck and collarbone, sending repulsive shivers down my spine, until he finally paused on my upper right arm. He gently stroked the skin on my arm, prodding and examining its texture with careful thought. 'This skin will be just fine. Now, this will hurt, but try to stay still. I'll be as gentle as I can.' He raised the scalpel and sliced deeply into my skin. The pain was strangely contained and sharp at first, but then morphed into a fierce, cold burning that screamed through my body as he continued slicing. He made the same rectangular shape as the cut on Peter's forehead. My body trembled with pain. I desperately tried to retreat to the depths of my mind, but the searing cuts kept pulling me back as clammy sweat dripped across my head and neck. Then the scalpel pressed deeper into my skin at the corner of the rectangle. I screamed as Velor slid the scalpel underneath and began cutting the rectangle away from my arm. My brain was on fire and couldn't focus on anything except the all-consuming pain that battered me. The pain went on for an eternity, then I felt him peel the skin off. Bright stars of pain burst in front of my eyes and a muffled, prolonged scream escaped my lips. I reached for my internal blue spark to focus on, but found nothing. There was only pain and an encroaching pulsing darkness, so I let the darkness take me.

I woke with a start and inhaled a giant breath. My heart was racing, and my nerves fired, ready to do something...anything. Velor was standing over me, a large needle in hand.

'Sorry Rachel, I need you awake for the tests, so no passing out. Otherwise, I have to keep doing this,' he said, showing me an empty adrenaline shot, 'and that's not very fun or sustainable.' The air felt too thick as my lungs struggled to breathe. My whole body was buzzing, but I had no outlet for it. A tightness gripped hold of my chest as panic settled over me. 'Don't worry though, the effects will pass soon. But until then, you may be a bit uncomfortable. You'll be happy to know that I'll be using anaesthetic for the rest of the tests. I promised everyone I would look after you, and I will, but I couldn't resist adding you to my collection. I have a perfect spot up here just waiting for you.' He stroked his horrid flapping mask tenderly and indicated an area under the right eye where the skin was starting to shrivel. 'This area needs some reinforcement. You can help strengthen up the remnants of what was my first patient. They've become quite weak over time.' Bile rose up in my throat. It was all too much. I wanted to pass out, but my body wouldn't let me as it buzzed on the adrenaline.

The next few hours passed in a horrid blur. Velor conducted test after test, collecting as many samples as he could by poking, prodding and cutting into me. There were vaginal swabs, cheek DNA swabs and bone marrow extraction to retrieve stem cells. The most disconcerting was when Velor insisted on undertaking an egg retrieval procedure that involved a needle being inserted through the vagina and into a follicle to remove what must have been one of my last few eggs. At least Velor was true to his word and used anaesthesia throughout it all. It made the whole thing less painful, but I was left with a horrible, disturbed feeling as I knew something terrible was happening, but since I couldn't feel it, my mind filled the gap with phantom pains.

Sometimes Velor and Serena, who had been a much too enthusiastic observer of Velor's work, would leave for long periods of time, replaced instead by a blank-faced guard dressed in very expensive black body armour. A small part of me was jealous of the guard's kit, but mostly I just wanted to forget about everything and go to sleep. With my eyes closed, I reached internally and found the hovering blue spark. It was weak and slowly dimming, so I gently caressed it and once again sent it out to find anything it could connect to, but there was still nothing. The metal mesh lining the room prevented it from going any further, and Velor had taken care to only use non-electrical equipment. Even the guard had only brought in a low-tech weapon with no electrics, and they must have left all their comms outside. The only thing I could sense was the localised battery of the bright light above me that made my eyes water every time I opened them. I flicked the spark towards it and once I had a connection, I ever so subtly reduced its capacity, causing it to dim just enough so the light was more comfortable on my eyes, but not enough for the guard to notice. It was a small victory, and I happily owned it.

The door to the room opened and I craned my head to see what was happening. A horrid cyclical squeaking sound filled the room as Velor wheeled in a bed like the one I was strapped to. He wheeled it in front of me, and unstrapped the band across my forehead so I had a clear view, and there, strapped to the bed, was Sam. His eyes were wide with fear and a red rectangular strip across his forehead oozed just like Peter's had, and just like mine was.

'As you can see, I've added your lovely son here to my collection. I've never had a family pair before. It will create such beautiful symmetry,' Velor said, tenderly stroking his horrid mask. I pulled against my restraints, but they didn't budge. My muscles screamed at the effort, nerves firing wildly as they fatigued from immobilisation.

Serena entered carrying a silver tray with a tool perfectly positioned in its centre and placed it next to Sam. A tool I unfortunately recognised too well. 'There are a few tests I want to run with the two of you here. I hope that's alright,' said Velor. He reached for the tray and tenderly picked up the intel-wrench and examined different spots on Sam as though he was deciding where to begin. I reached out with my power to the intel-wrench, hoping to do something, but they had done something to the wrench and adapted it somehow, as I couldn't feel any buzz of electricity running through it.

'This will hurt a bit,' said Velor before flicking the switch to activate the intel-wrench and placing it against Sam's neck. A sudden blast of electricity pulsed from the wrench straight into Sam. His body twitched and shuddered in response, his face contorting in a grimace of pain. Blue crackling waves of electricity sparked across his body. I screamed and instinctively reached for Sam with everything I had in me. I needed to get to him. The wrench and lights in the room suddenly exploded, sending shattering sparks over Serena and Velor. Darkness enveloped the room, broken only by a small flickering flame from the tip of the destroyed wrench that Velor still clutched in his hand. The tiny blaze threw eerie red shadows across the room as I looked at Sam. His body was limp, but his eyes were blinking and shining in the faint wispy light, his chest rising and falling in great heaves. He was alive.

The electricity buzzed under my skin, crackling smoothly as it lay await-ing my command. Unfortunately, with the intel-wrench destroyed, and the room's metal cage blocking all signals from outside, there was nothing elec-trical for me to connect to. With nowhere to go, the electrical tingling began to build in my hands and a strange blue glow lit up the room. I strained against my restraints to see where the light was coming from as my fingers burned with a buzzing feeling. I looked down and saw a sparking blue light bouncing across the surface of my hand, with small bolts arcing between my fingers. Velor and Serena stared at me intently, a hunger burning in their eyes.

'Well now, that is interesting,' said Velor with a smile. I flicked my hand towards him in a rage. He dodged the small bolt of electricity that flew through the air and slammed into the wall of the metal cage behind him. The bolt arced and spread across the surface of the cage, illuminating everything with a crackling glow. Tendrils of electricity reached outwards before snapping back to the cage walls. 'Very interesting indeed!' I could hear the excitement in Velor's voice, and I hated him for it. My insides felt bubbly as a heated pressure built around my neck.

Without a care for what could happen, I reached for the electricity and willed it towards that disgusting man.

A loud scraping thump came from across the room and the sparking electricity disappeared before I could launch it at my target. 'You were right, that did turn out to be a useful switch,' said Serena from the shadows by the entrance door.

'I told them, an earthing switch is always a good idea for a faraday cage.' Velor flicked on a new battery-powered lamp and walked over to a bench to retrieve a small spray bottle. 'I have so much data to process. Thank you for that. We'll leave you both now while we get some work done.' He used a small spray bottle to douse the flames of the tiny electrical fire flickering at the end of the intel-wrench. 'Your power has impressed me, and I look forward to seeing how much it can be stoked.' He turned and, with Serena by his side, left the room, leaving me and Sam strapped to the tables.

Sam was awake but exhausted, his eyes fixed solidly on something. I followed this gaze to my hand where small blue crackles of electricity were still sparking. My whole body felt alive, like a live wire. I needed to calm down and think. I closed my eyes, found my centre and cycled through some calming box breaths. My body settled in response, and regained control of my instincts. I looked down at my hand and watched as the small sparks dissipated until they were completely gone.

'How did you do that?' Sam's voice was hoarse but clear. 'I want to do that.'

'I don't really know.' My arms burned with dissipating energy that morphed into a blunt ache that spread through every limb. 'Your father could have told you the specifics of what he did long ago to create this power in me. It obviously reacts to stress since it only emerged after you were taken, and now it seems almost instinctual, but I'm still not sure what to do with it.'

'What does it feel like?'

I looked at him. His eyes were so keen, so focused, with a hunger for information. 'I guess it's like a fast buzzing. I imagine a blue crackling light that flares up and out through me that reacts to my will. Why do you ask?'

Sam looked down at his hand. Small, soft waves of blue light suddenly danced across his skin, gently flowing as Sam rolled his hand. 'For me, it's more like...like a vibrating wave.' He suddenly looked straight at me. 'Mum, what is going on? What is this?'

I couldn't speak. I couldn't feel the blue light wafting over Sam; it wasn't connected to me. It was coming completely from him. My stomach dropped with the realisation. What had I done to my son?

'Mum, how can I also have this?'

My mind was racing, but I found my voice through the fog of thoughts. 'The experiments. They altered my DNA. Your father experimented with splicing bio-electrochemical genetic material into live DNA, and he had a lot of success. When he came to the Agency, he was ready to begin human trials, and I volunteered. The experiment must have worked before you were conceived. Miles warned me about the change being irreversible and about its potential to be passed on to future generations. I had thought it was a failure though, so didn't even think. I'm so sorry Sam, I should have told you everything sooner. It was stupid to keep it from you.'

'Told me that my mum was a super spy with super powers? Yeah, you should have, and now because of it all, Lilli is dead!' Sam let his head flop back against the table as tears started streamed down his face. 'She's dead.'

Tears welled in my eyes. 'I'm so sorry, Sam.' A long silence fell between us as my mind started trying to grapple with the reality of our new world.

'Do they know?' I asked.

'What?'

'Do they know about your powers?'

'Yeah, they do. I only discovered them when I accidentally blew a light while they were experimenting on me.'

'They want to know how we ended up like this, how your father made me into whatever I am so they can replicate it.'

'Did Dad leave files or paperwork or something?'

'No. Like the Master said, he had a failsafe. Your father ensured that if anything happened to him, all his work was wiped. He thought the threat of the failsafe would keep him safe. They either didn't care about it, or forgot, because they killed him before they could get a copy of his files. That makes us the only remnants of his work. But I refuse to let us be their lab rats. We need to get out of here.'

I squirmed and wriggled, thrashing about as I desperately tried to break free, but nothing worked. We couldn't escape our restraints. Time started to slip by. Seconds becoming minutes, minutes becoming hours. It all blurred together as a feeling of hopelessness grew heavy in the pit of my stomach. We were trapped, and I couldn't find a way out.

The door to the room opened and Velor entered, dressed in a full-body rubber suit with just his flesh face mask showing. 'Time for another round. Those last results have me excited.' I saw his lips crinkle in a twisted smile through the gaping mouth hole in the mask. 'Let's see how the son here reacts to watching things happen to his mum.' Fear started ripping at my insides as Velor walked towards me holding a syringe filled with a white pearl opalescent liquid. I looked at Sam and tried to be stoic as Velor stuck the needle into my arm and pushed. As the liquid spread through my system, an undulating pain washed through me as though everything was on fire. Like the fibres of every muscle were being slowly torn apart. An involuntary scream left my mouth as pain clouded my vision, and my body shut down to nothingness.

My head throbbed. Everything throbbed. A painful pounding ache pulsed through my body as I worked to sift through the fog in my mind until one thought crystallised and pulled me back to myself. I needed to help Sam. My eyes flew open, and I searched desperately for him. I found him off to my right, still strapped to the table, but with his eyes closed and his head drooped to the side, the clear liquid oozing from his forehead towards his ear. I didn't know if he was alive or dead. A cold shiver washed over my body and my heart skipped a beat from panic.

'Sam!' I croaked. He stirred and opened his eyes. My lungs heaved out a breath as the cold shiver subsided into a numb tingle. He was alive.

'Mum! You're okay.' The relief in his voice was palpable. 'I wasn't sure you'd wake up again.'

'I'm here sweetie...I'm here. Are we alone?'

'Yes. How are we going to get out, Mum?'

233

The question made me pull against my restraints. I still couldn't make them budge. 'I don't know.' The words left me in a whisper. I barely wanted to hear them myself.

We both lay there, quietly dealing with our pain and fear. 'He did things to me, Mum,' said Sam into the silence. 'He wanted to see what would happen. To find out how I could make my power work. We need to get out, Mum.'

His voice quivered and was pulled so tight, I felt if I asked him what happened, he would break. My son needed me more than ever, and I was powerless. I couldn't do anything. He was the one important thing in my life, the one thing I desperately wanted to protect, and I couldn't do it. Tears slipped down my cheeks. 'I know, sweetie. But I don't know how.' My voice caught on the last word as a sob bubbled up in my throat. I couldn't let it out, though. I couldn't give into it. If I crumbled now, what would happen to Sam?

The lock on the door clicked and swung open. Two figures entered the room swiftly and closed the door behind them. My insides squirmed in response. I wasn't sure I could handle another round with Velor.

One of the figures rushed over to Sam and started doing something to his table, while the other approached me. Their face was hidden in the shadows of the room. Fear spiked in my belly, but as they came closer, I saw their face, and that fear turned to hatred. It was Peter.

He moved quickly and after a moment the restraints around my wrists fell away. I instinctually moved and stretched my hands, the joints cracking from the effort, then I glared at Peter.

'You don't need to give me that look, Rach. I know,' he said, while continuing to release the restraints. 'You can't say anything to me that I haven't already thought to myself. I'm a massive dick and I'm sorry. Now let's deal with that later and focus on getting you two out of here.'

I looked over and saw a woman with Sam. A woman with short spiky hair and a swooped fringe. My mind raced to understand what it was seeing because that woman was dead. Wasn't she? Megan worked quickly to release Sam and help him sit up. I looked back at Peter. Only a moment ago I couldn't see any way out, so I would be an idiot to refuse help when it came along. Part of me screamed that it could easily be a trap again. But whatever they offered had to be better than being a lab rat. And somehow Megan was alive! I couldn't process what it meant in that moment, but there was obviously more to unravel in the whole messed-up situation.

'Fine,' I said briskly. 'But I'll need your help standing up.' Peter helped me into a sitting position as my body started inadvertently shaking from the pain. Noticing it, Peter pulled out a canister I was all too familiar with.

'I know you've had a lot lately,' he said, indicating the adrenaline shot he held in his hand. 'But we need to get you guys out of here. We'll patch you up on the other side of it all.' I nodded, and he jabbed it into my arm. The sting made me flinch, but the desired effect was instantaneous, as the drugs pumped through my body, causing my heart to race. I looked over at Sam and saw Megan jab an adrenaline shot into him. Then, after Peter helped me to stand, I hobbled over to Sam on shaky but energised feet and embraced him in a tight hug.

'I love you,' I whispered.

'I love you too,' Sam said.

'Come on! There'll be time for that later,' commanded Peter, as he handed us our clothes and guns. Once dressed again, with Old Blue wrapped around me and a gun held tight in my hand, Peter led us to the door, and out into whatever came next.

22

Escape

I RAN OUT THE door on shaky legs and around the motionless body of a guard. Sam flinched at the sight, but didn't miss a beat as we continued our hurried hobbling. One whole side of the hallway was carved out of rock, which I didn't recognise. I didn't know where we were or where we were headed. All I could do was follow Peter and get as far away as possible from that terrible laboratory. A bubble of panic grew up in my chest at the thought of trusting Peter, but I had no other option.

As we ran, I looked around desperately for security cameras, worried we would be caught instantly if I didn't eliminate them. I spotted one further down the hallway, but its shape was strange. Once closer, I noticed it had something stuck to it; a small, round disk with an antenna poking off the top. I remembered those disks. They interrupted a camera's feed and piped in what you wanted it to see, like an empty hallway, instead of what was there. We used them all the time when I was at the Agency. They did exactly what I had done with my power, so why the hell hadn't we used them earlier? Unless they had wanted me to use my powers. I glared at the back of Peter's head as he led us swiftly onwards. I didn't trust him, but everything was confusing. I didn't understand what was going on, and it terrified me.

Peter paused at a corner and indicated for us to do the same. He poked his head carefully around the edge, then pulled back to the safety of cover. His free hand moved to a pouch on his belt and pulled out a small, rounded disk with an antenna, along with a thin laser pointer. After another quick check around the corner, he holstered his gun, stepped out into the hallway, and pointed the laser at something, before throwing the disk and pulling back around the corner. He pocketed the laser pointer, then checked something on his wrist-comm. He paused for a moment, then fluidly unholstered and charged his gun, spun around the corner and fired two shots. It all happened in the space of a couple of breaths. He nodded to us to continue following him, and we ran around the corner and into the next hallway. We passed the body of a guard who had taken one shot to the head and one to the chest. They would have been dead before they hit the floor. I had to admit; it was expertly done by Peter. I glanced up at the camera in the hall and there was the disk, its magnetic force having pulled it to the exact spot Peter aimed the laser. It really would have been much easier to have used these coming in, but I guess that would have meant I wouldn't have been as drained and tired, which probably wasn't what Vivian, the Master and Peter had wanted. If I had been at full strength, there was no way I would have let them kill Lilli and then take us. The guilt and pain of that washed over me, but I bit down on it and forged onward.

We continued down endless white, clean hallways, taking our time to be careful as we went. Suddenly, a swooshing sound from a door sliding open came from behind us. I turned around and saw a guard step into the hallway.

'Hey! What are yo—' the guard's head cracked backwards, never letting him finish his sentence. He sunk to the ground, blood dripping out of the small wound between his eyes. I looked back over my shoulder and saw Peter standing with his gun raised.

'What the hell!' came a voice from the room behind the fallen guard. We all held our weapons, poised to attack the first thing that popped out the doorway, but instead we heard a thud as something hit a wall inside the room.

'Intruder alert! Corridor 59E. Man down. I repeat, man down,' came a panicked voice from within the room.

Red lights flashed above us, and a robotic voice, unnervingly smooth and calm, sounded across the hallway speakers. 'Alert. Alert. All guards to corridor 59E. Alert. Alert. All guards to corridor 59E.'

'That can't be good,' Megan mumbled.

'RUN. NOW!' commanded Peter. We hurled ourselves down the hallway, while a small part of my brain continued screaming at me for blindly following a man who, not long ago, had betrayed us all. Following him seemed like the stupidest thing to do, but what choice did I have? Even with synthetic adrenaline pumping through my system, my arm was fatiguing from holding a gun, and my legs were wobbling from supporting Sam. When I looked properly, though, I realised Sam was in front of me, holding my arm. He had been helping me, not the other way around.

We turned a corner and came face to face with a group of four guards. Peter and Megan fired immediately, taking two guards down. The other two guards raised their weapons just as a loud bang sounded from Sam's weapon. One of the guards crumpled, clutching desperately at a leg wound. The guard's screams risked drawing attention; without losing a beat, I aimed and squeezed my trigger, dropping both guards before they could react. The encounter was over in the blink of an eye. I turned and looked at Sam. His gun was still pointed towards the bodies. He looked at me nervously and I gave an encouraging nod. His aim was off, but he had acted in the moment, and that counted for a lot.

'Keep coming!' shouted Peter, and we continued onwards, jumping over the pile of bodies.

'Hope you know where you're going!' yelled Megan at Peter.

'Not too much further! Should be just up ahead. Keep running.'

My chest was heaving. Every breath was burning my throat, but I pushed on. Escaping was all that mattered right now.

We came to a door where Peter stopped and entered a code into a keypad. Its small light turned from red to green with a beep, then the entire door slid open, revealing a huge room filled with different vehicles, along with a group of guards standing in front of us.

I grabbed Sam and pulled him behind the edge of the doorframe, while Megan dropped to the ground, aimed and fired her weapon. Peter whipped out a secondary gun and started shooting both weapons at the guards. Staying low, I edged around the corner of the doorframe, holding my gun ready. Three guards were already on the floor, and after another burst from Megan's weapon, it quickly became four. I felt my body react almost instinctually as I let off two shots that dropped another guard. I changed my aim to another guard, but their head snapped backwards before I could squeeze the trigger. The bullet had smashed through their jaw. It wasn't clean, but it was effective. Sam was next to me with his gun still aimed at the fallen guard, a look of shock on his face. Shots suddenly hurtled towards us from the three guards still standing. Sam and I pulled back behind the edge of the doorframe as Megan rolled across the floor and took cover on the other side. From my half-obscured vantage point, I saw Peter rush sideways into the room, and fire another two shots. Two more bodies fell, leaving only one guard. I leant out and readied my weapon, took a breath, then fired a shot at the remaining guard. He was distracted by Peter, so the guard never saw it coming. My aim was true and smashed into the guard's temple. They didn't even have time to process what had happened before crumpling to the ground.

The door behind us suddenly opened and two guards rushed out and grabbed hold of Sam, smashing his weapon out of his hand in the process. I couldn't risk shooting in case I missed and hit Sam, so I put my weapon down and let my body take over. I launched myself at the guard near me and grabbed hold of the front collar of her uniform. Using my weight and whatever strength I had, I yanked her towards me, then lifted my legs to let gravity do its thing. Her balance slipped, and we fell to the ground. The impact sent a jarring wave through my body, but I rolled as I landed so the guard fell next to me rather than on top. Once on the ground, I sent a punch flying at her face, but she turned at the last moment, and my hand smashed into her cheekbone. My hand screamed from the impact, but I whipped up my gun from the floor and fired into the guard's head.

Sam was still wrestling with a guard who was trying to aim their weapon at his head, but he kept moving and knocked the weapon out of the guard's hand. In frustration, the guard grabbed Sam around the throat in a choke hold. That's when I threw myself at them. I tackled them around the waist, but when my shoulder connected with the guard's midsection something in my joint popped and ground unhappily as I knocked them to the ground. As we fell, I raised my gun, and using my memory of the guard's height, weight and the force of the tackle, aimed where the guard's head should be, and squeezed the trigger. Before we hit the ground, half of the guard's face was blown away. I landed heavily on top of their chest, but they didn't care. They were already dead.

I rolled off and pushed myself up. My shoulder pulsed with a burning pain that told me something wasn't right. I didn't have time for that now, though. I gritted my teeth, grabbed hold of Sam and pushed us both onward through the doorway.

We entered the metallic-framed structure and took in the sight before us while dodging the bodies of the fallen guards. Numerous vehicles gleamed in the light of the phosphorescent strip lights that ran the length of the cavern. There were four lo-vehics and at least six armoured land e-vehics optimised for traversing the Wastes. The lo-vehics drew my attention, as low-orbit vehicles were a rare sight on Tir-na. The energy needed to fuel them was too high for common use, especially on our world, where everything needed to be conserved, so only the Agency and police forces had access to them—or so I thought.

We joined Megan and Peter at the top of a set of stairs that led down to the vehicles.

'Flying it is', said Peter, finishing some conversation with Megan that I didn't hear. She nodded and started descending the stairs. My brain was fuzzy, and thoughts weren't coming easy, so I followed, letting Megan do the thinking for us.

'Look,' Megan said, pointing to small boxes attached to the roof over each vehicle. 'They're all connected to a proximity sensor. I've seen those before. If you try to move them without the right access, you trip the sensor, and it locks the hangar door. If we can't decouple the sensors, we won't get out.'

'Well. We better find a way to do it then,' said Peter. We hobbled to the lo-vehic closest to the hangar door. Once on board, Megan started examining its defence weapon systems, while Peter plonked himself down in the driver's chair. 'Hey Rach! Any chance you could do some of that weird hoogitty boogitty stuff and get that box decoupled?'

My stomach sank. I could barely stand as my body pulsed with pain and adrenaline. I lowered myself into one of the passenger seats and sucked in a breath to get the courage to admit what I knew to be true. 'I really don't think I can.' Three pairs of eyes stared at me. 'I don't think I have it in me.' My voice caught on the last word. I looked down and my hands were shaking. I couldn't feel the light buzz of power waiting under my skin anymore. It had retreated somewhere deeper inside me and wouldn't respond without effort. I stretched my hands and flicked them a couple of times to get rid of the shakes, but it didn't work. So, I gripped them together and placed them in my lap.

'I can help, Mum.' Sam crouched down in front of me, drawing my attention to him. The rectangular wound on his forehead still shone a damp red, and the healing cut on his cheek was an angry pink, but the rest of him looked calm and alert. 'Show me how to control my power so I can do it.' He took my hand in his and squeezed, and I knew I had to at least try. Sam looked at me expectantly, waiting for me to start teaching him, but I barely knew how to use the powers myself.

I fumbled for a moment as I figured out where to start. 'Close your eyes,' I told Sam, 'and find that spark inside you. Deep inside that dark internal void.' Sam closed his eyes and focused. 'Let yourself drift deeper until you see or feel the spark. Then, once you see it, reach out and let it latch on to you. Let it become you.' A heart beat later, Sam's hands flickered with shimmering blue currents. Sam opened his eyes and looked at his hands. He turned his hands slowly to examine the electric sparks shooting across his skin. The lights then slowly subsided and disappeared.

'It's strange,' he said, looking up at me. 'I can't see it anymore, but I can still feel it.'

I nodded. 'It's there, ready to use.' With effort, I reached and grabbed my own tiny flicker of light. It was so small and depleted now that my energy was drained. I pulled it upwards and sent it through my hand into Sam's. A small arc appeared between our fingers, and Sam flinched with surprise.

'I can feel your energy reaching into mine, trying to meld with it,' he said. I could feel his energy, too. It was different to mine, though. My power felt fierce, like a sparking, live electrical wire, whereas Sam's was smoother, like a steady, flowing current.

'I don't have much left,' I said, 'but if you let our powers join, I might be able to help direct your powers to decouple the box.' Sam nodded, and his power extended a link to mine. Then I was there with him, connected. 'Do you trust me?' I asked Sam.

'Of course I do.' His reply was so simple, so assured, that it caused a bubble of emotion in my throat. I nodded and pushed the bubble down. Then, with the small spark I had left, I directed his energy and encouraged it to expand towards the sensor box above our lo-vehic.

'You need to know what you want to do, and then direct your power to do it,' I instructed. Sam's power twitched, then reached into the sensor box. I let mine flow with him until he found the connection to the main control centre. He severed it, rendering the sensor redundant. With the job done, I gently guided his power back into him, then let go of our connection and slumped back in my chair. I could barely keep my eyes open.

Sam shook my shoulder. 'Mum?'

'I'm okay honey,' I mumbled as I sat down. 'I just need to close my eyes for a while.'

'What happened?' Megan asked.

'We decoupled the sensor,' Sam replied. 'We should be good to go.'

'Awesome job, kid,' Peter shouted from the pilot's seat. 'Any chance you can also open the hangar door?'

'I can try,' Sam replied. I could hear an undertone of uncertainty in his voice. I reached out and squeezed his fingers, trying to give some reassurance and support. He closed his fingers around mine as I let what was left of my tiny sliver of power reach out to him. His power grabbed onto it hungrily, pulling it in before melding with it and sending it out on an invisible wave. His power wasn't gentle or delicate this time, instead it came out in a roaring wave. It smashed forwards into multiple electrical sources, causing loud cracking explosions throughout the garage.

'Holy shit!' Peter exclaimed.

I opened my eyes and saw Sam in front of me. His eyes were closed, and he shimmered with power as he held my hand. I looked out the front window. Every sensor on the roof above the vehicles had exploded, showering the space in electrical sparks, but through the bright bursts of electricity, the huge metal hangar door rolled open.

'If they didn't know where we were, they certainly will now,' said Megan. 'Get us out of here, Peter. Now!'

'Yes ma'am,' saluted Peter.

Our lo-vehic lurched forwards, throwing Sam off balance. The falling electrical sparks ignited the engine of one of the other vehicles. As our lo-vehic shot out into a wide valley in the canyon system surrounding the base, a deafening explosion echoed through the air, shaking the very foundations of the towering cliff faces.

'I'm going to stay low, so this may get a little hairy,' called out Peter.

I helped Sam up onto the seats and strapped him into a harness before he sank backwards, exhausted and spent. Then I strapped myself in too and held onto him for my own reassurance as we rocketed forwards.

Red streaks suddenly flew past the front windscreen, followed by a loud thump at the rear of the lo-vehic that sent us swerving sideways.

'They've got laser cannons mounted on the base!' exclaimed Megan. 'This thing's got a pretty good shield that should hold, but best not to test it too much.'

'Shit. Get up here, Megan. Pull up the sensor map and help get us out of here,' yelled Peter as he straightened up our flight path. He sounded more stressed than I had ever heard him. I guess flying was something he only did when there were no other options. I clung onto Sam, who appeared to be drifting in and out of consciousness, as Megan rushed to the co-pilot chair. She tapped at a screen that sprang to life with a shocking green glow. The screen pulsed and displayed a rudimentary three-dimensional map of the surrounding area that showed that the wide valley was about to change into two narrow gorges.

'Incoming! Cut left now!' commanded Megan. The lo-vehic lurched sideways as three more blasts streaked past the front window and impacted into the rocky cliff between the two gorges. A stream of rocks tumbled from the cliff face and crashed on the valley floor.

'Right or left, Megan?' asked Peter.

'Right. Down the wider gorge,' she replied.

Loud thumps from falling rocks battered the lo-vehic as it flew past the crumbing cliff face.

'Shit!' yelled Peter as the lo-vehic suddenly flipped sideways. My harness cut into me but held as I watched a huge boulder fall past us, only missing the front of our lo-vehic because of Peter's manoeuvre. Sam's limbs flailed wildly with the movement while his harness held him securely in place. Small rocks battered the lo-vehic in a loud maelstrom, but the hull remained intact thanks to the shields. Once through the falling rocks, Peter levelled out the lo-vehic and it raced along the right-side gorge, curving around a corner and out of the way of the base's weapon systems.

'We're not out of this yet,' yelled Megan. 'Two lo-vehics coming up behind us. I've activated stealth mode on this thing, which will cover us from any scanners, but that won't stop them from visually spotting us!'

'I thought Sam destroyed all the vehicles!' I yelled.

'There's another hangar in the base,' stated Peter. 'Megan, you take over. I don't want us to die because I didn't admit you're the better pilot.' Megan nodded, then reached forward to the controls in front of her seat. Peter hit a switch, and the two swapped roles, with Megan now piloting and Peter viewing the map. 'There are two coming up on our tail. Rach, can you man the defence system? You're a better shot than me.'

My muscles screamed with every shifting of my weight, but I sucked it up, as this was too important. 'I'm on it.' I released my harness and gave the top of Sam's head a quick kiss, being careful to avoid his forehead wound. He was completely out of it, which was probably for the best. I pushed myself up and, with great difficultly and a lot of grasping onto handholds, stumbled my way to the back of the lo-vehic. I strapped into the controller's chair and fired up the defence system. Multiple three-dimensional feeds sprang to life, displaying a visual of the world outside. My brain took a moment to configure where everything was spatially in the real world, and to remember the controls, but after that, I was ready. I gripped the joystick with my right hand and, hoping they hadn't changed defence systems too much since my time at the Agency, readied my left over the switches controlling the onboard weapons. After that, I let muscle memory take over.

'They're right behind us. Rach, take them down!' bellowed Peter from the front cockpit.

The pursuing lo-vehics came into view, the two of them streaming up the ravine at an intimidating speed, dodging and twisting through the rocky gorge with ease. I imagined the pilots had flown these paths often, putting them at an advantage. Megan started standard evasion manoeuvres, flicking us from side to side. Nausea rose up my throat, but I held on and just focused on the screens in front of me. The front lo-vehic fired at us, but its shots went wide as Megan looped us around. I moved the joystick and aimed at the closest pursuer. Its twisting movements made it difficult to get a lock, so instead I focused on our surrounds, the obstacles of the ravine, and the pattern of the lo-vehic's movements. My brain crunched all the data inputs into a workable model that helped predict the lo-vehic's next step. I moved the joystick and my targeting circle changed from red to green. I flicked the switch for the rear cannon and fired two shots. The first one hit the lo-vehic straight in the nose, but its shield protected it. The second shot went wide, missing both targets and instead smashed into a rocky cliff in a cloud of dust. In response, the two lo-vehics pulled into a dual formation and fired at us. Megan ripped us upward, causing three shots to miss us, but the last smashed into our wing. I looked out the small side window to assess the damage. The wing was okay, but the shot had taken out our shield, meaning another hit would rip right through us.

I focused and moved the targeting circle back onto the closest pursuer. The circle flashed green, and I fired the cannon twice, closely followed by a stream of shots from the auto-guns on the bottom of the wings. The first shot from the cannon smashed into the target's right wing, destroying its shield. The second hit the same wing, and ripped it apart, causing it to bank to the right, directly into my stream of auto-gun fire. The gun ripped apart the cockpit in a spray of blood, and the response was instantaneous. With the pilot dead, the lo-vehic plummeted downwards and crashed into the base of the gorge.

The second pursuer flew past the fiery wreckage and let off a sequence of cannon and auto-gun shots. Megan expertly manoeuvred, ducking, weaving and twisting us out of the direct line of fire. My throat burned with bile as my nausea rose up again. I sucked air in through my nose and pressed my lips shut, determined to not let anything out. I started analysing the feeds on my screens again, hoping the mental effort would distract from my nausea. The world flashed by in a blur as I scanned for information, desperately searching for options. Then I spotted it, a rocky overhang further ahead that we could go under.

'Head under that overhang!' I yelled at Megan, trying to make sure she heard me over the rumble of the engines and weapons.

'What?' yelled Megan.

'The overhang ahead! Go under it!'

Our lo-vehic responded instantly as Megan pushed us forwards even faster. I looked at my screen and saw that our relentless tail was gaining ground. It let off another round of shots. I fired interceptor blasts to counter their cannon shot, and they smashed into each other in a ball of fire and smoke. Our pursuer's auto-gun blasts hit us though, right next to where I was sitting, missing me but only a hand's width. The close call filled me with rage, and I pulled on the joystick harder than I needed to, playing out the scenario in my head as I aimed our auto-guns.

We lurched downwards and under the rocky overhang. I readied myself as the pursuing lo-vehic started descending to follow us. I let off a stream of auto-gun shots aimed just below its cockpit. The only way they could avoid the shots was to move upward, right into the rocky overhang. With a thunderous crash, the vehicle slammed into the rock face, sending a plume of dust and dirt billowing into the air. The impact caused the front of the vehicle to crumple instantly, and its engine erupted in a fiery explosion. As the wreckage tumbled down into the ravine below, a shower of rock and dust rained down upon the canyon floor.

'Yeah! Awesome job Rach!' Peter called out. I sat for a moment looking at the damage I had caused and desperately searched my screens for further threats. Megan piloted us along the base of the gorge and focused on getting as far away as possible. We all sat poised for another attack, but it never came. Everything was calm behind us. Finally, feeling confident the immediate danger was gone, I turned myself to assess the damage. A series of holes had punched through the metal frame and were sucking out our oxygen-rich air in a horrendous hurricane of noise. I went over to an oxy-mask cache and grabbed four. I put mine on and hit the button to start the air flow, then did the same for Sam, who was still unconscious, and handed the last two to Megan and Peter.

We raced through the ravine, staying low and out of the line of any scanners as I stood in the cockpit.

'Where are we going?' I yelled so the others could hear me over the raging winds.

Peter's eyes were still completely focused on the sensor map, giving a running commentary of the geography ahead so Megan could pilot us through the twisting ravine. 'I don't know,' he said between instructions. 'I hadn't really thought that far.'

'I know a place,' said Megan, as she zoomed us onwards at speed. 'If you trust me, I think it could work. It's a safe place where we could lie low for a few days.'

'I trust you. Let's do it,' said Peter a little too quickly, with an awkward eagerness in his voice.

They were both waiting for my answer, and I realised then that they were leaving the choice for me. I looked back at Sam. He was still unconscious, and I wanted to join him. We needed to find somewhere to rest. I was spent.

'If you think it will be safe, I trust you,' I said, with my eyes trained on Megan. I could feel Peter looking at me, but I ignored him. I wasn't ready to deal with that.

'Okay, then. Peter, get me out of this ravine so I can get us the hell out of here.'

I went and checked Sam's harness was secure, then settled into the seat next to him as Megan rocketed us onwards.

23

Hidden Truths

M Y HEAD BOUNCED UNCOMFORTABLY as the lo-vehic landed, rousing me from a dreamless, dark, exhausted sleep. Waking from that world of nothing, it took a moment to process where I was and what was happening. Sam was still asleep next to me, and I thought I should be doing the same. Every muscle in my body ached. Every joint crunched and throbbed with any movement, and my arm, where Velor had peeled off my skin stung. The adrenaline boost Peter had given me had thoroughly worn off, leaving me like a hollow shell, stripped of all substance. I looked out a small window on the far side of the cabin and saw endless rolling dirt. Not the type of place I would have expected Megan to land. Curious, I twisted around and looked out the window next to me. There was a rocky cliff with a large dark opening cut into it that lead into a cave. I didn't think I could handle another night sleeping in the dirt, especially in a place that reminded me of losing Miles again. There was so much I still hadn't processed. Compartmentalisation was great for getting through, but at some point, things needed to come to the surface, because if they didn't, they could drown you. I sighed and pushed my compartmented feelings back down inside me. Once again, I didn't have time to deal with it. Survival had to come first.

'This is it,' Megan said as she powered down the lo-vehic and locked it in place. She casually reached to something down the side of her chair, then whipped her hand up and pointed a gun at Peter. The audible prepping of the weapon rang through the cabin.

'Woah! What the hell?' Peter said, staring at the gun.

'If you so much as say a bad word to one of us again, I will kill you. Understand?' Peter froze, and I watched the micro-movements of his facial muscles as they twitched and constricted uncomfortably. 'Lilli's death is on you, Peter. No one else. Remember that. You've got a long way to go before they trust you again,' Megan nodded in our direction, but her eyes never left Peter's, 'before *I* trust you again, and goodness knows you already had a long way to go to get my trust back.' Peter nodded as a raw sadness flashed across his face.

'We really should talk about that,' Peter almost whispered. 'You know, about everything that happened, before all this stuff.'

'No. We shouldn't. There is nothing to say about it. You were a dick when I needed you the most and there is nothing you can say to fix that. So, what you can do is get your arse out of the cockpit and go check the damage. See if you can patch it up. Then, when we go in there,' Megan pointed at the cave entrance, 'you will follow my lead, say nothing and maybe, just maybe, you won't get yourself killed, by them or me.' Peter looked like he had been slapped. He took a moment to process, as Megan began fiddling with the controls again. I quickly closed my eyes and pretended to be asleep, feeling like I had walked in on something private. Peter stood without a word, left the cabin and closed the external door gently behind him.

'I know you're awake back there,' Megan called towards me. Feeling caught out, I sat up straight and unhooked my harness.

'I didn't want to intrude.'

'All good. Nothing for you to intrude into. It's all pretty black and white. Peter's a dick, and he needs to be treated as such.'

'Fair enough.' I walked forward and sat heavily in the seat where Peter had just been.

'Crap! You really look like shit. Like you fell out of a lo-vehic without a chute.'

'Thanks...I think. That's certainly how it feels. This shoulder isn't right.'

'We'll get the two of you some proper treatment once we go in.'

'Where are we, by the way?' I said, staring at the cave entrance.

'Somewhere with people who can help us.'

I nodded at her reply. 'I trust you.'

Silence fell as Megan started fiddling with controls to power the vehicle down. My head swarmed with questions, so I picked the most burning in my mind to start unravelling my confusion.

'Megan,' I said, drawing her attention to me. 'What happened back there? I thought he killed you.'

'Peter, kill me? Ha! He wouldn't dare. Wouldn't have the guts to do something like that.'

'Then what happened? Because of him, Lilli is dead. He's lucky I haven't killed him. I'm really trying to search for a reason not to beat him to a pulp.'

'That is completely on him,' she acknowledged, 'but I know he didn't mean for it to happen, and he feels shit about it. After he pushed me through the door, I was certain he was going to kill me. I thought he had finally grown the balls to get rid of me, so he didn't have to think about the past ever again. He pushed me through the door, and I turned to face him, so he had to look me in the eye before killing me. As soon as it shut, he put a finger to his lips, telling me to stay quiet, then fired a shot into the wall away from me, and threw himself onto the ground. Of course, I was confused. He ushered me into a small back corridor and got me to hide in a cupboard. He told me he would be back when he could and then left me in the dark. I don't know how long he was gone. Apparently, he told Vivian and the Master that he pushed my body into the garbage chute so he could be done with me forever. Because of our history, they ate up his lies. He eventually came back and found me, then we got scheming on how to get you out. And here we are.'

The story made sense. It actually made more sense than what I thought had happened, as I couldn't quite believe Peter could turn into a stone-cold killer. However, I also never thought he would betray us, but that happened. I started questioning everything I knew and realised there was something I still didn't understand. 'Megan, what happened between you and Peter?'

'There's just...a lot of baggage around our history. Too much to be together, and too much to be rid of each other.' Megan left it at that and instead changed the topic. 'Think you can wake up Sam?' Megan said, looking back at the still-sleeping figure of my son.

'I'll try. I don't really want to, though. At least while he's asleep, he doesn't have to deal with the reality of everything. I remember after Miles died, I didn't want to do anything but sleep, because then I was free from the pain and grief. Being awake and aware was painful. Sleep was an escape.'

'I know what you mean,' replied Megan, her eyes fixed on some unseen point outside the window.

I moved back to Sam and brushed his hair off his forehead like I did when he was a boy. 'Sam,' I said gently. 'Sam sweetie. You've got to wake up now. We've got to get moving.' I saw his face twitch and slowly he started moving his limbs.

'Mum?' he murmured.

I kissed him on top of his head, then moved to give him room. 'Yes, sweetie. It's time to get up.' He sat up and looked around, eyes glazed and confused. I left him on his own to have some time to become functional and instead hobbled off to see if there was anything useful on the lo-vehic to take with us. I found a bag and started loading it with spare oxy-canisters, ammunition, food and water packs. Then, once satisfied, I went and joined the others outside.

Sam still looked shaky on his feet, but he had gotten out of the lo-vehic without falling, which I was proud of. His face was frozen in a blank, emotionless stare, but I could tell underneath he was seething with feelings. It was his 'I need to get on with the job right now even though I'm not okay' face. I'd seen it before, usually over little things like when I had made him scrub the bathroom before he could go out with friends. He had set his face in that same emotionless gaze and got on with it, and I knew he would do the same now.

'Alright, where are we going?' I asked.

Megan, who had been standing and talking to Peter in quiet tones, turned and indicated the cave in the cliff face. 'In there. You'll need these.' She threw each of us a light. I checked mine was working as Peter slammed the door of the lo-vehic shut behind us. I looked over at him, but he still couldn't meet my eye. We had a lot to hash out at some point.

'Follow me, and keep an eye out for beasts,' commanded Megan.

The roar of the wind cutting across the Wastes softened and eventually disappeared as we trekked deeper into the cave, being replaced by an echoing liquid drip from somewhere in the dark. The path we followed forked a number of times, but Megan was unflinching in her directions and never faltered. We sometimes popped out into larger underground caverns, but Megan would simply lead us through and back into another narrow tunnel. I couldn't tell how long we had been walking as everything blurred together. Eventually we turned a corner and emerged into a small alcove area where three figures stood pointing weapons at us.

'Hail brothers and sisters. The underground is dark, but it brings the light,' said Megan with her hands held in a peaceful, placating manner. The guards lowered their weapons.

'Megan,' one guard replied with a deep, rolling voice. He moved forward and clasped hands with her in a sign of acknowledgement and friendship. The man had grey braids woven back over the crown of his head, offset by a shaved section that wrapped around the back from ear to ear. He was easily over six feet tall, with broad shoulders and a barrel-like trunk. 'I didn't think you were due back for another eight days.'

'I had something pop up, Lucas. Something I need help with. Is Calista here? I need to speak to her.' Megan spoke with the comfort of familiarity, and I felt like there was a much bigger story within these caves than Megan had let on.

'She is. Who are all these people?' Lucas asked, pointing to us with his weapon.

'They're with me. I vouch for them. This is Rachel Tomsen, Sam Tomsen and Peter Brand,' she said, indicating each of us in turn.

'Peter Brand, you say?' Lucas asked Megan.

'Yep.'

'Hmmmmm', said Lucas as he stared at Peter, making some sort of internal judgement. 'Alright.' Lucas nodded in acquiescence. 'Any consequences are on you, Megan.'

'Of course,' Megan said, nodding in agreement. 'Also, there's a lo-vehic above that needs to be hidden.'

'You definitely don't do things by half, now do you?' Lucas said in an amused tone. 'Cal, can you look after the lo-vehic?'

'Yes, sir!' said an overly eager young guard.

'Well, alright then.' Lucas turned then and addressed me and Sam. 'Lucas Evans is the name and you'll be wanting to stick close and follow my path exactly. Can be some tricky things in these caves, but if you stick with me, I'll get you to Calista.'

We gave our thanks and Lucas paused for a moment to give a hard stare at Peter, before turning and walking off deeper into the cave system. We all followed close behind. The passage wound deeper, and I was thankful for the extra oxy-canisters I brought with us. A cave system this deep and intricate, in a land with little surface oxygen outside of the terraformed regions, would be a death trap without the canisters, and I had no idea how long we were going to be down here.

I followed dutifully, trying to keep a map in my head of all the twists and turns, but even I lost track after the eighth turn. We suddenly popped out of a narrow tunnel and what I saw before me took my breath away. The tunnel opened into a huge cavern, with a winding metal staircase along the wall that led down into what looked like an underground village. The immense space was lit with poles of different heights scattered across the cavern floor, each topped with a sphere emitting a green-tinged light that seemed to ooze its way across the damp, textured surface of the cave. Littered across the bottom of that cavern were ramshackle structures and tents where people pottered about their day. There were crooked paths winding through the village, kids playing with a ball in an open community space, cooking areas filled with steam rising off huge pots, and in the centre of it all, a well-worn bridge that spanned the small stream that cut the cavern in two and filled the air with a rhythmic babbling sound. I couldn't believe what I was seeing. An entire town stood before us. An entire underground community hidden in the Wastes.

Lucas reached up and removed his oxy-mask, then took a deep breath and released a huge sigh.

'Ah!' he said. 'Nothing like breathing in the real stuff.' He must have been able to read the confusion on my face as he went on to explain, 'The cave walls are covered in an oxygen-producing algae. They create enough to fill this cavern. Which is why we set up home base here. Come on. The supply meeting should be about to wrap up so we can catch Calista after it.'

Lucas led us down the metal steps down to the cave floor. I stared at the furry, spongey algae as we descended the stairs. 'Were these algae already here or did you bring it with you?' I asked Lucas, curiosity getting the better of me.

'Already here, but it needed our help to grow. It likes the chem-lights,' he said, pointing at the green spherical lights. 'They give off just enough energy to help the algae bloom. We spent a long time exploring these caves to find somewhere to fit us all. We couldn't believe our luck when we found this place with water running through it. And then when our own lights helped the algae grow and produce oxygen, well then, it was like it was meant to be. Also helps that those Waste beasts can't breathe the oxygen so they tend to stay away and leave us alone.'

I was amazed. I had always thought of everything outside the terraformed regions as a death zone with no oxygen, so the idea there could be areas naturally producing it after a simple reaction to chemiluminescent light was completely mind-blowing. The entire planet was apparently fully scanned and assessed as unliveable for humans by the first planet scouts, but obviously their data wasn't as good and detailed as they thought it was. You never really could trust those scouts. A bit too much gruff and bravado for my liking. Terraforming had turned into big business on the Tir-na continent. I couldn't imagine the implications of native chemiluminescent-activated oxygen-producing algae. More importantly, why hadn't these people told anyone? I had too many questions, and no way of obtaining answers. All I could do was watch and absorb as Lucas led us through the town.

The people who lived there came from everywhere. There were elements of Craynian and Grovian textile styles and artistry throughout the dwellings and the makeshift fabric curtains that passed for doors on the tents. I even spotted some Uishkan and Aeirian embellishments. The smell permeating the space was a mix of stale human stench and fresh oxygen. It tickled my nose, but I ignored it. We were greeted with many hesitant and judging eyes as we wound our way through the camp. After all, we were strangers, and in such an environment, that was enough to make us a threat.

Lucas stopped at the edge of a wide opening and indicated for us to wait. In the centre of the space, there was a circle of boulders where people sat deep in conversation. It was a meeting place, so we watched quietly, too far away to hear their conversation, until the people nodded and left. An older woman with a long grey braid remained behind and turned her eye in our direction. Lucas gave a small wave, and she nodded, indicating for us to come forward and join her in the circle. This must be Calista. We approached as a group, then each perched ourselves on a rock while Lucas took up a guarding position behind the woman.

'Megan,' said Calista with a soft, kind voice, 'I see you've brought strangers into our home. I assume there is a very good reason, as you know it is not permitted without council approval.'

'I know Calista, but it was necessary. We are being pursued by the Master and I believe the Entity is involved. They kidnapped Sam,' Megan said, pointing at Sam, who seemed more interested in our surroundings than the conversation, 'then lured and captured his mother, Rachel. They experimented on them both before we freed them. We came here as I couldn't think of anywhere else safe for them. It appears the Entity's web has effectively spread throughout Crayn as we can confirm that both the Agency and La Panta have Entity links.'

'So, they finally got their claws into the Agency,' said Calista as the frown lines around her eyes deepened. 'It explains a lot about the Master's sudden boost in weapons technology.'

I sat silently and patiently through this interaction, but my mind was pinging with connections, thoughts and more questions. 'I'm sorry,' I held up my hand in a placating manner. The fact Megan had been using such a respectful tone spoke volumes, as obviously this woman held the power in this place, and I didn't want to be disrespectful. 'But who are you all? And what is this place?'

'We are the dispossessed. The homeless. Those with nowhere to go. Those thrown out and discarded. We are those that have encountered the Entity and lost, and together, we have forged ourselves a new life as we continue to keep fighting the unseen fight against the most powerful of foes. We call ourselves the Hidden.'

'If the Entity is so bad, why not just go public?' I asked. 'Go on the stream and tell everyone.'

'There are those who tried such a thing, but the Entity is everywhere, so all it did was cause the deaths of those brave souls who tried to expose the truth.'

Calista paused and genuinely looked sad. 'This is a place to call home for those who need it,' she said, gesturing at the camp, 'for those who want to fight and make a difference. This is their refuge. The only preconditions to join us are a desire to help sustain our community, and a willingness to fight for truth.'

Calista's voice was melodic and filled with such conviction and love, and it made me understand how she had ended up in charge of this place.

'I'm sorry to interrupt again,' I said, forcing the conversation in a new direction, 'but who is this Entity you spoke of earlier? And how is it connected to Vivian, the Master, La Panta and the Pleasure Spot dealers? Are all of them working together?'

'They're working together, Rach, because they all work for the Entity,' said Megan. 'As far as we can determine from our sources, the Master is a high-ranking Entity official. We believe he reports directly to the Entity council, an anonymous group of three who oversee it all. They are a secretive bunch, though, who prefer to operate through their trusted leaders, like the Master. So, technically, all the others work for him, and through him they work for the Entity council.'

All of them were connected. The lengths involved in setting something up like that, and not having details slip to anyone, were mind-boggling. I couldn't figure out how there could possibly be a group in charge with the foresight to orchestrate something so wide-reaching and extreme. I've met lots of people, and from my experience, on the whole people are people. They're flawed, messy and emotional, so the idea of hundreds, if not thousands, of people being coordinated and efficient enough to make it all work seemed impossible. There were so many questions I wanted to ask, so I started with the biggest one.

'Okay, but who is the Entity and what do they want?'

'The Entity is everywhere, and it is interested in everything,' said Calista. 'It seeks power and control, spreading its tendrils across the planet like a plague. No one really knows where it came from, but it's rumoured to have begun during the first colonisation of Tir-na in Aeir. It's said that when those first floating settlement ships were put into position above the continent, it was decided Tir-na would be slowly and carefully colonised, only terraforming enough of the planet to produce enough oxygen for survivability. The rest of Tir-na would remain untouched, to respect what was here before us. But not everyone agreed. There were those that saw the potential for power and wealth in the un-colonised regions of the planet. An uprising ensued, and those enthralled by the call of wealth and power stole a terraforming drop ship and landed some-where on the continent. With the entire story of the uprising disappearing into the whispers and rumours of history, no one knows exactly what hap-pened next. What we know is that at some point, the members of the uprising re-entered society and started silently working within the system to build their power and strength. They forged networks across Crayn, Uishka and Aeir by recruiting people in powerful positions to use for their own benefit. They are the secret puppet-masters who direct the entire show. The Master may appear to be in charge, but he is only one small drop in a terrifyingly big bucket.'

'But what do they want? Why do any of this?' I asked.

'Power. Control. A feeling of being important,' said Calista. 'I've often said that one of the most dangerous things in the universe is an unchecked ego. People who draw others in with their enthusiasm and the appearance of accomplishment but have nothing of substance apart from their posturing. Those are very dangerous people indeed.'

'Sounds like you've known a few in your time,' I said.

'Haven't we all encountered people like that?' continued Calista. 'People with an ego, too much bravado, not enough substance and an inflated sense of self?'

'You're not wrong,' said Megan, throwing a look in Peter's direction.

'Okay. So, there's this big ego-driven, power-hungry group of people who want to control the planet for their own unknown purposes, and they are behind everything going on,' I said, trying to pull my thoughts together.

'They are not behind everything, but they're often a driving force behind big decisions or actions carried out on this planet. Let's just say they know how to influence effectively,' replied Calista.

A terrible thought crossed my mind. 'Do they control the Collective?' The Tir-na Collective was a harmonious committee of leaders from the continent's cities that guided the development of Tir-na and ensured adherence to Tir-na's collective ethos. The idea of it being tarnished or influenced by personal gain made my skin crawl.

'We don't know if they control it outright, but they definitely have strong influence over it,' said Calista. 'As the Grove's representative and the lead for terraforming efforts the Master is a member of the Collective, so we know they at least have significant influence over it, if not full control. How many of the other members are part of the Entity? Well, that's harder to know. But we expect a couple more are in their ranks. After all, why wouldn't they target the most influential forum on Tir-na?'

I let Calista's story sit for a moment and instead took stock of Sam and Peter. Sam was staring at something on the other side of the clearing near what appeared to be a fix-it shop while his foot nervously bounced. The muscles around his neck were taut, and he looked paler than before. Peter, in contrast, sat perfectly still, his eyes fixed on the ground. I could tell he was listening intently, but he had the foresight not to look at anyone. I hoped he was stewing in his shame. He had blindly followed ego-driven people, and had led us into danger, causing the death of a young girl. The base of my neck and my fingers tingled with anger, but I silently sucked in a breath and held it before letting it go in an attempt to calm down. I would need to deal with Peter later.

Calista stood slowly, pushing herself off her stone seat with a small grunt of effort, her white hair swaying with the movement. 'Come, I can see you are all tired. If Megan vouches for you, I trust you and you are welcome here. Please, rest, eat, get the medical attention you need, and then we will talk more. Megan knows the way to the empty tents where you can stay. Now, if you'll excuse me, I have a meeting with the head cook. Lucas, if you wouldn't mind helping an old lady?' She held out her arm, and Lucas wrapped his bulging forearm around hers and escorted her as she slowly hobbled away.

Megan stood up. 'She's right. You all look terrible. Let's get you some medical help and some rest to regain some strength, then we'll figure out what happens next.'

'I need to do something first,' said Sam, standing up with his eyes still fixated on that funny little fix-it shop. 'Mum, will you come with me? I need to do something and would like you there.'

Completely unsure of what was happening, I did what any parent would do when your grown child asks you to do something with them. I simply agreed and followed his lead.

24

Fix-it

RANDOM BITS AND PIECES of broken machinery were sprawled everywhere in front of the small ramshackle fix-it shop. What drew my eye, though, was the small display out the front of the shop showing off mechanical animal toys made of whatever metals and materials the maker could get their hands on. They were cute in a messy way, and I had seen something like them before. My heart sank at the memory of a small rodent-shaped robot of the same design skittering across Sam's desk at home. A present from Lilli, he had said. I looked at an old sign above the door that looked like it had been hastily removed from its previous location and tenuously attached to its new home above the little shop. It read, in messy painted font, '*Zinke's Fix-it*', and next to the words were three colourfully painted handprints. Two big, and one from a small child.

I looked at Sam as he stopped in front of the small shop. 'I think it's Lilli's parents' shop. She always said it was in the Grove, but it's here. I don't understand how it's here.' His eyes drifted down and fell on the mechanical toys. 'Her father must have had made the robo-rodent she gave me.' His eyes filled with tears. Alarm bells started ringing in my mind. Lilli was supposed to have been spying for the Master through the Den goons, but now her family was here in the Hidden. It didn't make sense, but now was not the time to unpick that mystery. Sam needed me.

I didn't know what to say, but I understood what drew him over to the shop. We had to tell them. We had to deliver the worst news a parent could ever hear. My stomach began twisting at the thought. Sam took a deep breath, then walked towards the colourful front door of the tiny shop where a beautifully painted *Open* sign hung pride of place. I followed without thinking.

A melodic tinkling sounded as Sam pushed aside stands of rope hanging from the top of the door frame, each one covered in small metal objects that when knocked together made clear and sweet musical chimes.

'Be with you in a moment,' a happy and practical sounding voice said from somewhere behind a heap of machinery bits and bobs. There was a grunting noise as something heavy and metallic hit something before a motor spluttered into life. 'Yeah! Thought you could conk out on me, huh? Well, not today!' said that same voice. He sounded kind and fun, and I felt terrible for what we were about to tell him.

'Mr Zinke?' Sam asked in a tiny voice. I truthfully was impressed he could say anything.

'Yep, that's me. How can I help you?' Around the corner came a squat man wearing a well-worn green apron with a huge tool belt hooked around his middle. I couldn't fathom how it even managed to stay up. It was so big. He had tiny bits of grey hair sprinkled around his ears, and deep wrinkles creeping outwards from his eyes and mouth, making it look like he had spent a lot of time smiling. A sad thought popped into my mind. If Lilli and Sam had married one day, he would have been my in-law. But that was impossible now.

'Mr Zinke...'

'Oh, my gosh. Sam? It is you, isn't it? Lilli has sent us so many photos. Wow! Please, call me Elias. I'm so thrilled to meet you.' Elias Zinke rushed forward and grabbed Sam in a huge hug. Sam looked taken aback for a moment, but then something broke inside him and he began sobbing on Mr Zinke's shoulder. 'Hey now, what's...' He looked at me and his face fell and twisted with creases of concern. I needed to tell him.

'Mr Zinke, I'm Rachel Thomsen, Sam's mum. I have some terrible news.' I couldn't stop my own tears, but I pushed through them. He needed to be told. 'Something awful has happened.' I sucked in a breath in preparation for having to say the next awful part.

'Lilli's dead,' Sam whispered to Mr Zinke. 'She got shot at a base in the Wastes, and...and she died.' Sam's tears ran even more freely, and he held onto Mr Zinke with everything he had. I watched carefully with concern as Elias's face crumbled through the emotions of disbelief, confusion and, finally, agony.

He let out a howl of pain and crumpled into Sam's arms. 'Lillian!'

A door at the back of the shop opened and a small woman with a greying black braid and a warm face rushed in. 'Elias! What's wrong?' She rushed over and put a hand on his shoulder. Elias Zinke instinctively turned and held onto the woman, who looked extremely concerned and confused.

'Sam?' she asked in surprise. 'What's happened?'

Sam couldn't say anything through his overflowing tears and heaving sobs.

'Lana,' said Elias Zinke. 'Lilli's dead.' The last word was half lost as his voice faltered.

I watched the same disbelief wash over her face. It was like someone had thrown a stick into the gears of her mind, causing it to grind to a halt. Everything was trying to work, but there was a new unbelievable, unmentionable thing in the way. The couple held onto each other for dear life as they tried to process the bomb we just dropped on them. It was heartbreaking to watch, and the worst thing was some deep part of me couldn't help but think, *Thank goodness I'm not them!*

I walked over to Sam and guided him back towards me to give Lilli's parents some space. Part of me wanted to flee, but we needed to stay. You couldn't say something like that and just leave.

'How?' Lana Zinke asked, her eyes suddenly staring at me with an alarming clarity.

'She was shot at a hidden base in the Wastes. She was helping us, and I couldn't save her.' My tears welled up again. 'I'm so sorry!'

Lana Zinke stared at the ground, then suddenly and fiercely, with cold, clear eyes, looked up and said one word. 'Who?'

'She was shot by a woman named Vivian Wyrmstead. She's the current Head of the Agency in Crayn and it appears she was working in league with the Master of the Grove.'

Lana Zinke nodded. 'Thank you.'

'I was with her,' said Sam. 'I was with her, and I couldn't help her. I tried to reach her, but...' his words evaporated into tears again.

'Thank you for telling us. We knew joining the Hidden and letting Lilli volunteer as an informant was a risk, but I never imagined...' Her words disappeared on her lips as her face crumpled. She took a breath and settled herself before speaking again. 'We need some time to be alone now.' Elias Zinke was still sobbing in her arms as she spoke in a voice that was suddenly and uncomfortably filled with repressed emotions. 'We will want to talk more, but not now. Are you staying here?'

'Yes. We're being put up in one of the empty tents,' I said.

'Good. We will find you when we're ready. But now, we need to be alone.' She began leading Elias Zinke to the back of the shop, but then paused. 'Would you mind turning the shop sign to *Closed* on your way out?'

'Of course,' I replied, then ushered Sam out of the shop. The couple shuffled their way out of the room to face what I knew would be the worst night of their lives.

I turned the shop sign to *Closed* on our way out, then walked to Sam and pulled him into a hug. There were no words. Nothing could be said or done to make anything better, but I needed him to know I was there, and he wasn't alone.

We walked off, wiping tears from our faces in silence, to join the others who were still standing by the stone seats. They looked at us with concern, but I shook my head at them, as any conversation about it could wait. For now, we needed to get to these tents, and finally rest.

Once comfortable inside one of the large empty tents, the doctor checked us over. I'll never forget his flinch at the wounds all over my body. It wasn't that they were gruesome, but more how methodical they were. Luckily, there wasn't any damage that wouldn't heal with time—he agreed that my shoulder wasn't right, but it was quickly, and painfully, relocated and would settle down—but the doctor insisted we needed to rest. I also pulled the doctor aside, out of Sam's hearing, and confided that Sam's girlfriend had been killed in front of him, which led the doctor to giving us some sedatives to make sure we got the sleep we needed.

Sam slept soundly on his bed, the half-empty tonic vial left on a small table near him. I walked over and pulled his blanket up out of habit more than any need. There were dried streams of tears staining his cheeks. It made my heart crack at the sight. I gently kissed his head, then went to rest myself, but sleep wouldn't come. My body was exhausted, but after everything, I felt like I couldn't be unconscious. I needed to be awake in case anything happened, which was stupid, as we were probably in one of the few situations where we were safe to rest. My mind haphazardly wondered how long it had been since I slept in a bed, and with surprise, I realised it was when we were at Megan's apartment in the Grove. It actually wasn't that long ago, but so many awful things had happened since then. All of it started playing through my mind, having to say goodbye to Miles again, seeing Lilli killed and Sam being tortured. It was too much, and nothing good could come of dwelling on those thoughts. I grabbed the last half of the tonic and drank it in one gulp before settling into bed. Things would seem better when I woke up. At least, I hoped they would.

· · · · · · · · · · ·

Sam stood in the middle of a dark room as blue electric sparks flickered across his skin, throwing a pulsing light across the small space. All around his feet in the dark were crumpled figures. Dozens and dozens of lifeless bodies scattered across the floor, and at the centre was Sam, his arms outstretched and his head tilted upwards with a cold, dangerous smile cutting across this face. This was not my Sam. This dark, twisted version of Sam locked eyes with mine. 'Look what we could be, Mother.' His warped, trickling voice cut through the darkness. 'We could be so much more. We could be whatever we want to be.' The dark Sam's smile broadened, and he flicked his hands forward, sending a huge bolt of electricity into my chest.

I sat upright in bed, panting. The space was dark and quiet. I gripped the blankets with my fist, letting reality seep back into my mind. Sam still lay where I had last seen him, completely unconscious to the world in his bed, with a healing strip firmly attached to his forehead. I threw my covers down, and while still trying to shake off the echoes of the dream, went outside the tent. The chem-lights were dimmed, simulating nightfall. Cool cavern air brushed against the sweat around my neck, and I smelled something cooking. Something rich with spice. The smell drew me towards it, and my stomach started grumbling. I had no idea how long I had been out for, and I was hungry.

Led by a saliva-inducing aroma, I found the communal eating space where a pot with something delicious-smelling in it happily bubbled away on a fire, surrounded by a ring of rocks that were used as seats. The pot was tenderly cared for by a young man who stirred its contents with a calm reverence, while two familiar figures sat on nearby rocks, hunched over their bowls, contentedly sampling the pot's contents. I hesitated for a moment, but my hunger drove me forwards in hope that Megan and Peter could hook me up with some food. I knew that there were also a lot of conversations I couldn't put off any longer. I needed answers.

Megan was the first to notice me emerge from the darkness and urged me to the seat next to her. 'You feeling better?' she said as I rested my sore joints on the cold rock.

'Yeah, I am actually.'

'You must be starving. Hold on a sec.' Megan walked over to the young man at the steaming pot and started getting me a bowl. My stomach grumbled in anticipation. While she was gone, a strained silence stretched between me and Peter as he continued to avoid eye contact. Megan returned with a bowl of stew, and I fell upon it with excited enthusiasm. The hot stew was comforting, and I soon felt more like myself, meaning I couldn't put off my questions any longer.

'Obviously there's some sort of understanding or shared knowledge between the two of you I don't know about, otherwise I can't explain how you're so forgiving, Megan. Not after everything.'

'You're right,' said Peter, bolstering himself and finally looking at me. 'There is more you need to know.'

'Have you both known everything this whole time, and just chosen to keep it a secret? Was watching me struggle and fight to survive through everything fun for you? Or was it some sort of sick consequence of wanting to relive your golden days? Tell me the truth about everything!' The words came out with more venom than I meant, but I was mad and the food had re-energised me. I hadn't wanted to re-enter a world with danger at every corner. I just wanted a quiet life with my son, and these people had somehow dragged me into this ridiculous, violent, painful and politically messy web. My son was hurting because of it, and I was mad.

'Peter didn't mea—' started Megan.

'No, I need to tell her everything. I owe her that,' said Peter. 'Yes, I've known about the messy politics and power plays since the start. A while ago, I started hearing rumours of secret meetings Vivian was holding with various companies and political figures. I didn't think too much of it until I noticed that a lot of our new assignments involved targets that were threats to either La Panta or the Grove. Sure, the targets were guilty and charged with legitimate offences, but the pattern ate away at me. I knew Megan was helping some underground movement or something, so I tried to get in contact with her as the more I looked into things, the messier and more disturbing it got. The Agency wasn't operating like the Agency that I love. Megan sent someone from the Hidden to meet me, and they told me everything about the Entity and their suspicions of how far its reach had stretched on Tir-na. They thought even the Agency had fallen under its influence, and that idea terrified me. The Agency exists to help keep the peace and protect people from untoward interests. That's what I signed up for and what I believe in. So, to make sure the institution I believe in, and that means so much to me, isn't used for nefarious purposes, I started passing bits of information to the Hidden. I would visit the Grove under the pretext of trying to recruit new Grovian informants, but really, I was meeting contacts from the Hidden. I didn't even know the name of the Hidden contacts, as they always changed. We went along like that for five months until your name popped up. We had an order in the Agency to confirm your location and establish a pattern of life for Vivian. Around a month later you came barrelling into the Agency office. That's when I knew something was up. I didn't know exactly what was going on, but I knew I didn't want you facing it alone. I'm so sorry Rachel. I should have told you, but at the time, I thought it would be better to keep it from you until I understood why it was all happening. I'm an idiot, I know.'

266

'And when you betrayed us and turned us over to that demented pervert who tortured and experimented on me and my son? What was that? Did you know that was going to happen? You had already experienced what he could do, and you just left us to it?'

'I never knew that shithead Velor was involved until we were captured in La Panta. I had no idea about their stupid plan of using stress to activate your powers. Then, at the base, leading you to Vivian and letting you be taken was the only way I could save you. Well, save as many as I could. It made me sick to do it, but they knew we were there and, reading the situation, we would have all been killed if I tried anything else. There was no way out of that, so I made a way out. I still feel sick about it all. I couldn't save Lilli. I still see her face. Then I couldn't get to you and Sam for a couple of days. I can't even imagine what you went through with that sick son of a bitch. What you both went through. I'm so, so sorry Rachel.' Peter put his face in his hands and roughly wiped away tears.

I took a moment to absorb everything. It was all so messy, but I knew who had caused all this pain and suffering. 'Is Vivian part of this Entity group?' I asked.

'We think she's vying for a position. They make potential members prove themselves before full admittance,' said Megan, matter-of-factly.

'And the Master is in charge of the Entity?'

'Not quite, but he's pretty high up,' Megan replied.

'So, what are we going to do about it?' I asked. Peter looked up and I could see in his eyes both pain and the hope that there was something he could do to fix everything. I knew it wasn't helpful dwelling on what had happened, so instead I tried to figure out what to do next.

'Well,' said Megan, 'we have some ideas, but what are you thinking, Rach?'

'I'm thinking we take these bitches down and make them pay.'

25

The Road Home

W E SPENT THE NEXT week plotting and scheming, and I had to admit, having access to the resources of the Hidden was extremely useful. They knew details about bases, patterns of life and security systems we never could have known. Calista also proved to be an extremely gifted and reliable leader. She knew so much and her eye for detail was meticulous, so each time we came up with a plan, she would examine it and point out any potential faults or risks. She was able to mobilise and encourage people like no one I had seen before, and simultaneously offer them the care and attention they needed. I could see why people stayed here, and why people fought for her.

After waking from his drug-induced sleep, Sam had split his time between our planning efforts and helping at the Zinke's fix-it-shop. I checked in with him a couple of times to make sure he was okay about being there, but he said it made him feel useful, that helping keep the little shop going seemed the one thing he could do for them. He also wanted Mr and Mrs Zinke to know someone truly cared about Lilli, and they weren't alone in their pain. It was during his time working at the shop that he learnt the full truth about Lilli. She had received a scholarship through the Master to attend university in Crayn, and she had started informing on us because of threats to her family. All of that was true. What we didn't know, though, was that the Zinkes were already part of the Hidden. They had used Lilli's position as a scholarship recipient to their advantage, and reported everything she knew back through Calista's network of informants. The Zinkes had moved their little shop from the Grove to the Hidden's cave after the questioning from Raph Merton's goons became a bit too intense and personal.

They had known something was up and were smart about keeping themselves safe. During those hours spent in the shop, Sam learnt that Lilli had been so much braver and more complicated than any of us ever realised, and it made the pain of losing her even more potent.

In our spare moments, Sam and I would seek a private spot in the cave system to practice using our abilities. We learnt a lot about our surroundings by practising our 'sonar', discovering that the Hidden had a separate cavern filled with transportation vehicles, including lo-vehics and e-vehic trucks. There was even a server room hidden off the main living cavern, which was mostly set to receive mode, with messages coming in regularly, and very few going out. Out of curiosity the two of us poked around a bit in the messages coming in and found that they were almost exclusively reports from on-the-ground operatives with little snippets of information about various Entity targets. One specific message caught my eye. It mentioned Serena Fabrica becoming increasingly annoyed that the Entity hadn't come through with its promise of delivering their next upgraded AI, said to be OmniAI. The agent reported that Serena even threatened to withdraw La Panta resources if the Entity didn't fulfil their half of the contact soon. My son, being who he is, became fascinated with the presumed-mythical OmniAI and spent a fair bit of his spare time rummaging through the servers, gleaning anything he could, until he found out what none of us wanted to hear. OmniAI was the system the Agency used. No one knew if OmniAI was developed in-house at the Agency or if it was gifted from somewhere, but it enabled the organisation to sidestep any system protection or safety protocols to access information about anyone and anything. It also proved the horrible depths of Vivian's betrayal, as OmniAI in the wrong hands would threaten the freedoms and safety of all citizens.

By the end of the week, my head was throbbing from tracking the connections across the tangled web we were caught in, but the information about the AI made things click together. The motivations finally made sense. What would motivate a powerful conglomerate to assist an unseen, nebulous organisation like the Entity for decades? The promise of constant access to the most advanced AI systems available to ensure economic domination would probably do it. Then there was

Vivian and her connection to it all. She had always been extremely capable, and even though we didn't like each other, I had always thought she was smart and highly skilled, but I never would have imagined her in a leadership role at the Agency, let alone its Head. It had been a meteoric rise for Vivian. The previous Agency Head was quite young when he retired. Through Peter, I found out there had been rumours of an affair and blackmail surrounding his departure, which was strange, as he didn't seem like the type for that kind of thing. The Entity obviously needed access to the Agency's OmniAI to maintain the cooperation of La Panta, including having access to La Panta's vast resources. That was when a sick feeling hit my stomach as a thought took root in my mind. Vivian's promotion and the agreement between La Panta and the Entity for OmniAI were connected, with the Entity also involved in Vivian's rise to power as the Agency's Head.

This realisation only intensified our resolve. These people would stop at nothing to achieve their goals, and it looked like Sam and I were directly in their sights. In that moment, I had two options: we could either flee and hope hiding was enough to keep us safe, or we could do something to make sure we stayed safe. I had run away before, hoping for a quiet life, but it hadn't lasted. My old life and the past had caught up with me, so this time I was determined to make sure my son was safe to have the life he deserved. Not as a test subject for some power-hungry, faceless organisation, but as a free person. I would do anything to give that to my son. So, I planned and plotted with the rest of our small team. I still didn't trust Peter, or maybe I just couldn't forgive him for what he put my son through. Either way, he was useful for our scheming. His knowledge of the targets was impressive, but I guess that comes with working in a place that can provide you with information about any target with the swipe of a finger.

After many arguments and discussions, the plan was finally set. We were going to take them down, and with the support of the Hidden, we might actually pull it off.

The day before we put our plan into action was a quiet day. Sam spent most of his time with the Zinkes again, and I found myself in the company of Calista.

'What will you do after this, Rachel?' Calista asked me while we chopped tubers for the nightly meal in the community kitchen.

'I truthfully don't know,' I replied. 'I've thought about me and Sam staying in Crayn, but I don't think I feel comfortable there anymore. The Grove isn't for us, and I don't think we can stay here with you. Even though it would be great, I think there are too many painful ghosts here to give either of us a real chance of a fresh start.'

'You speak of the terrible loss of Lilli Zinke.' No question in it from Calista, just a statement. We both looked up from our rhythmic chopping in the direction the Zinke's fix-it shop. We couldn't see the shop from where we were, but I knew that's where Sam would be.

'I think Sam feels guilty about what happened. We all feel guilty, but I think he feels it more sharply. If we stayed here, I'm not sure he'd ever be free of it.'

'I believe you might be right. I have noticed him often at the Zinkes', helping them with their shop. He has been so very kind to them, but it would be a shame to see such a bright, smart and kind young man tinker away in a fix-it shop and never realise his full potential. I believe the drive to see their child reach their full potential is what led to the Zinkes letting Lilli go to Crayn, despite the risks. They had faith in her and were determined to do everything in their power to secure a brighter future, not only for Lilli, but for all children. After all, doesn't every parent want to see their children take hold of opportunities that were never available to them? To live the dreams we could never have?'

'You're not wrong.'

'And I believe that's why they joined us here at the Hidden, and why I hope in time, they will continue the fight alongside us.'

We let the conversation drift away and sat, chopping in silence, letting our own thoughts consume us.

'Have you thought where you'd go if not back to Crayn?'

'Truthfully, I haven't. I haven't let myself make plans too far ahead since everything has been so uncertain.'

'Well, there are some beautiful cities on Tir-na. Cities without dust that clings to your clothes.' Calista slapped some dirt out of her skirt. 'I'm told some of them are really a sight to behold and are also big enough for people to truly start a new life.'

'I'll think about it,' I simply replied and went back to my chopping. And think about it, I did. I wondered and speculated while cutting each tuber. Calista left to do her rounds of the camp and I started weighing the pros and cons of Aeir and Uishka, the other large cities on Tir-na. Two beautiful cities I had only passed through on missions. I even considered the idea of heading off-world, but I didn't think I was ready for that. I hypothesised about what each option would mean for Sam and what type of life it could give him. But I mostly thought about how we could start afresh in a place where no one knew us. It was an interesting and exciting thought that I took to bed with me that night, holding it as a promise that there would be something bigger and better for us after tomorrow, if we survived tomorrow.

· · · · · · · · · ·

The next day, our plan swung into action. Kitted up with oxy-masks, we headed back to the surface. Coming out of the cave system was a shock and my eyes winced painfully from the bright daylight. A fearsome wind had picked up and was lashing us with grains of sand. I pulled Old Blue around myself a little tighter and rushed over to our stolen lo-vehic with Sam, using one arm to buffer my face from the sandy gale. Only Peter and Megan came with us on this trip, as we didn't need many for this part of the plan. Lucas and his team had already loaded the stolen lo-vehic with explosives. It was now Sam's job to use his skills to program the lo-vehic so that in perfect synchronisation with our advance on the Palace, it would fly haphazardly around the Wastes before returning to its home base with a bit too much enthusiasm.

We ran over to the side of the lo-vehic and opened it up, then rushed inside, happy to escape the blasting abrasive winds of the Wastes. After coughing and spluttering to clear the sand from our throats, Megan and Peter took up defensive positions in the body of the lo-vehic while Sam and I headed for the cockpit.

'Alright, you know what to do?' I asked Sam after settling into my seat.

'Yep. I studied transport coding last term, so this shouldn't be too hard. I just need to send it home, right?' He said with a half-smile.

'Don't forget, we need the timing to work.'

'Yes Mum, I remember. Don't worry. You just do your thing to keep us safe.' He closed his eyes and settled back. His breathing becoming slower and more rhythmic. He looked like he was meditating. I realised this must be what I look like every time I used my powers.

'Oh! Almost forgot, kid,' said Peter suddenly. 'You'll need an access ID. Hold up.' Sam looked at me quizzically, but I had no idea what was happening. Peter started tapping on his wrist-comm, then suddenly said, 'Remember this number, 573592.'

'573592,' repeated Sam.

'Yep. You got it. Welcome to the Agency, kid. You're now an agent with your own ID and everything.' Sam looked stunned.

'How...how did you do that?' I asked.

'You got your abilities, and I got mine, and sometimes it's best you don't know how I do what I do.'

'Alright then,' I murmured.

I settled back, closed my eyes and found the quietness within me that contained a little spark. I held onto it and caressed it before throwing it outwards, letting it expand as far and wide as it could. My job was to make sure no one knew what we were doing, so I let my powers feel the space as far out from us as possible. And there I waited, sensing and reaching for any electromagnetic signal. Anything that might pose a threat. But the sky stayed clear, and before I knew it, I heard a voice calling to me through the haze of my powers.

'Mum, it's done.'

I stopped pushing my powers out and let them retreat into me. I opened my eyes and found Sam looking at me. There was a small patch of sweat on the side of his temple and the scar on his cheek was flushed a brighter pink.

'Was it harder than you thought?' I asked.

'A bit harder, but I got it. I must say, that ID code came in handy.'

'Told ya,' piped up Peter's voice from the back of the cabin.

'I've set it to take off in three days,' said Sam. 'That should give everyone enough time to make sure it's ready, and for us to make our way to the Palace. It has enough fuel, so no need to worry about that either.'

'Fantastic! Great work sweetie,' I said and pulled Sam into a hug. 'I'm so proud of you.'

'Mum, stop,' was the only reply I got as he tried to push my arms off him while hiding a smile. Satisfied with our work, we headed back into the caves to prep for the next stage.

···•••••···

Having an underground intelligence and reconnaissance group on our side proved extremely helpful. They already knew tunnels hidden throughout the cave system that could get us most of the way to the Grove. Lucas also kindly offered to come with us, to show the way and help however he could. I never got his story out of him. Nothing about how he ended up with the Hidden, or about the man with kind eyes I had seen him eating meals with and suspected was his partner. Not even why he seemed so keen to take down the Entity. But Lucas was a big help to us, and that was enough for me, so I left him to his mysterious secrets.

The trip was hard, with the nights uncomfortable and the days long and tiring. There were no natural light sources away from the Hidden's main cavern, so we travelled by the light of glow torches. We spent two full days hiking through the cave system in the dark. It was tough, but gave me time to practice. I would often send out what I thought of as a radar ping to build my stamina with my powers, but also out of curiosity to see what was around us. I thought of it like a muscle I needed to keep working in order to strengthen it. Down in the depths of the tunnels, though, the only things that pinged back were devices carried by our group. I found I could easily reach for my spark now, stretching or directing it as precisely as I needed. It was a relief to finally have some cognisant control over it, rather than just using intuition and hope. I still didn't understand the full breadth of what I could do, and part of me was terrified to find out.

Early afternoon of the third day, we finally emerged into blinding sunlight. A strange stillness sat across the Wastes. Usually winds ripped across the landscape, but not today. It was unnervingly quiet, like it had been waiting for us. I ignored my nerves and followed Lucas out of the caves, pulling Old Blue around me a little tighter. Lucas had organised covert means to get our small group into the city. He had organised for one of his people who worked as a sand hauler to provide us transport to the Grove. Sand haulers spent their days digging out the giant sandbank that built up along the side of the Grove's wall from the fierce Waste winds. They used a sand-mover to scoop up a load, and transport it out into the Wastes somewhere, and then repeat that process ad infinitum. Without someone doing that, the Grove risked getting buried by the sand, and it would be impossible when it came time for the Grove to roll forward again. A sand-mover was therefore a common sight and the perfect incognito transport from our location in the Wastes to the Grove.

We met the sand hauler at the organised spot behind a rocky outcrop and piled into the sand-mover to get on our way. Sand-movers are big, but their cabin areas are only designed for four people, so with five of us and the sand hauler squished in, it quickly got uncomfortable. I spent the next hour with the edge of a small toolbox jammed into my hip and Sam's elbow in the back of my neck as the sand hauler conducted another sand collection run. The extra run helped ensure we didn't draw attention, but my joints groaned at having to stay in the awkward position for longer. The sand-mover finally began its slow approach to the Grove's wall, and when it parked to fill up another load, we said a quick thank you and hustled out of the cabin to duck behind the cover of the giant sandbank. It would have been suicide to climb the sandbank itself, as the risk of an avalanche was too high. Instead, we crouched and ran, using the sandbank's hulking expanse to shield us from unwanted eyes. Our target destination was a small, forgettable door in the wall around to the left, a door the Hidden had created with a laser cutter the last time the Grove moved. I had no idea how they managed it without being caught, but I was thankful for it.

The door opened into the belly of the wall and Lucas ushered us inside to the right. Within the wall was a latticework of beams smashed together to hold the thick, mismatched rusty metal sheets against the brunt of the fierce winds. The space we were in stretched both forwards and upwards, soaring high above us to the top of the towering wall. The structure was completely hollow, with just enough room inside for a person to duck and climb their way through the web of beams. For some reason I had thought the wall would be solid, but it was simply a facade with a few strong supports propping it up. A dark chuckle at the similarity of this structure and the Grove's eclectic master escaped my lips.

With Megan leading the way, we ducked and wove our way through the wall, heading towards the Palace. We moved silently, scared to set off any sound in the metallic-lined structure. Lucas knocked something off a beam at one point. The clang bounced off the side of the wall and pierced through the confined space, echoing back and forth between the metal sheets stretching far above us. We all froze. On the other side of these metal sheets was the Grove, where exactly I wasn't sure, but since it was mid-afternoon, it was highly likely there was someone with ears on the other side. We stayed silent and still for a long time, many of us frozen awkwardly mid-duck or weave. Poor Lucas just stayed on top of the beam, desperately trying to not make more sounds. Once deemed safe to proceed, we continued our cautious and claustrophobic journey through the bowels of the wall. I couldn't see past Peter, who was in front of me, so when we finally halted, I had to pull myself up to not crash into him and Sam almost lowered himself down on top of me as he finished climbing over a beam. With the entire line paused, we finally heard why we had stopped. Megan had found the door.

Peter suddenly turned to me and whispered, 'Check there is no one before exiting the door. Head right and group up behind the storage crates. Pass it on.'

I saw Megan peek out the door, then smoothly slink out. Next was Peter, who tentatively looked out but quickly pulled back and froze, alerting us that there was something out there we didn't want to see. Then, after another peek, he rushed out the door. It was then my turn. I looked up once more at the web of beams stretching out above me, taking in the strange sight for the last time, then with my weapon gripped tight in one hand, I cracked the door and peered out into the waiting twilight.

26

Into the Palace

THE EVENING TWILIGHT GAVE off a strained blue light that washed over the cluttered storage yard in front of me. Littered with containers and crates, it was hard to see clearly across the expanse from the doorway, but there on the other side rose the strange, multi-coloured, multi-styled Palace. It stretched ominously into the sky, casting a huge, stretched shadow in the evening light. I scanned the yard for movement but saw nothing, so sprinted to where Megan and Peter were crouching behind a large pile of crates. It seemed too quiet, and that's when I felt something. It was a vibration in the air followed by a swinging, piercing slice, and my heart sunk at the realisation I had felt that before.

'Bot!' I whispered fervently at Megan. She locked eyes with me for half a heartbeat and then put her hand up, signalling for Sam and Lucas to stay behind the door. Sam's head quickly pulled back into the protection of the wall and the door closed behind him.

'Where about?' asked Megan.

'Off to the right, just coming round the corner.'

'How many?'

'One that I can sense.'

'Well, that explains why there aren't any guards. No need with bots flying around. If we get pinned down by the bots and can't get in the Palace, our whole plan is out the window. Can you do anything?'

'You got any EMPs?'

Megan gave me a dry look. 'We're not that well stocked at the Hidden.' It had been wishful thinking anyway.

I took a deep breath and reached out to the vibrations coming from the floating bot. Suddenly, a second goosebump-inducing tingle caught my attention. 'Second bot just appeared from the left,' I warned.

I opened my awareness and pushed out a force that wove itself into a secure net around the bots to disrupt their communications and ensure they wouldn't sound the alarm to summon Palace guards down upon us. With the comms secure, I attempted to push even harder, willing my power to penetrate deeper into the core systems of the bots and disable them completely. But I didn't have time. The first bot was barrelling towards us at frightening speed, and the sight of it made the recently healed scars from metal daggers tingle across my body.

'On our right, bot approaching fast. We can't stay here,' I said to Megan. She responded instantly, barking orders at Peter to prep his weapon, and spread out. He raised his gun and began eyeing off other crates to move behind, but there wasn't time to move safely with the bot streaming towards us.

I jumped up to the top of the crates and on an instinct, sprinted across the top of the crates and launched myself at the bot. Landing on top of it with a thud, I gripped onto it as my weight pushed the bot off course. It wrenched to the side but stayed in the air, my weight not enough to pull it to the ground. I held onto it for dear life as the bot swung around in a half circle. A loud ping sounded off the other side of the metal bot as a sharp piercing and familiar pain hit my left thigh. I looked up and saw the second bot hovering nearby, aiming directly at me. The second bot shot another volley of daggers. I pulled my bot sharply sideways to get out of the bot's range, but it left me exposed and in pain. I needed to end it quickly. Without thought, I slammed my palm down on top of the bot and started forcefully pushing and pulling at the electrical signals in the bot's internal network. My hand shimmered and sparked with blue crackling energy as I ripped apart the bot's internal mechanisms with surges of electricity. An ominous crackling noise hissed from inside the bot. I didn't have much time. I pulled my weight backwards, causing the bot to drift closer to the ground, then once at a manageable distance, I let go and dropped the last couple of metres. The dagger still embedded in my thigh tore at my flesh as I landed in a crouch. The bot erupted in sparks that engulfed its form in a blinding cocoon, before plummeting to the ground in a dusty explosion. A muffled swear word escaped my lips as I pushed up, ripped the dagger out of my thigh in frustration, and started racing towards the other bot.

My thigh screamed as I ran towards the second bot with my hand outstretched. I latched onto and yanked at the waves inside the second bot. Surges of energy rushed towards me, pouring out of the bot, and I gathered them in my palms, forcing the electromagnetic waves into a warbling, sparking ball. I continued to pull and pull, ripping the energy from the bot. Once stripped of all its energy, it fell from the sky and crashed into the ground, inert and defunct. A third set of vibrations in the air appeared behind me from around the corner of the Palace. I spun and released the giant ball of energy straight at the third bot. The warbling electric ball sailed through the air and stuck true, blue energy crackling and sparking across the bot in a shimmering cloud that overwhelmed its systems and rendered it useless. After the third and final bot crashed into the dusty ground, I turned and limped back to Megan and Peter. They both still held their weapons at the ready, but their eyes just stared at the crashed bots littering the yard.

'That was...interesting,' said Peter.

'I thought I would try something,' I said as I limped past them, heading for the pack I'd left behind the crates.

'Alright then,' said Megan, her initial surprise turning into action. 'Get yourself patched up, Rach. Peter, let Sam and Lucas know it's safe to come out of the wall. We need to move.'

I busied myself with applying wound seals from a med kit to stop the bleeding from my thigh as Sam finally emerged from the wall and came to help. The wound was clean but deep, and I knew it would cause me grief for the rest of the day but would heal up nicely. Sam looked at me through worried eyes, but I just popped some pain relief and pushed myself up to stand next to him and placed my hand on his shoulder in a comforting manner. Megan was right. We needed to move, so any conversations would need to wait.

With the bots eliminated, and our guns at the ready, our group ran across the expanse towards a side door to the Palace.

'Sam, can you deal with the cameras?' I asked as we ran. 'Just as we practised.' Sam nodded, then, while still running, he sent his power out to manipulate any cameras along our path. I sensed the change in the surrounding electromagnetic waves almost instantly and knew he had done it. Pride bubbled up inside me as a small smile spread across my face.

We reached the side entrance into the Palace and paused briefly to reassess. 'This is it,' said Megan. 'Once inside, Sam, you're with me and we're heading to the server hub.' Sam nodded and gripped his weapon a little tighter. 'Rach, Peter and Lucas, you're going after the Master and Vivian. As we've said, from what we know of the Palace layout, they will be on the top floor. Remember, don't let them get to the Master's lo-vehic on the top level. If they get away, then we've lost our chance.' There was a silent pause as we all readied ourselves for the next stage of the plan. 'See you on the other side,' said Megan with a smile.

I quickly pulled Sam into a tight, fast hug. 'Remember what we've practised and stay safe. Do everything Megan says,' I commanded, 'and remember, I love you.'

Sam hugged me back. 'Love you too, Mum. I'll see you soon.' He smiled at me with a confidence I wished I shared and a warmth that stopped my heart. I held onto it and locked the feeling away, sending a silent prayer that he would be safe, and I would see him again soon.

Megan appeared at my side. With her hand on my shoulder, she whispered, 'I'll get him back to you,' her hand tightening as she spoke. I turned to face her and forced a hug on her. She wasn't the type for mushy stuff, but I didn't care. I trusted Megan, more than I had trusted anyone in a very long time. Part of me ached at the idea of what could have been the life and friendship we might have shared if we'd crossed paths twenty years ago. Maybe we both wouldn't have been alone through everything, but there was no point in dwelling on could've-would've-should've thoughts, as that way pain and sorrow lay. Anyway, if anything changed in my past, I wouldn't have Sam, and nothing was worth losing him.

'Let's get a drink when this is all over. I think we could both use a good girls' night out.' I smiled at her.

'Sounds perfect,' she replied. Then, with a confirming nod between our little group, Megan slowly cracked the door and instantly let off two stun shots. The bodies of two guards crumpled to the ground, and after a scan of the surrounding area, we hurried into the hallway, avoiding the twitching limbs of the fallen guards.

We hit an intersection, and there our party split in two. I squeezed Sam's hand briefly and then he was gone. I sucked in a breath, steeling myself for what we needed to do. Then, with Peter and Lucas by my side, we began moving forward towards our goal.

'Just like that raid on the Capelson family,' said Peter as we hurried down a hallway towards an intersection with our guns at the ready. 'We keep it tight, fast and together, and remember, I've got your back now just like I did then.'

I spun towards him and let off two stun shots over his left shoulder, dropping a guard that appeared from around the corner. 'I've got your back too,' I said with a slight smirk.

We hustled through the labyrinth of passageways and stairwells, pausing now and then to nullify the security cameras, until we suddenly found ourselves in a large, open mess hall. Around ten guards were there drinking coffee or having food. They stared at us in confusion for a moment until Peter and I started firing. With our guns still set to stun, the two of us took down four guards before they even reacted, their bodies crumpling to the ground in a spasming pile. Another four were faster than their compatriots and shot back, forcing us to take cover behind the tables and food carts. Lucas let off two perfect shots that dropped two more guards, their limbs twitching as they fell to the ground. That only left two still shooting at us, and another two that had the good sense to run out of the room.

In a coordinated effort, the three of us concentrated our fire on the remaining two guards, and it wasn't long before they too lay unconscious on the floor. With that threat eliminated, we made a move to leave but were stopped in our tracks. Five black-clad figures emerged through the doorway in a too fast and too coordinated manner to be regular Palace guards. Everything about their movements and defensive positioning was familiar. These weren't guards, they were agents.

I rolled to the ground behind a table as two small spongy cubes sailed over my head and landed on either side of Lucas. A heartbeat later, Lucas was engulfed in the warbling golden energy of a silencer trap. He tried smashing through the energy field, but it was no use. Agency silencer traps were the best but were really shit if you were on the receiving end of one. More cubes sailed through the air towards me. I rolled sideways and leapt behind the cover of another table. They landed where I had been and activated around thin air.

Peter was crouching and weaving through the room, staying out of the agents' sight. He was trying to get the jump on them, but with one of us already contained, it was two against five, which weren't great odds. Peter needed a distraction if he was going to make it. A horrible, stupid idea planted in my mind. I swore to myself and I hoped my years as a movement teacher paid off.

I leapt up and over the table and ran at the agents. More cubes flew at me, but I grabbed one and threw it back before it could activate. I shot at the agents as I rushed towards them and managed to stun one who crumpled to the ground. The surprise attack caught the agents off-guard and with their attention now on me, Peter emerged behind them and smashed the butt of this gun into one of their temples, knocking them unconscious. I fired a stun shot at another but missed, then launched myself and tackled the closest agent. We spun off each other, and I landed in a crouch facing them. It was a young woman, practically a child in my eyes, but she looked hungry and determined. I guess that's what I looked like when I was her age, until life and too much experience had broken my naïve perceptions.

In my periphery, I saw Peter fighting the other two agents, but his movements didn't look like they usually did. He was pulling his punches. That's when I realised these were agents he probably worked with every day, and most likely trained himself. There would be some interesting conversations around Mission Hub after everything was over.

The agent I faced used my moment of distraction and smashed their leg into my ribs. The blow was painful, and it sent me off balance, but I used it to propel myself back up and retaliate with a kick of my own. My leg connected with the side of the girl's face, and she stumbled from the impact. She recovered quickly though and spun to face me; her frame braced for a fight. Whoever had trained her had done well. She lunged with a flurry of attacks that had me on the defence. I countered, but a single punch to my throat slipped through. It left me gasping for air and pissed me off. I launched myself and smashed my forearm into her throat, elbowed her solar plexus and kicked her groin. As she was already gasping for air and struggling to move, I fell back into a defensive pose. The poor girl looked rough.

My vision filled with a warbling golden light. I glanced around and noticed an agent watching as the power from the two sponge cubes he'd thrown connected, locking me in a silencer trap. I reached out and felt the electrical burn from the energy field course through my finger. It stung but also called to a part of me.

Trapped, I looked around to assess the situation. Lucas was stuck in a silencer trap, pointlessly bashing on the electrical wall with the butt of his weapon. Peter had been overrun, and an agent had him pinned to the ground. This was looking bad.

My throat was burning from the punch the agent got in, and I knew from experience that my voice would be rough for days. I ignored it as my mind whirled. We didn't have time for this crap. If we didn't succeed, Sam's life would be under threat forever. It needed to end today.

The anger of the entire situation filled me, as my spark of power burned deep in my core. I grabbed onto it and flamed it with all my anger. It grew bigger and bigger until it consumed me, and spread outwards, latching onto the silencer trap electrical barrier surrounding me. Then I lifted my hand to the barrier and willed it to join me. The electricity coursed into me and I drew it towards my central spark. My entire body shimmered with bright, crackling blue streams of light. My outsides finally reflected the constant turmoil and anger I felt inside.

I sucked all the electricity out of the silencer trap, rendering it useless, then turned to face the agent holding Peter and the one that threw the trap. They were staring at me, and I saw the whites of their eyes expand as I flicked my hands out and shot two bolts of energy towards them. One hit the agent on top of Peter, knocking them to the ground with an incapacitating surge of electricity. The other agent rolled out of the way and watched as the ball of energy smashed into the wall behind them in an explosion of sparking energy. I reached my hands behind me and pulled at the electricity from the silencer trap surrounding Lucas, letting it flow into me.

'Get the cubes!' I yelled at Lucas and Peter with a husky, sparking voice.

Peter rolled into action, rushing over and grabbing the two cubes next to me. He threw them on either side of the female agent I had been fighting. With a blast of energy from my hands they sprang back to life, trapping her in a golden cage. I walked towards her and then through the golden barrier. The currents listened to me now and were no longer an impediment. I grabbed her wrist-comm and removed it so she couldn't deactivate the trap. She was still hunched over and struggling to breathe so didn't put up much of a fight, but her eyes stared at me with an intense fear. I left her inside the trap and went to Lucas, who was holding the two sponge cubes from his now defunct trap.

'Surround the agents with the cubes.' I commanded. 'Peter. Get their wrist-comms.'

With difficulty, Peter subdued the remaining agents and ripped off their wrist-comms as Lucas positioned the cubes. Once clear, I released streams of energy, and the silencer trap sprang to life, trapping the agents. They gaped at me with a strange fear in their eyes, but I ignored their looks and made my way to the exit. We needed to keep going.

27

Takedown

I WAS BUZZING FROM the encounter and felt strangely excited for what I could come next.

'Rach?' Peter said, causing me to pause at the threshold of the room and turn to face him.

'What is it, Peter?' I asked, my voice still raspy from the hit to the throat.

'Ummm, you feeling...okay?'

Frustration flared within me. Why was he asking such a stupid question? It didn't matter what I felt like. We needed to get this done. I bit the anger back as I responded, 'I'm fine, Peter.' I turned to leave, but he ran up beside me.

'I just thought you should know that your eyes are glowing. Also, your whole body is covered in blue sparks...you sure you're alright?'

I looked down at my palm, and he was right. My entire body was covered in crackling energy, but I wasn't scared of it. Strangely, I hadn't ever felt stronger, more determined, more in control and or more like myself.

'Ha!' I exclaimed, more at myself than anyone else. 'Well, I guess we're learning what I'm capable of. Perfect timing, really.' I smiled and put a hand on the door. Peter hesitated for a split second, but then moved to my side as we carefully opened the door and peeked through.

There was a camera. With a flick of my hand, I sent a wave of jolting energy down the entire hallway, shorting the circuits of every camera in the vicinity, rendering them useless. After what had just happened, there was no point in being covert now.

'We need to head this way, then up the stairs to the left,' whispered Lucas. 'Up a couple of flights, then down the hall to where the Master will be. Our little encounter back there would have activated his evacuation protocols, so that's where he'll be. The guards the Master keeps close to him are professional killers who won't hesitate to eliminate you, so don't hesitate with your stun shots.'

I looked at my two companions. Both stared at me with a cautious curiosity, but their faces were determined. It was the final push now, and we all knew it. I took a breath and felt myself relax into who I was and what I had become. I had always shied away from the fact I was a trained ex-agent with a kill count, and my new powers scared me. But they were both part of me. Part of my history. Just as being a mum, and a movement and meditation coach, who simply craved a quiet life, was also part of me. It was all me. A rich tapestry. I held layers of complexity and contradictions, but all of it wove itself together to become me. With this acceptance, I let myself embrace my power.

We moved into the hallway in a tight formation and worked our way up a stairway on the left as I eliminated the cameras ahead of us. We emerged at the top into a larger hallway that led to a huge, ornately decorated golden door. Three guards, with their weapons at the ready, stood in front. They started shooting when they saw us, forcing us to drop and roll out of the way. Lucas grunted in pain, then aimed his weapon and returned fire, hitting each of the guards squarely in the chest. They fell almost as one, their bodies twitching as they crumpled to the ground. I had clearly underestimated Lucas.

'You okay?' I asked.

'Just a graze,' Lucas said as he pulled a medi-patch from his front coat pocket and slapped it on his thigh, where a large blotch of red had started spreading. He stood up and his face twitched in a silent grimace. 'See. Nothing to worry about. Now let's get moving.'

We rushed forward, the feeling that our quarry was close driving us onward. We paused only long enough to assess our weapons, then together, we pushed open the grand doors.

Inside was a cavernous dome-shaped room adorned with gold chandeliers, rich burgundy carpets, billowy cream couches, glittering stained-glass windows and intricate colourful tapestries showing the Master in various majestic poses. It was an opulent transport waiting room, used I presumed by the Master and his companions to await their lo-vehics. It was a horrific juxtaposition to the dirty, crazy, chaotic streets of the Grove outside the Palace walls. Off to one side was an open-air exit to a currently empty launch pad, where lo-vehics could land. In the middle of the over-the-top domed room, seated on a sumptuous couch, relishing the luxurious environment, was the Master himself. He sat snacking on some fruit, looking contentedly at ease, while behind him stood four agents alongside a very alert and pensive Vivian.

Things happened quickly then. The agents lifted their weapons ready to fire, but before they could act, Peter sent a stun shot at one of them, while I threw a bolt of energy from each hand that slammed into two of the agents. All three collapsed to the ground in quivering heaps. The last agent hesitated slightly, giving both Peter and me the chance to shift our sights to them, but Lucas was faster and dropped the agent with a single stun shot.

With Vivian now firmly in my sights, and a grudge to settle on Lilli's behalf, I started walking towards her as two more electricity bolts grew in my hands.

A silver cage made up of beams of light sprang from the floor and sur-rounded me, and too late I realised my mistake. Distracted by my own confidence, I had walked into Vivian's trap. I reached out and tested one of the beams. It burned my finger and sent pain pulsing up my arm, causing me to jump back away from the bars. I tried throwing a bolt of energy at it, but it just skittered along the beams of light before bouncing back into me. Nothing could get out. The cage blocked electromagnetic fields, which meant my powers were redundant. I looked up at Vivian. She stood in a depressing grey pant suit with a smirk stretched tight across her face. In her fingers, she held a small remote aimed at the cage.

Two more agents charged through the main door and launched themselves at Peter and Lucas. Peter parried one of their attacks but was hit by a punch that left him winded and shaken. I couldn't do anything to help them, so with Peter and Lucas locked in their battles, I turned my attention back to Vivian, and the slightly unhinged presence of the Master. He rose to his feet, drawn towards the action.

I grimaced as his face stretched into an overly enthusiastic smile. He seemed to savour the chaos unfolding around him.

'Like my little trick, Rachel?' asked Vivian in a smug voice. 'I had it made just for you.' She always did like drama, but my tolerance level for theatrics was zero, so I ignored her.

A crackling sound emitted from the communications system in the corner of the room, drawing everyone's attention.

'Hey Mum, can you hear me?' came Sam's voice from the speakers.

'Yeah, we can Sam,' I replied.

'Great. I can hear you through the comm speaker. We're all done here. I managed to release the AI, as well as some very interesting documents that I'm sure some people would have preferred to keep hidden. I also thought it might be good for everyone to see this.'

Vivian and the Master flicked worried, unsure glances at each other as the room's large comms screen suddenly turned on. A wave of pride rushed through me as I realised Sam had really done it. The screen showed footage from the cockpit camera of the lo-vehic Sam had programmed. It flew above the Master's hidden base, giving us an aerial view of the entire compound.

'I decided to give the AI a couple of little jobs before releasing it,' said Sam, 'and you should see one of them on the screen in three, two, one.'

The entire screen filled with a huge fiery ball as the base exploded.

'That's right,' came Sam's voice through the speaker. 'Your arses are smoked!'

I smirked at Sam's terrible turn of phrase, but then focused again on the screen. There was no sound accompanying the visual, so the room was eerily quiet apart from the sounds of Peter and Lucas dealing with the agents. After the explosion settled, the lo-vehic suddenly dropped from its hovering position high above and flew directly at the base's last standing structure. It gathered speed as it charged towards the structure, then the camera cut to black. I could only imagine the explosion that would have decimated the place from the impact. Nothing would be left of the base but smoke and ruins.

'What have you done?' Vivian demanded as her cheeks flushed with rage.

'What we needed to.' My voice was still a raspy husk, but I replied with a calmness that even surprised me.

'You had everything!' Vivian yelled. 'This was *my* time. *My* chance to be the powerful one, the envied one. The one everyone wants to be. You had your time, Rachel!'

'What are you talking about? You're the Head of the Agency.'

'Everything just comes so naturally for you, doesn't it? I always had to scrape and connive just to survive. They only promoted me through the ranks because of everything I knew about them. I made some great money too, selling our equipment to the highest bidder. Then when I set my sights on the top job, I luckily had some new friends to help me. All they wanted in return was access to our AI,' she said, gesturing towards the Master who was still staring at the blank screen. 'These friends helped the old boss through his early retirement. A terrible shame and such an embarrassment to him and his wife after those nasty rumours started spreading, but it did provide an opportunity for me, and I took it! And I won't let you take any of it from me!'

What she said was unsurprising, but still shocking. My brain didn't know where to start. 'I've never felt like a natural at anything Vivian, I just didn't know how to say no when it came to my career. So, when someone suggested I should do something or give it a go, I just did it. Look at the consequences of that.' I lifted my hand, showing her the blue streaks of energy dancing over my skin. 'None of this would have happened if I had known how to say no.'

'You're right. This is all your fault. If the Entity had never found your file on our system, then none of this would have happened.'

'If the Entity hadn't found my file? Do you hear yourself? Vivian, all of this is because of you. You could have said no, but instead you wanted power and you didn't care what it took to get it. Then you helped kidnap my son, killed his girlfriend and had us both tortured. All of this is because of you. Because *you* couldn't say no. You haven't changed at all. My instincts have always been right. I never hated you Vivian, but I knew I didn't trust you. That's why you never did well as a field agent. You had skills, but you couldn't be relied on to help anyone else. You were selfish back then, and you're selfish now.'

'How dare you!'

'You're an embarrassment to everything the Agency stood for. I don't care what messed-up reason you have for what you did. Whether it was for power, out of jealously, proving a point to someone, I don't care. What you did was wrong, and I won't let you do it to anyone ever again.'

'You just try to stop me,' spat Vivian. 'You're trapped. We made sure the cage worked perfectly to contain your powers.'

'Oh, it does work perfectly to stop any of this escaping,' I said as I sent a shock of energy into the bars. It bounced around, jumping from point to point around the cage, then jumped back to me. 'But you forgot something, Vivian. Before all of this I was an agent, and an agent always has a backup plan, and luckily for me, I'm not alone in all this, unlike you.' I turned my attention back to the room's comm system. 'Sam! You still here? I could use some help to get out of this cage thing.'

'On it!' came Sam's voice from the comm speaker. A moment later, the surrounding cage winked out of existence, and I attacked.

I rushed at Vivian, leaving no time for her to realise what had happened before I was on her. I threw myself into the attack, letting loose a flurry of kicks and punches. Some of them hit, but even wearing heels, Vivian was more agile than I had hoped and managed to block or duck most of my attacks.

'You're sloppier than you used to be,' Vivian taunted as blood trickled from a split on her lip where one of my punches connected.

'You're just the same as I remember,' I mocked, then threw myself into another attack. I feinted blows and kept my attacks varied as we moved through the room. Vivian kept up, and even landed a couple of blows, but I was angry and was channelling all that anger into my attacks. I noticed my hands starting to shine with a faint blue light, and as I landed a solid body punch, a small spark jumped from my hand into Vivian. She gasped and took a step back, visibly surprised by the electric shock. It gave me the opening I needed. While she was distracted, I directed a solid kick straight at her sternum. The kick landed true and, with a little added electric shock, sent Vivian flying backwards, head over arse, towards one of the huge beautiful stained-glass windows lining the room.

I gathered my breath as remnants of electricity tingled across my hands. Vivian pulled herself back to her feet with a look of pure hatred that made me flinch.

'You bitch!' she screamed. 'Why can't you just die?' Rage pulsed off her as she stood shaking. I let the energy in my hands gather and build in response. Vivian wiped her sleeve across her bloody lip as she flicked off her high heels.

As I stood there, my power growing and ready to attack, Vivian took a step forward and caught her foot on one of the discarded heels. She stumbled backwards and fell. I waited for her to catch herself, but she didn't and instead the huge stained-glass window shattered as Vivian fell through it. I rushed over to the broken window, my anger still pulsing in electrical surges that flowed across my hands, but when I got there, it was too late. All I saw was Vivian free-falling through the air, before abruptly hitting the ground far below with a sickening and deadly smack. I hadn't realised this room was at the absolute top of the Master's spiralling Palace until I saw how far Vivian had fallen.

I was relieved—and shocked—but anger still swirled inside me, desperate for a release, so I took a breath and turned to face the next threat.

Peter and Lucas had subdued the remaining agents, whose bodies lay unconscious on the floor, but both were now locked in a deadly fight with the Master, who was a surprisingly lithe and competent fighter. That man really was the definition of secrets. I watched for a moment and saw the fight shift back and forth. Neither Lucas nor Peter had their weapons, and I watched as the Master parried several blows before lashing out in a flurry of kicks, flips and punches. It was mesmerising to watch as he had a unique style that was fluid but lethal, and often used his opponent's weight and momentum against them. Peter and Lucas locked eyes with each other, then, after a slight nod, charged and combined their attacks into one. With a surge of brutal strength, they overwhelmed the Master and pinned him on the ground, their combined weight crushing his limbs. The Master squealed a high-pitched yelp of pain.

With the fight over and their quarry detained, I sauntered over to the Master, who was writhing with pain and embarrassment under the hold of Peter and Lucas. His panicked eyes wildly looked around until he noticed me moving towards him, then he just stared at me.

'You might take me down, but you'll never get rid of us.' The Master spat the words at me in his tight, whiny voice, his head tilting back ever so slightly in a desperate show of defiance. 'Each one of us is like the trees we so desperately plant. As each one grows, it drops seeds that slowly take root and spread. You might cut down one tree, but you'll never be rid of the forest.'

Anger still bristled under my skin, burning to be let out as I bent down to be face to face with the Master.

'I don't care,' I said. 'I don't care about you, or your "Entity", I just want to make sure you leave my son alone. But you've shown that's impossible. Thing is, though, you've underestimated just how far I'll go to protect my family.'

I lifted my hands, with all the pent-up energy and anger from the unsatisfying fight with Vivian, and placed them on either side of the Master's head as though I was cradling his face. I closed my eyes, inhaled a deep calming breath, then started pulling on the small warbling blue energy pool at my core until it cracked and leaked out. I gripped onto the escaping power and channelled it through my hands to each side of the Master's head. Following his neural pathways I guided it carefully and precisely to the small area of his brain where I could short-circuit his long-term memory, erasing myself and Sam from his mind forever. The power flowed easily out of me, trickling and curving to my will. The energy was warm and seductive, and it began to grow, quickly morphing from a trickle to a torrent. I willed it to stay small, thin and precise, but it wouldn't listen. I couldn't rein it in and stop the oncoming flood. It was like a dam had burst.

The power had grown out of my control as it raged out of me. The effect was horrific. The Master's eyes locked with mine, then slowly they lost focus as his face twisted in a silent scream, his tiny facial muscles twitching and trembling in a grotesque dance. A gut-rolling smell of ozone mixed with burnt flesh filled the air as my power fried the Master's brain. I vaguely registered a voice next to me, screaming something, but I was lost in the shocking force of my own power. It flickered across and under my skin, shooting through my cells in a manic wave. It was wild and erratic, and I couldn't control it. The power consumed me until I felt nothing but its bright energy.

A huge shoulder slammed into me, knocking me to the ground. I swung around, ready to attack the assailant. Peter was crumpled on the ground next to me, his body shaking uncontrollably. I froze. The power still coursed through me, but it was no longer flowing into the Master. A sickening feeling punched me in the stomach as I realised my powers were flowing into Peter. He had used his own body to break my connection to the Master, and the lethal energy was now surging into him. Panic gripped my heart and with all my might, I yanked back on my power, trying to suck it back in. It felt as though I was trying to block a burst dam with a pebble, but I was determined. I couldn't let the power control me. I heaved on my powers, pulling them back. Through pure grit, I felt my small pebble of defiance grow into a rock, then a boulder, and finally a dam wall that halted the torrential flow. Crackles of energy raced up my arms, disappearing somewhere around my chest as I pulled all the escaping energy back to my core, willing it to retreat into me. Peter's body went limp on the ground and fear burned through my blood. What had I done? Shocking streaks of blue energy still crackled across my skin, preventing me from reaching out to check if he was okay. Instead, I yelled at Lucas.

'Lucas! Check he's okay!' As Lucas rushed to Peter, I focused on drawing back the energy further, sending it to my core where it could once again be locked away, dormant. With a final burst of effort, I pushed it all back into its pool, and opened my eyes to find my skin its normal colour. Sweat dripped down my forehead, but with my power back under control, I threw myself towards Peter.

'He's breathing...barely.' When Lucas looked at me, his eyes were filled with accusation and fear. I ignored the heavy punch that look landed and focused instead on checking Peter's vitals. Satisfied that my check aligned with Lucas's, I risked a glance over at the motionless form of the Master, and instantly regretted it. Either side of his head had been singed away, leaving only giant blackened holes with exposed, cooked muscle and sinew poking out. The smell of smoked flesh filled my nostrils, and I just managed to turn away from Peter and Lucas before vomiting all over the floor.

'Yep, that's nasty,' croaked a voice.

I looked back and saw Peter pushing himself up on his elbows. My entire body sagged in relief.

'Thank goodness! I—'

'Help me up, Rach,' Peter said, cutting me off and waving away whatever it was I was about to say. I swallowed my words of apology and hoisted him to his feet.

'You took away our chance to bring him to justice!' snapped Lucas. I didn't know how to respond. His words turned my blood cold, as the reality of how out of control I had been slapped me in the face. The feeling of being completely helpless and overwhelmed by that pure, wild power still tingled through my body and terrified me. 'Then you almost killed your friend who tried to sto—'

'Ease up Lucas,' interrupted Peter. 'She knows.' He turned back to me, 'You okay?' he asked softly, 'I thought we lost you there to all those sparkles.'

'Sparkles?' A small, stressed smile creased my lips, but didn't reach further. I looked at Peter as the terrifying clarity of what had happened settled in my mind. 'I think you did lose me there for a moment.' Fear began eating at my heart. 'Peter, I couldn't control it.' I confided desperately. 'If you hadn't—'

The door of the room swished open and the three of us to jump into defensive poses. Megan burst into the room, gun raised, ready to take down any adversary in her path.

'It's clear,' she said over her shoulder after she assessed the situation and lowered her gun. Sam popped out from behind the door, his pistol held firmly in his hand with a too tight grip. He rushed over but pulled up short when he spotted the burnt corpse of the Master behind us. I quickly stepped in front of him to pull his attention away from the body and grabbed him in a hug.

'You're not hurt, are you?' I asked, as I began desperately sweeping my eyes across him, making sure everything was as it should be.

'I'm fine. Mum, I did it. I think we'll be okay now,' he said, with an assuredness I hadn't seen in him before. 'I posted copies of all the documents linking the Agency and La Panta to the Entity on every major community forum. Then I released OmniAI by posting a copy of its base code everywhere I could think of. If everyone has it, then no one can use it to their sole advantage, and with the code available, people will be able to build protections against it.' The words tumbled out of his mouth, and I smiled despite myself. 'But,' he continued, 'I got it to do one thing for me before releasing it.'

'And what's that?' I asked, my curiosity and concern piqued.

'I sent it on a mission to delete every record it could find concerning the two of us and anything to do with...well...this,' he said, raising his hand and releasing a small spark into the air. 'I also may have snuck in a small instruction embedded in every copy of the code to auto-delete any file or piece of information it ever finds about us, from now until forever. We're going to be okay, Mum. No one will ever know about us.' I placed my hand gently on the side of Sam's face, as my lips quivered in a shaky smile that reflected the torrent of emotions I held within.

Multiple figures simultaneously appeared in the doorway and let off a volley of gunfire that echoed through the chamber and crumpled Lucas like a rag doll, his body ripped apart by the assault. I dived onto Sam and pushed him to the ground to shield him with my own body. My vision seared with a bright pain as a bullet tore through my left shoulder. I swallowed a shocked scream and grabbed onto Sam as I rolled the two of us to lie behind the decimated corpse of the Master. Hoping it would provide enough cover, I pushed the body up to create a barrier. Bullets pummelled into the corpse, covering us in a red mist. The noise was deafening as more bullets cracked into the wall behind us with explosive force. Our makeshift shield wouldn't hold out long.

I risked a quick look around the room and saw Megan and Peter pinned behind the couch where the Master had been sitting, letting off their own bursts of gunfire at the advancing attackers. Satisfied that they were still alive, I turned my attention to the assailants. There were at least ten black-clad figures filtering into the room in a sweeping pincer manoeuvre. They had our backs to the wall and were coming in fast. If we didn't do something now, we would be overrun in a matter of moments. A terrifying idea popped into my brain, but I didn't have time to second-guess it.

'Drop to the ground and stay there!' I yelled at Megan and Peter. They looked at me briefly, then dropped flat.

I grabbed Sam's hand. 'Sam, I need you to channel everything you have into me. Now!' I commanded. He didn't hesitate and latched his hand with mine. I sent a silent prayer of hope to the void and opened up my core to his power that began instantly pulling as Sam let his internal power flow into me. I hoarded it, letting it gather in an ever-growing warbling pool of crackling blue energy, then when it was close to bursting, I stood up, and released it as I threw my arms to the side and turned my face to the sky. At that moment, I was nothing but pure energy as I gave myself to the power wholeheartedly.

A wave of sparking electricity shot out of my chest and arms, shooting across the room in a shocking circular blast that slammed into everyone and everything in its path. The assailants were knocked to the ground, their bodies twitching and shuddering from the blast. The electricity wave skimmed above the flattened forms of Megan and Peter and smashed into the couch, flinging it across the room, where it burst into flames. Energy flowed out of me in relentless, undulating waves that crackled through the air. I couldn't control it, so I just watched as the strange and amazing power coursed out of my body, until finally the pool went dry. My mind wasn't my own, but I heard a voice from somewhere say, *Enough,* just before I collapsed to the ground, completely spent. My body was shaking, and I felt as though my insides had been ripped out, leaving nothing but an empty shell. The smell of burning flesh once again filled my nostrils. I rolled onto my side and saw the lifeless bodies of the assailants twitching on the ground, the remnant crackling energy dancing across their skin until finally going out.

A hand grabbed and squeezed my arm. 'Mum?' Sam's voice was strained and devoid of energy.

'I'm alright,' I croaked out. My mouth was dry, and my tongue swollen, making it hard to form the words. Rushing footsteps drew my attention, and I looked up into Megan's face.

'You still alive?' she said.

'Barely.'

'I'll take barely. Think you two can stand? We need to get out of here.' Her strong arms hoisted me to my feet. Peter helped Sam up, then together we hobbled towards the Master's personal lo-vehic landing pad, zigzagging our way through the still-smoking bodies of the assailants. The flaming couch drew my attention, but then I saw the body of Lucas near the couch as a dark pool of blood steadily spread out beneath him. My heart contracted at the sight, causing my legs to falter and stumble. Megan caught me and we locked eyes. She glared at me with a force of determination that told me no matter what, she would get us out of here. I rallied, buoyed by her strength, and we rushed out to the launch pad just as a lo-vehic was landing.

We made sure to stay out of the pilots' line of sight as Peter and Megan stood poised and ready to act as soon as the lo-vehic door opened. The air was taut with anticipation as we lay in wait for the lo-vehic to power down. The door popped open, and Megan sprang into action, neutralising the pilots with terrifying ease. She removed the unconscious pilots from the vehicle, then ushered us inside. I felt like I was outside of my body, just watching the events unfold before me without being able to interact with them. My footsteps were so shaky and laboured I wasn't sure I would make it, but with effort and the support of Sam, I made it inside and collapsed into a passenger seat. I heard a dragging noise behind us and turned to see Peter and Megan heaving the lifeless form of Lucas into the lo-vehic. They had gone back for him, making sure we didn't leave anyone behind, and I was thankful for it. They secured Lucas's body and closed the door with a loud clunk. Megan raced past us into the pilot chair and began flicking switches to power up. Peter hobbled past and plonked himself down in the co-pilot chair. A flood of guilt washed over me as I saw burn marks across his body, injuries I had caused, that made him heave and grimace with every movement. With the lo-vehic prepped and ready, we suddenly lurched upwards as Megan took us into the air. I turned and looked out the window as we pulled away from the Palace, its eclectic structure with strange domed points and towering spires slowly disappearing below us. As we went higher, I saw the streets and buildings of the Grove stretch out below us, and I wondered what would happen now the Master was gone. It was a dangerous and complex thought, the type of thought I didn't have the energy to contemplate, so I let it go and instead just hoped we had done enough. Enough to keep us safe, enough to falter the corruption and enough to justify the death of Lucas. I hoped it was all enough, as I finally wrapped Old Blue around me and let myself be pulled down into the darkness of sleep.

28

Plans

I woke up and stared at a familiar, rough brown canvas fabric. Its texture rippled in an unseen breeze, bouncing little specks of light off the rugged fibres. It was mesmerising, and a welcome distraction from the pain undulating through my body. I closed my eyes and focused on my breath to block out the relentless pain and to centre my buzzing thoughts. Fragments of a dark and violent dream flashed through my mind. Blood splattered across the floor. The smell of ozone and burnt flesh in my nostrils. The lifeless figures of lives cut short. The flash of energy and pure power exploding out of me. A lump of dread grew in the pit of my stomach as I realised these images weren't from a dream.

'Mum?' came a familiar voice from somewhere in the hazy dappled light of the tent. I turned to locate the source, but the movement made my head swim and filled my vision with tiny sparks of light. I closed my eyes until the wave of pain and vertigo subsided, then ever so hesitantly started letting the world come into focus, until the clear image of Sam solidified. He was sitting in a chair in the corner of the small tent. The skin under his eyes looked dark and puffy, and he suddenly looked so much older than a boy of twenty. With his scarred cheek, scruffy beard, and concerned, knowing eyes, I realised this was no boy. This was Sam as he truly was now, a fully grown man with the weight of the future on his shoulders.

I reached out, and he moved forward, grasping my hand in both of his palms in a comforting and gentle manner, much like you would with your elderly parent. Part of me inwardly cried at the thought.

'Mum, just take it easy. You've been out for two days, so the doctor said you need to let your body slowly adjust. Do you want some water?' I nodded, and he carefully lifted a cup to my mouth, supporting my neck as I sipped. The water was cool and invigorating, and my parched lips couldn't get enough. 'Easy Mum. You just need to sip.' With my thirst sated, I rested back into my cot and closed my eyes.

'Where are we?' I asked.

'Back at the Hidden camp, in the same tent we had last time. It was a bit of an effort for everyone to carry you back in from the lo-vehic, but we did it, and once we got you in your bed, you pretty much haven't moved. The medic has been in a couple of times to check you over. No permanent damage was her diagnosis.'

I nodded, which I regretted immediately as it sent a cascading wave of pain through my body. I bit back a groan and instead asked the most burning question in my mind. 'Are you okay?'

'A bit tired but getting better. That was...that was really something that you did back there. I didn't know we could do anything like that.'

'Neither did I.'

'What did it feel like?' I opened my eyes at his question. I wasn't sure how to answer in a logical manner, but I stumbled on anyway.

'It felt like...like I didn't exist as me anymore. I was just part of the power. I could feel it growing and growing, and I knew that if I let it, it would consume me. The flood of electricity out of me was harrowing and intoxicating. It's the only way I can describe it. I killed all those people so easily, and it terrified me. It felt like I lost myself and became nothing but the power. Untamed and raw power. But then there was something, a voice maybe, that...you're going to think I'm crazy, but it sounded like your dad, and he said "enough." So, I listened to him and let the power go.'

'Mum, that wasn't Dad, it was me,' said Sam, smiling. His words surprised me, but of course it had been him. I felt ashamed and silly for thinking it was anything else.

I looked at him and realised he had been watching me as I spoke with an eager interest, absorbing every word. Something in his look sparked a wave of concern and worried me, though, as he seemed a bit too curious.

'Sam…I'm truly scared of this power. What happened just shows that it's not safe; it's too much for one person. I saw the true depths it can suck us down into, and I don't want you pulled into it. I know the temptation is overwhelming, but we need to be careful. We need to learn to control it. If I have it, and you have it, then there is every chance that if you have children, they will also inherit it. So, we need to keep ourselves safe, and we do that by being careful, being quiet and learning how to manage these powers. And we do this together, okay? Don't go off being reckless. I know you; you're too easily consumed by curiosity and will want to figure it out. We do need to figure all this out, but we can't risk anyone knowing about it. I see now why they were after us. These powers in the wrong hands would spell disaster for so many. So, we will figure this out together and keep each other safe.'

'You're right, Mum. Truthfully, what you did back there scared me. I could feel you sucking my power into you, and it left me feeling empty, but I was more scared of what it would do to you. It's strange though. That feeling of power is already so much a part of me that it felt wrong having it taken away. But you're right. This power in the wrong hands is unthinkable, so we need to keep it secret. I was thinking though; too many people here know us. Even after wiping all records of ourselves, it's not going to eliminate the fact that multiple people know who we are and what we can do. We can't wipe their memories, so what if we leave? Head to Uishka or Aeir and start a new life there under different names. I don't want to stay in Crayn. It has too many painful memories.'

A sad smile swept across my face. He really was all grown up. 'Running doesn't get rid of those memories, Sam. Trust me, I've tried that before.'

'I know. Lilli will always be a part of me, just like Dad will always be part of you. But as you said, we need to keep this safe.' He flicked his fingers and threw a tiny blue spark into the air. It floated gently through the air and my eyes tracked it as it moved in a dazzling dance before winking out of existence. It was beautiful and such an inaccurate reflection of the true power that lay beneath.

'Well…I guess there is only one thing we need to figure out then. Do you want to live in the sky or near the ocean?'

'Let's go ocean,' said Sam. 'I'm not sure I would get used to the heights in Aeir.'

'Uishka it is then. A quiet life in a house by the water sounds perfect.' We smiled at each other as excited determination filled me. We would have a new life, my son would be safe, and we would figure out how to control our powers together.

'Knock, knock,' came a voice from the door. We both looked and saw the warm, kind face of Calista. 'Okay if I come in?' she asked. 'I just wanted to check in on how our patient was doing.'

'I'm fine,' I said, a reciprocal smile spreading across my face.

'Don't listen to her,' said Sam with an authority I hadn't heard before. 'She just woke up and needs to keep resting.'

'I won't keep her long,' promised Calista, 'but I would love a quick chat if she's up for it.'

'Alright. A quick chat. Then you need to rest again,' Sam said, pointing at me. 'I'll go get you some food while you two have your chat.' He headed towards the opening, awkwardly squeezing past Calista as she made her way to the tent's only seat and gripped the armrests tightly as she gently lowered herself onto it.

'So,' Calista began once she was settled, 'you're taking my advice and heading to a new city.'

'How did you—'

'Hear?' Calista offered, finishing my question. 'It's a tent, dear, with fabric walls, and I didn't want to interrupt such an important conversation, so I just let it continue its natural course until a moment came when it would be okay for me to come in.'

I wasn't sure I liked that she had been listening, but there was no getting away from it.

'Did you hear where we're going?'

'Yes, I did. But don't worry, I have no interest in letting anyone know about you. That is, unless you pose a threat to me or my people.' It was a statement but also a question and she stared at me, waiting for an answer. It seemed that something important depended on the answer I gave.

'I have nothing against any of your people, or yourself. You have all been so generous. You gave us sanctuary when we had none. I just want us to start again somewhere so we can try to build a life. That's all I want.'

301

'And that you will have. We will help you on your way. We have someone that can provide new identities. Have you thought of a different name for yourself?'

'Well...we had to choose between water or air for where to live. So, what about the name Skye? Since I won't get to live there, why not take a name inspired by it?'

'Skye. I like it. But Skye who?'

I didn't hesitate with my answer, as I knew Miles wouldn't mind me taking some inspiration from him. 'Shaw. Skye Shaw.'

'It's definitely an option,' Calista nodded, pulling an unsure face. 'You've got time to think about it, though.' Her rejection of the name hurt, but I barely had a moment to process it before she continued. 'There is a memorial this afternoon for Lucas. If you are strong enough, I would like you to be there.'

'Of course.'

'Ah! I think I hear your darling boy back already with food. Eat, get stronger and I will see you at the service.' Calista patted my arm before rising and shuffling to the exit. Before leaving, she paused and half mumbled to herself, 'Skye Shaw...sounds like a made-up hero's name. Maybe it's actually perfect.' Then she left, letting the tent flap fall behind her.

Sam reappeared not long after, laden with bowls of stew and simple, fire-baked bread. I jostled my way into a sitting position, biting my tongue as my muscles groaned at every movement. Sam handed me the bowl of stew and I pounced on it, devouring it like a wild animal as I dipped in the bread and scooped up chunks of vegetables. It was hot, and hearty, and exactly what I needed. We ate in silence as I let my body and mind just enjoy the flood of nourishment. Once finished and re-energised, I handed the bowl back to Sam and asked him a question that had started bouncing around in my mind.

'What's going on back in the real world after everything? Have there been any reports about the Master or Vivian?'

'Yeah, there have been. Word spread pretty fast about an assault on the Palace and the resulting death of the Master, but the details are hazy. The reports just say the Master's body was found near his private lo-vehic pad by a Palace cleaner, and officials haven't yet been able to identify who's behind it. There are rumours, though. One suggests it was worker organisations finally acting against the terrible conditions experienced by the Grovians. Officially, the Tir-na Collective is "investigating the issue" and will release their findings once complete. The reports are also saying Vivian was just unlucky and got caught in the attack, just an innocent bystander. I must admit, whoever came up with that story knows what they are doing as it plays well in the comm feeds, and more importantly, doesn't point to us.'

'What happened to the freaky doctor and his perfectly groomed babysitter? Do we know if they were at the base when it exploded?'

'Unfortunately, it looks like they got out before it blew up. No one has seen Velor Closman, but from all accounts Serena Fabrica is already back at work doing whatever it is she does at La Panta. The two of them are wrapped up in so many layers of protection provided by La Panta that it's going to be almost impossible to make anything stick.'

'Even with you releasing the details of their connections to the Pleasure Spot dealers and the Master?'

'Kind of unsurprisingly, that information has somehow been buried so deep that it hasn't registered with any comms networks. Perks of having a rich and powerful corporation behind you, I guess.'

'Well, that's annoying. I hate loose threads; they make me uncomfortable.' I rubbed and pinched the bone between my eyes as a headache started pounding in my skull. 'Any news on who will replace Vivian and the Master in their positions?'

'No news yet about who will lead the Grove and all the terraforming activities. One of the Master's staff has stepped into the role as a temporary measure while the Collective takes their time to appoint someone officially.'

'Makes sense,' I said.

'As to who will step into Vivian's position? Well...I'll let you talk to Peter about that later.'

'Peter?'

'Yeah. He can give you the most accurate update on that situation. He'll be at the memorial this afternoon. You can talk to him after that. In fact, that's probably not the only thing you two should talk about.'

'What do you mean?'

Sam sighed. 'Look, from what I can tell, you two used to be close. You were partners for many years.'

'Yeah,' I replied hesitantly. I was wary of where the conversation was going.

'I'm just saying, you two have a lot of history, and used to share a deep trust. That's now been shaken. You need to figure this out, and I don't think we should leave until you do, for your sake.'

I hated to admit it, but he was right. I needed to figure out where I stood with Peter. If we just left, it would leave everything unresolved, and those unknowns would haunt me for the rest of my life.

'When did you become so smart?'

'My mother was an excellent role model.' Sam smiled a cheeky grin, then stood abruptly. 'All of that is for later, though. Right now, you need to rest. I'll come get you when it's time for the memorial.'

'Thanks, sweetie.'

'You know. I think this might just all pan out. I'm actually excited about our new life.'

'Calista said you need to think of a new name for yourself.'

'Really!?'

'Nothing stupid, Sam!'

'How about Keith?'

'No.'

'Douglas?'

'Sam!'

'I know, Aled!'

I just looked at him with an amused dead stare.

He laughed, 'I'll have a think and come up with something good. Rest up and I'll see you soon.' Then he left, leaving me to carefully lay down in my cot again. Thoughts kept swimming through my mind. A new life. A new name. Would it all be too much? Was I even ready to leave my old life? Truthfully, I didn't think I ever could really leave it. It was a part of me. It made me who I was, so even with a new identity, the core of me would stay the same. All the good, all the bad, all the softness and all the hardness, it was all me. Maybe this new life would be a chance to forge a life as I truly am, as my messy, complex self. Now that was a thought that excited me, and on that happy thought I closed my eyes and let myself drift off to sleep, pulled along by visions of a happy future where I could truly be myself.

29

Farewells

THE GROWING SOUND OF slow footsteps and muffled conversations moving past my tent woke me from a heavy and fretful sleep. I sat up and put on my shoes, my joints aching at the effort of tying up the laces.

The tent flap opened, and Sam stuck his head in. 'It's time, Mum.'

I nodded and got to my feet, half shuffling, half stumbling as I walked across the small space and reached for Sam's offered arm for support. Part of me hated that I was the one needing help; he had always been my boy, and for twenty years it was my job to help him. The tides had changed though, as they inevitably should, and now I needed him more than he needed me.

We walked out into the low-lit encampment, the eerie green glow from the chem-lights painting everything a sickly colour. Multiple people were passing through, all heading in the same direction, much like a flowing river, so we let ourselves drift along with them. We wove our way through the Hidden's camp until we reached the large open expanse at its heart. There, the crowd slowed and gathered as one. The central ring of stone seats were occupied by the same group of individuals we had seen talking together in those seats the first day we arrived, and there in the centre, dressed in flowing grey robes, her long, braided hair pinned in a loose coil on the side of her head, was Calista. The crowd fell silent as everyone trained their eyes on Calista, waiting for her to begin the service. I looked at the people gathered and couldn't help but notice how their eyes were filled not just with a solemn sadness as appropriate for the occasion, but also with an idolisation of Calista. She was their leader, their mother. The power she commanded without any show of brute strength or political cunning was inspiring. She led her people with truth and love, and they loved her in return. I wished I had time to learn from her.

There were still a few people trickling into the area, and as I looked around, I spotted the Zinkes at the front of the crowd clutching each other's hands. Looking further, I saw Peter and Megan hovering at the back of the crowd, their faces solemn, their bodies still. Once all the Hidden were present and settled, Calista opened her mouth, and her heart, to begin the service.

'My friends. My people,' she began, letting her soft voice carry across the space like a warm blanket enveloping her children. 'We are here together, in the heart of the home we have built, to remember and honour our fallen family, Lucas Evans and Lilli Zinke.' She paused for a moment, letting the names hang in the air, like her words were summoning their spirits to be with us. Sam reached out and grasped my hand. I held it tightly, hoping I could send what little strength I had through my hands and into him. I hadn't realised the service would also be for Lilli. 'Lucas was the bravest and most fiercely protective man I've ever known. Having no family himself, he found his family in us, and also found true love here with Jamie. For Lucas, our world was everything, and he gave his life in the hope of building the better world we dream of. So often he would come to me and talk about the amazing life he could see for all of us at the end of our struggle, at the end of our mission to bring truth to the people. He longed to live in that world with his love, Jamie, and we will honour him by making sure his dreams for us all become truth.'

Calista lowered her head and paused, giving time for our minds to embrace the memories of Lucas. 'Lilli was the smartest of us all and had the biggest heart. When her family was threatened, she didn't shy away from the situation, but instead did what she had to do to ensure their safety. It was only from her efforts that her family found their way to our camp, where they now have a safe home. Every action ever taken by Lilli was motivated by one thing: love. Love for her family, love for Sam, love for all of us.' I heard Sam suck in a sharp, quiet sob, and I gripped his hand tighter as Calista continued. 'She sacrificed so much by doing what needed to be done. She showed bravery and courage beyond her years, all for the dream of a better life for us all. Lucas and Lilli won't see those dreams become reality, but you will. The world they dreamed of belongs to you now, and we all must do our best to honour their memory by living. Not just getting by, but truly living.' She reached down to the ground and picked up in her slightly shaking frail hands a green glowing globe made from the same material as the lights scattered throughout the cave. She raised it above her head, throwing a rippling green glow across the crowd. Everyone responded in kind by pulling out similar globes and copying Calista's movement by lifting them above their head until the crowd became a sea of glowing orbs. It was beautiful in its simplicity, and overwhelming in its meaning. They were a family, and together they would mourn the loss of their loved ones. 'Lucas and Lilli, you were the best of us, and the two of you will live on in our hearts forever. May you both find peace.'

'May you find peace,' the crowd responded as one.

Calista lowered her light orb and placed it in the exact centre of the stone circle she was standing in. She shuffled to the side and indicated for the Zinkes to come forward, along with Lucas's partner, the kind-eyed man called Jamie. Lilli's mother and father slowly moved to the centre of the circle, with tears streaming down their cheeks, and placed their orb next to Calista's. Jamie was next, and he lowered his light with shaking hands as a sob escaped his lips. One by one, everyone made their way forward and laid down their orbs in expanding concentric circles, with Calista's orb at its heart. A kind soul in the crowd noticed that we had no orbs, and after a small fuss, they acquired one each for us so we could take part. Then, with orbs in hand, we walked to the circle, and I added mine to the ever-growing pattern that grew brighter and brighter with each added light. Sam hesitated for a moment and stared at his orb, lost in what could have been a thought, a memory or maybe a wish. He closed his eyes, raised the orb to his lips, kissed it briefly and then stepped forward and added his to the final circle to complete the pattern.

Everyone stood for a moment and soaked in the sight of the glowing circles. It was a collective display of love, hope and remembrance, and it was beautiful.

'Thank you, one and all. Our community is small, but it loves with its entire heart. Remember your love and hold on to it as it will always guide you home.' With that, Calista bowed her head, and the crowd parted, creating a path for her.

Calista slowly walked through the crowd, followed by the Zinkes and the other community leaders. As they passed us, Elias Zinke paused, walked over to Sam and pulled him into a giant hug. He then pulled Sam by the hand to join himself and Lana. Sam momentarily looked back at me, but I nodded in encouragement to join them as a tear that had been swelling in the corner of my eye finally escaped and streamed down my cheek. Sam walked with the Zinkes through the crowd, their backs straight and their hands locked together in a show of solidarity. Everyone watched, then bowed their heads as they walked past. Once the official party had left, everyone followed suit and filtered out of the space. I stood for a moment, unsure where to go. My body was screaming out for more sleep, but my mind was too awake for that.

'I've never actually seen one of their services before.' Megan appeared at my side, with Peter close behind. I noticed the streaks of dried tears on Megan's face but didn't draw attention to them. 'It was beautiful.'

'It was,' I agreed, looking back at the circles of glowing orbs.

'How's Sam holding up?' Peter asked.

'Truthfully, I'm not sure. I imagine he'll spend some time with the Zinkes now and be strong for them, but after that, I don't know how he'll be.' They both nodded in understanding, then turned their heads to look at the orbs. 'He was parenting me this morning. Was fussing about me getting enough rest and food.'

'Ha!' laughed Peter. 'And how did that make you feel?'

'Old.' They both smirked at my response.

'That's 'cause we are old,' said Megan.

'Speak for yourself. I'm in the prime of my life.' Peter reached up and made a show of tousling his hair with his hand, making his annoyingly always-perfect hair look that bit more bouffant and perfect. I could practically hear Megan's judging eyebrow raise in response, but Peter just laughed.

'I really hate your hair,' I said to Peter. 'Have I ever told you that?'

'All the time, Rach.'

'It's just so...so...'

'Irritatingly perfect,' offered Megan.

'Yes! I used to hate rocking up to work with my crazy hair barely contained in some sort of ponytail that took me a good ten minutes to create, and in would walk this guy whingeing about how he didn't have time to do his hair and of course it looked perfect! Even on windy days, it would look immaculate, like the wind sculpted it for him. Bloody nature itself helps make his hair look good!' Megan let out a small laugh, and I turned back to Peter to see him smiling at me again. 'And that's why I hate your hair,' I said pointedly to him.

'I can't help it if the universe wants me to be pretty. I am who I am Rach. No point in fighting it.' I laughed at him, then a happier, comfortable silence fell over us.

'On a serious note, though, are you okay, Rach?' Peter asked.

'Me? I'm fine. What about you? I almost killed you.'

'Just a little shock to the system, no biggie.' I looked from Peter to Megan to try to gauge the accuracy of what he was saying, but Megan had turned and started walking over to the orbs.

'I can't say sorry enough, Peter,' I said in earnest.

'It's me who can't say sorry enough. I should have told you everything from the start. If I had involved you from the beginning, we could have figured out another way to do everything, a smarter way, just like the old times.'

'We've both made mistakes, but it's how we move forward that counts, right?' Peter nodded in agreement and placed a hand on my shoulder as his eyes went glassy. I moved forward and pulled him into a hug, only the fourth since we had known each other.

I pulled back, and we looked at each other as a silent, shared understanding passed between us.

'I hear I'm supposed to ask you what's going on with the Agency after everything,' I said, refocusing the conversation.

Peter took an extra step back and rubbed his hand through his hair, a nervous tic of his I had noticed years ago. 'Well...some people from the Collective decided they couldn't trust Agency leadership once all that evidence of Vivian's schemes and deeds was released publicly. So, they looked for someone else to put in charge for a while, someone with experience.' Peter paused as a strange look I couldn't read crossed his face. Was it excitement? Fear?

'And...' I said, trying to drag more information out of him.

'And, so, they asked me to do it.'

'You? The Head of the Agency?'

'Yep.'

I was astounded. Peter knew the business better than anyone, but he hated bureaucracy. I couldn't help but giggle. 'Are they really that desperate?' I said, laughing.

'Ouch, Rach, ouch. I'll remember this next time you come knocking at our door looking for a favour.'

'Fair,' I said with a smile. 'But seriously Peter, congratulations. You're probably the perfect person for it. They need someone who genuinely cares about the mission and its people. Speaking of, what are you going to do about the agents we had to fight in the Palace?'

'Well, all of them are good agents, and I wouldn't want to tarnish their careers just for following orders. I'll start an investigation into them. Any who didn't know about Vivian's plan will be put back on regular duties, and any who did, well...I'll figure out what to do when it comes to it.'

'Sounds reasonable and right. You know, you might just be the change the Agency needs.'

'Thanks Rach, that's kind of you.'

'So, how bad are things out there after everything got released?'

'Well, let's just say all the investigative bodies in Crayn are flat out, and La Panta's shares have certainly taken a dip.'

'I can imagine.'

'The most important part, though, is that none of the investigations involve, or mention, either you or Sam. You guys are in the clear, and I'll make damn sure to keep it that way.'

'Thanks, Peter.' Megan wandered back towards us, obviously deciding she had given us enough time. 'What about you then, Megan?'

'What?' she replied.

'You going to rejoin the Agency with Peter here? Help it get some real leadership?' I smirked in Peter's direction; he didn't bite, though, and instead just enjoyed the banter.

'No, actually,' said Megan. 'I think I'm going to stay around here for a while. Help figure out what these guys want to do next, and also keep an eye on the Grove. There are a lot of people in that city who could use someone keeping an eye out for them. If I can help them in even a tiny way, then I'm happy with that.'

'That's actually a relief,' I said. 'I was worried about the power vacuum we left back there, but it's good to know you'll be here to help make sure things are better than they were for the people of the Grove.'

'I'll do what I can,' Megan responded frankly. 'And what about you and Sam? You going to stay around too.'

'Us? No. We're going to leave. Make a fresh start somewhere, somewhere away from the Agency and everything to do with this mess.'

'Sounds perfect.' Megan smiled.

I looked at Peter and noticed his eyes were shiny; it made me smile.

Peter noticed me looking and wiped his eyes quickly. 'Well then, we better make use of the time we have left together. So, first things first, let's go get a drink. Pretty sure I can hear the remembrance party starting to kick off.'

'A drink sounds like a great idea. Reckon they have the ingredients to make a couple of Starfires?' I joked. Peter laughed as the three of us walked off to finally just sit down and enjoy a drink together.

· · · · ● · ● · · ·

The next few days flew by in a blur. Calista came through with her promise of providing us new identities, which Sam registered everywhere citizen details were recorded. Every record of our old lives had been deleted by the AI, so if anyone ever went searching, they would find nothing about Rachel or Sam. We were now Skye and Aidan, and they both had long histories stretching back to Skye's old school days in Crayn.

I slowly regained my strength as the days passed, and I even had enough stamina to spend time with Sam experimenting with our powers, either in the privacy of our tent, or in a quiet spot in one of the cavern's off-shooting tunnels. I also spent hours talking with Peter and Megan about everything and nothing, both of which I enjoyed wholeheartedly, while Sam spent time with the Zinkes, which resulted in him picking up some tinkering skills. It was a lovely few days, but sooner than we realised, it was the morning of our departure and we had to say farewell to the sanctuary we had found there.

Our goodbye with the Zinkes was tear-ridden and heartfelt. I could tell there would always be a bond there, with a shared love for Lilli at its heart. After saying my goodbyes and giving a farewell hug, I left Sam to take his time. I couldn't hear all the whispered conversation between Sam and the Zinkes, but I did catch Mrs Zinke telling Sam to go and live a life full of love and laughter, just as Lilli would have wanted. The relief flooding my system from hearing her say that caused my muscles to weaken, and I hadn't realised until then that I had been holding a fear deep in my gut. A fear that Sam would forever be stuck and never be able to live a full life. It was something I couldn't fix as his mother, but Mrs Zinke could. As the mother of Lilli, the power of her giving permission for him to go out into the world and live again could not be understated, and it was the kindest gift she could possibly give. I caught Mrs Zinke's eye and gave her a soft smile, and mouthed the words *thank you*. She smiled back and gave a slight dip of her head in a motion that acknowledged the gravity, hardship and joy of our shared experiences as mothers.

We next said our goodbyes to Calista, who piled us up with bags of food, clothing and money to set up our new life. I tried to push the money back at her, knowing full well that Sam had already transferred all of my savings and his holo-tournament prize money into accounts under our new identities. He had even managed to sell his e-vehic remotely and move the money to our new accounts. We would be completely fine, but she was insistent. Her intricate grey braid even waggled around with the velocity of her refusal to take it back. Not wanting to offend her, I acquiesced and promised to use it for something good, something important. Then I gripped onto Calista tightly as we shared a final embrace.

'I can't thank you enough,' I said.

'You don't need to thank me at all.' We held onto each other for a moment longer and I tried to channel all my appreciation into that embrace. 'Now go,' Calista pronounced. 'Go and live your lives and be happy.' We smiled for a moment longer, then I turned to Sam and we headed to grab our bags, only to find Megan and Peter standing with them.

'You can't escape us that easily,' said Peter with a smile.

'Doesn't seem like it,' I said.

'Here, hand me that,' Megan said, indicating the supplies Calista had just off-loaded onto us. 'We're going up to the lo-vehic with you guys.'

'You don't need to,' I began protesting.

'No, but we want to.'

It was a slow walk to the surface through the cave system. The walk gave me time to think, and I realised I truly was excited for the fresh start—although it had been a while since I had breathed the pure oxygen of the oxy-masks, so there was a chance that was making me a bit giddy, not just the excitement. We finally emerged to the surface and saw the Master's lo-vehic parked in front of the cave entrance.

'You sure you wiped all geo-location capabilities, the registration and anything else that could link this thing to the Master?' I asked Sam.

'He did a great job,' said Megan. 'I came up with him when he did it to help make sure we covered all bases, and this thing is 100% all yours now. No linkage to the Master at all, it's completely clear. Even gave it a fresh coat of paint. It's also got enough fuel to get you to anywhere on Tir-na, so you're good to go.'

I nodded, and we loaded all our belongings into the lo-vehic. It was bigger and more spacious than the one we had stolen from the base in the Wastes, and the sale of this lo-vehic at the other end would probably buy us quite a nice house in Uishka. Maybe even a house on its own island.

With everything settled, there was only one thing left to do, and it suddenly felt like the hardest thing in the world. So, instead, we hovered around each other, wishing there was a way to avoid what had to come next.

'Rachel,' said Megan, instigating the inevitable, 'it's been an absolute pleasure.' Megan extended her hand, but I knocked it away and pulled her in for a hug.

'I can't thank you enough, Megan. You saved us.'

'I think in some messed-up way, maybe it's actually the other way around.' Megan stepped back slightly and held onto my forearms while staring at me. 'If you ever need anything, you know where I am, so don't be a stranger.' She squeezed my arms one more time, then let go and walked over to say goodbye to Sam, leaving me to turn my attention to Peter.

'Well...' he said. 'It's been a ride, hasn't it?'

'Just like old times, huh?'

'Yeah, just like old times. I'm not going to say goodbye, cause knowing you, you'll pop back into my life just when I least expect it. So, instead I'm just going to say, work on your right hook, it's getting sloppy.'

I couldn't help but laugh, even as a tear slid down my cheek. 'Thanks for everything, Peter, and don't stuff up the Agency too much.'

'Maybe I'll instate mandatory dawn pack marches for everyone, even for the tech newbies.'

'Peter...'

'Lunchtime fighting competitions?'

I just shook my head and enjoyed the moment of comfortable, light-hearted banter. 'Look after yourself, okay?' I said looking at him in earnest.

'I will. And you too. I don't even know where you're going, and I don't want to know. But that means I won't be around to help if you get into trouble again, so how about you just...don't. Don't get into any more trouble, okay?'

'I'll certainly do my best.' We both smiled, and I pulled him in for a hug that contained all my thanks for our shared history together, and the future that only existed because of him. I didn't know what would have happened if Peter didn't circuit-break my powers at the Palace. Maybe I wouldn't have survived. I was certainly glad I didn't know.

Sam said his farewells, then we loaded into the lo-vehic's cockpit and prepared for take-off. The lo-vehic roared to life, and I engaged the hover booster that blew the dirt and sand everywhere. We slowly rose into the air, and I paused for a moment to look down at Megan and Peter, who were standing at the entrance to the cave, shielding their eyes from the sand. We exchanged a final wave, then I turned to Sam.

'Ready?' I asked him.

'Yeah,' he said. 'Let's go have a new adventure.'

I smiled, then looked to the horizon as I engaged the thrusters and flew us onwards to our new lives.

Epilogue

A QUIET LIFE

Fifteen months later.

THE FRONT DOOR OF our whitewashed house swished open, and I stood in front of it, ready to say my farewells to the quick-witted, and lovely natured, blonde young woman who had been visiting.

'Thank you so much for a lovely evening, Mrs Shaw. The food was delicious, and your house really is beautiful. I should get you to come run an eye over my place sometime and offer some advice on how I could make it look nicer.'

'I'm sure your place is beautiful, Cari, otherwise Aidan wouldn't spend so much time there.'

'Mum!' Aidan protested, but Cari and I just laughed at him.

'I would love to come visit your place sometime. It really was lovely to finally meet you.'

'You too, Mrs Shaw,' said Cari.

'Please, call me Skye. Mrs Shaw makes me feel old.'

'You're fifty, Mum.'

'Yes, but you don't need to remind me about it. That's just mean,' I said, doing my best to fake offence.

'If I had to guess, I would have said you were in your late thirties. Maybe I should start coming along to some of your movement and meditation classes. It obviously works well.'

'See, I knew I liked this girl,' I said conspiratorially to Aidan. 'Alright, you'd better get going. I know how those water taxi captains can be. If you're not at the dock exactly on time, then you're dead to them.'

'You're not wrong,' said Cari. 'It really was lovely to meet you, Skye, and I'll hopefully see you soon.'

'I'll walk Cari to the dock,' said Aidan.

'Sounds like a great idea. Bye Cari! Come again soon.' I waved them off and watched for a while as the two of them strolled down our little winding stone path to the small dock at the bottom of the garden. I loved living on our private island. It sounded exotic, but it was just the way things were in Uishka. Admittedly, the sale of the Master's lo-vehic helped put down a sizeable deposit on the place, but it was worth it. I loved this little house with its bright white walls and spindly plants growing all around it. And the privacy! I liked being with other people and sharing laughs as much as anyone else, but I loved coming home to my privacy. And I realised I had come to love the way of life in Uishka. It was more relaxed, and more community focused. Everyone seemed to look out for each other, and part of me wished I had been brave enough to move here long ago.

The white, low-hulled water taxi pulled up at our little dock and my lips curled into a cheeky smile as I saw Cari pull Aidan in for a goodbye kiss. Cari seemed like the perfect mix of humour, smarts and guts. Aidan was lucky to have met her during a work experience placement at Rimre. I was so proud of him when he was one of five Uishka University students selected for the four-week placement in the research department of the most advanced tech company on Tir-na. Then, for him to meet someone like her while on placement, well, a mother couldn't ask for more than that.

The taxi pulled away and Aidan waved farewell, as Cari's long blonde hair streamed out behind her.

'Cup of tea?' I called out to him as he walked back up the path.

'Yeah, why not? We have practice scheduled for tonight so I could use it.' We walked into the homey kitchen, and I began the automatic movements of making tea, reaching for the cups and leaf mix without a thought.

'She's really nice,' I said to Aidan while pouring his cup.

'I think I'm going to break up with her.'

'What?'

'I don't know. It's just not right. I don't feel like we click. She's nice and all, very pretty and smart too, but it's not right.'

'Since we moved here, you've brought two other girls here to meet me, and none of them were right either.' I took a sip of my tea, then decided to be brave and say what I was really thinking. 'None of them are going to be like Lilli, if that's what you're looking for.' I saw Aidan's body visibly slump. It hadn't even been a year and a half since we left the Wastes, and so much of it was still so raw and real. I was also scared he had taken Mrs Zinke's advice a little too much to heart and was now forcing himself to get out there when he wasn't ready.

'I know no one will be like Lilli, Mum. I promised I would try to live and do normal things a guy my age does. But it's not easy having to pretend none of that happened.'

'You should never pretend it didn't happen.'

'I know, but Aidan has never experienced watching his girlfriend die in front of him. That was Sam, and Sam doesn't exist here.'

'I understand what you mean. It wasn't easy for me either when I had to start over after Miles died, having to constantly explain away your absent father to everyone I met, as though I hadn't watched him die in front of me. I get it, sweetie. I just...I think you should be kinder to yourself and give yourself more time. There's no rush when it comes to this stuff, and you need to do what's right for you.'

'Thanks, Mum.'

We both sipped our tea, lost in our own painful thoughts and memories.

'Alright. Enough moping around. We better get to work so we have better control over this stuff,' I said, sending a tiny spark of power off the end of my finger that sailed through the air and extinguished itself mid-flight.

'Are you teaching the early class in the morning?' he asked as we headed out of the kitchen to the basement door.

'No, not tomorrow, so we can make it a late one if you like.'

'I do have a lot of energy to burn off.'

I nodded and flicked on the lights in the basement before descending the stairs into the cosy underground room we had set up. It was our hidden place, our sanctuary, a place we could be ourselves and practice controlling our powers in secret.

'Where do you want to start today?' asked Aidan.

'Why don't we begin with some slow, focused practice? I think we could both use that.'

We sat and began creating balls of pure energy that floated in front of us. Aidan created hundreds of small balls that floated around three large ones that I had formed. The balls of energy lit up the room like it was filled with hundreds of tiny stars. It was mesmerising, watching the beautiful dance of the stars that echoed the beauty of the universe itself. It was magical. Smile lines crinkled my face, deepening the wrinkles around my eyes in just the right place.

My wrist-comm rang with a sharp chirp, breaking my concentration and causing the energy spheres I had created to disappear. I looked at the screen and saw an unknown caller ID.

'Hello?' I answered, unsure. I made a habit of not giving out my contact details, so I could count on one hand the number of people who knew how to get hold of me.

'Rach? It's Megan. We need to talk.'

Acknowledgments

Well, that's it. We got there! My first novel done and dusted. I hope you enjoyed reading Agent. Mother. Other. I can't express how thankful I am to everyone who has taken time out of their lives to enjoy Rachel's story.

Rachel emerged from an assignment for an Australian Writers Centre course I completed and quickly took on a life of her own. I needed to know more about this strong, complex, and layered woman and the terrible thing that had happened to her to spur her into action. In many ways, Rachel became a means to explore the strange experience after becoming a mother of losing what I thought composed my identity. I felt like I was thrown into a situation where I had to become a different version of myself, one I didn't recognise and was called "mother." It took time and work to reconcile the different parts of myself and accept that I am composed of various aspects, but all of them are essential to form the complex tapestry that is me. I'm sure I'm not the only woman to experience this after becoming a mother, so in many ways, this is a story for all of you. You can change who you are multiple times, but you should never hide parts of yourself. Without them, you wouldn't be who you are, and you, my friend, are perfect, just as you are.

This isn't the end of the road, though. I am currently working on book two of the Tir-na Saga, with everyone's favourite kick-arse woman, Megan, front and centre this time. Stay tuned to my socials to know when book two is good to go (apologies, I'm a slow writer, but I will get it to you as soon as I can!).

Thank you to everyone who has been with me on this journey. So many friends and family have supported me over the last few years. Sometimes it was just by asking how the book's going, and I am so grateful to all of you.

Thank you to the other half of Invoke Creations, Andy Mac. You gave me the required kick in the butt to actually start taking myself seriously, and to sit myself down and do the work. You should all check out his story Star Ranger! It's a wild and fun ride!

To my breakfast writers' club whose common and supportive goals made it possible to get the words down on the page, while enjoying some delicious poached eggs on toast.

Huge thank you to my amazing cover designer Nikki. You really helped capture the feeling of the story and made it look so much cooler than I could have imagined.

To my fantastic editor Beth, whose input helped tighten the plot to make the story shine.

Thank you to my kids with their endless energy and joy. I wouldn't understand the crazy journey of motherhood without you. And finally, thank you to my alpha reader and husband, David. You always have my back and you definitely have more belief in me than I have in myself. I couldn't have done this without your unwavering support, so thank you to the moon and back and beyond.

Writing and publishing my first book has definitely been a wild ride, but I hope it is the first of many. See you all on the other side of book two!

About the Author

Sharn Lee is an Australian author, who lives, works, and dreams on Ngunnawal Ngambri land in Canberra, along with her husband, two boys, and an overly spoilt doggy fur baby. She has held various roles across both government and industry organisations throughout her career, and in her spare time, between writing and working, she is also a keen D&D player, music hobbyist, and podcaster. Sharn is currently hard at work on the second book in the Tir-na Saga.

To stay updated with Sharn's latest adventures, follow her on X @SharnLeeCreator. You can also catch her co-hosting the podcast 'Bards Lost in the Metaverse,' available on your favourite podcast streaming platforms.

Also By

For more details about Sharn's work head to www.invokecreations.com

· · • · • · • · · ·

To keep up to date with all the happenings in Sharn's creative life, follow Shan Lee and Invoke Creations on Facebook.

· · • · • · • · · ·

To chill out and relax with Sharn's musical creations, either head to Invoke Sounds' YouTube channel https://www.youtube.com/@invokesounds, or check Sharn out on your favourite music streaming service.

· · • · • · • · · ·

To hear about Sharn and her creative partner in crime, Andy, talk about creative processes, self-publishing and the emerging world of Web3 technologies, check out our podcast Bards Lost in the Metaverse. Available now on your favourite streaming service (Spotify, Apple Music, etc).

Or follow the podcast on X @invokecreations to get alerted when new episodes are released and see some behind-the-scenes details or extra content.

www.ingramcontent.com/pod-product-compliance
Lightning Source LLC
Chambersburg PA
CBHW031948130726
47904CB00012B/349